# THE STAR FROM CALCUTTA

Books by the Author

### THE PERVEEN MISTRY SERIES
*The Widows of Malabar Hill*
*The Satapur Moonstone*
*The Bombay Prince*
*The Mistress of Bhatia House*
*The Star from Calcutta*

### INDIA BOOKS
*India Gray: Historical Fiction*
*The Sleeping Dictionary*

### JAPAN BOOKS
*The Kizuna Coast*
*Shimura Trouble*
*Girl in a Box*
*The Typhoon Lover*
*The Pearl Diver*
*The Samurai's Daughter*
*The Bride's Kimono*
*The Floating Girl*
*The Flower Master*
*Zen Attitude*
*The Salaryman's Wife*

# THE STAR FROM CALCUTTA

## SUJATA MASSEY

Published by
Soho Press, Inc.
227 W 17th Street
New York, NY 10011
www.sohopress.com

Copyright © 2026 by Sujata Massey

This is a work of fiction. The characters, dialogue, and incidents depicted are a product of the author's imagination. Any resemblance to actual events or persons, living or dead, is entirely coincidental.

Library of Congress Cataloging-in-Publication Data is available.

ISBN 978-1-64129-509-3
eISBN 978-1-64129-510-9

Interior design by Janine Agro, Soho Press, Inc.

Printed in the United States of America

10 9 8 7 6 5 4 3 2 1

EU Responsible Person (for authorities only)
eucomply OÜ
Pärnu mnt 139b-14
11317 Tallinn, Estonia
hello@eucompliancepartner.com
www.eucompliancepartner.com

*To Sylvia Bhattacharya*
*Reader, Writer and Artist*

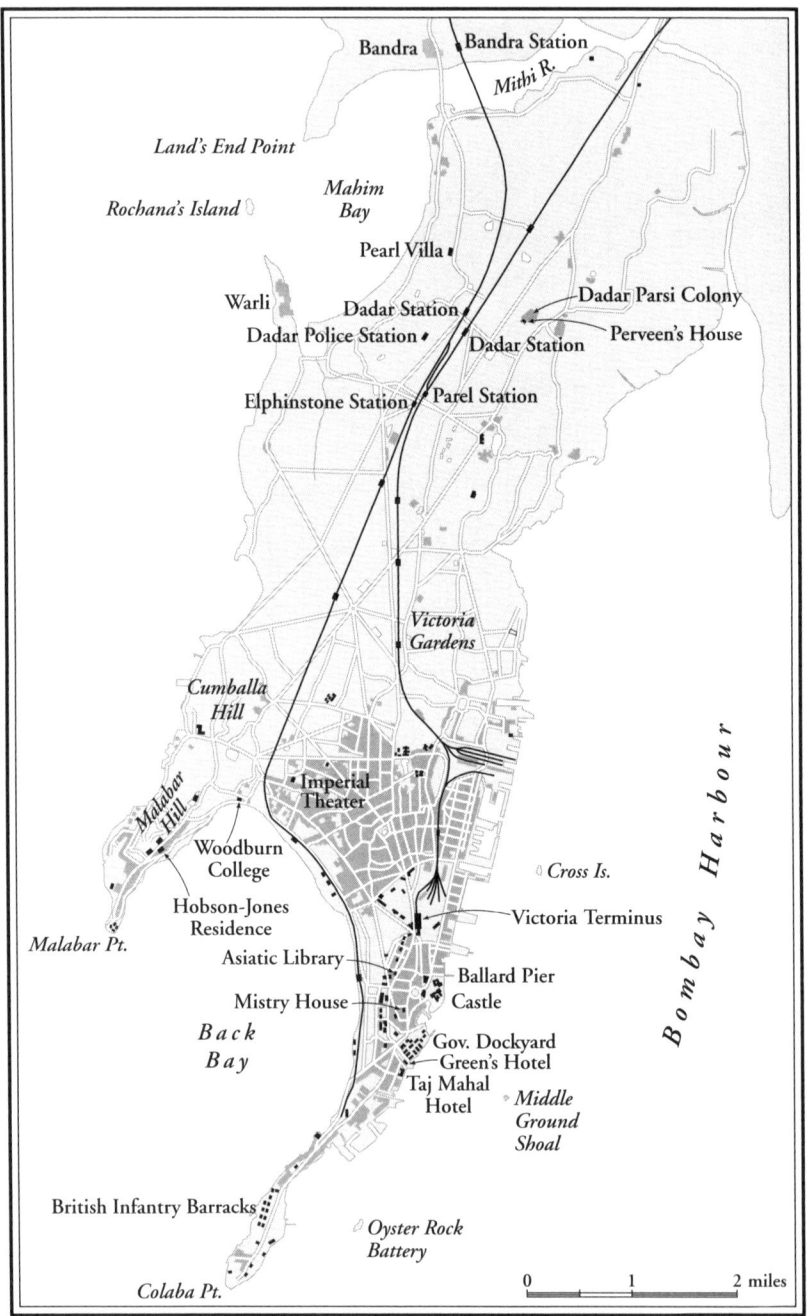

# 1
## CALL TO SET
### Fall 1922

Sometimes Perveen Mistry felt like the only person in Bombay who didn't care for the summer monsoon. Yes, the rain was a relief after springtime's burning temperatures and thick humidity. A solid deluge was necessary for the life of plants and animals. Yet every year, from June through September, the ferocious rainfall brought floods that washed away shanties, houses, and even people. One couldn't hang laundry in the morning without knowing whether it would be wetter by day's end. Rainy season was like the worst legal opponent: someone with unlimited resources to draw out the battle.

Therefore, when Perveen awoke on a mid-September morning to a hammering sound on the roof, she was irritated. Three days had passed since she'd been able to get to the law office in South Bombay. She imagined a pile of damp, unread mail was moldering to bits inside. In that pile could be necessary work to finish . . . and perhaps a discreet letter from someone special.

She smiled, thinking of Colin Sandringham, in his flat close to the city center. By now, her secret paramour had probably finished his morning exercises and was either on to the newspapers or any one of the letters she'd sent him during the rainy season, when chance meetings between them seemed all but impossible.

Resolutely, Perveen swung her feet from the bed down to the

soft Agra carpet. She tied on the light summer-weight cotton dressing gown and trod along the black-and-white marble checkerboard hall and stairs.

The rain had been too fierce for the newspaper boy to come, so she had to make peace with rereading yesterday's *Bombay Chronicle* and *Samachar* lying on the dining table. As usual, the family's chief maid, Gita, had meticulously refolded the pages after her father's inspection. Jamshedji Mistry, who was also the senior partner in their family law practice, always got the first read.

She wasn't seated long before she heard the swift, soft footsteps of Hiba. The household's baby-ayah carried in Khushy, who despite the early hour was already wearing a spotless white muslin frock and the creamy remnants of porridge on her cheek.

"Good morning!" Hiba greeted Perveen while placing the four-month-old on a small cotton mat on the floor for morning exercise. "Khushy's glad to see her aunty's come down. Rustom-sahib isn't yet awake."

Perveen smiled. Her older brother—Khushy's father—was an infamous late sleeper. She picked up the small red ball that Hiba handed her and began rolling it back and forth with her bare foot—a morning exercise that benefited both aunt and niece, in a small way.

"Gah!" Khushy chortled, her tiny brown eyes fixed on the ball.

"Ball," Perveen proclaimed in English, although the baby manual said that Khushy could not be expected to speak for several more months. "You are a clever one, aren't you? Ba-a-all."

After stretching out the word, she became suddenly uncomfortable.

"Let Khushy know her mother tongue," Rustom had scolded Perveen and her parents at the dinner table a few nights earlier. The word "mother" had made Perveen wince, because Gulnaz, Rustom's wife, was estranged from him and, at the moment, enjoying Paris with her parents. The fact was, the Mistrys had always spoken more English than Gujarati around the house—even Rustom himself. This was typical for ambitious Parsi families, who raised each generation to work and socialize closely with the British. Their staff, who were all from different religious and ethnic groups, spoke a mixture of English, Hindi, and Marathi.

Perveen kept rolling the ball as she turned to the newspaper. Amid advertisements for fail-proof umbrellas and anti-mildew powders, she saw a continuation of an article about the cotton market. Bombay's chief commodity had lost value in recent years, and the impact of monsoon had been a slowing of orders worldwide. It was fortunate for the Mistry family that their specialty was in another field: construction. Perveen's father, Jamshedji Mistry, had worked hard to persuade his family to let him take up the practice of law. But lawyers could work, regardless of weather, while her brother, Rustom, now in charge of the construction business, couldn't keep his men working during the rains.

A sound in the hallway drew her attention away. Jamshedji Mistry had emerged from his study. It was his policy to be correctly dressed for a day of work, rain or shine. Today, he wore a lightweight gray wool suit that picked up the silver in his thick head of hair. Although fifty-four, he had the trim appearance and movements of a younger man.

Khushy turned her head to take in the sight of her handsome grandfather, who bent to ruffle the baby's short curls.

"Good morning to you, Khushy-jaan," he said as the baby made a sound of recognition from her place on the blanket. Looking at Perveen, he said, "We have a business prospect."

Perveen closed the newspaper and smiled up at him. "Tell me."

Gita, the slender young Bengali woman who served the meals prepared by John, bustled in with the silver coffeepot and poured a cup for Jamshedji, who said, "Our prospective client asked if we could meet them at their office. You're free this afternoon, so I'm calling you along."

Perveen shook her head at Gita's murmured offer of more coffee. "A meeting today, in these rains?"

"Only in West Dadar. No reason to worry."

Gita gave Perveen a quick, intense look. She probably was recalling how the family's Daimler had been almost swallowed by a flash flood a week earlier. Although Perveen had exited the car safely with the chauffeur's help, it was days until it was operable. When Gita had left the room, Perveen asked, "Tell me, who is this new client?"

"Champa Films. We will meet with the owner, Subhas Ghoshal, and his wife, an actress from Calcutta. They've got a new film called *Queen of Hearts* coming out in a few weeks."

With about two dozen theaters providing Bombay's restless middle class with a social outing—and refuge from rain—cinema was one of the few businesses that could defy monsoon. Thousands of people turned out regularly to watch pictures imported from Europe and especially those produced by Indians in the new studios being set up in Calcutta, Madras, and Bombay. The studio he'd mentioned, Champa Films, was becoming as well-known as Madan Theatres, Royal Indian Pictures, and Kohinoor Film Company. "No introduction needed! I'm familiar with his films and the Calcutta star he's married."

Jamshedji's salt-and-pepper eyebrows arched upward. "You are?"

"Rochana is very famous. Why, she happens to be Alice Hobson-Jones's favorite actress!"

"Miss Hobson-Jones watches Indian films?"

Perveen understood his puzzlement, because the vast majority of the films screened in India came from America and Britain. Perveen and Alice, who'd been steadfast friends since their days at Oxford, had always been filmgoers, particularly enjoying those made by Charlie Chaplin. Indian films were something else entirely. "It started when I brought Alice to see a film based on a story from the Mahabharat called *Nala and Damayanti*. And then, there are these other kinds of pictures: modern stories with villains and perilous situations in which the heroines are the ones who prevail."

His mouth quirked. "Oh dear, that sounds a bit like you."

"No, no," Perveen said quickly. "Rochana's involved in sword fights and riding runaway horses and car chases. She's quite famous for being the best at it. When Alice saw Rochana at the races in Poona last winter, she even got her autograph."

"So, it sounds as if Mrs. Ghoshal gets about in society?"

Perveen sensed some skepticism. Film was considered a dubious profession for most women in India. This was the reason that most of the stars in India had international backgrounds. Jewish girls like Ruby Myers, now called Sulochana, and the Anglo-Indian Patience Cooper rode high on the top of the theater marquees. Perveen mused, "Rochana sounds like a name that could be Hindu or Muslim, doesn't it? But she is quite fair—she might have European blood."

"All I heard from Mr. Ghoshal is that his wife is now serving as the studio's executive producer. Perhaps she's given up the stage lights for propriety."

"Oh." Perveen felt conflicted about the idea. Although Bombay needed more women in professional roles, she would miss the vicarious thrill of seeing Rochana win so many sword fights. "Pappa, if time allows, maybe we should go together for an early screening of Rochana's current film, *Train in Trouble*. Then you can see the creativity of the Ghoshals before meeting them."

"No, thank you. Moving pictures are a marvel, but they don't stir my emotion." Jamshedji dramatically pressed his hand to his heart. "There's nothing like Parsi theater, with flesh and blood people wearing colorful clothes singing songs and speaking words."

He was referring to the lively musical plays that their own community, Zoroastrians from Persia who'd long ago settled in India, excelled in.

"I wonder if there's a link between Parsis being prominent not only in theater but law," Perveen mused. "Both require commanding a stage and sometimes making a spectacle."

He chuckled. "That may be true. Now, tell me something about *Train in Trouble*, so I will be able to compliment them."

Perveen summarized the storyline. Rochana's character had raced to defeat a pair of bandits in a scene filmed atop a moving train. "It was a damned fine debut picture for Champa Films. I've also watched some of her earlier films from Royal Indian Pictures. Do you want to hear about those?"

Jamshedji waved his hand, the gold of his thick signet ring catching the table lamp's glow. "No need. Given the depth of your enthusiasm, I'm thinking that you'd be well suited for lead counsel."

Perveen felt herself swell with joy. As if to punctuate the declaration, a clap of thunder broke out.

"Baa!" Khushy said from the floor.

"And she calls my name!" Jamshedji boasted, beaming at the child.

"Are you sure?" Perveen spoke casually, rolling the ball back toward the baby with her foot. "She's looking at the ball."

"Yes, you heard it as clear as day, she is trying to say Bapa-vaji. It will take some time to get all of it expressed—but she is a quick study."

His granddaughter's supposed flattery had diverted him, so Perveen said, "Yes, of course she is! But could putting me forward as lead counsel diminish the likelihood the Ghoshals will hire us?"

Before she could answer, Perveen turned to see her mother, Camellia Mistry, had joined them.

"Everyone's up so early!" said Camellia, who at forty-nine,

still had the physique and thick, black hair of a younger lady. Because of the early hour, her hair fell loose to the middle of her back, and she wore a softly draped pink silk robe embroidered in the blooms that were her namesake.

"Good morning, Mamma!" Perveen said, wondering why it was that her mother always managed to look better than everyone else in the morning.

Camellia crouched down to pick up her only grandchild. "Khushy-jaan, you'd like your sweetheart to stay home with you today, isn't it?"

Perveen felt her back go up. Camellia longed for her daughter to play Mamma just as vehemently as Jamshedji thought she should work hard as a solicitor. "Mamma, I can manage work and still love Khushy."

"Of course. It's just that you are her special one!"

"No." She swallowed hard. "We mustn't pretend I'm her mother."

"And I am here, too. You misunderstood me," Camellia protested fervently.

Perveen relented, remembering how much her mother had loved Gulnaz. It must have been a shock to have had a daughter-in-law walk out of one of the most kindly and progressive families in Bombay's upper-class Zoroastrian community. Gulnaz hadn't left because of anyone's cruelty. Doctors said that Gulnaz's problems were tortures made by her own mind, an inscrutable condition that had revealed itself only after Khushy's birth.

"Perveen is fully right," Jamshedji said briskly. "She is still the sole female solicitor in the city, and it would be a shame for the city to lose having her. And if Mr. Ghoshal would grant his actress wife the position of executive producer, he is far from conservative. I think that if we play our cards right, Perveen could have *Queen of Hearts* and much more on her table."

THE APPOINTMENT WITH their prospective client was at two that afternoon. Although the drive would have normally taken fifteen minutes, Perveen requested that Arman, the family's chauffeur, be prepared for them at one-thirty. But Jamshedji had tarried on the telephone, so they were not able to leave until one-forty-five. Hiba and Gita stood by the doorway, bouncing Khushy between them, waiting for the goodbye moment that the baby was used to when her grandfather and aunt went out on business. Finally, kisses were delivered, and they were out the door.

"We will hardly make a good impression leaving the house at the time we were expected to arrive," Perveen grumbled as they got into the car.

"Creative types will be late themselves," Jamshedji said dryly. "And it's only Dadar West."

"I'll do my best," Arman said. "But there are plenty of ditches full of water. The rain has not given me a break; it was heavy all the way into the city and back."

"And why were you in the city today?" Perveen asked.

"Rustom-sahib needed a ride to the Willingdon Club."

"When the rain ceases, his business will pick up, and there will be no time for midday clubbing," Jamshedji said sternly.

The raindrops lessened as they entered the district of West Dadar, an affluent neighborhood that was building up rapidly for city commuters as well as those in the film business. The car chugged past a cluster of charming tiled-roof cottages and they came to a long, eight-foot-tall wrought iron fence.

"The address is right, but it doesn't look like a place of business," Jamshedji said as Arman drew the Daimler to a stop at a tall gate with ornate but partially rusted ironwork. Behind the gates, tall trees and overgrown shrubs seemed to form a forest.

"Perhaps not. The name on the signpost says A.D. Nanporia." Perveen pointed to the faded brass marker on the post set next to the gate.

"I could turn back and ask at a shop?" Arman inquired.

Perveen checked her watch. "That would make us even later."

As if she'd been overheard, a gray-haired guard with a stooped posture slowly emerged from the forest. Taking a key from a chain at his waist, he laboriously unlocked the gate. He approached and spoke to Jamshedji through the rolled-down passenger window. "Are you Mr. Mistry?"

"I am indeed!" Jamshedji declared.

"Sir, you are late. At the end of the driveway, you will come to a large house. Someone will let you in."

"But is this Champa Films or the Nanporia family home?" Perveen felt anxious. She'd envisioned a studio to look more businesslike than an aged countryside bungalow.

"Mr. Ardeshir Nanporia has leased the property to the studio. Mr. Ghoshal has been here for more than a year."

"Perhaps he will change the sign on the gate, then?" Perveen asked, trying to get a better sense of the tenant's relationship to the property owner.

"They prefer it that way." The guard lowered his voice. "Not so many interruptions."

"Thank you." Perveen supposed that hordes of young people wishing for their chance at stardom might present themselves at the gate, creating an annoyance.

"Try not to argue with a watchman," Jamshedji murmured as they drove on. "He could make your life difficult later on."

"Do you know Mr. Nanporia?" Perveen paused, thinking an awkward situation could arise if the reason they were being called was that Ghoshal wanted to press a case against his landlord.

"Yes; we've had business in the past. His forebears made a fortune shipping to China. Now the Nanporias have their hands in many businesses."

"I see." Perveen suddenly remembered Shireen Nanporia, an older girl from school who came from the family. Not her friend, but a popular girl. "Don't you think the watchman had cheek to mention the time? It's just five minutes after two."

"Bad weather brings bad moods," Jamshedji counseled. "Now, put a smile on your face and put your mind back in the right place."

Arman slowed the car as they proceeded up a stone driveway lined with coconut palms. Beyond the palms lay an impressive array of trees: very old ones, like banyan and peepal, combined with amla and ashoka that looked recently planted. On a sunny day, the property would look magnificent. Perveen also caught sight of numbered wooden buildings. Some also had hand-lettered signs in English that said DRESSING ROOM and FILM PROCESSING. Some distance from the road, in a grassy area, stood low wooden platforms that, she guessed, could be outdoor stages.

"Zoo!" she said aloud, catching sight of a sign and a high iron fence and gate. "My goodness, there might even be an elephant here. I saw one in that last picture!"

Jamshedji peered through the rolled-up window. "Any wildlife seems to be sheltering from the rain."

Perveen's ear caught a strange sound: a low, rolling snarl in the distance.

"Did you hear that?" When he nodded, she ventured, "Do you think it was a lion or tiger?"

"Any beasts are sure to be caged," her father said in a comforting tone.

"But it sounded so close!" As she stared through the rain-drenched trees, she wondered if the tiger had seen the car and was making a protest to defend its territory.

"Now, those small cottages over there—could they be for servants or actors?"

He was trying to distract her. Perveen followed his pointing finger to the low white stucco cottage and noticed a curtain twitch in one window. As they continued, they passed another cottage, well-built of stone and looking original to the property. This cottage had a veranda with a half roof, and on it, a thin gentleman was standing with a cigar at his mouth. Perveen was surprised to see that the man had blond hair and fair skin. Despite the hour, he wore a vest and pajamas, as if he had been lounging or asleep. The man turned to look at their car, and although he likely could not make out their faces through the window, he stepped back through the open door into the cottage as if not wanting to be seen.

"Who could that be?" Jamshedji mused.

"Certainly not anyone named Nanporia or Ghoshal!" Perveen said. "Maybe he's an actor from Britain."

They passed a long, oval pond of concrete that had a variety of potted plants around it; Jamshedji guessed aloud that this was probably used for water scenes, and Perveen agreed, remembering the Champa Films picture about Lord Krishna wherein a group of young actresses playing milkmaids had all emerged wearing soaking wet saris. She'd felt embarrassed for them—as well as for herself, hearing the lusty howls from men in the audience.

A nearby large, rectangular building reminded Perveen of a horse barn. Perhaps that had been the original use, judging from the line of half-sized doors on each side of the building. But she could see electric light shining from the interior, and the shapes of figures moving about. What magic was going on inside? Dancing, sword fighting, even kissing . . . Her pulse raced.

The car dipped down on an incline, and when it rose up, the original bungalow presented itself. No disappointment here: It was vast, two stories high and built of golden Porbandar limestone. Majestic arches framed both the lower and upper verandas. The arches seemed like a perfect frame for someone like Rochana to pose herself, but nobody at all was outside.

"Those look like Romanesque arches," Perveen said, gesturing toward the building. "So I'd say the bungalow's probably dating from as early as 1900, don't you think?"

"It could be even earlier than that," Jamshedji told her. "The

Nanporias have been rolling in money for decades, and they are known to be on top of every fashion."

Shireen Nanporia's uniforms had been made by a French seamstress, while most of the other girls got theirs from the school shop. No matter how hard Perveen scrutinized her while standing in line, she'd not seen a difference in Shireen's attire from her own.

The Daimler stopped. Arman slid out of his seat and came around to open the passenger door. Jamshedji exited first, hurrying up to the shelter of the house, with Perveen following, moving slowly to avoid puddles.

The front door opened without anyone knocking, even before she had ascended the veranda. Standing in the doorway was a golden-skinned Indian gentleman who appeared to be in his late thirties, wearing Western clothes and with hair slicked back. *As handsome as Rudolph Valentino*, Perveen thought as she watched him hold out his hand to Jamshedji. The two men shook, carrying out the British behavior that was commonplace among Indian elites. She'd seen photographs of Subhas Ghoshal before, but charisma could not translate to black-and-white.

Ghoshal's expression changed from ecstatic to perplexed when he caught sight of Perveen.

This reaction, followed by a sudden, rushed smile, made it apparent that Jamshedji hadn't said anything to him about his having a female partner. *Another client who won't want a lady solicitor*, she thought, preparing herself as she moved forward.

# 2

# A PAIR OF STARS

"I'm Subhas Ghoshal," he said, as if this was not an obvious fact. "Asmaa will take your umbrellas and coats. You must have run into trouble getting here."

As they entered a wide, black-and-white marble tiled floor, a very slender woman in her late thirties, with a dupatta covering her hair, came forward. Jamshedji eased off his coat and handed it to her. Perveen did the same, noting the dignity with which the woman held herself.

Jamshedji said, "Thank you. Because of these rains, my partner at the practice, Miss Perveen Mistry, had suggested that we should come earlier—and she was right."

"Miss Mistry, I am delighted!" Mr. Ghoshal put out a hand and gripped hers firmly. Nodding at the two of them, he said, "Your surname is the same. Do I see a family resemblance?"

"Without a doubt, the nose," Jamshedji said with a chuckle.

"And there's more!" Perveen wanted to prove she was more than a token. "We both read law at Oxford and emerged as solicitors."

"But not at the same time, I hope?" the man said, chuckling at his weak joke. "I am reading you as father and daughter. At least, that is how I would cast you in one of my pictures."

"You are correct," Perveen said with a forced smile, remembering what her father had advised her to do. Asmaa was watching as if she sensed Perveen's discomfort, but she looked away sharply when Perveen turned toward her.

"Please come into the library. It's the most comfortable place." Subhas waved his hand toward an arched doorframe.

Perveen was surprised to see that the large room was designed in the European manner and even had a fireplace with logs set aflame. The fireplace was an odd element for a house in Bombay, but perhaps the architect had responded to a desire of the Nanporias for European glamour. The room might have held their family furniture, which appeared moderately aged, yet well-made with ornate Gujarati carpentry. She proceeded through the large room, disappointed that Rochana wasn't present.

"Something to drink?" Subhas said, striding toward a mirror-topped cart cluttered with bottles holding liquids of gold, brown, and even red liquids. "I've just opened a bottle of excellent white rum. It's very nice with pineapple juice and grenadine."

"Isn't that just like a Mary Pickford?" Perveen said, before she could stop herself.

"Yes, that's what it is." When he smiled, his teeth flashed white. "You certainly know your way around a cocktail bar."

"Who is this Mary?" Jamshedji cut in.

"Miss Pickford is the star of stars in America, and I've heard talk about a cocktail named in her honor. I'd be honored to try a very mild version of the drink." Perveen wanted to make sure Subhas saw her as a modern woman and not a sheltered daughter.

"And so you shall have it!" Subhas clapped his hands together. "Some people are calling Rochana India's Mary Pickford, but I prefer to think of her as a bit more alluring. Mr. Mistry, would you also like a Mary Pickford?"

"Sir, please remember?" Asmaa's voice was low.

"Right, right. Our housekeeper cannot even touch a bottle of alcohol due to religion." His eyes rolled upward, and he gave Perveen and Jamshedji a sarcastic grin that made Perveen feel sorry for the servant.

"Actually, a cup of tea is truly what I crave on a day like this," Jamshedji said.

"Well, then you're in luck. Asmaa makes tastier chai than anyone outside of Bengal." Looking directly at the lady, Subhas added, "Bring the tea and tell Rochana to come in and fix the drinks."

"Yes, sahib." Asmaa's eyes, before she lowered them, were cool. Perveen thought they were luminous, well-shaped eyes, the kind worthy of a film heroine. Yet unlike a siren, Asmaa moved stiffly out of the room, perhaps from arthritis or irritation.

Perveen glanced at her father, who had made the conservative drink choice. Was his order meant to ease the situation for Asmaa, or was he trying to position Perveen as the modern choice of solicitor?

Perveen decided to press forward. "Before we talk business, I must compliment you on *Train to Trouble*. I am still thinking about the hair-raising sword fight between Rochana and Master Nishant. They made it look so realistic."

Grinning, Subhas leaned forward. "It was absolutely real! Rochana studied fencing as a girl. Her father served in the British Army and made sure all his children were quick with weapons."

"No, darling. Not all weapons. Only swords, knives, and bayonets."

When Perveen turned, she saw a slender woman a few inches taller than her, draped in a modish violet silk frock. Her hair was beaded with rain, and the short boots on her feet were damp, as if she'd just come in from outside. Yet if she'd worn a coat, it had been abandoned; she appeared ready to serve as a party hostess.

Perveen had wondered about Rochana's voice; she'd only ever seen screen images of her mouth moving. It turned out that she spoke English in a low-pitched, sweet tone with a veneer of proper Britishness. Girlish, although there was a maturity around her startling blue eyes that made her seem possibly older than the twenty years of her official biography.

The actress came forward toward her husband, squeezed his hand into hers, and then turned to look benevolently at Perveen and her father. "I was coming in from the zoo and heard I was needed for a drinks party. Welcome, whoever you are!"

"Our future solicitors are here," Subhas said. "Behold Mr. Jamshedji and Miss Perveen Mistry. May I present my wife, Rochana?"

Rochana's violet-blue eyes—so European in color, but Indian in shape—seemed to intensify as she studied the Mistrys. Turning to Subhas, she said, "Has it really come to pass?"

"Don't worry." He pursed his lips, as if sending her a kiss through the air, and Perveen felt a little shock at such a display of public affection. "The Mistrys are here to help us right the drifting boat."

Perveen murmured hello and her father put forward a hand. Rochana came forward and shook his hand, but when she came to Perveen, she reached upward to her face, pushing back a strand of hair from her forehead. The touch felt sensual and sent a shiver through Perveen.

"Your waves are exquisite," Rochana murmured. "And such a strong brow. You are obviously highly intelligent."

Perveen couldn't think of a rejoinder to the flattery, which had made her feel like she was being considered for a film role. The edge of her forehead was damp from the stamp of Rochana's hand and the brief, exciting moment.

"Tell me, what will you have to drink?" Rochana paused, looking appraisingly at her. "Or are you a teetotaler?"

Perveen suspected Rochana was trying to get a read on whether she was traditional. "I imbibe every now and then. Your husband lured me with a Mary Pickford, and I think he's having the same."

With a giggle, Rochana said, "Why not? Subhas is alluring, isn't he?"

"Isn't that an adjective more often used for ladies?" Subhas commented, smiling back at his wife. "But never mind."

"I suppose I'll make the same drink for myself, too." Rochana glided toward the bar cart and started handling bottles, clearly used to the process.

Asmaa reappeared silently with a tray holding a pot of tea, a cup, and enough Brittania biscuits for all four of them. Rochana paused, watching the lady lift the small pot of tea and start pouring. When Asmaa finished, Rochana gave her a soft look, as if to thank her, before Asmaa departed.

"Well, then, let's convene." Subhas patted the empty space next to him on the settee.

Rochana brought over the finished drinks, handed them around, and sat down. "Cheers, everyone."

Perveen tasted her drink, which was strong and overly sweet. She wouldn't be able to finish it, but she had indicated interest to Subhas and didn't want to offend Rochana.

"I want to tell them about that letter we got from Royal Indian Pictures last week," Subhas said gently to his wife.

"Why do we have to do something right away?" Rochana pouted at him and took a sip of her drink. "I can tell you from my experience ABC becomes upset about things and makes a fuss—and then a few weeks later he forgets about it."

Perveen wanted to understand what "ABC" meant, but she disliked jumping ahead when Rochana was anxious. She squeezed the glass, letting its coldness steady her. "This is only a meeting to learn more about why you think you need help."

"That's right." Jamshedji leaned back in his chair, as if to give the anxious actress some distance from him. "And please know that we will keep your confidence, whether or not you decide to retain us. I've been in practice for a quarter century in Fort. Perveen joined me two years ago."

"Very good," Subhas said briskly. "Now, if you didn't know—the man Rochana spoke about, the infamous ABC, is properly known as Abhijit Bipin Chatterjee."

"Mr. Chatterjee is the owner of Royal Indian Pictures," Perveen said for her father's edification. "And Miss Rochana's former employer."

"Chatterjee founded Royal Indian Pictures in 1917, around the same time I was raising funds to start Champa Films. Naturally, I watched him with admiration—and some envy. Rochana was a star at Royal Indian Pictures from the very first picture. Six months ago, she resigned to marry me"—he smiled self-consciously—"and come over as star actress and a co-producer. We didn't hear a peep about Rochana's move until a month ago, when ABC wrote telling me that Rochana has broken their existing contract."

"And don't forget—he also wanted bubbles!" Rochana added.

"Bubbles?" Perveen inquired, wondering if this was a reference to alcohol, or just more film slang.

Rochana's eyes welled up, and she murmured, "Bubbles was my baby."

"Oh!" Perveen felt both confused and horrified by her misstep. "I am so sorry. I just didn't know."

"Let me interject that Bubbles is—was—a dog," Subhas said, his expression serious. "He was Rochana's pet who appeared in some films with her at Royal Indian Pictures and also in my own picture *Train to Trouble*."

"Oh, I remember having seen him," Perveen said. "What a terrible shame."

"Bubbles was a second employee, then?" Jamshedji asked as he began taking notes. Typically, this was Perveen's job, making her think that the switch was to allow her to assume the leading role in this consultation.

"No more an employee than any of the tigers and deer in our

film company zoo," Subhas said. "We certainly don't have contracts with them. They are akin to company equipment, though Tora seems to think she's Rochana's child."

"Tora's the best tiger we have," Rochana said, giving her husband a reproving look. "She arrived to the studio a few months before I did, and our zookeeper, Sridhar, and I have been training her. You must take time for a zoo tour, Miss Mistry."

"Is this zoo the place where Bubbles stayed?"

"No, no, Bubbles stayed with me. You see, Bubbles was *my* pet—ABC didn't buy him. And just like our Tora, he is a being, not a piece of equipment," she said, throwing a scolding look at her husband.

"When did you acquire Bubbles, then?" Perveen asked.

"I know for certain that it was November 11, 1918." Rochana glanced at Subhas, who gave her an encouraging nod. "We were celebrating war's end with a party at the Great Eastern Hotel. A small white poodle ran into the salon with a waiter chasing him. The staff said he'd been abandoned by a previous guest and that they couldn't force him from the hotel. Clearly he was no street dog! I scooped him up there and then. Subhas named him Bubbles, because we were drinking champagne."

"I was at that party—only because ABC did not know what a rival I would become," Subhas said. "After Rochana began bringing Bubbles from her flat to set, she suggested adding him to some of her scenes. And thus, a star was born."

Rochana's eyes shone with tears. "His last film will be *Queen of Hearts*, releasing end of the month. You'll see him in that."

Perveen was confused. "Was Bubbles quite old then—did he die of natural causes?"

"No, he was quite spritely," Rochana said, wiping her eyes. "He started off last Wednesday morning in the highest of spirits but became listless in the afternoon."

"He took his last breath before dinnertime," Subhas said soberly, putting his hand over Rochana's—an act that again made Perveen envy the couple's easy physicality. "Sometimes quick is better—less suffering. But I miss him also. Darling, I'm so sorry."

Rochana gave her husband a soft look. "Bubbles was going to play in our next film, and we'd rehearsed a sequence where he picks up a dagger between his teeth and carries it to me."

"A dagger in a sheath," Subhas said. "We could find a new dog."

"Dogs are highly prized studio assets. It takes at least a year to train one to be able to work in film." Rochana walked over to the grand piano, where she picked up a silver-framed photograph that she brought to Perveen. "Our cinematographer shot this a few months ago."

Perveen sighed, looking at the picture of a small white poodle playing with a ball in a garden. The small dog seemed to be smiling, but perhaps that was because of the way light and shadow played in the picture. "He's very sweet. You must have brought so much joy to him, too."

"My mother used to say he was like my baby," she said, shaking her head. "And what could that studio demand from us, now that he's dead?"

"Don't worry about that, Rochana," Subhas said crisply. "You are of far higher value."

Shaking her head, she said, "I had to get away from them—I would be dead, or close to it, if I'd stayed."

Perveen scrutinized her, wondering if the actress was using hyperbole or speaking an actual truth. "Do you mean—there were attempts on your life?"

"She is saying that their work was very risky," Subhas cut in. "Rochana had a scene in the sea for one of ABC's films on a day that the waves were high. She was swept up and it took a Royal Navy crew to rescue her."

"Shocking!" Jamshedji said.

Rochana nodded and said, "I'd thought the water looked

quite fierce, but I'm a strong swimmer. I agreed to go in. When I knew I was losing strength, I screamed to be rescued. From the way I kept being swept under, anyone could tell that I wasn't acting. But they kept on filming at least two more minutes!"

"Was that film *Victim of Fate*?" Perveen recalled how she'd felt while watching this recent film's suspenseful scene of Rochana disappearing in the waves and then finally rising out of the water to swim to shore.

"An apt title, wasn't it? I was almost drowned."

Subhas pursed his lips. "And at no time did Royal Indian Pictures ask Rochana if she preferred a stunt actress take the scene!"

"Why would they ask?" Rochana asked. "No true female actress working in India can swim like me."

Jamshedji raised an eyebrow. "True female?"

"Until recently, very few Indian girls were allowed by their families to perform on camera. At least, no girls from *refined* families," Subhas added, glancing fondly at his wife. "Therefore, most lady characters were portrayed by slender fellows with fine features. In fact, we have one young man retired from being a lady who works these days in cinematography for us."

"I understand now. Many actors play women's roles onstage in Parsi theater," Jamshedji said. "Quite some talent there!"

Rochana rolled her eyes. "Action scenes in films came into fashion because of what's being done in America. Tremendously brave actresses who race cars backward, ride horses at breakneck speed, and so on."

"Like Helen Holmes," Perveen said, thinking about the American film *The Midnight Limited*, in which the actress hung from the railings of a bridge and jumped onto the roof of a moving train.

"Yes!" Rochana answered. "And there are others. Have you heard of Helen Gibson, Mary MacLaren, and Mary Fuller . . . ?"

Jamshedji looked bemused. "All these actresses with the same first names? Why is it?"

Perveen thought that Rochana's name was awfully similar to that of Sulochana, a slightly better-known actress, but decided it was better not to point this out.

"Names are given for marketability. For instance, the pretty girl known as Seeta Devi, who debuted in the German-Indian film *Light of Asia*, walked onto the audition stage with the simple name Renee Smith."

Perveen looked expectantly at Rochana, waiting for her to reveal her original, possibly dull, name. Rochana merely gave her a wink.

It wouldn't have been right to press her. Four years earlier, Perveen had married a handsome young man who'd come from Calcutta to Bombay to seek a wife. Cyrus Sodawalla had been a sweet talker, but he and his family had wanted nothing more than an endless stream of Mistry money to finance their failing bottling plant. When the truth had finally come out and violence ensued, she'd fled his family house in Calcutta to return to Bombay. Perveen had returned to using her maiden name in both work and social life. Quite likely Rochana had chosen a new name to protect herself from past associations.

Her father's crisp voice broke into her thoughts. "Miss Rochana, what happened after your film with the near drowning? Were you injured and unable to work for some time?"

"I had some cuts and bruises. But I didn't work for two weeks."

"Were you unpaid during this time?" Perveen asked, thinking of a possible countersuit.

"No, ABC still paid me," she acknowledged. "But as I waited during my recovery, I began thinking about how to leave. I'd met Subhas at that party you heard about. He was often at film world gatherings, and we had become quite friendly. After my accident he called on me at my flat and sent the best doctors to see me and had so many thoughtful gifts delivered! When he proposed marriage, I knew in an instant I wanted to be with him. He promised me a better life. Action scenes would be done safely, and I wouldn't only have to be on camera. I could use my intelligence to help him create ideas for new films."

"What came first, working at Champa Films, or the marriage?" Perveen wanted to be clear on this point. It would be hard to argue that Rochana was leaving Royal Indian Pictures because of their negligence for her safety when she might have really left because of a romantic attachment to a man.

"We married at my family temple in Calcutta one afternoon and started work the next day!" Subhas answered.

Perveen knew from Subhas's first and second names that he was a Hindu—and she'd surmised because of Rochana's parentage, she was likely a Christian. What had her parents thought about the marriage? Although this was the question that sprung to her mind, she could hardly ask it. Instead, she turned to Rochana. "So, it sounds like you are still acting, obviously, and have some administrative responsibilities?"

"But of course," Rochana said. "Having done film work for three years already in Calcutta, I know all about the responsibilities behind the camera."

"Rochana has every kind of freedom with me," Subhas said. "If she wants to star, well and good, because she's a top marquee name. But she's proven generous enough to give a hand to other females. We plan to build out our studio with a number of leading ladies and gents."

"How are you giving a hand?" Perveen asked, noticing Rochana's pleased expression at her husband's words.

"I have been nurturing a sweet little starlet: Marisa Young, the daughter of Master Nishant," Rochana purred. "The girl plays supporting roles now but may get to headline one day."

"And who is Master Nishant?" Jamshedji asked, making Perveen wish she had prepped him further. Master Nishant was a famous actor: the Indian version of Douglas Fairbanks.

"Master Nishant is the most impressive example of manhood

in India," Subhas said, with a hint of humor. "He was a bodybuilder before he got into films. He can lift whatever you hand him. Sometimes he is Rochana's adversary, other times her partner. They look very nice together," Subhas added.

"I agree," Perveen said, remembering the dashing maharaja the man had portrayed in *Train to Trouble*. "Returning to your situation, Rochana, have you kept your copy of the contract with Royal Indian Pictures?"

Rochana edged closer to Subhas. "No. When I decided to leave the studio, it was very quick. I had just two suitcases of clothes and, of course, Bubbles."

"Do you recall putting pen to contract, though?" Jamshedji pressed, reminding Perveen that this should have been the first question.

She paused. "I'm not sure there was a contract. He told me my salary, and I was so happy. And after making two pictures, I began receiving more every two weeks."

"Paid in cash, then?" Jamshedji asked. When she nodded, he asked, "Where is your home?"

"Here, of course." Tittering slightly, she asked, "Where else would you think?"

"I mean in the past. You had a flat in Calcutta—what did you do with your possessions when you left? Are they in your family's flat?"

Rochana fiddled with the fringe on the sofa throw. "It was a furnished flat that I shared with another lady. And when I left, I only came away with my pictures, my dog, and a few favorite dresses stuffed into a trunk."

"She and the parents are not on good terms," Subhas said, patting Rochana's hand. "No fault of her own, but of prejudice."

"Race and religion," Rochana said in a low voice. "No matter how famous he is—he is a Hindu Bengali. That's the way it works."

So Perveen had supposed correctly that Rochana's parents hadn't approved—yet the actress had gone forward and married. She tightened, imagining her own father's likely reaction if he found that she yearned for Colin or, come to think of it, *any man*. Although separated, she was still legally bound to Cyrus, likely for eternity.

"Never mind, then." Jamshedji waved a weary hand. "Miss Rochana has no contract to show us, but that is not the end of the world. We can certainly endeavor to help, if you would like to engage us. Let's start with the letter."

"Very well. And I must say, Mr. Mistry, that it's exemplary for you to make your daughter a partner in your practice. It shows both your respect for her, and your progressive nature." Rochana sprang up to move, catlike, toward the desk, where she rummaged in the drawer. "Sweetie, where is the letter?"

"That's right—I almost forgot. I gave it to Ardeshir."

"Who?" Perveen asked. "Do you mean to another lawyer?"

"No, no," Subhas said, smiling expansively. "I'm friends with the fellow who owns this place, Ardeshir Nanporia. He is my chief financial backer, and a shrewd businessman, so I thought he might have an opinion. He rang this morning and suggested that I call a lawyer, and your father's was one of the names given."

"You must trust Mr. Nanporia's judgment," Perveen commented, watching him. Her opinion was that showing signs of legal trouble to a funder exposed a vulnerability.

"With my life!" Subhas touched his chest. "And he is not the only angel in my life. Aside from dear Rochana, the whole team makes my films possible."

Perveen seized the opening. "Speaking of your team, we passed a European-looking gentleman standing outside a cottage as we came onto the property."

"That's Hans Becker; our cinematographer," Rochana cut in eagerly. "He's also the fellow who photographed Bubbles. A world-class talent!"

"Yes, indeed he's European—from Switzerland," Subhas said with a hint of pride. "We met some years ago, because he had come already to India to do filming for a French company by the name of Pathé. He said he liked our Bombay weather better than that of Zurich, so I invited him to become our cinematography director." Laying a hand on his own fine lapel, he said, "It's my heart's desire for you to meet him and the rest of the company. Both of you! Do come tomorrow evening; we're having a party to celebrate the completion of *Queen of Hearts*. The festivities start at five."

"How kind." Jamshedji gave an apologetic smile. "However, I must give my regrets—I have a previous obligation."

"But what about you, dear? Do bring a companion, if you'd rather." Rochana regarded her with sympathetic eyes, as if she thought Perveen wasn't used to going places without an escort.

Perveen hesitated. Because of Jamshedji's dinner meeting at the Ripon Club, she'd covertly promised to meet Colin Sandringham for a lecture. However, attending the party could be an important way to build a bond with both Subhas and Rochana. "Yes, I should like that very much. Thank you!"

Jamshedji cleared his throat. "Before we part, may I explain how Mistry Law operates?"

Without waiting, he delivered a summary. He and Perveen would research the grounds on which ABC's letter was based, and from there, any legal liabilities or advantages of Royal Indian Pictures. Jamshedji asked for a retainer of one hundred rupees and described the hourly fee structure of twenty rupees per hour for his services, and fifteen for Perveen's.

Subhas's brow creased. "Is the price difference due to a difference in qualification or expertise?"

"My rate is higher due to co-qualifications as both barrister and solicitor, and my limited availability," Jamshedji said. "Miss Mistry is a licensed solicitor who's had a more recent legal education than I have at our alma mater, the University of Oxford.

Furthermore, she's familiar with personalities of the film world. I will always be available, but I believe it would be more appropriate for my eminently qualified daughter to be your chief counsel."

Perveen felt her eyes dampening. Her beloved father had put her strengths ahead of his own.

"A lady lawyer will suit us perfectly!" Rochana clapped her hands together. "But Miss Mistry, how formal must things be? How do you prefer to be called?"

Perveen couldn't stop smiling. "I'd much rather be Perveen."

"And you must call me Rochana," the actress said, making a kissing pucker with her mouth.

"Who is the contract with: my wife or me?" Subhas interrupted.

Perveen flinched at his reaction, especially because he was looking at her father. Had Rochana overstepped, when Subhas didn't actually want to work with her? "The contract will be with you, Mr. Ghoshal, as you are the owner of Champa Films, and the letter is directed toward you. It's a bit complex because Rochana is the one who allegedly broke a contract and thus might face trouble. Our intention is to nip that in the bud."

Subhas glanced at Rochana, whose playful demeanor had changed to a more serious one. "That's all right, then. I know she's been worried about things. A beauty should not have such troubles marring her expression."

Jamshedji opened the brass locks of his Swaine Adeney briefcase, the same model as Perveen's—in fact, she'd brought it for him as a gift upon her return from her studies in England. He pulled out the boilerplate contract and handed it to Mr. Ghoshal. "Please read it carefully and ask any questions you have. No need to sign today, just before we begin our work together."

"I'll write you the check, though," Subhas said, going to the desk and taking out a checkbook. "And Ardeshir Nanporia is coming to the party, so I'll certainly have the letter back by then."

As the man wrote out his check, Perveen had a sudden idea. "Mr. Ghoshal, perhaps if Rochana looks at the employment contract she signed with you, it might jog her memory about whether she ever was given a similar document when she worked in Calcutta."

There was a pause, and Rochana looked toward Subhas, her forehead creasing. "I don't remember you giving me a contract, dear."

"A contract is not needed when one is married. What's mine is hers, isn't it?" Subhas said.

Perveen looked from the husband to wife, thinking that would be the case, as long as the two stayed married. But it had only been six months. That was about the length of her co-habitation with Cyrus Sodawalla: a scandal in Parsi circles. "Under Hindu law, widows do not automatically inherit a man's property. To do otherwise, one needs to specify in a contract or will."

Perveen glanced at Rochana, whose engaging smile had faltered.

Subhas took a last sip of his drink. "I'd rather not think about my or anyone's prospective death when so much of the real world keeps me busy. But what I've heard so far, I like. Let's work together. If you can get us out of this little irritation with ABC and ensure our next picture opens without trouble, there will be plenty of time to get every scrap of paper in order."

He was trying to deflect, Perveen thought. Was he trying to promise the world to them, just as he might have done with Rochana?

# 3

# THE ALICE CARD

"By not paying his leading lady a salary, he is cheating her immensely," Perveen fumed on the ride back down the driveway. It was raining hard, and she could hear the tires struggling through mud—just as she, too, was struggling with her emotion.

"Hold on with your outrage." With a relaxed sigh, Jamshedji settled back in the passenger seat. "The husband said he plans to share profits with her."

"Not exactly. He just said, 'What's mine is hers.'" Perveen stared out the window at the estate's trees bending under weight of rain. "Without a contract, the words are meaningless. Imagine what happens if the marriage fails. And Hindu marriage laws don't allow for divorce!"

Jamshedji looked curiously at her. "And why are you predicting such ills for them?"

"I'm not. It's just that contracts make good business, especially in family situations," Perveen muttered, thinking of how in her own situation, her father could easily change his mind about how much she received for her work. Recently her father had named her as his partner; but there was no contract, and she certainly hadn't received a larger paycheck.

"I'm pleased you are available to attend the party. Whom will you bring as your companion?"

"As I mentioned, Alice is Rochana's great admirer, although I don't know if Rochana will remember meeting her."

"She might. A six-foot-tall blonde lady with a booming voice is not to be forgotten!" Jamshedji said with a chuckle. "In the meantime, draw up the employment contract properly and have it sent to Subhas; perhaps he will even have it signed by the time you arrive at the party."

"And we can't do anything without having the letter from ABC that's in Mr. Nanporia's hands." Perveen was already slightly frustrated. "Why did it take five months after Rochana's departure for ABC's threat to arrive? I wonder if it's because he's had a sudden change of fortune."

"It might be financial pressure," Jamshedji agreed. "However, he must realize that Subhas Ghoshal is unlikely to have much to give him. Filmmaking is a very difficult business!"

"It's a stereotype that films are risky business," Perveen expounded. "While in reality, the profits from one typical picture being shown in theaters and even tents around the country can be quite large. ABC is right in thinking that without Rochana, his profits will shrink. He may have seen it already."

"Ah. I see your logic," Jamshedji said. "The question remains: How can we mollify him without them having to pay for it?"

WHEN THEY ARRIVED in Bruce Street, the rain was hammering down. Perveen and Jamshedji hustled out of the car and up the stairs to Mistry House, the high-roofed stone mansion decorated with gargoyles that was a former family home but now served as a grand law office.

"Too much rain," Mustafa said as he opened the door. The tall, handsome Pathan man served as Mistry House's majordomo; he lived in and attended to matters large and small. His years as a former high-ranking soldier had given him the advantage of speaking English almost as well as Hindi and Punjabi. Ten years in Bombay meant he also knew its native language, Marathi. Perveen smiled her thanks as Mustafa gave each of them a towel to dry off. Words were not always needed between Perveen and Mustafa, who was almost like an uncle to her.

Sitting on the mahogany bench in the hallway, Perveen changed from her wet sandals into dry slippers and recalled Rochana's stylish short boots. So practical, and also modern. Where could one buy them—and could they be worn with a sari?

Jamshedji had changed shoes more quickly and got upstairs ahead of her. When she finally made it into the first-floor study, her father was already seated at the partners' desk with his notebook open, reading through the notes he'd taken during the Champa Films meeting.

Perveen wondered whether she might find news about Champa Films and Indian Pictures in the papers. A carved mahogany shelf near the room's entrance held a full month's newspapers: The variety delivered to their office was larger than those that came to the house in the suburbs. She found no editorial features. Still, a paper from the previous Sunday had an advertisement that proclaimed: *Coming Soon to the Imperial—Queen of Hearts!* The rectangular space had a closeup of Rochana's big eyes shining out from behind a fanned deck of cards. Here, she looked much more coy than she'd appeared in person.

Step two was getting Alice involved. This was almost a certain yes. Perveen went back downstairs into the hall for the telephone. To her surprise, it wasn't the household butler who answered, but Lady Gwendolyn Hobson-Jones.

"Perveen. I suppose you're ringing for Alice?"

"Yes," Perveen answered. Who else would she ring? Alice's mother was always cool with Perveen. She'd imagined it was because Gwendolyn didn't like her daughter being close to Indians, especially the one who'd helped her daughter land a position teaching mathematics at Woodburn College. Now

Alice had been appointed dean of students, but this promotion was unwelcome news for a woman who dearly wanted her free-spirited daughter to get married.

"It may take a moment. She's not come down yet today."

"Oh! Is she feeling poorly?"

"Not at all. She was playing tennis for most of yesterday and then was out to dinner. It was a late night, probably, and she's sleeping in. And how are you faring these days?"

The personal question was a surprise. "I'm living a bit more quietly than that. Because of monsoon, I'm only at the office when the roads are passable. When I'm home, my niece Khushy keeps me busy. She's just four months old and she's—"

"Govind—go tell Alice there's a call!" Gwendolyn interrupted what Perveen was going to say about her niece's ability to hold tight to things. Her voice was sweeter when she returned to Perveen. "Sorry. I've got a charity meeting—must run. I'll leave the phone off the hook, and surely Alice will pick up in a minute."

Gwendolyn set down the receiver in such a way that Perveen was left hearing the staccato barking of Diana, the family's dog. Diana had joined the household eight months earlier after Alice had taken her from the streets. The small terrier sounded much larger than she was. A moment later, the barking stopped, and Alice spoke into the phone.

"Good morning! What are you doing awake so early?"

"It's mid-afternoon already, Alice. I didn't know you were such a sleepyhead."

"The last few weeks of the college's holiday," Alice said. "I'm knackered from tennis and the heartiest dinner with Kitty Daboo at her house. Can you believe they didn't serve till ten-thirty?"

"Remind me who Kitty is?"

"Her good name is Roshan and she teaches literature at Woodburn College. You met her once. She lives in Breach Candy, and we've seen each other quite a lot during the break."

"Yes, it has been hard catching you—when the rain breaks you always seem to be out playing tennis."

"Yes, Kit and I are tennis partners. If we get rained out, we just loll around and talk, do this and that. I'm so glad you called; now I know the phone's working again. I tried to ring you yesterday afternoon, but we had no service. The rains ruined the junction box in Malabar Hall."

"It must have been very hard for your family to manage with the line down."

"Mummy was annoyed, even though I told her she needn't worry—if anything went wrong in Malabar Hill, it would likely be fixed before anywhere else in Bombay, save the police headquarters and the secretariat."

"All places where your father gets to spend his days," Perveen said with a chuckle. "But there's no need to be sour. I've something important to ask you—it's got to do with my work. Are you up for coming along to a party tomorrow evening?"

"Sure, unless I loathe the people. Who's giving it?" Alice's voice dropped an octave. As the daughter of one of the Bombay governor's councilors, she was one of the most socially connected people in the city.

"Rochana and Subhas Ghoshal. They gave me an invitation to bring someone to a private prescreening at this party. I don't suppose you'd like to come?"

Alice sucked in her breath, the sound rippling down the line. "You mean—to see Rochana's film before it's actually released? Of course, but—well, I'll disappoint Kitty because we'd planned to attend the Thinkers Lecture at the Royal Asiatic Society. But those lectures occur monthly, and this is an extraordinary opportunity! How did you get the invitation?"

Because of past work Alice had done for Mistry Law, she had a legally protected status and was one of very few people who could be informed that Subhas Ghoshal had retained Mistry Law as his company's counsel.

"He must be—your most famous client yet!" Alice said excitedly.

"Not as famous as his wife. But the one who will hopefully give us years of business."

"And to think I'll be at the party with you! Did I tell you about the time Rochana and I met?"

"Only about a dozen times," Perveen said with a laugh. "At the Poona racetrack, wasn't it? You were with your father for the celebration of the new clubhouse, and—"

"She was dismounting her horse. She's a fantastic rider—you'll remember that from films we've seen. Seeing her there, wearing a proper riding habit and behaving like anyone else, I was gobsmacked." Alice chuckled and said, "I almost couldn't get it out of my mouth to say hello to her, let alone ask for her signature. I do hope she remembers me—but of course, stars meet so many people. Probably to her, all the English look alike!"

Perveen snorted, knowing Alice was being snide. Her friend had rued the inability of her mother to remember the identities of their servants and other Indians she'd met repeatedly. That kind of carelessness was one of the many byproducts of colonialism that made Alice uncomfortable. "Even if Rochana doesn't recall you, I'm sure she'll be pleasant. She doesn't think herself above helping anyone: In fact, she even made everyone cocktails at our meeting."

"Sounds like quite a meeting. Tell me everything!"

"I will—and I was thinking you might be able to help me with some background research? I mean, could we go over what you might know about Rochana's career, et cetera?"

"Rather! With so many rainy days, I've little better to do than sort my film scrapbooks. Could you join me soon—for breakfast, maybe?"

"Not breakfast, you goose. By the time I get there, it will be late afternoon," Perveen said, looking at the grandfather clock in the hall. "And don't put Govind to any trouble. I'll bring some pastries from Yazdani."

"Ooh, goody. Nankhatai, please!"

AN HOUR LATER, Perveen had gone uphill to the Hobson-Jones bungalow. It was a grand house with three stories, but with the heavy rain, mold had begun to mar the pale yellow stucco, just as her own white stucco house in Dadar had a dingy brown growth on its edge. The patch on the second story level was fresh, and not too large. No repainting could be done until after the rains; it was a fact of Bombay life.

Govind, the butler, opened the door and took away the box of sweet butter biscuits Alice had requested to be properly plated. Alice came down the stairs, barefoot and still in her linen dressing gown, a bluebell color that enhanced her eyes. Alice's luminous, intelligent eyes were inherited from her father, along with his height and strong build. Her figure was too broad for the current fashion but looked just right for someone who was six feet tall. Her dirty-blonde hair was cut in a bob that stuck out in all directions; clearly, she hadn't combed it, a sign of how quickly she'd hurried downstairs.

Her arms full of paper and other objects, Alice beckoned for Perveen to follow to the dining room. Two places had been set on the glossy mahogany table. Perveen eyed the china, which was etched with gold and a delicate pattern of baby pink flowers and bluebirds. Probably Spode. Yet the elegance of the luncheon setting vanished when Alice set down a vast pile of newspaper pages and a large, dog-eared scrapbook.

"It's so lucky for me that you have all of these," Perveen said, carefully picking up the clipped newspaper pieces. Some of the papers were damp and already starting to disintegrate. "It seems like you've collected information about films from quite a few countries."

"Yes—anything that's screened here is of interest to my

students' film club. And about half the club members can't afford to go to theaters, so they treasure looking at the ads and articles. They will be spiffed to hear about me getting to chat with Rochana."

Perveen put down the clipping and chose her words carefully. "Dear, you mustn't share about the party with the students. Professional discretion is needed because one never knows what might be repeated."

"Of course." Alice's voice dropped an octave as she added, "The Ghoshals aren't being charged with a crime, are they?"

Perveen shook her head. "Nothing of the sort. Just between us, I'm aiming to protect them against a potential lawsuit from Rochana's former employer."

Alice's eyes glowed even deeper blue. "You must mean Royal Indian Pictures."

"Yes. Tell me, did you ever hear about Rochana almost drowning while filming something for them?"

Alice's pale brows drew together. "Not that I can recall. The main story was a question about her background, whether she is of royal blood, mixed blood, something like that. We're most likely to find it in one of the Sunday papers."

"At our meeting, Subhas intimated that Rochana comes from a military family," Perveen said. "I don't know anything more except the parents were displeased with her marrying Subhas and are still at odds with her."

"Well, I suppose it doesn't matter whether her parents are terrible because she's paying her own way as a film star." Alice had stopped at a page of the scrapbook. "Ah, here is something. While working on her fourth film with Royal Indian Pictures, Rochana was rescued from drowning. So that story's true."

The article mentioned the accident that Rochana had described, except it didn't mention the actress being unable to work afterward. Reading this account reminded Perveen of another misfortune—the recent death of Bubbles. This she explained to Alice in brief.

"What a terrible situation." Alice's eyes shone with empathy. "I can't imagine losing Diana—I'd have nobody warm to sleep with at night and nobody to kiss good morning." Alice's words made Perveen think of Colin, and she silently agreed that her friend was lucky to have a pet. As if understanding, Diana came over to kiss Perveen's ankle with her wet nose. "Bubbles was such a delightful sidekick for Rochana. Did you hear whether she's got a replacement?"

"She didn't mention one. Truly, she was quite broken up about the death. Crying quietly."

"Oh, dear," Alice said, and Diana whined, as if in sympathy. "It's all right, Diana. Be a good girl and bring me your ball."

As Diana instantly quieted and padded out of the room, Perveen said, "She's very well trained; it seems quicker for you to get Diana quiet than I can with Khushy. Now, getting back to our situation. You'll come to the party, and I—"

"I'll make a grand second impression on Rochana!" Alice interrupted. "I was mourning all the comments I didn't have a chance to make when we met in Poona. Now's my chance."

Perveen had a sudden, horrific picture of Alice delivering a monologue to Rochana. "Alice, you are so very enthusiastic. I must warn you this party should have many businesspeople who are important to the Ghoshals. They must circulate and talk with everyone."

"I won't embarrass you. I promise!" Alice said firmly. "You'll see."

"That I will." Perveen stood up, readying herself to leave, but was almost knocked over when Alice leapt from her own chair to embrace her.

"Oh, how I love you! Since coming to India, this is the most exciting thing we'll be doing together."

"The feeling is mutual," Perveen said, hugging back her

friend's solid, reassuring frame. This would be a very mild excitement compared to some in their past. At their student days at St. Hilda's College, they had marched for suffrage, holding their own against a line of formidable police with batons. In India, they had also come close to trouble with the police, as they'd tried in vain to defend a student undergoing a beating. Sometimes they'd helped achieve justice; other times, they counted themselves fortunate to have escaped serious harm.

Holding her even tighter, Alice kissed her cheek but in the next minute sprang back quickly, dropping her arms from Perveen's body.

"What is this?"

The clipped tone of Gwendolyn Hobson-Jones rang through the room. Alice's mother had appeared in the doorway. With her blonde hair styled in a lacquered bob and a plum silk frock decorated with white pearl beads and embroidered orchids, Lady Hobson-Jones was a vision of fashion, the opposite of her casual daughter.

"Good afternoon." Perveen forced a smile. "Lady Hobson-Jones, you have returned from your outing."

"Obviously!" The woman glared at Perveen, making her point that niceties didn't work.

"Who's here?" Sir David's voice boomed, and in seconds, the handsome, silver-haired man in his fifties appeared, filling the room with his strong presence. "If it isn't our dear Miss Mistry! It's been far too long since we've met. How's business at the family firm?"

"Busy." A slight exaggeration, but it was important to keep up appearances.

"Bully for you and your father. If things slow, I've always got ideas for you," Sir David added. "In the meantime, why not join Alice and me for a canter around the club one morning? The rain's so much lighter today that I feel optimistic about tomorrow."

Perveen had never done well with riding, so she made a quick excuse. "Riding doesn't agree with my back—though I do enjoy watching the horses run."

"You heard her," Gwendolyn Hobson-Jones said. "She's really not interested."

Perveen tensed, sensing that she'd given Alice's mother an opening to dismiss her even further.

"Another time, then." Sir David had an easy manner with Indians; probably because he spoke Hindi well and had spent over three decades in country. Perhaps it was because of Gwendolyn's lack of happiness as an idle wife in India that he supported Alice's foray into work and had praised Perveen's position as the city's first woman lawyer.

"Where are you two coming from?" Alice asked, affecting a casual air while scooping together the scrapbooks. "It's a surprise to see you together before the evening."

"I did the flowers for tonight's Evensong at the cathedral with my committee, and your father stopped by to give me a lift home. It appears that you both took advantage of my absence."

"Sorry. Must run!" Sir David said, giving a sort of salute to Perveen before he stepped back out into the hall. The main door creaked open and closed heavily. Shortly afterward, Govind appeared and Lady Hobson-Jones thrust the lilies at him. Perveen saw that her hand was shaking. Govind took hold of the flowers gently and, without looking at anyone, disappeared, presumably to find a vase.

"You should count yourself lucky your father didn't see what you just did!" Gwendolyn said in a tight voice. Perveen flinched, wondering if she was talking about her white daughter embracing an Indian friend.

"Mummy, what on earth do you mean? It's just scrapbooks," Alice protested. Diana had come close to Alice and was whining, as if she too were frightened.

Gwendolyn's eyes swept over the table and the news clippings, then at the briefcase near Perveen. "Did you bring this filthy detritus with you?"

"I—" Perveen was cut short by Alice's quick retort.

"It's all mine, Mummy. You know that I keep scrapbooks about music and film."

"I hadn't realized they were in such a deplorable condition." Gwendolyn shook her head disconsolately. "You and your obsession with actresses and sword fighting. I'd rather you had come with me to the cathedral this morning—it draws a top-drawer group of girls who are doing something meaningful with their lives."

"Their purpose as I understand it is to marry stuffy men and spend their days piddling with others like them!" Alice shot back. "Your friends look down on me, Mummy. They only care about being with like-minded wives."

Perveen's heart was racing now. Ever since she'd known Alice, her friend had only expressed loathing for her mother. Perveen always strived to avoid commenting on the woman, no matter how much she privately disliked her. She didn't want to make things worse.

Gwendolyn's cheeks now had two spots of bright color. "If it weren't for the flower committee, St. Thomas Cathedral would be a very dull place. Attendance would be lower, and people would not have their spirits raised in these dreary days."

"I know that you believe you are doing God's work," Alice said glumly. "But all the while, you ignore the two real women workers at your table, both of whom have fought tooth and nail to have paying jobs, jobs in which we serve people who actually need help."

"It wasn't work that I saw you two doing—"

"I'm quite sorry. I've come at a difficult time." Perveen arose, thinking the longer she stayed, the worse things would become.

"Better take it away before she disposes of it," Alice said bleakly to Perveen. "When you're through, bring it to my office at the college. I'm elated that the new term is starting, and I can get out of this hellhole!"

Perveen snapped shut the brass clasps on her case while Alice and her mother stared venomously at each other. Awkwardly, she said, "Goodbye, then."

"Yes, I'll see—" Alice bit her lip. "Goodbye."

Perveen guessed Alice had been about to say: *See you tomorrow.*

But she didn't want her mother to know.

# 4

# INTRIGUE AT THE ASIATIC

By Tuesday morning, Perveen had gotten through most of Alice's clippings. There was a lot to see: dozens of film reviews and scads of photographs of headstrong actresses on galloping horses or posed toward the camera with guns pointed. She paused at the advertisement for *The Sheik*, a film released the previous year. In the picture, fair-haired Agnes Ayres was pulling away from the embrace of Rudolph Valentino. It wasn't the first time Perveen had thought Alice looked like a taller version of Agnes, but it was hard to imagine her in anyone's arms. Frankly, it was refreshing to be with a friend who wasn't always hinting how sad it was for Perveen to live in a world where she had failed at pleasing a husband and now could never join with another.

Lady Hobson-Jones had all but said those words, but in a joking manner, to Perveen a few months earlier. Perveen had responded with dead silence, because what else was there to say? The experience had only built her sympathy for Alice.

Shaking aside the memory, Perveen concentrated on the articles that Alice had saved. One story detailed how the government remained resolute in not allowing banks to finance films on the basis of being an insecure investment. Another article was an interview with Subhas Ghoshal, where he had decried this decision as an act meant to suppress the availability of Indian films to a hungry audience. A news feature about G.K. Thadani, a Marathi businessman, announced his investment in Champa Films. She found an article about the creation of a film censor board in Calcutta, and another one about the agreement of the Bombay government to follow the same direction and take up censorship, too.

She found plenty on Rochana, but nothing deeper than pictures of her performing stunts and an interview she'd done in Calcutta a year earlier about how excited she was about an upcoming picture.

In the late morning, Arman drove her and Jamshedji to Mistry House. Her father went off to court, and when the car returned, Perveen signed some money out of petty cash, put it in an envelope, and asked Arman to drop her at the Royal Bombay Asiatic Society.

"It might take a half hour—but perhaps less," she said.

"I shall be waiting in front. And be careful! Those steps are very wet."

It was true that the august library's wide, tall promenade of marble stairs shone with the wetness of the morning's downpour. Perveen stepped up carefully, raising her sari a few inches with her left hand and carrying the folded umbrella, a waterproof cape, and briefcase with her free hand.

Her first stop was the newspaper library. Electric fans whirred on the high ceilings, and the windows had been opened to let in the fresh air. Only a few people sat at tables reading; she was gratified to see her old friend, Mr. Dass. The retired postal clerk was seated at his favorite spot, just out of direct view of the room's clerk, but close enough that bringing newspapers to and from the desk wouldn't be too taxing.

He looked up at the sound of her footsteps.

"Miss Mistry!" His small, wizened face was alight with surprise.

"Mr. Dass, what luck for me to see you here! Morning is not your usual reading time, is it?"

"There was a break in the rains, so I made haste. I haven't been here in days. And what are you researching today?"

"Please come into the hall with me," Perveen said, having already noticed the head librarian, Mr. Nambudripad, looking their way. "We mustn't disturb anyone with our conversation."

"Most certainly." Mr. Dass fumbled for his cane and slowly arose. As they walked down the hallway, she noticed the stand with an announcement of an upcoming Thinkers Lecture to which Colin Sandringham, a vice president at the society, had invited her. *When Does History Begin? A Panel Discussion with Honorable Guest Speakers Mrs. Sarojini Naidu, Mr. Joseph 'Kaka' Baptista, and Mr. Henry Stavely Lawrence.* Colin was moderating, though he was too modest to suggest his own picture be included. Yet Perveen could picture him perfectly in her mind, and the image made her feel warm.

Remembering Mr. Dass at her side, she looked toward the rare book room. "That looks more comfortable for us."

"Very well," Mr. Dass said, following her with his slow, rocking gait.

Even though the room was vacant, she chose a table in the back, near the windows, which were closed against the pelting rain. Perveen pulled out a chair for Mr. Dass and he sat down, balancing the cane against the edge of the table. "Did you bring me here because you don't want anyone listening?"

Putting a finger to her lips, she said, "I wonder if you might be able to spare a few hours to do some research for me."

He beamed. "In retirement, many hours lie idle. It would be a pleasure."

"Thanks. My first question to you is whether you are following anything about film?"

"Going to pictures is too expensive on my pension," he said. "I've done some reading about the business, though. The city government wants to tax films made here for the reason of gathered people causing a danger to society." He shook his head. "They truly don't like us consuming anything that doesn't come from England."

"That's interesting. I'm hoping to learn more about a few entertainment film companies. Are you familiar with Champa Films or Royal Indian Pictures?"

After a pause, he said, "I believe the latter is based in Calcutta, and Champa Films is here. The head of Champa Films is named Subhas Ghoshal. He's a Bengali, and as the stereotype goes, those people are genius at the creative arts, but not so much with money."

Perveen sat up straight. "Did you read that Mr. Ghoshal has lost money?"

Mr. Dass paused, and his already wrinkled forehead furrowed deeper. "I might have read that he's got plenty of financiers. But I've read that about other filmmakers, too."

She didn't like to take rumors as gospel. "The information I have from Mr. Ghoshal is that Ardeshir Nanporia, a local Parsi, is one of his benefactors. And a news story mentioned that G.K. Thadani also assists him."

"A well-known Marathi name," Mr. Dass said with a nod. "It's rumored that G.K.'s father bought him a seat on the Bombay Stock Exchange. Young G.K. is supposed to drive up cotton futures, but he can hardly do that singlehandedly when the demand for the stuff has greatly diminished."

Perveen was already impressed by what the retired postal clerk knew. "I want to find out more about Subhas Ghoshal, especially if it's related to business. Also give me whatever you can collect on Abhijit Bipin Chatterjee, who owns Royal Indian Pictures in Calcutta. Now, have you heard of an actress named Rochana?"

He shook his head. "Isn't the name Sulochana?"

"Sulochana is another leading lady," Perveen explained.

"Rochana is a rising star who came from Calcutta to marry Subhas Ghoshal and act and coproduce for Champa Films. Before that, she was at Royal Indian Pictures. I'm curious about her."

"Three Bengalis you've given me; this will be a pleasure! I shall search the last two years in other cities' newspapers: not only Bombay but Calcutta and Delhi."

"As much as you see fit. Now, here is an advance payment—for this month's work." She produced the envelope with the five rupees that she'd carried in anticipation of this opportunity. Quickly she wrote out an invoice and gave it to him. "Please sign this. It's the record that you are officially joined to Mistry Law."

He looked at the money and then shook his head. "What need have I for this money? My life's dream is already here: open days full of reading."

"Of course," Perveen reassured him. "But if I pay you, that connects you to Mistry Law. This protects you from possibly having to testify about anything in a court of law."

"Why would anyone go to court about film companies?"

Perveen hesitated, not wanting to say too much. "As a solicitor, my hopes are to settle problems between people without litigation. But sometimes, unexpected things happen."

"That's right. Like a visit from you, on a rainy Monday." Smiling, he signed and gave her back the paper. "Will I be required to come to your office to report?"

Perveen got the sense that perhaps this was something he secretly wanted to do. Yet she imagined his walking stick sinking into six inches of water, or worse. "Please telephone first, because I might not be in."

"But I don't have a telephone."

In her eagerness to make his life easier, she'd forgotten that very few in the city had the technological luxury that she had. "You can always send me a note. And if you are in the library, perhaps Mr. Sandringham will help you make the phone call?"

"Ah, yes." Mr. Dass smiled broadly. "The only Britisher I know who greets me by name! As a twenty-year member of the library, I was the first to nominate him for his vice presidency, you know."

"Well, the next to be nominated for an important role should be you!" Rising to her feet, she said, "I'll go downstairs to let him know you may wish to use the telephone sometimes. Would you like to come with me?" Secretly, she wanted at least a moment alone with Colin, but it was important to include her helper.

"I don't like going down those spiral stairs on rainy days. In any case, I must return to the reading room to make sure nobody absconded with today's *Times*. But will you please give Mr. Sandringham my best regards and tell him that I'm coming to the Thinkers Lecture?"

MR. DASS'S FOREBODING had been correct. The marble floor shimmered with at least a quarter inch of water. She had to step carefully to avoid the hem of her sari getting wet; her feet, in the damp leather sandals, were already a lost cause.

The door to the vice president's office was half open. Colin Sandringham was standing near his desk, examining the contents of a large wooden box. Everything that might have been on the floor had been placed atop chairs and tables for safety from the water.

"I should have brought a mop!" Perveen said by way of greeting.

Instantly, he whirled around, almost losing balance. As he steadied himself on the desk, he chuckled. "What an excellent surprise! Do you have time to come in?"

Perveen smiled back at the tall, thin man with a shock of dark hair that fell across his wire-rimmed glasses. Since the onset of rains, he looked a bit thinner; perhaps he was dining out less frequently, or his servant Rama had less access to the market. Having known Colin for more than a year, she had a heightened awareness for changes, although she knew better than to comment on it. And the relationship was impossible, both because of her marital status and their disparate backgrounds. Still, in another world, they might be together. After all, Colin's tan from three years under the Indian sun sometimes caused local people to think he was mixed. Or should she think of Kashmir, because of the green-brown color of his eyes? Always, she tried to rationalize what made him different; but the fact was, he could not be categorized.

Colin asked, "Were you researching something upstairs?"

"Yes, I saw Mr. Dass, and he sends his regards. But first I need to make an apology—I shan't be present on Wednesday evening for the Thinkers Lecture."

He gave a wry smile. "Well, that's a shame! It's such a controversial topic—and you are an admirer of Sarojini Naidu, isn't it true?"

"Yes, I am very glad you invited such an important female writer to be part of the panel. What's the controversy this time?"

"It sounds very simple on the outset: When does history begin?" His eyes flared, and he beckoned for her to move closer. "Some Asiatic Society members suggested we acquire a book of photographs from the last war, and I ordered it. But not everyone in the Asiatic wants to keep it. They are saying the photographs are neither art nor true history."

Perveen shook her head. "If we truly just experienced the war to end all wars, photographic evidence may be very important."

"Quite," Colin said crisply. "The book's photographs were taken by a mix of war photographers and officers in Africa, the Middle East, France, Germany, and the Balkans. I suspect the real problem is that some of the pictures reveal British men in the embarrassing position of captivity."

"Such images could make Britain look weak. Is that the accusation?"

"Yes, but I don't think everyone will agree. That could be a reason for some people, but I don't think it's all of it. This evening, we'll hear all the opinions. I would truly hope you could be there . . ." His voice trailed off.

"I got called to a party given by a new client." She felt silly saying there would be a film screening. Colin was such an intellectual that he probably had no idea who Rochana was.

"A dinner party?"

"Not exactly. It's in Dadar West, not far from me. Alice is coming along."

"Well, then." He gave her another wry smile. "Of course I understand—but I'm disappointed. I am grateful for any chance to be in the same room. Even if we are twenty feet apart."

Perveen shut her eyes for a moment, recalling their last private meeting. It had been at his place in Harriman Road just a few weeks after the onset of rain. She remembered what it felt like, lying against him on the creaking settee in the sitting room. Strong gusts of rain had breached the open windows, sprinkling them, as they kissed. She opened her eyes and looked straight at him, all the while savoring the memory of stolen pleasure. And Colin was looking back at her as if he knew her thoughts: an unspoken intimacy that made her feel warm everywhere.

Once again, she was relieved that Mr. Dass hadn't accompanied her downstairs. Huskily, she said, "I'm here now. And you did promise tea."

"Certainly, madam." Colin gave her a long look. Moving past her to look out the door, he called down the hall. "Hello, Varun! Please bring two cups of chai with milk but no sugar."

Perveen smiled as he returned to stand a few inches away from her. "You've bent to my sugarless way?"

"Lady Gwendolyn Hobson-Jones also says fewer sweets are better for the teeth, and I must concede she's right."

She'd been about to take his hand, but now she stopped, feeling a tightness as she remembered the mother-daughter confrontation from the day before. "When did you last see the lady?"

"Last Friday. My flat flooded and I had to take rooms for a few days at the Yacht Club residency. It's still uninhabitable, in fact."

"Oh, I'm sorry to hear that!" Perveen asked, just as Varun, the peon who took care of odd jobs on the ground floor, came into the room with a tray holding their cups.

"Thank you," Colin said, taking the tray from him while Perveen cleared a spot on the desk for it to be placed. After Varun departed, Colin continued his tale. "I don't know how long I'll be at the Yacht Club. Lady Gwendolyn has taken pity and asked me to stay, which is free, and thus entirely better."

Perveen felt her spirits sink. "Really?"

Alice's mother had been charmed by Colin ever since their first meeting at the Government House the previous November. Sir David had said outright to Alice that "someone like that Sandringham chap" might be a suitable husband for her. Perveen privately thought that a man as handsome and kind as Colin would be more than suitable for most women. Fortunately, Alice wasn't looking.

"Yes, she nattered on about my taking up residence in their carriage house," Colin said, then sipped his tea, wincing at the heat. "She believes that I shouldn't be living in the Fort District because it's bad in the rains. I had to point out that I don't have a budget that could allow for living in Malabar Hill and hiring a car to bring me down here six days a week. That led her to send her driver to give me a lift to my physician the next day. Nothing's wrong," he added. "But I have to be more careful about things when it rains."

Perveen had noticed how much more stiffly Colin swung his right leg—the one with a prosthesis that started underneath his knee—since the rains had started. "Rainy season is something we yearn for, but after a month, it becomes tiresome. Every day I go out knowing I might not reach my destination!"

"And how is your family?" A rote question, but the warmth in his hazel eyes showed true interest.

"Khushy can sit up without being held for a few seconds now, and she recognizes everybody with big smiles. My mother's got very involved in a maternity hospital fundraising. She's doing what Gulnaz would, if she were still in town. Rustom is at loose ends, spending too much time at the Willingdon Club because his construction business is virtually halted during the rains."

"I've never met your brother." Colin sounded pensive.

"Yes, I know. Better to keep it that way!"

Looking at her challengingly, he said, "Why don't you want me meeting your brother?"

"One of the few characteristics he shares with my father is a strong sense of suspicion."

"Really? I rather think you've got that trait as well. I mean— that's why your cases have gone so well. You read people." Colin drained his cup of tea.

"If that's true, it's a skill I learned too damned late."

Colin shook his head, not understanding, but she was not going to elaborate. How stupid she'd been at eighteen to believe that someone like Cyrus Sodawalla was worth marrying. And now, because of the complicated laws governing marriage and divorce in colonial India, she could live apart from him but never get divorced. Colin knew about it, of course; it was as much an obstacle to their happiness as their differing races and religions.

Colin must have sensed her melancholy, because he steered the conversation back to small talk. He told her about the water damage in his apartment, and she counseled him that buckets and towels were the only strategy until the rains ceased. As someone receiving his flat for free—the building was owned by a library trustee—he didn't like badgering the landlord.

Perveen pointed out that the landlord would benefit from being able to save his building before it collapsed, as many places did around the city. Privately, she wondered if Colin might think it virtuous not to spend money on creature comforts.

She knew so little about him. His clothing had always bordered on aged and occasionally shabby. In any case, they were an afterthought. But he was hardly poor; she knew his father had been a respected general physician in London, and he was the third generation of men in his family to matriculate at Oxford. Yet Colin had no interest in medicine—he had entered intending to read history but left midway to serve in the war. When he reenrolled at war's end, he shifted his studies to geography. After coming down, he'd passed the examination for the Indian Civil Service, chosen Marathi as his required language, and then shipped out to serve as a junior officer in the Bombay Presidency in 1920.

Colin truly loved India. He had stayed on even after a snakebite had resulted in the loss of his right calf and foot. He'd given part of his body to the country; but against all logic, he'd quit the civil service to become an unpaid vice president at the Asiatic.

In a way, Colin was as much a cipher as Rochana, she thought as she finished the last drop of tea, put down the cup, and rose from her chair.

"Going so soon?"

Perveen looked into bottomless hazel eyes and felt an inexorable draw. "I'm afraid what I might do if I stay longer."

"That sounds like a challenge." Colin looked from her toward the closed door. She understood his silent message: If the room was closed off from view, they could kiss each other goodbye.

"And if we close the door, someone's bound to arrive to investigate!" she predicted.

"Can your eyes see through doors?" Colin grumbled, rising. As he continued to look at her, the magnetic pull became stronger.

*This is right*, she thought, as their lips met, and he gently closed his arms around her.

The kiss was just beginning to intensify when the knock came.

"Damnation!" Colin swore in a whisper.

"I'll answer," Perveen said, going hastily to the door and opening it onto the face of Mr. Dass. To her relief, he smiled, appearing utterly innocent in his thoughts.

"Good afternoon, Mr. Sandringham. I thought—I thought I should state my case, you know, about the telephone—"

"But of course!" Perveen blurted, realizing she had forgotten entirely what she'd come to say.

## 5

## A SMALL LEAK

The night of the party, Perveen stood in the front hall of her family house, taking advantage of the light from the south-facing windows. It was always a struggle to fasten the tiny clasp of her pearl necklace. Eventually she got the thick strand secured, but in the meantime, she'd had time to study herself. The turquoise chiffon she wore seemed to have brought out bluish-black shadows under her eyes. Did she look older than her twenty-four years?

The silk sari, with its elaborate petit point border of tiny birds, was the height of Parsi fashion, but wouldn't come close to whatever modern cocktail frocks Rochana and her friends might wear. If a woman wearing a knee-length frock walked into a Bombay salon, every lady wearing a sari would fade into the wallpaper. She supposed she shouldn't care—she was there on professional business, not to catch anyone's eye.

"Hey! There's a mongoose in the garden—with a leash."

Perveen turned away from the mirror and her brooding at the sound of Rustom's voice. Her brother was standing near the parlor window, cradling Khushy in his arms. He repeated in a babyish voice, "A mongoose, followed by a European and a Parsi lady. What a parade!"

There was a sharp rapping sound at the door. Perveen opened

it to see Alice holding a mud-spotted dog: her beloved Diana. Behind her was a woman a bit taller than Perveen, fair-skinned but with the wavy hair and strong nose typical for Zoroastrians. She wore a straight skirt and lace blouse, rather than a sari, looking a bit like a schoolmarm. Was this someone Alice planned on bringing along? Perveen went rigid with disappointment at Alice's presumptuousness.

Rustom broke the tension by chuckling. "Aha! That animal's not a mongoose but a mongrel!" Rustom chuckled in delight. "Do come in, Miss Hobson-Jones and—all of you!"

"Ho, sir, that's no way to greet my sweet Diana!" Alice teased back. "Perveen, you must remember Miss Daboo—Kitty Daboo, who teaches at the college. She was kind enough to give me a lift so my parents would remain oblivious!"

"Oh, she's just dropping you, then!" Perveen felt relieved, recognizing the woman as a literature lecturer at Woodburn College she'd met who'd been present at the college's viewing stand for the Prince of Wales's parade a few months earlier. Kitty must be a nickname, though she couldn't see why—unless it was for her luxuriant head of hair. "Miss Daboo, I do recall you, but wasn't Roshan your good name?"

"It still is," Roshan Daboo answered. "I'm disappointed that Alice can't come to the lecture tonight—but of course, she loves Rochana's films and can't miss the chance to see her in living color."

"So, Miss Daboo—" Perveen was intent on keeping formality, since Rustom was present. "May I introduce my brother, Rustom?"

"Charmed. Are you of the boatbuilding Daboos?" Rustom said by way of greeting.

"Yachts," Kitty corrected. "My father and brothers and grandfather own Tip Top Sailing."

"Very good," Rustom said, giving her an approving nod. "A long time ago, we Mistrys started out that way—"

Like so many other Parsis, the British had recruited from Gujarat to Bombay. Perveen cut him off, looking directly at Kitty. "Are you keeping Diana with you while Alice is out with me, then?"

"No, I'm bringing her along!"

"What?" Although Perveen was fond of the dog, she couldn't imagine what Alice was thinking when they had a high-status party to attend. But Alice didn't seem to be listening; Khushy had started to coo with excitement, and Diana, now with feet on the ground, took a few steps toward her.

"Didn't you read the article about Rochana's love for dogs?"

"Yes, but—"

"I know that Diana will be a hit with her."

Perveen wanted to remind Alice that Rochana's own dog had recently died, so now might not be a good time—but she hesitated to say too much about a client in front of Kitty and Rustom. Instead, she said, "I don't think dogs were invited."

"This isn't Watsons," Kitty cut in, and Rustom laughed. Watsons was a hotel where there was rumored to have been a sign at the entrance that said NO DOGS AND INDIANS ALLOWED. But the truth was, Perveen had never seen the sign. It could be mythology.

"Meet the dog, dearie!" Rustom said, bringing his baby closer to Alice and Diana.

Perveen joined them, picking a broken section of passionflower vine that was still caught in Diana's collar.

Alice looked at the flower and winced. "Sorry about her going through the flower beds. That's such a ripping shade of blue—or is it purple?"

"Whatever you want to see," Rustom said. "I believe the English name is passionflower. I think the Indian name is Krishna Kamal. Because Lord Krishna's skin is the same blue."

"So says the Hindu pandit!" Perveen teased, because her brother was anything but a priest.

"If Diana is party bound, you may as well take her to the little washroom down the hall. You may wish to do your own washup as well. That's a smart suit, but the dog has done her best to soil it."

Perveen frowned at him. It wasn't right for a man to point out a lady's deshabille; but perhaps, because Alice was wearing trousers and a jacket, he was thinking of her more like a Douglas Fairbanks character.

Perveen made small talk with Kitty about the activities she'd taken up during the academic break—mostly tennis and reading. She seemed a pleasant enough sort of woman, and that made Perveen wonder if she could subtly persuade her into offering to hold on to the dog.

"I suppose you can't keep Diana with you for a few hours?"

"No animals in the Royal Asiatic Society, unless they are carved from marble!"

A few minutes later, Alice and her dog emerged from the lavatory. The Englishwoman's mussed blonde hair had been slicked behind her ears, and her green linen jacket and the edges of her matching trousers had been brushed off. Diana was free of foliage and walking sedately beside her.

"Why don't I add this passionflower to your buttonhole," Perveen said, realizing she still had the flower bud in her hand. She desperately wanted to give Alice, who had no jewelry, some ornamentation.

"Fine." Alice took the purple flower from Perveen and fixed it herself in the top buttonhole of her double-breasted jacket.

"I'll be off, then," Kitty said, wiggling her fingers at Perveen. Alice puckered her lips in an air kiss. Kitty's face pinkened as she smiled back and stepped out the door.

"She's driving herself," Alice said as the rumbling sound of an engine started.

"Goodness," Perveen said, going to the window to see. But it was too late: Kitty had already roared off.

"Now, before I go, Rustom, let me show you Diana's tricks." Alice whistled, and Diana turned away from the footstool she was sniffing to look at her mistress. Bending slightly toward the dog, Alice held up her index finger. Diana immediately lay down. "Good girl," she said, proffering a biscuit.

"What else can she do?" Rustom asked, looking as underwhelmed as Perveen felt.

"She will fetch things, roll over, and come when called. I hope that she'll make a good show for everyone tonight!"

Standing a few feet away, Rustom was smiling as if he could anticipate every one of his sister's fears. Giving him a cautionary frown, Perveen spoke. "Well, we're off. Rustom, please tell Pappa we aim to return before midnight."

"Before you leave . . ." Rustom fetched a folded wool lap blanket from the hall shelf and held it out, smiling sweetly. "For the sake of Alice's fine suit."

"Thank you kindly!" Alice said, taking the blanket from Rustom, her smiling face showing that she was unaware of his teasing. And this, in turn, made Perveen grab the largest umbrella in the stand and hold it protectively over her friend as they stepped outside.

"Your brother's a lot friendlier these days," Alice said as they went along. "And he's very sweet with Khushy."

Still annoyed, Perveen said, "Rustom might be more attentive because the rains keep him home more days."

"He's getting used to the idea he's a papa. I'll only ever be a dog's mummy, but I do love Diana," Alice mused as she stroked Diana's small golden-brown head. "One look from her bright eyes, and I will do whatever she wants. Imagine a close-up of her face on film." She paused. "I thought bringing her was a good idea—but lately I've been mucking everything up."

Perveen thought about the recent fight between Alice and her mother. It clearly had to do with her. "Do you have any idea why your mother was so angry?"

"Don't let's talk about her. I came with you for the adventure of my dreams." Alice pressed her lips into a mournful line. "Do you think—do you think Diana's good-looking enough?"

Perveen strove to be honest. "She's quite a dear dog. With the asymmetrical blot on the face, she looks very different from most of the standard pretty canines in pictures and films."

"Those damn purebreds," Alice said with a snort, as if she herself were not exactly that.

AS IF TO welcome guests, the gate to the grounds of Champa Films was wide open, and they sailed through without having to be checked off from a guest list. As they rode through the property, Perveen told Alice about the cast and crew living in small houses on the property. Although it was just five, the lamps outside the house were already lit, with jasmine garlands twining up the poles.

"Goodness, it's a large estate. Right here in the city too!" Alice exclaimed.

"I shall be in the parking area," Arman said, tilting his head toward a stand of trees, where five cars were already parked, and a few chauffeurs lounged outside, gossiping. "How long do you think you'll be?"

Perveen looked at her watch. "It's just five. Probably nine o'clock?"

"Ten if it's a very good party!" Alice added.

Arman parked the car close to the entrance, just as he had done before. This time the villa looked especially festive, with many small lights glowing in welcome. A handsome gentleman in a pink and silver suit with matching turban came from the house to open the passenger door. Diana immediately sprang from Alice's lap to cross Perveen's and jump down. The man stepped backward in shock, and Perveen stepped out of the car quickly to catch Diana, who was prancing toward a set of bushes.

Alice followed and took the leash from Perveen. "Sorry! She's not minding her manners."

The gentleman had followed behind them and was watching Diana relieve herself under the bushes. "What is that?"

"Diana," both women said in unison.

"And she's some kind of hound. Well, then." He bent and took the dog's paw in his hand and spoke in a reedy voice. "Diana, my name is Nishant. Master Nishant, to be official."

"My goodness—you are the star! I'm sorry, I didn't realize!" Perveen felt herself blushing. Because the man had opened the car door, she'd not even looked at him, assuming that he was a bearer. "Master Nishant, my name is Perveen Mistry. I've admired you in a number of films."

"Quite charmed." He took her hand and kissed it. "I've been told to tell everyone the screening of the film begins at six-thirty, in the ballroom, which is upstairs. Until then, mix and mingle and tipple to your hearts' content!"

"Well, thank you," Alice said.

Nishant turned to Alice and smiled, revealing two decks of straight, pearly white teeth. "I didn't know they'd hired a European actor for the new film."

"I'm not!" Alice answered shortly, pulling the lead so Diana was closer to her.

Perveen guessed that her friend was offended that Nishant thought that she was a man. A quick glance at Alice's height and dress might have confused him. It was best to set things to rights immediately. "Master Nishant, may I introduce my friend Miss Alice Hobson-Jones? She owns Diana, who actually might be suited to film performance."

"Ah, an animal trainer! Good for you, Mr. Jones," Nishant said, holding out a hand to Alice.

Ignoring the gaffe, Alice shook Nishant's hand. "I hope to introduce Diana to the Ghoshals. I heard they're looking for a dog—"

"Yes, perhaps they are. Good luck." Even though he was speaking to them, his gaze was beyond them. Without excusing himself, he stepped along to the car that had pulled up behind them, disgorging an Englishman and an Indian, both dressed in evening suits.

"Mr. Caruthers and Mr. Patel. What an honor to welcome you both, Bombay's most esteemed theater owners!" he called out, rushing to take their hands.

"Well!" Perveen said, turning back to Alice. "Watching him on-screen will never be the same. I didn't think he'd have such a pip-squeak voice."

"And eyes and ears that are so"—Alice paused—"ridiculously weak!"

"Except when it comes to recognizing the very important people," Perveen said.

The friends linked arms and stepped through the door, where Perveen was thrilled to see many people, Indian and European, mingling with gayety. This was not the buttoned-up society of the British, nor was it the hierarchal formality of the majority Marathi Hindu community. Somehow, the Ghoshals had invited the kind of people who laughed and drank and danced—yes, there was a Victrola blaring somewhere. Impulsively, she lowered the pallu that had covered her hair, which had been pinned up. Now she took out the pins, letting her hair fall to her shoulders.

"Receiving line," Alice said in her ear, and Perveen was nudged back to the present and walked with her friend to join the queue. First in the short line of party dignitaries was an Indian gentleman in his thirties wearing a cream business suit stretched to the limit over a round belly. After him came Subhas Goshal, slender and sharp in a black tailcoat and pinstriped trousers. Then came Rochana, dressed in a banana-colored silk gown, beaded in gold and black, with an irregular hemline. She wore a heavy gold choker at her neck, and golden feathers made a tall fan on the headband that topped her shining black bob.

"She's glorious," Alice said in a whisper. "Simply glorious!"

A thin European man in his late twenties was just ahead of them in line. The guest quickly passed through handshakes with the first gentleman and Subhas. When he reached Rochana, he took her hand and looked intently at her. The actress's smile went stiff as her arm, and she was seemingly trying not to look directly at the fawning man.

After Perveen and Alice had shaken hands with the portly gentleman, who turned out to be G.K. Thadani, they arrived at Subhas.

"Miss Mistry! I'm very glad you came. I have everything ready for you, as we discussed previously. We must get together for a few minutes, at least, after everyone's arrived." He spoke warmly, and taking in the sight of Alice, he said, "How nice for us that you've brought a companion—"

"Dearest Perveen, you must keep showing your hair like that. It's gorgeous!" Rochana interrupted, pulling her hand from that of the white guest who was still lingering. The man stood awkwardly for a moment but then moved on. As he did, though, he shot a resentful glance toward Perveen, as if faulting her for the interruption of a tender moment. Probably this happened to Rochana constantly, Perveen thought as she focused on introducing Alice.

"Madam Rochana, I don't suppose you remember me?" Alice blurted. "We met in Poona at the races. My name is Alice Hobson-Jones?"

Rochana's head reared back, as if she'd been punched. But in the next instant, as her eyes focused on Alice, her apparent shock relaxed into a glowing smile. "Of course I recognize you! Of all the luck—Perveen, I didn't imagine you'd know Alice."

"Well, Bombay can be a very small town sometimes," Perveen said.

Alice's face flushed with excitement. Rochana had put her on a first-name basis: It was an incredibly intimate honor. Asmaa, who had been circulating with a tray of cucumber sandwiches, was now watching Alice intently. Could a white guest really be so important? Perveen felt slightly miffed at Alice's sudden rush to stardom.

"I hope you don't mind me bringing Diana along," Alice said, drawing Rochana's attention to the dog, who was sitting patiently at the end of the lead. "I heard you lost Bubbles, and I'm so sorry about it."

"Yes, I've been very sad." The actress looked down at Diana with a wistful smile. "What a dear little pooch. Did she travel with you from England?"

"No, she's a Malabar Hill stray. And so clever! She understands many commands—I'm thinking of putting her into film and theater roles, in fact."

"What a sweet little face. The spot over her eye!" Rochana trilled.

"Chaplin's dog Mut has a spot surrounding his left eye," Subhas said, crouching down to take a close look at Diana. Diana gave a low growl, and Alice jerked her back on the lead.

"Might I hold her?" Rochana asked.

"Of course!" Alice lifted the squirming dog into Rochana's arms. Diana took a good sniff, burying her nose in Rochana's bosom. Perveen felt considerable relief.

"She is taking liberties! But I must say, she seems naturally fond of you." Subhas clapped his hands together. "I know! Darling, what do you think about Diana trying out as your new costar?"

Alice squeaked, as if she wanted to say more but was trying to control herself. Rochana paused in scratching behind Diana's ears. "You mean—for Alice's dog to take on the roles Bubbles would play? It's an idea, but . . . I'm not sure any dog outside of Chaplin's could perform as brilliantly as our Bubbles did."

"It's worth a try, dear. You seem to be making inroads with Alice's pet. Before the night is over, make sure Hans sees him."

"Her! Diana is female," Alice said. "And oh, she would just love to perform!"

Perveen looked at Alice, trying to telegraph both her amazement at Subhas's offer as well as caution, because as Rochana placed the dog back on the ground, she had an expression that Perveen couldn't read. Maybe she'd felt insulted by what Subhas had said about whom she had chemistry with. Surely it wasn't a comment on their relationship, or how she came off on-screen with Master Nishant.

Someone standing behind them made a rough throat-clearing sound.

"Oh! We're holding up the receiving line," Perveen apologized.

"I'll enjoy chatting with you later," Rochana said, the smile from her films back on her face.

Perveen and Alice proceeded toward the next honoree, who was Ardeshir Nanporia, owner of the property. He was a small, thin man in his fifties, with the characteristic strong Parsi nose and graying curly hair. Nanporia politely nodded when Perveen commented on the beauty of his home; she sensed his mind was elsewhere. At least he wasn't commenting on Diana's presence. The dog was sitting nicely at the end of her leash, in clear obedience to Alice.

Perveen recognized the blond gentleman she'd seen in the cottage area at the very end of the line. Close up, he was older than she'd expected: somewhere in his thirties. Yet there was a vitality to his eyes and a smile on his lips that were pleasingly youthful.

"I am Hans Becker, the cinematography head," he said while delivering a crushing handshake to Perveen. "Miss Mistry, I know you are a solicitor. And is your friend here an actress?"

"No," Alice answered, slowing her typically rapid speech, as if in response to his soft continental accent. "I'm Alice

Hobson-Jones. Until now I have been a lecturer in mathematics. And I have my dog, Diana, with me. Mr. Ghoshal wants you to see if she has what it takes!"

His brow creased as he looked down at Diana, who was sniffing around his trousers. "What did she take?"

"Oh sorry!" Alice put a hand to her mouth. "That was just a play on words. He wants Diana to have a screen test with an eye toward becoming a member of the next film's cast."

Perveen cringed at Alice's exaggerations. But Hans didn't seem to think it sounded unusual, because he merely stepped back to look at Diana. "Turn her to the side, please."

Alice did so.

"She's not pretty, is she? But she has character."

"That's what they say about me," Alice said cheerfully.

Chuckling, Mr. Becker said, "You are quite funny, Miss Hobson-Jones. Are you sure you're British?"

"Yes!" she said with a wink. "Though Diana's from the streets of Bombay."

Perveen could barely keep up with how fast things were going—and in Alice's favor.

"All right, I'll screen-test this furry urchin tomorrow. We can try her alone on camera, and then in a scene with Rochana. Can you come to the Stage Two building at seven o'clock?"

Alice blinked her eyes and hesitated. "Might I come later?"

"Seven might be a bit early to reach. Alice lives in Malabar Hill," Perveen explained.

"I wish I could be flexible, however tight timing is a necessity of the business. Come if you can. Very pleased to meet you, and . . ." He trailed off, surveying the room. "Let me show you into the library!"

Perveen had thought he was on the verge of excusing himself from them, but instead, Hans walked between the two of them deep into the party throng of well-dressed guests, all of whom seemed to be holding drinks and chattering boisterously. There was even a couple sitting in the wing chair that Jamshedji had occupied just two days before; the woman on the man's lap, a scandalous intimacy, yet nobody was gaping. Now she wished Colin hadn't been involved in the Asiatic Society lecture. She could have told him to meet her here, and then they would have had a rollicking time with cocktails and dancing without being the slightest bit controversial.

Perveen did feel grateful, though, that some other women at the party wore saris. Threaded through the crowd were a number of ladies wearing fine silks with glittering silver and gold embroideries. All the women had chosen instead to drape the sari's end over the shoulder, thus revealing the tender backs of their necks and lustrous hair coiled in various styles; puffy buns, elaborate French twists, and even shoulder-length marcelled waves.

One pretty young woman, with thick, sleek braids coiled around her ears, extended one hand toward Perveen and the other to Alice. "Welcome to Champa Films, pretty ladies! I'm Marisa Young. The daughter of Master Nishant. Both of us are in *Queen of Hearts*, the film you'll see tonight."

So, this was the actress Rochana had mentioned taking on a false surname to help her remain an ingenue. Marisa was dressed in a pale blue georgette sari with borders of heavy silver zari stitching. Her silver necklace, punctuated with blue stones, matched her elegant, heavy earrings. Perveen wondered if they were truly sapphires or glass.

"My name is Alice!" Alice spoke more casually than she had to the men in the receiving line. "I'm a huge film buff, but I'm not sure if I've seen you on-screen before. Have you played in any previous films?"

She shook her head. "No, it's my big debut! And I am currently playing a part in Champa Films' next production—we just started shooting it last week."

"I hope it's the picture in which Diana might costar!" Alice said, picking up her dog and nuzzling her. "Go ahead and pet her if you like, Miss Young."

"Do call me Marisa! I'd like to hold her—but there's the matter of my sari," Marisa said, looking nervously at the dog. "It must stay perfect tonight—no crumples or stains."

Perveen imagined the starlet's sari and jewelry might be borrowed from the costume department, or even a wealthy person. "Wise thinking. I'm Perveen Mistry, the lawyer who's doing some work for the company. Tell me, what role are you playing in *Queen of Hearts*?"

"A younger sister in great peril! I am the crux of the story."

Alice scrutinized her. "Younger than Rochana, you mean? What's the age difference?"

"I will play girls any age from age twelve to sixteen, Subhas-sir says, although I just turned eighteen. Rochana's probably at least twenty-six, although her biography says she is twenty . . ."

Marisa trailed off, and Perveen promptly understood why. Rochana was beside them.

"Oh, here you are!" Rochana's gaze landed fondly on Alice. "I'm getting a drink. I see that you don't have anything yet, dear."

"Ooh, I'd love to find a drink. And Hans wants to test Diana—but the hour's just a bit hard for me to reach here from Malabar Hill."

"Oh dear. We've got to figure out something. But first, drinks." Rochana took Alice's spare hand in hers, and the two, accompanied by Diana, moved off.

"Well, well! The queen has found a favorite," Marisa said archly.

Perveen felt shocked that Rochana hadn't invited her along, but she didn't want to reveal her emotion to the obviously envious young woman. Bowing her head, she said, "What a pleasure to meet you. Now, I see Mr. Ghoshal is beckoning to me; I'd better go."

She wasn't fibbing, because she'd noticed him standing in the doorway, looking at her. She threaded her way through the crowd to him.

Subhas's eyes darted here and there, as if he was anxious. "Let's just go off to the side for a moment. I want to tell you something."

Subhas took her down a side hall, where she could see into a kitchen. Asmaa was setting out canapés on a tray, and a handsome waiter in a tuxedo was sniping at her about taking too much time.

He reached into his jacket's inner pocket and withdrew an envelope. "As promised, here is the letter from ABC and also the legal contract your father gave me."

"Thank you very much!" It was a good sign that he'd been prompt with the papers. She took the envelope, wondering where she was going to put it safely until she could get back to her car.

"There's one other matter." Subhas had lowered his voice. "An uninvited stranger has come. I'd like to know who he is."

She answered in the same quiet timbre. "I'll do my best to speak with him. What does he look like?"

"He's one of the very few Europeans here and was just ahead of you in line," Subhas said. "He's tall and has light hair. He's wearing a wide striped jacket. He mumbled something like 'Morris' or 'Morgan' when we met. Out of etiquette, I pretended to know him. Perhaps we have met, or he came in someone's stead—but I don't recall any Morgan on the guest list."

Perveen understood why he wanted her help. The British could quiz Indians about their motives, but Indians could not usually do the reverse. The trouble was, she was also an Indian, and, to boot, a woman. "Might Rochana know? He seemed to linger at shaking her hand."

"That's right," he said. "It was unseemly."

"I had guessed that he was a very zealous fan."

"Yes, he could be an admirer. But he might be from a newspaper or spying for another film company—"

"Like Royal Indian Pictures?"

"That did cross my mind. And there's one other thing."

"Yes?"

"I was very pleased to meet your English friend. I feel as if I've heard her surname before." With a wink, he added, "Is she connected to Lord Hobson-Jones?"

"Yes. Sir David is her father." Perveen spoke reluctantly because Alice hated the idea of being judged by her name. Now she recalled how Rochana had momentarily frozen upon hearing the surname during introductions. It could be that the actress had picked up on it already.

"One of the governor's inner circle—I must say I approve!" Subhas sounded gleeful. "Well, I think we have discussed what is necessary. We mustn't be away from the party too long."

"Of course."

As Perveen set off, intending to safeguard the contract before doing anything more, she saw Marisa Young was standing at the corner where the back hall intersected the great hall. Meeting Perveen's gaze, Marisa gave an exaggerated turn of her head before sauntering back into the teeming hallway.

Maybe she'd been suspicious Perveen was reporting on Marisa's sniping about Rochana's age. Or was it something else?

# 6

# A SHOCKING INVITATION

Perveen made it through the packed hallway, only after suffering a champagne shower down her shoulder and then almost tripping over a couple necking in the stairwell. *Am I really in India?* She wanted to pinch herself, but there was a drink in one hand, and the other hand was busy protecting her sari. She squeezed through more bon vivants, heading for the doorway to take the contract out to Arman for safekeeping. As she exited, she was glad to see the rain had lessened, and she hastened across the damp ground to the cars.

Arman was leaning against the car, a cup of chai in his hand.

"Oh, that's nice!" she said.

"There's a canteen here. One of the staff members made a big pot of tea. Are you leaving so soon?"

"Not at all." She showed him the envelope, and he quickly opened the door and put it on the seat. "See you when we are ready in a few hours."

Inside the main hallway, Perveen spotted Alice and Rochana and Diana at the center of an exuberant circle of people. Even though Alice's head rose above the crowd, she didn't seem to be looking anywhere except downward toward Rochana's marcelled curls. A man leaned in—the very handsome Master Nishant—and Rochana playfully pummeled his shoulder before stretching up on her toes and pressing her lips to his cheek in a kiss. In turn, Nishant squeezed his costar into a brief embrace that sent the people around them into gales of laughter and a few catcalls. As Nishant stepped back, and Rochana made a seductive pout, Perveen tried to make sense of what she'd seen. Nishant and Rochana often embraced on-screen—but that, of course, was scripted. This intimacy seemed surprising—but she was beginning to understand that film people had an entirely different social code.

In the library, the crowd had also become very thick. Most were concentrated around the bar, which was manned by a young man in his early twenties with a wheatish complexion and hair slicked back like a matinee idol. Dressed in a highly embroidered sherwani coat and English trousers, he seemed the very picture of mixed elegance, and he chatted affably with his customers, an act atypical for a regular waiter. Gold-rimmed glasses slipped on the barman's long nose as he poured fruit juice into a silver shaker and then added a dash of red liquid from a bottle.

"May I ask what that is?" she inquired.

"Maraschino cherry, imported from America!" The barman sounded gleeful. "The house drink tonight is the Mary Pickford. Want one?"

"The white rum is from the Myers distillery," Perveen said, reading the label of the bottle. "A British company, isn't it?"

"Yes, Miss Mistry. The very best!" The barman handed the drink off to a waiting guest before giving Perveen his full attention. "But if you would like, I'll make this drink virgin."

Was this an assumption because she was too properly dressed? "I should like the typical Mary Pickford. And how did you guess my name? I feel at a disadvantage not knowing yours."

"I'm Ajen—Ajen Biswas, if you are writing me up in your report. I heard the company's just hired a lady lawyer."

He was smiling as if it were all a joke, but she sensed an edge to his commentary. Softening her tone, she said, "I'm only here to get a drink. This isn't your typical job, is it?"

"Sharp!" He winked. "I'm only playing the role of bartender because the butler walked off. I'm an actor sometimes, but I prefer to be the one doing the filming."

"That's quite a range of work," Perveen said, watching him clumsily pour rum into a shot glass. "Which characters have you played, Mr. Biswas?"

He rolled his eyes in a way that seemed to say: Only old-fashioned people use titles. "Do call me Ajen. In my first film in 1917, I played Queen Sita in the *Ramayana Legend*. Did you see it?"

"Yes, along with most of India. I was so taken with the trick photography and costumes that I didn't pay very close attention to the credits."

"You wouldn't have known. The credits listed me as Miss Ajanta, one of my several stage names." He waved his fingers in front of her. "See? Slim hands. And I've got the perfect neck. This was my way into Champa Films."

"You are a man of many talents."

"And I can't help but think you could do more than practice law. What pretty hair you have."

Perveen blushed, realizing that her exposed hair might make her look as if she desired recognition among the crowd. "I'm not trying to act! I just want to learn about the film world. I've met Master Nishant—"

"Once named Noman, just as his daughter, Zareen, has been recast as a starlet named Marisa." Winking at her, he added, "Can she really make it, though? The largest contingent of females in film are Anglo-Indians like Rochana and Renee Smith, and Jewish girls like Patience Cooper and Sulochana. The pretty girls you see lighting up the room are mostly friends of Rochana's, some acting and others just . . . let's say, those who enjoy parties."

"You're a very good tour guide to the room." Perveen affected a teasing tone. "There are quite a lot of men here—and not all of them as handsome as those in the film company."

Ajen rewarded her with a chuckle. "Most of the gents are on the other side of the business—film distributors and theater owners. Their badly behaved sons are the fellows canoodling in the corner with minor actresses."

Perveen followed Ajen's gaze and saw the unthinkable—a young woman sitting in a man's lap, locked into a deep kiss.

"Voila, darling!" He handed over the finished drink.

She sipped the drink, which burned her throat. After she'd finished coughing, she said, "Your Pickford packs quite a punch!"

Ajen chuckled. "Sorry if it's too much. I'm no expert!"

"It's a special honor for the guests to be personally served by the film company principals," Perveen reassured him. "All of you must be pitching in. Master Nishant even helped me step out from my car—"

"That's because there's a strike on amongst the estate's servants. It's the reason you were summoned, isn't it?"

A jolt went through her. Subhas should have told her that labor trouble was afoot. "I can't address specifics of my work, but can you tell me when the strike began?"

"It started today," Ajen said, his voice lower. "About ten aren't working."

"I didn't see guards at the gate tonight," Perveen murmured.

"Some of the actors were supposed to fill in there," Ajen said. "Perhaps Subhas had something else for them to do."

Perveen wondered if Subhas had meant to mention this but had become sidetracked by the issue of the mysterious guest. "Why are they striking?"

"They're demanding back wages. Not just the household people, but some fellows that Subhas hired to do things like move equipment, get necessary film supplies, and run the zoo. Then there are the ones working for Mr. Nanporia originally."

Perveen remembered the tiger's roar she'd overheard when

driving in with her father. "Yes, I heard there are large animals housed in the studio's private zoo."

He gave her a slightly patronizing smile. "Right, but it isn't a proper zoological garden like the one near the Prince of Wales Museum. Just some pens and cages. For filming, we must keep various animals—a tiger, deer, horses, and the like. There are several tanks for fish and a crocodile."

She wasn't sure whether she felt more nervous about the tiger or the crocodile. "Do you think this will be a short strike?"

"I hope so. It's just a delay in salary—all of us in the company know about these things. The money will come after the opening weekend of the new film."

"What was your contribution to the film we're seeing tonight?"

"Everything! I play a part in the film—I'll let you see—but I also shot many of the most technically difficult scenes."

"That's quite a variety of skills, isn't it? What's your specific training?"

"Oh, it's typical to jump between jobs while at a studio—there's never enough money to have the crew and cast. I started out as an actor and learned to film during my entry to the industry in Calcutta. I worked at two companies before joining this one," he added with pride. "When Mr. Becker came to Champa Films, I first thought: Why? He knows nothing about India and our stories. But the truth is, he's brought with him good cameras and some stage-lighting strategies to make our actresses look even more fair. Now we are players on international screens."

Ajen inclined his head, and she turned to see where he was looking. Hans Becker and Marisa were together. He had his hand on the wall and another on Marisa's arm; their heads were close, and they were speaking in a most confidential manner.

"I've briefly met Mr. Becker, and he didn't mention that," Perveen said, thinking it was foolhardy for Ajen to natter about fairness when speaking to a lady much browner than most of the other ladies. "I saw him standing by the cottages on Monday afternoon. I suppose one can't film much when it rains hard."

"If he went to the cottages in the afternoon, it might mean he was napping... or privately coaching someone!"

Perveen felt like she was being drawn into a centrifuge of intrigue; it was hard to find the boundary between what was necessary to know for work purposes and what was salacious. She shouldn't let herself fall in, but it was impossible to resist the pull.

A cough behind her alerted her to the fact that someone was waiting for a drink. Perveen turned to see a tall, thin blond man in a gray and blue striped suit; the man who'd been just ahead of them in the reception line.

He scowled at Ajen. "Give me a French 75."

Ajen's smile faltered. "Will you be kind enough to tell me how exactly you like it, sir?"

"It's a champagne and gin cocktail. Everyone knows it." The man's mouth pursed in contempt. "Go on, don't be cheap. Open the bottle of champers for an honored guest."

The man's accent was rough; clearly, he wasn't part of the British elite, and it had been Perveen's experience that Europeans who were on the lower end of the social spectrum worked extra hard to put themselves above Indians. If Subhas was right, he'd had great audacity to crash the party. Perveen watched Ajen slowly rotate the cork on the neck of a bottle of Moët, all the while his lips pursed. She realized he might not know how to make the drink.

"Isn't a French 75 two parts champagne, one part gin?" Perveen said, turning and smiling shyly at the probable Mr. Morgan.

"Quite right!" Morgan blinked, then gave her a devilish smile. "My lady, you seem to know the English language and drinks so well?"

"I've had that scintillating beverage before, sweetened with a bit of sugar syrup and lemon juice," she added for Ajen's benefit. "Lots of people were drinking in Paris to celebrate war's end."

"Paris! Did you serve as a nurse?" His voice lowered, becoming slightly more respectful.

"Not quite so noble as that," she said with a chuckle. "I went to Paris on holiday after I'd finished my studies in England."

"I had that drink in the early days of the war—well before my platoon was captured in Dordogne. I'm Joe Morgan," he said, putting out a free hand to her.

"My name is Perveen Mistry," Perveen said, taking his hand, which had a firm grip: hot, but fortunately not sweaty. "Are there other soldiers here tonight with you?"

"Oh, no. I'm out of the military and enjoying my lazy days on the film censor board."

"Oh! Can you watch all the films for free, then?" Perveen tried to sound innocently curious, aware that Ajen's face had tightened following the man's declaration. "I only got the invitation for tonight because of a chance meeting with the studio owners. You must know everyone in the Bombay film world—it's supposed to be like a little Hollywood, isn't it?"

"I wouldn't use those words, because Britain makes better quality films." Morgan sounded smug.

"I must say, I didn't know about a new fellow in the censor department!" Ajen cut in and beamed obsequiously. "How do you like it?"

"I've only been in town two months. It's disgraceful that a forthcoming film is being advertised and even screened here, when you have yet to submit it for censor review."

A rebuke—again in that same contemptuous tone in which he'd ordered the drink. She felt herself tense; because in the brief moments she'd spoken with Joe Morgan, the loudness of his voice made her think he was already under the influence of alcohol. Wishing to distract the Britisher from bothering Ajen, she asked, "How did you hear about the screening?"

"Oh, I heard about it from Rochana." Morgan smirked after the name-drop.

Given Rochana's seeming disinterest in talking to him in the receiving line, she doubted his declaration. But it wasn't her role to challenge him, so she parried, "Isn't Rochana a smashing actress?"

"Oh, she's nothing special, really. All show and no blow. But she's got it coming."

Looking at Morgan's hard mouth, Perveen wondered exactly what he meant. Perhaps he was making a sarcastic comment about Rochana not chatting long enough with him in line. But now she at least had an answer for Subhas: The stranger in the room was an incredibly nasty film censor who claimed Rochana had told him about the party.

A high-pitched ringing cut through the din of voices. Perveen turned to see Rochana and Hans Becker standing at the library's entrance, each holding a brass temple bell. As the ringing sound died, the crowd quieted, and Rochana cried out, "Once again, welcome to everyone who was kind enough to come. And now it's time for the premiere screening of *Queen of Hearts*!"

"There is plenty of seating upstairs in the ballroom, and the film will roll in ten minutes," Becker said.

Perveen glanced at Morgan, who had already drained his drink and was clutching the empty glass tightly as he stared at Becker. As Rochana and Hans turned and left the room, he muttered something that sounded like "shy mule."

"Sorry?" Perveen asked. She had pegged his accent at last as that of Northern England, maybe Manchester. If he'd said something in his native slang about Rochana, she wanted to know what it meant.

Morgan coughed and said, "Who's the hon?"

Had he called Rochana *honey*? This was entirely inappropriate. Softly, she asked, "What do you mean?"

"The bloke with Rochana."

"He's Hans Becker. And he is actually Swiss," offered Ajen, who had come out from behind the bar and was taking the apron off to reveal a regular dinner suit.

Morgan shook his head. "Swiss and a Miss."

Nonsensical child-talk; he was indeed a drunk. Perveen said, "Shall we all follow directions and go upstairs before the film starts?"

Instead of answering, Morgan turned back to Ajen. "Is Herr Becker Rochana's new paramour?"

"No, sir!" Ajen said, and Perveen saw from the young man's pursed lips that he was offended. In a rush, he said: "Rochana is the highly esteemed wife of our studio president. Hans is our chief cinematographer. You will see his work and mine on the screen."

Morgan's voice had dropped, and he gave Perveen a sidelong glance. "Can you believe it, Miss Mistry?"

"Yes, I certainly can. And I hope you enjoy the film!" Perveen was already angling to get away from Morgan. She'd done her job for Subhas and was eager to catch up with Alice. She'd heard enough malicious comments for the evening. She wanted to step back into the happy madness of the film world; it was high time for the show.

A WIDE FLIGHT of pale blue carpeted stairs led them to the first floor, a mahogany hallway lined with lamps and doors to what she presumed were bedrooms and other private quarters. One more flight up led to a massive ballroom with adorned charming beaux arts moldings and giant Belgian crystal chandeliers. As Perveen entered, she noticed two men conferring over a film projector on an elevated stand; then, her attention was drawn to a small band of men who were seated on a platform at one side of the room. She strolled closer: Between them, the musicians had a fine tabla, a sitar, and several other instruments, including cymbals and a xylophone. From attending films in theaters, she knew that these instruments would be played to enhance the storytelling. But unlike in a theater, the seats for guests were not attached in rows; these were dozens of gilded dining chairs loosely arranged, most likely possessions of the Nanporias or borrowed from a catering company. A white-painted screen was propped on a frame almost like a painter's easel, but at least twenty feet wide, at the front of the room.

Alice and Diana were already nestled in the front row of seats closest to the screen. Perveen hastened toward the few empty seats at their left.

"Oh!" Alice said, looking startled. "There you are. I lost track of you downstairs."

"Sorry—I got into quite a few strange conversations. I can't wait to hear what you've heard." As Perveen moved to sit down, Alice's hand shot out over the chair.

"I'm really sorry, but Rochana asked me to save it."

"Oh, of course!" She flinched, feeling embarrassed. "What about the other chair?"

"That's for her husband. Apparently, everything's reserved." As she spoke, Alice's voice slurred the r's. "Actually, the seat I'm in was supposed to be *yours*, but Rochana changed her mind and wanted Diana and me. She thought you might be able to find something just behind us."

Perveen looked behind and saw the row was already filled. "I'll have to go elsewhere."

"Another thing." Alice spoke cheerfully, as if the seating situation was over and done. "Because of the screen test, Rochana invited us to stay overnight. She's already showed me our room—it's very comfortable."

"You can't stay! Your parents are expecting you home tonight, aren't they?"

"But I . . ." Alice's voice trailed off. "I might need help with that little matter. But let's talk about it later, all right?"

Clearly, Alice didn't want to discuss family matters in public.

Feeling shaky, Perveen stepped back the way that she'd come. The musicians burst into a joyful melody, making her feel even more disjointed.

She felt a slight pressure on her shoulder and turned.

"The curtain's about to rise." Ajen said cheerfully. "Will you sit with me?"

"How kind of you!" she said, following him to the far end of the second row, where he waved toward a pair of empty seats near some portly Indian men wearing Western business suits.

Subhas and Rochana sailed down the aisle toward the front row. Applause grew in volume as Subhas waved to the audience and went to sit alongside Mr. Nanporia. Rochana waved at the audience before gracefully alighting on the empty chair next to Alice. As Alice turned toward her, Rochana kissed her cheek, and Alice put her hand to the cheek. *Would Alice ever wash her cheek again?* Perveen wondered.

Ajen smoothed his jacket as he settled in beside Perveen. "And now we begin! I want your honest opinion at the end."

"Of course." She smiled at him, gratified by the last-minute help he'd given her. "I wonder where Mr. Morgan's sitting."

"Hopefully in the back!" Making a face, he added, "It was very good of you to step in with the drink receipt. That's why I want you near me. I don't like censors, least of all him."

"I'm not an expert, but I'm glad I knew that one," Perveen said. "So, what's happened in the past with censors?"

"They spoil our films—take out anything that's exciting or relates to the current moment," he said.

"Such as?"

"Well, these days one can't show a bald male actor wearing a dhoti," he said in a low voice.

Perveen thought about it. "Are they thinking of a resemblance to Mahatma Gandhi?"

"Not stated explicitly, but yes. There's a rule prohibiting

characters and storylines that might incite sedition. It's not only happening to our studio." Ajen craned his head to look behind them, but the lights dimmed. "I don't see our villain. But shhh—it's starting now."

The music changed, too, to a quieter strumming of the tabla. The screen glowed in the darkness, lighting up the room with the title *Queen of Hearts*. The actor and actress names followed, then the lotus flower emblem for Champa Films.

NOT LONG AGO, THERE LIVED A FINE FAMILY, WELL RESPECTED IN THEIR TOWN, read the next title card in Marathi, Hindi, and English.

Scene one opened in an old-fashioned kitchen. Rochana appeared dressed in a modest sari, coming into a quaint parlor with a pretty, young-looking teen actress that Perveen thought she recognized from the party—now dressed as a ten-year-old in a school uniform and carrying books in her arms. Seated at a table in the center were an actor and actress several years older that Perveen hadn't noticed downstairs who were playing husband and wife. The title card introduced Rochana as Leela, the daughter in a merchant family, who had just brought her younger sister home from school. The parents were upset over a letter from a shop for a high bill charged by Rakesh, the family's reckless brother. The next scene was of Ajen playing Rakesh, wearing an English suit with great aplomb as he sprawled lazily at a card table in a gambling den.

"You!" Perveen whispered, nudging Ajen's side.

"Subhas didn't want to pay a star's salary," he whispered. "My last role, I hope!"

Ajen's gestures on-screen were broad and dramatic; this was all to be expected, but his facial expressions, purporting anger, were almost comical.

Perveen fell back into the story. Rakesh's gambling debts were threatening the family's stability so much that the parents were worried they had nothing left for Leela's marriage dowry, nor for their younger daughter's school fees. How unfortunately common it was for young people's education to end when families were in dire straits. And it was also highly realistic that eldest daughter Leela, a graduate of high school, was very concerned for the sake of the whole family and insisted something must be done to stop Rakesh's behavior. The father character revealed an empty cashbox with a thunderous rolling of drums. To the sound of a wailing flute, the mother collapsed, and Rochana rushed to embrace her.

In the next scene, Rochana took a horse-drawn taxi into the area near Apollo Bunder, Bombay's front bay harbor. When Leela stepped down, she caught the attention of a handsome man in a seaman's belted cotton coat and trousers, along with a fine cap, played by Master Nishant. Introduced in the title card as Promod, owner of a fishing company, he showed a comically lovestruck reaction with goggling eyes and a hand pressed to his heart. He returned to the boat and talked to his younger sister, a pretty teenager played by Marisa. After hearing her brother's tale, this young woman, introduced as Radha, threw down the fishing net she'd been mending and said her brother must be careful, because their parents wished him to wait for a properly arranged marriage.

All the actors seemed top-notch, Perveen thought to herself. Turning her head slightly, so she could see Subhas and Rochana in the first row, she wondered how that was for a husband—could he ever feel jealous of Rochana in her scenes with others? After all, Master Nishant was so handsome. But she couldn't tell much from the back of their heads; Rochana seemed to be whispering to Alice, anyway.

The story continued at a slow, suspenseful pace in the gambling parlor, where it was clear nice women weren't supposed to be present. Of course, Rochana's beauty was noticed by the leering gangster-type who was playing against Rakesh. As could be expected, the ne'er-do-well brother was immediately confronted by an evil-looking man named Vikas. Reading the English lines on the title card, she saw: YOU MUST PAY! EITHER YOU GIVE US YOUR FATHER'S SHOP, OR... YOU LOSE YOUR LIFE!

The shift from one film reel to another meant that about twenty minutes' time had passed; the visual drama had been so engrossing that Perveen had hardly noticed. She looked forward again to the front row. Rochana's head was resting against Alice's shoulder—and she doubted her friend would ever forget the thrilling moment.

On-screen, Rochana implored Vikas to give her brother a chance to raise money. WHO IS THIS BEAUTY? Vikas asked Rakesh.

MY SISTER. TREAT HER WITH RESPECT. But then he demanded: I AM LOOKING FOR A WIFE. GIVE HER TO ME, AND YOUR DEBTS WILL BE PAID.

A mournful sitar song played as Rakesh rose, taking his sister off to the side and apologizing. He swore that if she would save his debt, he would be through with gambling—and that if she didn't agree, Vikas might go after their youngest sister. The camera slowly closed in on Rochana's face, which was illuminated with goddess-like fairness, as her expression tightened with shock.

It must be Hans's special lighting technique, Perveen thought to herself—how intimate the actress's emotion seemed. She recalled how Rochana had spoken about wanting to help Marisa. How odd—these parallels between people and their screen personae.

Perveen's heart jumped into a jagged pattern as Rochana glumly agreed. She would submit to the terrible marriage if their parents wished it—and in no terms would her younger sister be mentioned as a possibility.

In the next scene, back at the family home, the parents deliberated with a dramatic wringing of hands, on the father's part, and the mother weeping. In the end, title cards told the father's decision that because Leela had made the mistake of entering the gambling den, it was her karma to accept marriage to Vikas.

*Horrible!* Perveen thought as a sitar sounded mournfully. Around her, the audience stirred and rustled with anxiety. *It's just a film*, she reminded herself; but she was not used to seeing family strife so plainly. Had Rochana helped write the story, she wondered; and did she use her own memories of discord to empower her tragic facial expressions?

More scenes played out: a painful one wherein Rakesh notified the gambler of the family decision, and another of Leela being counseled by her mother that a good wife can change a bad man for the better. There were some snickers at this, and Ajen made a big shushing sound.

"So rude!" he muttered to Perveen.

The wedding approached. The outside of the gamblers' den was bedecked with garlands, and in a shop close to the waterfront, villainous Vikas preened before a mirror as a long wedding coat was tailored for him. In the meantime, the fisherman Promod questioned workers at the gambling den and learned the full story about Rakesh's gambling debt and the forced marriage ahead.

The next scene showed Leela wandering sadly by herself through the streets and entering a small temple to pray.

And then, the story really took off—Promod approached Leela inside the temple, offering to help her escape her impending fate. Rochana showed distrust and her best haughty demeanor in refusing him. After the prayers finished, the fishing captain's younger sister played by Marisa arrived and took up her brother's case—and finally, Leela agreed to the plan. She would ask for money for Vikas to buy a wedding sari and ornaments, during which time Vikas would ready his boat.

Best-laid plans always go awry—and as Rochana set sail with Promod and Marisa, they were spotted from the gambling den's veranda and a chase ensued. The audience, who'd been respectfully quiet, began whooping and cheering. At last, the promise of an action scene with Rochana!

Perveen's pulse raced as the outraged villain and two followers seized a fishing trawler and took up a water chase, closing in fast. Promod rowed so hard he fainted from exhaustion. The audience's booing turned to cheers when Rochana took up oars herself and began rowing mightily—all the way to a small island.

"Finally, she's doing something!" Perveen said aloud.

In the seat on the other side, the businessmen chuckled in agreement. "High time for some action from her!"

Perveen guessed that the little cove they pulled into was one of many real islands dotting the Back Bay area—it had a lighthouse, which made her think of Bombay's former Portuguese conquerors.

Promod was now conscious and rose from the boat with the help of a few tribal people living on the island. Nishant convinced the men to give clothing disguises to Rochana and Marisa. Then came a scandalous moment with the two women going behind a tree and suggestively throwing off their clothes and emerging in pantaloons and tunic. *Clever*, Perveen thought—for it let the audience be witness to the women undressing without the actual on-camera show of skin or underclothing. *Mr. Morgan, what can you do with that?* Perveen wondered.

But all too soon the ballroom audience's whooping was drowned out by musicians pounding drums. Gangsters stormed the island and overpowered Promod.

After a title card reading, HE MUST BE DEAD, A VALIANT SACRIFICE FOR LOVE, a weeping Rochana reboarded the boat to escape with Marisa. But as the women cast off, Vikas swam through the shallow waters and boarded the boat, grabbed Marisa, and held a knife to her throat. Rochana turned sharply, jamming her body against Vikas and striking out so he fell into the ocean. A big-eyed crocodile emerged from the waves, and the next scenes were of one arm flailing helplessly, then sinking underwater.

"Crocodiles in the Back Bay?" Perveen whispered incredulously. "How was that managed?"

"Not in the Back Bay. Actually, the crocodile's name is Danta and he lives in our tank!" Ajen whispered back.

*And what did the Champa Films tiger think of Danta?* she wondered.

Rakesh threw away his cards, and remaining debts were paid with money Vikas gave Rochana for the wedding sari—and Rakesh returned, behaving modestly, to work in his father's shop. The final scene was of a wedding, with Promod and Leela circling the ceremonial fire, and her parents smiling happily.

Perveen clapped with the others as the lights came up. What had struck her most was the family drama—the reality of trouble caused by gambling and the difficult choices people made when there was no dowry available for a daughter's marriage. She would have liked to have seen a tiger in the film—Rochana's previous film had shown her riding a beautiful one—but the toothy crocodile was something new.

Around her, people chattered about the film's setting and characters. She caught comments about Master Nishant's enviable charisma, Rochana's beauty in the temple scene, and the power of the fearful climax with Rochana saving everyone's lives.

Truly, it was the crocodile who had saved the day, and that was just not as satisfying as Rochana having the final blow. Was she depraved to think this? She wondered what Alice thought.

Looking in the rows ahead, she saw Rochana and Alice with their heads still close together. And just as all the screen characters had mouthed unintelligible words, the same was happening before her own eyes. Perhaps it was about the film. Or maybe about Diana's possible screen test. She certainly hoped it wasn't about her.

AS THEY STROLLED out of the packed ballroom, Perveen tried to distract herself by delivering sincere compliments to Ajen on his acting and camerawork. "So kind of you, dear. I'm headed back for bar duty—but don't you rush downstairs. Hans is shooting pictures of all the stars and guests!"

As she passed along the hall, Perveen's journey was slowed by the knot of admirers surrounding Rochana and Nishant, who were posing in a loose embrace for Hans Becker, who was adjusting a large camera set up on a stand.

Perveen caught sight of Marisa standing amid the picture-taking queue. She touched the actress's shoulder. "Congratulations. I think you are going to be a very famous actress!"

"Do you really think so?" Marisa gushed. "Hans says I'm the face of the future. Now, why don't you have your picture taken? You're quite a pretty girl."

"Oh, I'd feel silly about it. I only stopped by to say hello to you—"

"Don't be so shy!" Marisa said, her face aglow with happiness. "You will get your picture later as a gift—a Hans Becker original. Look at all those businessmen posing for pictures. It's a bit of a reward for the money they put forward."

Perveen wondered where Subhas was; she wanted to tell him what she'd learned about the mystery guest. Now, she watched Mr. Nanporia shuffle shyly beside Nishant and Rochana. The costars stood close with just the right positioning to show the attractive lines of their slim bodies. Rochana looked up adoringly at her wide-jawed costar and wrapped her arm around his waist.

Shaking herself, she turned and spotted Joe Morgan standing nearby, his eyes like pinpricks as they focused on the couple. Feeling unnerved, she scrambled for something innocuous. "Are you waiting for a moment in the limelight, sir? I hear that Mr.

Becker is willing to take a picture of all and sundry who've come here."

"No! It was a poor film. I've got no interest." Not waiting for a response, Morgan turned on his heel, walking in a fast, irregular pace, not noticing the people who had to jump out of his way. Perhaps he was eager to get out, now that he'd seen the film. She felt herself start to sweat as she imagined him having made a decision to disapprove the film. But why the grudge? Was it because of something about Rochana, Hans Becker, or Subhas?

Perveen's body felt tight. She didn't like thinking about this when she already had her own concerns about getting the besotted Alice and Diana out of the party as they'd planned. She couldn't see how it would happen, because now Rochana was abandoning her poses and had linked arms with Alice to head downstairs. Diana's leash was caught between the two of them, and Rochana laughed as she untwisted it.

The crowds did not part for Perveen as they had for Rochana, Alice, and Diana, making her feel even more anxious as she threaded her way through the packed crowd to reach downstairs. Catching her breath, she peered into the library, which held at least twenty guests. Perveen saw Subhas waving his hands as he chatted with Mr. Nanporia. She tried to signal with her eyes that she wanted to talk to him, and he very slightly shook his head. *Not now*, the gesture said. She made her way toward Rochana and Alice, who were on a settee with Diana and holding saucers filled with champagne. As Perveen approached, Diana jumped out of Rochana's lap and came to her.

Rochana affected a pout as she looked at the dog. "I'm not her favorite, then?"

"She might wish to go outside, or just be in a quieter place," Perveen said, feeling a quiet bit of pride at Diana's recognition. "My warmest congratulations on such an exciting film. I was quite worried about how the situation with the gambling son would be resolved—and whether your character would go into a bad marriage. Very important social issues, actually."

Rochana murmured, "I agree. The best screenplays have a kernel of ordinary truth that everyone understands. Then we layer in flourishes that take the story to another level. I'm so pleased you both will be staying tonight."

"No, actually—"

"But there's a lovely guest room already prepared and close to Rochana's! We can be up all night, can't we, chatting and laughing?" Alice's voice was entreating. "A regular pajama party, if you can lend us some, dear!"

"You're such a hoot, Alice! As if my pajamas would go past your knees!" Rochana giggled as she hugged her.

"Do stay," a soft voice said in Hindi from somewhere behind them. Perveen turned in surprise to see Asmaa there, smiling and holding a tray filled with pieces of cake. "For you and Miss Hobson-Jones."

Perveen was startled that Asmaa had taken time to be kind to them, and it made her feel all the more pressured. "It's such a gracious invitation, but really, we can't. Maybe Alice could find a way to come back in the morning by herself for the screen test."

"I can't! Pa uses the car first thing every morning—you know that. Please do stick with me tonight, Perveen—otherwise what will I say to my parents?" Alice gave her an entreating look and then thanked Asmaa, who'd handed her cake.

"Why not stay, Perveen? Are Subhas and I not proper company?" Rochana's eyes flashed fire.

Slowly, Perveen said, "Nothing of the sort. You two are married; you can host guests without anyone thinking badly of you. But we are both unmarried and living with parents who have rules for us."

"Alice's father is such a clever, worldly man. He wouldn't mind!" Rochana shot back.

"Really, Mummy's the only obstacle. If I could reach home by ten-thirty tomorrow morning, she'll never know that I was out all night." Alice's voice had a faint slur, and with a catch, Perveen realized she almost sounded like Lady Hobson-Jones also did when drinking. "Mummy doesn't stir until ten-thirty or eleven most mornings. Arman can wait for us here overnight and then, after the screen test's done, drop me home first."

"I can't keep the car out like that. It's my father's property."

"Your father always liked me . . ." Alice closed her eyes, as if she were wishing for sleep.

"For goodness' sakes, you and your father are the lawyers serving the interests of our company!" Rochana interjected again. "I've made it entirely possible for this film test to be convenient for Alice, who's in her last few days of her holiday from the college. Why stand in the way? If your driver can't wait, I'll send you both home in my car tomorrow."

Perveen had initially felt excited by the crowded party, but now she felt a bit claustrophobic. She didn't wish to stay for hours in the loud, smoky house filled with too many people under the influence. But could an angry Rochana convince Subhas to ask her to return the signed contract? She had to stay. "That is not my intention. But because my father certainly needs our car tomorrow morning, I'll have to release our driver to go home. Alice, I suggest that you ring your parents—"

"In good time," Rochana said, and then turned to Alice, who was beaming her gratitude toward Perveen. "Darling, I'm so glad you're staying. Will you fetch us a second round of champagne? I must pay my regards to Mr. Nanporia, the most boring man . . ."

PERVEEN DIDN'T STAY to hear the rest. She felt stunned that Alice had taken over Rochana's attention so quickly, and vice versa. Alice's caution about not getting caught out by her parents seemed to have evaporated like a morning mist. Only she didn't want to be around the following morning to see what the weather was like in West Dadar.

Holding fast to the leash, she brought Diana out of the study, through the hall, and to the open door, where she pulled the plainest umbrella from the stand. Outside, the rain was falling hard. Diana balked, even though the umbrella covered more of her than Perveen. Diana sniffed the greenery while Perveen tried to push down her sense of alarm. Alice hadn't been so incapacitated since a long-ago dinner in Oxford when neither of them had realized the power of the claret being served.

Perveen made her way toward the car to speak with Arman, who was already standing at attention. After she explained the circumstances, he frowned and set into a volley of questions. To stay over with strangers at night? With Alice and the dog? Would the dog be allowed inside to sleep? In which room? And what could he say about it to her father?

"We will all be in a guest room together, and Diana is good protection. Truly, if you just give him those papers, he should be satisfied. Rochana said she'll send us back in her car tomorrow. My valise, please!"

Shaking his head, Arman retrieved the valise containing extra clothing and notebooks that Perveen always traveled with from the boot of the car.

*So much concern about my safety*, she thought to herself as she went inside again with Diana. It would be even worse if the chauffeur saw inside the house: the boisterous crowd, weaving to and fro, with some pairs even kissing or embracing in quiet corners of the hall and unused rooms. Why hadn't she gone to Colin's panel at the library?

Still, many of the guests were in the process of departure, gathering their wraps and umbrellas. Laughter faded amid the sound of umbrellas clicking. As she was collapsing her borrowed umbrella, a well-dressed Parsi gentleman stepped up to take it from her hand. Mr. Nanporia, the house owner.

"You took my umbrella." His expression was almost hurt.

"I'm very sorry, it was just for a moment—"

He shook his head, and murmured, "What a fool I've been!"

"No, Mr. Nanporia. It is my fault. I am very sorry!"

Perveen raised her hands in a placating gesture and the lead slipped from her hand, and Diana streaked across the vestibule toward an abandoned samosa. Forgetting about the disconsolate Mr. Nanporia, she hastened after the dog, who was finished with her treat and now was streaking upstairs.

# 7

# A TROUBLING NIGHT

Breath coming hard, Perveen chased Diana from the stairs along the first-floor hallway, a long expanse of dark mahogany flanked by doors with ornate moldings. Two white men were standing close together at the far end. After she drew closer, she saw they were Hans Becker and Joe Morgan.

Diana trotted toward them, and she had no other course but to follow—although the men hadn't yet noticed her. Morgan was delivering a long, intense stream of words, and as she got closer she caught the last two words: "Snide mule!"

Now she got it. The strange regional epithet she thought Morgan had uttered earlier wasn't exactly that. He wasn't saying "shy," he was saying "snide"—a term that she'd sooner apply to Morgan himself than anyone else. But Morgan was calling Becker a rude donkey, and this peculiar insult was making Hans Becker turn pale.

"I don't know what you mean, sir," Becker said rapidly. "It must be some mistake. In any case, we are glad you enjoyed the film."

"'We'? Who else is in league with you?" Morgan replied sarcastically. "How much do they really know?"

Diana whined. Morgan's shoulders shot up in surprise as he caught sight of Perveen. "Regards, Miss Mistry!"

"Please excuse me. I only came upstairs to catch this little runaway."

"Very good of you to catch our next star!" Hans Becker smiled as if he wasn't at all upset. To Morgan, he said, "Little Diana will make her film debut tomorrow. Miss Mistry, her call is seven o'clock at Stage Number Two."

"Thank you. I'll tell Alice." She shifted uneasily, trying to decide her next move. She didn't want to keep drinking and socializing downstairs. The best action was to retire and address Alice when she felt calmer. "Mr. Becker, do you know where the guest room is?"

"There are several spare rooms on this level, but I think I can guess where they're putting you. The Pink Room."

"The Pink Room! How naughty. Is it where they put all the girls?" Morgan chortled.

"Sir, you are misunderstanding. I am here doing business—" Perveen felt heat rush into her face, and Diana growled. She had not identified herself to him as the company lawyer. To do so now might add to the tension.

"I'll say!" interjected Morgan sarcastically. "It's just a business to all of you. Nobody is harder-hearted than an Indian female."

Perveen could not dignify him with a reply; she looked sharply away.

"Over there is the usual guest chamber," Becker said with a graceful flick of his hand. "The third door on the left, the one right before Mr. and Mrs. Ghoshal's."

Perveen felt discomfort at Becker's release of so much personal information in front of Morgan. But it was her fault—she'd asked the question. "It's just for the one night—and as I said, my friend and our watchdog will be in our room."

"Do enjoy the evening. I must meet someone downstairs." Hans bowed his head politely toward her and swiftly headed downstairs.

Morgan stared after him, his expression belligerent. Perveen walked past without bidding him farewell, keeping Diana's leash more tightly in hand.

Before, there had been a bustle. Now, there was nobody on the stairs coming up, and she felt anxious in the still hall, which was brightly lit by three chandeliers. The Nanporia villa was a beautiful place to stay; utterly elegant and respectable, she told herself. No need to worry.

Perveen walked softly along the hall, the dog lightly panting beside her. Maybe Diana had sensed her fear of the place and the men. She knocked on the doorway of the room that Mr. Becker had indicated, just in case. There was no answer.

The door opened a few inches when she turned the knob, and Diana eagerly pushed her small head into the opening. Inside, she switched on the light.

The room's walls were painted a rose color that glowed in the warm light from the sconces already lit on either side of the canopied double bed. It was almost as if someone had anticipated that guests would stay, Perveen thought as she set down her valise, noting a fragrant bouquet of roses on the dresser.

It had been a long time since she'd shared a bed with anyone. Since childhood she'd occasionally slept with others while visiting away from home—mostly with female cousins, and these nights had been filled with warmth and excitement. But now she considered the awkwardness of the situation. She was older. In a deep sleep, she might dream that Alice's lanky frame belonged to Colin. She could roll over and embrace her. Not that she had ever fallen asleep next to Colin, let alone been on a bed with him! Her heartbeat sped up at the thought. Truly, her anxiety was high enough that she probably wouldn't sleep at all.

She went out again and downstairs with Diana. Her eye was caught by the party debris that was everywhere—glasses, napkins, plates. The umbrella stand was turned over. The library was much less crowded. Only a dozen people milled about drinking and chatting lazily, draped on all pieces of furniture, and even lying on the carpet. Alice and Rochana were huddled together on a settee, giggling. Perveen tapped Alice on the shoulder to get her attention.

"Oh, hallo!" Alice trilled with the overexuberance that came with drinking and then fell into a laughing fit. Rochana joined her, mimicking the exact same laughing sound. The two of them made a powerful, headache-inducing racket. Perveen suddenly felt herself back in nursery school, when two classmates didn't want her to join their game.

"Enough!" Perveen's exclamation was fierce enough that their laughter trailed off.

"Do join us," Rochana said, although her smile did not reach her eyes.

Perveen spoke directly to Alice. "I told Arman to return home with the car. You got what you wanted."

"Excellent, my dear. Drinks are still going." As if oblivious to Perveen's discomfort, Rochana waved a hand toward the bar. Perveen wasn't sure if it meant she wanted Perveen to settle down, or just leave them.

"I've had enough and am going upstairs. The Pink Room appears to be charming."

Rochana clasped her drink tightly and said, "Yes, of all the rooms, I think that is the perfect place for you."

"So—we really are all staying!" Alice seemed to finally understand the conversation's topic. She ruffled Diana's furry head. "It will be like the old days, won't it?"

Rochana looked inquiringly from Alice to Perveen.

"We used to both stay at St. Hilda's College," Perveen explained, adding, "in Oxford."

"How well educated you are!" Rochana's tone sounded affected. "I had no choice but to sell myself to films."

"And now Rochana is the highest-paid woman in Bombay!" Alice said, as if she had also caught Perveen's sense that Rochana had felt dismissed.

"Actually, that was in Calcutta. Now that I'm part owner of a studio, I have to assume the same debts as my husband. We bear our burdens together." The actress raised her perfectly plucked half-moon eyebrows in an ironical manner.

"Don't be silly! You are on top of the world!" Alice interrupted.

"Perveen doesn't think so," Rochana purred. "Isn't that right?"

"Of course I do!" Perveen sensed from Rochana's words and expression that she might be thinking about the letter from Royal Indian Pictures. "Anyhow, you said there's a room for us. I'll go upstairs now to leave my valise."

"Let Diana stay with us. I must become better acquainted with this sweetie." Rochana held out her arms and Perveen deposited Diana, who seemed to have grown weary, because she nestled down and seemed content with Rochana.

"Goodnight," Perveen said, but nobody seemed to hear. At the doorway she paused, looking back. Subhas was lounging on the chaise with a small, rapt audience around him. This would not be a good time to give him the information that his guest was a film censor. Morgan had come into the room and was sitting in a chair, scowling, his eyes on Alice and Rochana.

PERVEEN WALKED SLOWLY up the staircase, thinking that she hadn't liked Mr. Morgan being in the room. Perhaps, because Alice was British, he wouldn't bother her the way he'd done Hans Becker. And if he did say anything to her or Rochana, Alice would surely dress him down. She wasn't afraid of anyone—excepting her own mother.

In the guest bedroom, Perveen went to the windows and drew closed the shutters; she could hear the gentle patter of rain, but nothing more. It was a soothingly familiar sound. She imagined her family hearing their own chorus of rain back in Dadar Parsi Colony—and Colin hearing it through the windows of his apartment in South Bombay. Such different worlds, and all touched by the same storm.

Locking the door, she undressed to her blouse and petticoat and went into the small marble en suite. Wishing she could clean her teeth, she found a glass and filled it with water from a jug standing on the counter. It was as if the Ghoshals were expecting people, all the time. After finishing the glass, she followed it with another, worrying about the prospect of headache. She'd had two drinks, more than her usual. She guessed that Alice would have many more.

Approaching the bed, she reached under the mosquito net and folded back the satin coverlet to the foot of the bed. It was too warm for anything but a sheet; if Alice were cold, she could pull up the coverlet when she came to bed.

But with the door locked, how could Alice enter? Climbing out of bed, she unlocked the door and also dragged the desk chair to be a few inches away from the door. When Alice came, the chair would make a scraping sound and delay her entry. That way she could be sure that it really was Alice; and if it was not, she'd have the extra moments needed to spring out of bed and come at the intruder, prepared to fight . . .

She stood shivering in the room's center, despite the heat, and tried to shake off her unease. Clearly, Rochana's scene of defense in *Queen of Hearts* had affected her. She turned her attention back to the luggage rack where she'd set down her Vuitton valise. Despite the case's elegance, it was small enough that she could only keep a few essentials: one soft silk and one silk-cotton sari, each folded flat like a package. Also, two coordinating blouses, two pairs of pantalettes and four long cloths tucked into a bag with an elastic belt—these, the necessities for female emergencies. The case also held her wooden hairbrush, extra hairpins, a set of pencils, a Mark Cross pen, a legal notebook, and a battery-operated torch given to her by Colin. Now she withdrew the torch and set it on her bedside table. Only then did she shut off the light and climb in. Suddenly she was hit with a rush of longing for Khushy, whom she kissed every night, the way Alice must do with Diana, before going off to sleep.

Sleep did not come easily, because she could hear a rumble of chatter somewhere along the hall. The sheep she counted in Gujarati turned into crocodiles. And then she must have been dreaming, because she saw her father and brother arguing with gamblers. They were the same fellows from *Queen of Hearts*, but the card table was outdoors in the middle of an island. Rustom made a threatening gesture with a fist and was quickly bashed in the face. She froze, watching the gamblers turn on her father. He staggered back from a blow. And then, she was wide awake.

Something was scraping the floor. Quickly, she switched on the bedside lamp.

The soft yellow glow showed that the chair she'd placed near the door was still there. Nobody was in the room.

She appeared to be safe. But where was Alice?

Perveen got out of bed and pressed her ear against the door. The scraping sound had ceased, but she heard a door along the hallway creak open. Then, nothing but the chirping of tree frogs and the soft falling of rain through the open windows.

Perhaps Alice was looking for the room in vain. Perveen had felt slightly contemptuous when she'd realized Alice was more than tipsy. Now she felt fear overlying her slight headache. Something might be wrong.

She went straight to the bathroom and took down a dressing gown she recalled was hanging in the attached lavatory suite. The rose silk crepe was faintly creased and carried the scent of gardenias, reminding her of Rochana. Unlike the dressing gown, the steel glass on the sink seemed fresh. Her mouth felt sour, and her throat dry from the night's drinking. She took the last of the water from the pitcher, although that would not be nice for Alice.

After she'd tied the gown over her petticoat, she went out

into the hall. A soft golden light came from a sconce on the wall. As she moved down, she thought she heard a sound—not from the rooms, but downstairs.

"Let's go."

It was Alice's voice in a half whisper. A feminine murmur followed. She guessed this was Rochana. So, the two new friends were on their way up to their rooms. The party was indeed over. It would be better for her to retreat unseen to the bedroom, so she wouldn't appear to them like a snooping mother.

This time, when she went back to bed, she didn't leave a chair in front of the door. Alice would be with her soon. With reassurance serving as sleep medicine, she drifted off quickly.

PERVEEN AWOKE WITH the light, an uncomfortable feeling of wetness on her hand. The wet feeling moved, and she shrieked, pulling her hand back. Something soft and warm brushed against her face.

"Diana!" she exclaimed. As Diana's tail gently thumped against her body, she stroked her back, noting that her leash and collar were off. The dog had come in—although Alice had not.

"Where is Alice?" she cooed, scooping up the dog. Presumably Diana had been sleeping with Alice, as she normally did.

In the best-case scenario, Alice had taken another room, perhaps because she wasn't feeling well. On the other hand, something could be amiss. Her stomach roiled with anxiety as she hurried into the bathroom to give herself the quickest of bucket baths. Then she opened her valise and unfolded the daytime sari, a green chiffon with gold zari work, and a white cotton lace blouse. After dressing, she combed her hair and fixed it into a very simple bun. Six-thirty meant that someone must have got tea ready downstairs, since the call for the film shoot was at seven.

SHE LEFT THE room, Diana following at her side with a pitter-patter down the grand staircase. The kitchen area was still in shambles with unwashed glasses and cups and dishes from the night before. To her dismay, there was no sign of a pot of tea anywhere—not in the kitchen, the dining room, or library. Perveen retreated to the main hall and chose a large umbrella from the stand near the front door, hoping she was not taking Mr. Nanporia's property again. As she opened the umbrella, a shower of drops fell, and Diana skittered off to the side.

"How can a Bombay dog be afraid of a few drops of rain?" Perveen teased as she opened the door—to significantly more rain, a gentle but steady downfall.

As if wanting to get things over and done with, the dog shot out, heading for the shelter of a tree, where she immediately crouched. As Perveen waited, a movement on the ground startled her, and she stepped back.

Snakes could be anywhere—and it was always in her mind that Colin had lost his right foot due to a cobra's bite.

But the animal that emerged seemed to be a type of lizard. A fascinating, motley creature, just shorter than her forearm. It had an imposing presence, with its ridged back and chartreuse skin that was dotted and striped with a darker green. Even the lizard's protruding eyes, which rotated to watch her, were patterned the same as its body. And then she knew what it was: a chameleon. She had never seen one in her own garden, so this was a treat. She was only sorry that Colin couldn't have seen it, too.

The chameleon skittered off quickly when Diana raised her head to look at it.

"Never mind chasing that dear thing. We're off to hunt for Alice!" Perveen tugged Diana away from her potential prey and walked toward the barn marked STAGE TWO.

But Alice wasn't there. A few men were drinking tea; their casual dress made her guess they were film technicians. Diana ran up to sniff at one of them with interest. Perveen considered asking if they had seen Alice, but she felt out of place.

Perveen walked along the gravel path she'd traveled the day before, the umbrella sheltering her well. Doing business with Subhas and Rochana had seemed like such a golden opportunity, but she was finding herself unsuited to the late nights and erratic behaviors she'd witnessed so far. If only the cast and crew were as one-dimensional and glamorous as they'd seemed on-screen!

Diana had been nosing close to the ground, and now, as if following a scent, she veered off toward the woods.

"Oh dear," Perveen said aloud.

Diana was a fast little creature, and it was doubtful she could catch her.

DANGEROUS ANIMALS and KEEP OUT signs in both English and Marathi were on a wrought iron zoo fence just off the path. Diana was running parallel, but the space between bars looked wide enough for her passage.

"Don't you dare!" Trying her best at Alice's dog-command language, she shouted, "Come!"

Diana paused for an instant, then ran on.

"Chalo!" Perveen tried instead. The dog ran on, not responding to the Hindi phrase for "let's go" any better than she had English.

Feeling miserable, Perveen hustled after the dog, hoping she wouldn't go all the way to the property's gate. The dog ran on, only stopping at a point where there was a turn in the zoo's fence. Diana glanced back and held Perveen's gaze.

*She wants me to join her.* Perveen walked rapidly, using one hand to hold the edge of her sari so it didn't trail in the muck. As she drew near, Perveen saw that they were a few feet from the half-open zoo gate. She hesitated, imagining that a large animal might be there, waiting for them both.

But Diana moved through the gate, again turning her head to look at Perveen.

*Follow me.*

Perveen felt a tumult in her chest—a fluttering sense of anxiety. Maybe Diana saw someone she wanted to visit, or worse yet, remains of an animal she wanted to eat. After all, she hadn't had breakfast. But as Perveen turned through the gate, she saw what Diana had found.

A long body, clad in a trouser suit with a blonde head streaked with reddish-brown blood.

*Alice*. Perveen's eyes darted away fast, not wanting to see anything more. She felt herself start to fall, so she clutched the fence. Behind her, she heard the sound of a car engine, soft and then louder until it had passed. A car reminded her that the day was going forward in a city that never paused. But all she could think of was this moment: that Diana had found her beloved mistress and wanted Perveen to help.

Tears streamed from her eyes; she gasped out for Diana to come back from where she had strayed along the zoo fence. Diana came trotting back, and as Perveen opened her arms, her eyes lit on a heavy shoe lying midway between the zoo fence and the body.

A man's brogue.

The shoe was not Alice's; Alice had worn a regular pair of ladies' pumps the previous evening, but the shoe could be evidence of someone who had left her here.

This word, evidence, was all too familiar. It meant everything in criminal law cases.

Perveen might be the first person to come on the scene. She should not take another step closer lest she conflict with any evidence. But then again—she took a deep hopeful breath—Alice might be hurt, but still alive. Slowly, she moved her eyes past the shoe and back to the body.

She caught sight of a muddied striped jacket and white cotton cuff, and a pale, large hand sprawled flat into mud.

Alice's hand was large, but this hand looked different—fatter and rougher.

Perveen closed her eyes and opened her mouth. She inhaled rain, earth, and the scent of dog. Diana nestled against her, as if she'd understood Perveen's need for consolation.

Perveen opened her eyes again and slowly rose. She walked along the outside of the fence a few more steps, and now she saw the full expanse of the fallen victim.

*Not Alice, but a man.*

A wave of relief rushed through her—so strong it overcame the horror that would have been the ordinary reaction. She took a few more deep breaths. There had been several European men at the party the previous night. It must have been one of them lying here.

Careful not to touch the opened gate, Perveen walked slowly and stopped again. The unpleasant face was covered with rough stubble and had the mouth slightly open.

Hans Becker, she'd thought at first, because of the light hair. But it wasn't him. The mud-spattered striped suit, and the vacant brown eyes, belonged to Joe Morgan.

# 8
# A BODY BY THE ZOO

Perveen wanted to put her thoughts in order, but her heart seemed to be exploding through her blouse. There was no time to wait. She stooped to put her fingers on Morgan's wrist. No pulse beat beneath her fingers. What had happened? Here he was at the zoo, but she didn't see any signs of attack by an animal. He appeared untouched.

Why was he here, so far from the villa? Wouldn't he have left the party in a car, like everyone else?

These were questions that the Bombay Police could ask. It would not be simple to report the crime. Being both a witness to finding the corpse and representing the film company's owner could raise ethical dilemmas. Lawyers had no responsibility to help the police solve crimes. Furthermore, they would know that her loyalty was to Subhas Ghoshal, the lessor of the property. The legal contract, now in Jamshedji's hands, established that fact.

The thought of him, just a few miles away, gave her a sense of hope. She had to reach him. But that telephone call couldn't be made until she'd alerted Subhas.

As she rose, she heard voices in the background. That's right—she had been on her way to the filming. She took a last look at the fallen man, trying to remember things as they were, then turned away from the body and started walking toward the voices, Diana loping a few steps ahead of her.

In the clearing, she saw four figures in raincoats. Drawing closer, she identified them as Subhas, Ajen, Hans, and Nishant. Following them was Alice. She was wearing the same clothes as the night before, but soiled: red wine, and orange and brown marks that Perveen guessed were dirt or vomit. She could tell from her friend's haggard expression that Alice wasn't feeling well. But here she was, no longer missing. For that, she was grateful.

At the sight of her mistress, Diana bounded up to Alice, who bent to take the dog lead out of her pocket and attach it to Diana's collar. She gave Perveen a weary but warm look. "So Diana was with you! I was looking everywhere."

Perveen felt a mix of emotions: the previous night's abandonment, and the great relief that Alice was not dead.

"You were told the time for call," Subhas said, glowering at Perveen. "Seven o'clock was ten minutes ago. Why weren't you there?"

She bristled at the reprimand. "Diana wanted to go her own way. She led me down to the zoo area and we found—"

"So you were looking at creatures for entertainment?"

"No! She picked up a scent." Perveen wondered how she could deliver the news quickly, but without too much shock. "You see—"

"She's a clever dog," Alice interjected. "No stopping her when there's a smell."

Perveen glanced at Alice, grateful that her friend was trying to save her. Then she swallowed and resumed the hard news. "There was—we came across one of the party guests lying by the zoo."

"What nonsense are you talking?"

"We found Mr. Morgan—he's the man you asked me about."

"Oh, God save us. He's a film censor!" Master Nishant moved forward, as if he were about to rush into a rescue scene.

"What a nightmare," Subhas said in a low voice. "Are you sure it's him and not another white man from the party?"

"I recognized his suit. We should call the police."

Alice bleated, "But it can't be! You must be mistaken—"

"I recognized his suit and his face. After that, I came straight back to notify you." As Perveen looked at her friend's aghast face, she thought of what it would be like if fate had played out the way she'd initially thought. If Alice was the one lying in the mud, the loss would have changed her life forever.

Ajen snorted. "Dead as a doornail, or dead to the world? Like Master Nishant's saying, he probably collapsed from all the drinks."

"He had no pulse." Now she felt irritation rising. "And there's dried blood."

"Dear God." Hans Becker's right hand moved before his chest, and he crossed himself.

Subhas pointed a finger toward Ajen. "Go to check if all is as she says."

Perveen stiffened. She was Subhas's lawyer—yet he didn't believe she was capable of understanding what had taken place? How strange that he wouldn't insist to look himself, but would send on a junior member of the crew.

"It's not a good idea to—" she began.

"Not me, sir!" Ajen shrieked. "I'm not his next of kin. And if he's dead in the zoo, maybe he was mauled. There might be loose animals roaming, and once they've tasted blood, they want more."

"My God!" Perveen put a hand to her mouth. She'd literally gone into a lion's den without thinking about it. "As I remember it, the gate was already open."

"Were the animals in their cages?" Hans asked worriedly. "You mentioned blood. It might be that he was attacked—"

"I didn't go in to look at the animals. But I tell you, his whole body was there."

Master Nishant crossed his arms, positioning himself like the solid hero he'd played in films. "Subhas, I have worked with the tigers before. I am willing to go in. The animals know my commands as well as the trainer's."

"Just a moment!" Perveen had to stop things from going further. "From a legal standpoint, sending Nishant down to look is reckless. Not only might the police give him extra suspicion, but the press would have a field day. Let me be the one who carries that burden."

"That's right," Alice said shakily. "Perveen always knows what to do. I promise you, she will make it better."

Perveen moved to Alice and slipped her hand into her friend's. Her palm was cold and clammy, but Alice didn't let go. Speaking to the group, Perveen said, "I only went up to him to check if he was still alive. I took care to keep things untouched. That will be important, in a police investigation."

"The telephone was out yesterday because of the rains," Alice said. Then, she addressed Perveen. "I meant to call home."

"You could drive to the police station in West Dadar to report," Subhas said, looking at Perveen. "My car's parked near the house, but the chauffeur is off work like the other lazy shirkers!"

And if he wasn't volunteering to drive, it might mean that he couldn't—just like her. Perveen had asked her father to teach her, but this was a freedom he'd refused.

"I can drive," Alice ventured. "If Mr. Ghoshal allows it."

"Unfortunately, you and the dog are needed on set!" Subhas was studying his watch as he spoke.

Perveen was stunned by the executive's quick turnabout. "But why? You can't be filming at a moment like this? And I can't drive."

"Terrible situation, yes," Subhas said soberly. "But if we don't shoot the scene with Diana this morning, and then the subsequent ones with Nishant and Rochana, we will lose a day."

His attitude was callous; did he have a heart for anyone? Clearing her throat, she asked, "Have you seen Rochana, then?"

"Not yet. But I'm sure she'll come. She wanted to see the hound," Hans Becker answered, and then gestured upward at the gray sky. "A storm is coming. Miss Hobson-Jones can drive Miss Mistry in my car to the station to make the police report. After Miss Hobson-Jones returns, we will screen-test the dog. If she's found suitable, we can then shoot the scene with the dog and Marisa and Nishant."

"Don't allow anyone to go to look at the body—or even walk into the zoo." Perveen was thinking out loud. "The police might suspect anyone who's been close to the scene."

"Right you are! And that is why I'm saying we must be in the studio," Subhas said. "Go and return quickly, please."

Perveen walked silently alongside Alice and Diana toward the parking area. She was uneasy, now that the men had put into question whether an animal had harmed Morgan. The estate was a wilderness of trees and shrubs, a far more desirable place for a tiger than a cage. Colin was a lover of tigers; he had refused to go on shikar with other ICS men who'd been invited by royals who kept private forests for their hunting pleasure. He'd said that tigers were shy, retiring creatures more interested in preserving their families than looking for trouble.

Alice's breath was coming hard and fast, as if she were climbing a slope, although the road was fairly flat.

"You've never driven me anywhere before. I'd no idea about this skill of yours," Perveen said, trying to keep her voice light.

"Pa taught me when we were up in Lonavalla." Alice's voice sounded almost plaintive. "We had a grand time. And he said, there's no better teacher than a curving road."

Subhas's car was a Hispano-Suiza: a long-bodied blue car with monstrously large wheels. Perveen glanced through the open window at the shining array of knobs and gears. "Do you really think you can manage this?"

"Don't know. If you want a ride, you'll have to trust me," Alice said.

Perveen glanced at Alice's face, which was downcast. A man was dead—and Rochana was missing. "Where did you sleep last night?"

Alice grabbed hold of the chrome handle on the driver's side and swung the door open. "I see the keys. Go over to the other side, and will you keep the dog on your lap?"

It was as if she hadn't heard the question. But Perveen had a sense not to push things. Reaching around to the back, she located a lap robe near a jumble of film equipment and umbrellas. She pulled it around herself, and Diana settled into her lap.

The engine roared to life, making both the dog and Perveen jump. Alice put the car in gear, and it jerkily proceeded down the long drive, following in the existing, well-worn tracks. Perveen wondered if she'd have to open the gate—but not only was it open, two people were coming through.

The intruders were a young woman of about twenty, with a light complexion and a bold red-and-orange striped sari, and a little girl wearing a frilly pink dress.

The young woman waved her hand frantically, and Alice slowed to a stop.

The woman peered through Alice's open window. "Oh! Madam, please—are you with Champa Films?"

"No!" Alice said. "Actually, we're in a bit of a hurry!"

"But we are wanting to have an audition—"

Perveen flicked her hand toward the street. "Please try another time. There is no space in anyone's schedule to see you today."

"But—"

Alice honked the horn, and the women sprang back as she went through.

As they drove through, Perveen said, "Hold on a minute. I'd better close the gate."

Alice slowed the car and Perveen got out, closing the gate. As she walked back to the car, her feet slowed. She was not looking forward to seeing the police.

Getting back in the backseat, she saw, in the rearview mirror, Alice watching her; but she did not speak.

"Take a left here, and I'll tell you when it's the proper turn for the police station."

"How do you know all this?"

"My father and I often pass by, taking better roads during the rains on our drive into town." The fact Alice had spoken gave her the courage to go on. "I do wonder about something, though. Mr. Morgan was a censor, so that means he's employed by the government. Do you know anything about him, or do you think your father might be acquainted?"

Alice abruptly braked, and Diana nearly fell off the backseat. Perveen gathered up the quivering dog and said, "Sorry to have caused a shock."

Alice sighed and resumed driving. "This is so dreadful. I thought I'd have got home by nine this morning, and now it seems unlikely to happen. This means my parents will wake up with me not at home *and* learn that I'm coming home from a place where a man died, and the police are investigating. And I don't think that my father knew him—I mean, a governor's councilor is at quite a distance from most."

Tightly, Perveen said, "Right turn up by that shop."

"I did try to call home last night, and the phone was truly out," Alice said. "My idea was just to say that our car was stuck somewhere in the rain, and by the time we got rescued it was only possible for me to stay at your home."

"My parents won't back up that story to your mother. They'll be quite angry with me, I'm sure." Perveen pointed toward the police station up ahead. Resentfully, she added, "We would not be here if you hadn't insisted on staying the night."

"Then why didn't you just go back home yourself?" Alice shot back.

"You seemed very drunk, so I was worried for your safety. Frankly, when I found the body today, my first thought was that it was you!"

"But why? I look nothing like that—that bastard!" Alice exclaimed.

"Come, now!" Perveen was startled by her friend's harsh language. "You are both tall and blond. Also, you were wearing trousers; it took me a while to recognize the striped suit as Mr. Morgan's. Then I was so relieved, I can't even tell you. I really don't want to be fighting with you, Alice—"

Alice was still driving, but her eyes had filled with tears. "I am really so sorry about all that happened. I didn't realize how many drinks I had until it was too late. I made a fool of myself in front of Rochana, didn't I? Can we let bygones be bygones?"

"All right," Perveen said. "Do you mind going around the corner and waiting for me?"

"Why can't I just stop here? There's space."

"A Hispano-Suiza is a very noticeable car. Someone might come out and want to know who you are, and where you came from. Especially since you look so disheveled."

"Right," Alice said with a sigh. "I wasn't thinking."

"Perhaps you can find some food for Diana. She's been awfully patient." Perveen was hungry, too, but she sensed any food was a long way off.

"I can manage that." Alice said. "Come round, past the bank, and I'll be waiting."

Perveen got out of the car, straightened her sari and approached the station, a one-story small stucco building with a tiled roof. Dirty floodwaters had stained the bottom three feet of the walls all the way around.

Yet inside, the red oxide floor was shining clean. The duty constable at the counter had his head on his arms. Perveen tapped the silver bell to awaken him.

"I've come from the Champa Films studio on the grounds of the Nanporia Estate. There's an emergency."

"Oh?" The constable straightened to a full sitting position.

"A man has died there. I saw him and have come to make the report. The body will need to be removed and autopsied—"

"Don't move a finger, John," said a bulky police officer with fading salt-and-pepper hair. "A doctor can make the pronouncement. Madam, is this a family member?"

"No." Perveen wished she had one of her cards, as she could tell from the stripes on his uniform, and its khaki color, that he was a superintendent. The nameplate MCDERMOTT was on his pocket. "The corpse appears to be Mr. Joseph Morgan, who visited the property yesterday evening. I'm a solicitor representing Subhas Ghoshal, who's currently leasing the property for professional and residential use from Mr. Nanporia. My name is Mistry—"

He interrupted her. "Miss Perveen Mistry, the lady solicitor?"

"Yes." Her name was becoming well-known in the city; she could only hope he didn't have an unfavorable opinion of what he'd read in the papers two months earlier about the shooting at the Ripon Club. "Murderous Attack on Ripon Celebrants," the headline had said, but it was far more than that.

"You should ring up your father. He called here last night wishing us to check for your safety at the studio. I told him that nannying was not our duty."

Her embarrassment was an exquisite pain twisting her empty stomach. "Yes, of course not. I'm truly sorry. He should have received word that I was staying out—"

"Staying out." He said the words slowly, as if to savor their indelicacy. "Well, madam, I suggest you ring him straightaway. After that, we will resume a discussion of this alleged corpse."

PERVEEN WAS USHERED through a door into the police chief's office, where a modern telephone set was on a side table.

The constable sitting near it, half asleep, was sent away, only to return quickly with a cup of tea.

Perveen thanked him, surprised by the courtesy. As she sipped the hot tea, Superintendent McDermott sat himself down at the main desk. He wanted to hear the phone conversation, she realized with annoyance.

"Thanks to God you are fine. Why didn't you return last night?" Camellia demanded when the call went through.

"Professional reasons," Perveen said carefully. "I'm so sorry you were worried. I told Arman to explain the situation."

"He tried, but it was not convincing. Are you still at the Champa Films studio?"

"Not at the moment. May I speak with him?" Perveen was determined not to use the word "pappa" in front of Superintendent McDermott.

Jamshedji didn't bother to greet her when he picked up the line. "To stay out all night shows nothing but loose character to your client. What nonsense were you thinking!"

"There's been a death at the estate."

There was a pause in which she heard only the crackling of the line. Then Jamshedji spoke in a lower tone. "Is our client dead? Or his wife?"

"No. His name is Joseph Morgan." Perveen took pains to state the name correctly for the sake of the police chief watching her intently. "I found him. I'm calling from the police station."

"So the police are nearby?"

"Yes." Now he would understand she couldn't say too much. "I came to Dadar Station to make the report."

"Shall I get you from the station, then?"

"No, we—I came by car. I'll return to the studio."

"I'll be on my way there, then. What's the weather like where you are?"

"Cloudy, but no rain at this moment."

"The wind's blowing strongly here. Rain will be coming soon."

# 9
# AN INVESTIGATION BEGINS

The telephone call had only taken a few minutes, but it felt much longer. As Perveen put down the receiver, McDermott said, "Good thing that your father's coming."

*Eavesdropper*, she thought, but gave him a terse smile. "Yes. Thank you for letting me call him."

"The constable has already gone up to the property. If need be, I'll come."

"Will the detectives come from downtown, then?"

"Of course. It's all in our hands now," he said coolly. "Is Mr. Ghoshal still on the premises?"

"Yes, of course." She knew Subhas Ghoshal would not leave the day's filming undone.

Outside, she went round the corner and saw Alice sitting on a bench near the parked Hispano-Suiza. A cluster of men was circling the car, eyeing its smooth curves. Alice, who would normally have enjoyed chatting with strangers about such a matter, kept to herself.

"Hello, you." Perveen thought Alice still looked quite sick, but it wouldn't do to rub it in. Her friend had shown remorse about the previous evening already. And now she was feeling sorry that she'd put Alice into such a bad situation, when she could have just as well come alone.

Alice's head jerked up and she forced a smile. "I found a hotel where the waiter pretended he didn't see me feeding my omelet to Diana."

"Are you saying that you gave Diana all your meal?"

"It didn't matter. I've no appetite yet. How was it with the police?"

"I hope Diana isn't going to be sick from the chilies."

Alice stood up, keeping Diana in her arms. "She'll be fine. How was it with the police?"

"The chief inspector was patronizing toward me, but at least he is sending someone to the death scene. And my father's on his way. He wants to be the primary speaker." Running her tongue over her dry lips, she added, "I don't think I gave away anything that could be used in court."

"Did you mention me?" Alice had reached the car, and its admirers drifted away, a few looking back curiously at the sight of a lady going into the driver's seat.

"No. And that's why I asked you to park discreetly," Perveen said, climbing into the other side.

Alice pushed Diana into Perveen's lap. "All right, then. Since your father's going to take care of things, do you think Arman could take us all home once he arrives?"

Perveen stroked the dog, trying to calm herself. She wasn't ready to run away. "But Diana's expected for her audition, and maybe even for a scene with Rochana later today."

"Diana doesn't care whether she's in a film or not." Alice had started driving and was maintaining a stony look straight ahead through the windshield.

"Subhas and Hans are expecting to test her." When Alice didn't react, she added, "Well, don't you even want to see Rochana when she drags herself up from bed?"

Alice shot her a scathing look. "What a strange thing to comment about."

"It's not!" Perveen flared, but as she spoke, she realized that her left-out feelings from the previous night hadn't gone away. Trying to recover, she said, "I think you can make a telephone call home to let everyone know you're fine and honor your commitment to the filming. The line at Pearl Villa might be restored. You should try," she said.

"No matter." Her expression, staring ahead, was grim. "I don't want to talk to them from a distance."

Perveen guessed that Gwendolyn Hobson-Jones would most definitely be awake before Alice rolled in. "Your houseman Govind usually answers the phone, doesn't he?" When Alice gave a cautious nod, Perveen said, "Surely you can speak to him."

The clouds broke open again as they approached the Dadar post office, which, like many other postal facilities, had a pay telephone. After giving a few coins for the telephone attendant, Perveen watched Alice move—limping slightly, she noticed—inside the building. She looked so different; not only was she moving slowly, but her shoulders were rounded as if to make her tall body smaller. Diana whined anxiously, as if she understood Alice wasn't quite herself.

Alice emerged after a few minutes, walking straighter. "You were right: Govind answered, lucky for me. Mummy had awakened already and was taking her bath. I told Govind that I was caught up on a film shoot that would make Diana a star, and I'd be back as soon as her scene is shot. I'm not sure he understood all that I was saying, but that's probably to my benefit."

"It's very good that you told the truth," Perveen said. Although it was a limited truth, the kind of truth that lawyers counseled their clients to give to avoid other lines of questioning.

WHEN THEY ARRIVED back at the Nanporia estate, a uniformed durwan was present at the entrance, coming out of the little booth to pull open the gates for them. Perveen couldn't see through the falling rain if the man was a true guard or an actor.

Farther up the drive, Perveen saw a police car, and a horse-drawn cart that was used for collection of bodies.

"There they are. I'll get out to let you go on to the filming location." Perveen grabbed hold of the spare umbrella on the car's floor.

Alice brought the car to a jerky stop. "I can't bear that you have to keep going on with this matter. Diana, you mustn't go with Perveen. Stay with me."

Perveen gave a half smile, acknowledging Alice's compassion. "It's my job."

Diana leapt into Alice's lap, and both of them watched through the window as Perveen exited. The car protested loudly when Alice put it into gear, its tires spinning in mud, before lurching back into motion. Now the police turned to look at the car disappearing toward the house, and Perveen left with them.

"Steady on," she muttered to herself.

In the hour and a half that had passed since she'd last seen him, someone had covered Morgan's body with an oilcloth, and two umbrellas were stuck into the earth on either side of the body, shielding his head.

Perveen hadn't wanted to look before, but now she knew this was a precious moment. She stood behind the police, looking carefully at the gash on the right side of the head. It didn't seem like what she imagined could be a crocodile or tiger attack. But nor did it seem accidental; the blood was on the left side of his head, and it was the right side of his head that lay flat against the ground.

A brash voice interrupted her thoughts. "This is police only."

Turning to look at him, she recognized the police superintendent who'd been so paternalistic. Seizing on this, she spoke demurely. "Superintendent McDermott, I'm only here waiting for my father."

"You could go to the house and get someone. It would be

most helpful to find someone in the Champa Films company to identify him."

She was reluctant to bring in Subhas without Jamshedji present. "I'm willing to do the identification. We have met before. I clearly recognized him by his face and clothing."

"Someone who knows him personally."

She thought he was nitpicking—and then she thought again. He was looking for a person on the scene who might have an existing motive to kill. And to establish a possible prior connection between Morgan and someone at the film company to investigate a motive. Flatly, she said, "Mr. Morgan had given me his name and told me that he's a censor with the Bombay Board of Film Censors."

McDermott's grizzled eyebrows shot up. "A censor?"

She nodded, realizing that the death of a government man was as bad a situation as she'd anticipated.

"Was he was coming in official capacity to the party?"

"I don't know why he came," Perveen said. Morgan had said Rochana invited him, and Subhas had intimated that the man had crashed the party. But mentioning either of these could lead to a false narrative.

A familiar put-putting motor was music to her ears. The Daimler was on its way up the drive. She turned to wave a hand toward the car, and it slowed to a stop. To McDermott, she said, "Mr. Jamshedji Mistry, my father, is the solicitor representing Champa Films."

"Did he know Morgan?"

"Not that I'm aware of," Perveen answered.

"Well, then, I suppose your father's here to retrieve you." McDermott sounded cheerful again, and she bristled.

Arman came around to open the door for Jamshedji, and accompanied him, holding an umbrella over his head. Jamshedji came to stand next to McDermott, looking at the draped body.

"Sorry news," he said, holding out a hand. "I am Jamshedji Mistry, chief partner at Mistry Law in Fort—"

"This is a closed police scene," McDermott interrupted. "Please take your daughter off."

Perveen waited, frozen, to see her father's reaction. She had experienced rudeness like this, but not seen her father in such a position.

Jamshedji's face was immobile. He made no response or apology, just a turn back toward the car, where Arman had already sprung out to open the passenger door.

He entered with grace, and she slipped into the car after him, not saying anything. It was as if by not acknowledging what had happened, it had less power. Her legal briefcase lay on the seat between them; she took it into her lap after she'd closed the wet umbrella.

"Straight up to the house," Jamshedji said in a level voice to Arman, who grunted his agreement.

And as the car moved slowly up the damp driveway, Perveen said, "Mr. Ghoshal is probably at Stage Two, rather than in the house itself. Arman can turn off in the clearing and stop there—do you see that barn? I think he's filming inside there."

As if seeking definite authority, Arman turned to look from her to Jamshedji, who said:

"You continue up to the parking area near the house. Perveen and I will go inside and find a place to speak."

Arman parked in the area under the trees where cars had waited the previous night. Jamshedji got out of the car and walked through the squelching ground toward the back of the house, where there was a closed door covered by a half roof. Perveen hurried to catch up with him at the sheltered spot, where he must have realized they could talk privately.

"You believe that, because I was on-site, the police may have the right to treat me as a witness," Perveen said when they had reached the sheltered position. "I agree that it's a complication."

Jamshedji glowered at her. "Actually, you might even be a

person of interest in the case. All because of you staying under the same roof at night!"

Perveen looked down, feeling a rush of shame, and saw a crumpled purple flower on the path. Krishna Kamal, the large passionflower blossom. Just like they had in the bushes at home.

"Don't you hear me? I said, they might regard you as a suspect!" Jamshedji repeated.

But Perveen's attention was on the flower. Could it have been dropped by Alice, who'd worn it in her buttonhole? Perveen felt uneasy remembering Alice's recent strange behavior, including the fact she had wanted to go home immediately and scrap the plan for Diana's role in the film. Yes, she wanted to get home before her parents arrived; but this fearful manner was in direct contrast to her behavior the previous evening. And now there seemed to be evidence that Alice had been behind the house.

"There's absolutely nothing tying me to Mr. Morgan besides a brief conversation overheard by a Champa Films employee named Ajen." Defensively, she added, "I only spoke to Morgan because Subhas Ghoshal requested that I determine his identity."

Jamshedji's eyes narrowed. "So, Subhas was concerned about him?"

"Yes. He said there was an uninvited European man, and he wanted to know his business."

Perveen went on to explain that Morgan had introduced himself to her as a film censor, and that he indicated that Rochana had invited him—and he had rounded things off by speaking rudely to Hans Becker. "If you ask me, he was abusing his position of power by crashing a party and then presenting himself in an intimidating manner."

"Possibly . . . looking to make trouble," Jamshedji mused.

"He said that the film they screened for us last night hadn't yet made it to the censor office. I'm afraid I haven't dug into the regulations around film censorship yet."

"How could we?" Jamshedji snorted. "The censor board was only established last year, and this is our first film client. I suppose the government could try to claim that it's illegal to show a film to people that hasn't got the censor stamp. Although if nobody was charged cash to see the film, and no public building was used, it wouldn't seem an obvious violation."

"I'm not sure if what we saw last night was the final version that Subhas and Hans would want to submit to the censor board." Perveen shook her head. "Such a mess!"

"That censorship process will surely go on with another employee looking at the finished film," Jamshedji said. "But you are right that Subhas could be held liable for anything related to the death—even a matter of unsafe walkways on which Mr. Morgan slipped and fell."

"If he's got a relative, they might file a civil suit!"

"Let's hope the autopsy shows cause intoxication, a state that could cause an accident anywhere in the city. But if it turns out that the blame for the man's death falls on someone within Champa Films, that will very likely delay the picture's release."

"Or possibly stop it altogether," Perveen worried aloud.

"And any number of people could easily have entered the property last evening and come upon Mr. Morgan. All because the regular guards were gone, and the actors who had been manning the gate made off quickly to the house once most of the guests arrived."

"Actors working at the gate? Who, exactly?"

"I can't say. Most of the property workers are on strike—since yesterday morning. Subhas hasn't yet paid them."

"Ah. So that's why the retainer check could not be drawn," Jamshedji said with a light snort.

"Are you saying he cheated us?"

"I deposited it on the same day we spoke with them—but I received a call from the bank yesterday afternoon saying that his bank had no funds to honor the check. I quickly assumed that this would be an error that could be cleared up. But now it seems—"

"We're working for free?" Perveen could not stop anger from rising within her.

"It would be unethical to cut him off." Jamshedji pressed his lips together. "He needs me for guidance when the police are ready to question him."

He spoke as if he planned to take over. He'd shunted her to the side, just as the police had done with her earlier. But still—she was the one who'd been there the night everything happened. The one with the connections. "He's filming now. Shall I bring you to meet him?"

# 10

# SUBHAS TELLS HIS STORY

Perveen's dour thoughts continued as Jamshedji gently pushed open the barn's door into a wonderland.

The original hooks on the walls that would have held reins and saddles were now draped with electrical cords and ropes. A few former horse stalls were packed with cameras, lamps, and equipment. In the center of the room was an elevated stage, which had a huge, three-sided painted screen, the type that was used in photographers' studios to create a false atmosphere of an elegant room. The background gave the impression of a drawing room, with the low furniture and potted plants typical of a comfortable Hindu household. A slender woman with her hair dressed in a simple bun and wearing a blue sari dressed with gold thread sat on the floor with her back toward the camera, holding an embroidery hoop. As Subhas walked across the stage, she turned her head to look at him, and Perveen saw the admiring gaze of Marisa.

"Is this good?" She held up the embroidery hoop.

"As long as you can make the sewing look real."

"But how close will the camera be?" Marisa touched her lips, as if to make sure the rouge was still there. "I've never had to sew."

Ignoring her, Subhas looked toward stage right. "Miss Hobson-Jones, one more time!"

Alice emerged from behind the screen with Diana in her arms. She was looking steadily more bedraggled and anxious. Diana seemed just as badly off and strained in her arms.

"Go two paces to the left—yes, that is where you stop. When Ajen says 'rolling,' you will set down Diana and tell her to run across the stage."

"But who's she running to, then?" Alice objected. "She's more likely to run to me, than from me."

"She will run to Marisa. Tell her."

"Could Marisa hold a treat?" Perveen suggested.

"Bubbles didn't need food as a bribe. He was professional!" Subhas said gruffly.

Seeing Alice put in a hard position, Perveen felt her anxiety. Clearing her throat, she said, "Wasn't Bubbles usually supposed to stay close to Rochana?"

"Yes. The two of them were quite a pair." Subhas shook his head. "My darling wife should be here by now. Didn't you call for her, Ajen?"

"Both Ajen and I knocked at the door," said Master Nishant, coming out on stage left, dressed like a businessman. "She's not answering."

Perveen felt a flicker of unease. One man dead on the property, and Rochana was missing? "Has anyone seen Rochana?"

There was no answer.

"I don't like it," Subhas said softly. "We must find her—"

"If there are police about, we should avoid them!" Hans said. "Stay out of their way. It could only cause more trouble."

"If she's sleeping and those coppers wake her up, they'll get a piece of her mind!" Ajen said cheerily, but the joke landed flat.

"Please. Everything is scheduled, and as we have heard, Miss Hobson-Jones and the dog can't be here all day," Hans said.

Subhas raised a weary hand. "Very well, we will try this scene another way. Miss Hobson-Jones will stand just beyond camera range at stage right. Ajen, come from the cameras. You hold the dog at stage left. After Nishant has given the scolding to Marisa, you let go of the dog. And Marisa, you must catch the dog on her way to Miss Hobson-Jones."

There was a murmuring, and Perveen held her breath until Ajen stepped forward.

"I'll want an extra fee," he said, chuckling as he took Diana in his arms. But Diana's head whipped around, and she snarled. Ajen immediately dropped the dog, who squealed in outrage.

"That's no stage dog!" Ajen pointed at Diana accusingly.

"You had your hand on her tail. She doesn't like it to be touched!" Alice retorted.

"Break!" Subhas said. "We can't be doing this now. I tell you, it's not right."

Jamshedji had been standing quietly beside her, but now he cleared his throat and spoke up. "Mr. Ghoshal, could I have a moment?"

Subhas glowered at the two of them. "What do you want from me?"

"A chance to help you," Jamshedji said gently. "I think you are becoming overwhelmed. Where can we speak with privacy?"

"The house," Subhas said after a moment. "But not for long."

SUBHAS WALKED AHEAD of them, his Wellingtons squishing loudly into the wet earth, making Perveen wish she had better footwear than her sandals. It was about five minutes' soggy walk to the house, where Asmaa, in a simple cotton sari, was at work picking up items left from the previous night's party.

Perveen seated herself on a bench to remove her own sandals, while Jamshedji and Subhas proceeded into the library, shoes still on. Asmaa gave Perveen a sidelong glance. "At least you are careful of the carpet."

"Yes. I was in the rain, and Mr. Nanporia's house is very fine," Perveen said, catching on to the lady's sentiment. She hadn't seen

Asmaa dressed so simply; but perhaps she was taking on more than her usual work. "Have you seen Rochana this morning?"

Asmaa turned away to pick up a plate. "I haven't heard from anyone that they've seen her."

Perveen thought the response rather convoluted. Did she bear a grudge against the star? "Do you mean that nobody's looked for her?"

"Rochana is lady of the house. She goes as she pleases," Asmaa said shortly.

It was hard to tell whether Asmaa's careless attitude was a sign of resenting Perveen's questions—or disapproval of Rochana. Perveen studied the slim, straight back of the woman walking briskly around the corner with a stack of dishes. She longed to go upstairs herself and fling open the door that Alice had said was the marital bedroom, just to find the star safely asleep. But she knew that it wasn't the time.

Subhas and Jamshedji were seated on wing chairs in the far end of the library. It was apparent that Asmaa had already cleaned this room very well. The only sign a vibrant party had occurred was the furniture arrangement, with chairs still lined up against the wall, and the bar pulled out to a prominent position. But there were no bottles on it at all—just a stack of papers. Glancing at Perveen, Jamshedji said, "We are establishing Mr. Ghoshal's whereabouts and actions from the party onward."

"I see." Perveen wondered how much could have happened in the minute or so she'd taken to join them.

"He's told me that his interaction with Mr. Morgan was limited to a brief conversation upon arrival, at which Morgan introduced himself. He doesn't remember seeing much of Morgan during the party and was unaware when the man left."

Subhas shifted in his chair. "I thought it better for me to keep a distance. I didn't want to put myself in the situation of making social niceties to someone who thinks his race gives him the right to crash an exclusive gathering."

"And now we know that he was a censor, so he did have tremendous power," Perveen said. She summarized the behavior she'd seen Morgan exhibiting, from his snippy conversation with Ajen to his argument with Hans. "The last I saw of him, he was in the library, staring at Rochana and Alice. That made me feel uneasy, but I was . . . tired. I went up to bed on my own," she said, realizing that she was in part testifying in defense of herself. But the fact was, she had been aware of something disturbing after she'd gone to bed. Should she raise it?

"Anything else of note?" Jamshedji's eyes bored into her, as if he thought the hallway had been crawling with suspicious guests.

"I didn't see anyone but . . ." She shuddered slightly, remembering her fear. "After midnight, I heard a thumping noise. I stepped out in the hall for a moment because I was concerned, but because it stopped, I went back to bed."

Jamshedji gave Subhas an inquiring look. "Did you also hear this noise?"

"Sorry, I did not," he said with a frown. "I went outside to smoke a cigar sometime after eleven, and then I retired. I slept in until my alarm clock rang at six-thirty. I made my ablutions, took a cup of tea, and then went out to the studio."

Perveen was surprised that he'd made the effort to smoke out of doors, but then she remembered the house was owned by a Parsi who happened to be present that evening. Smoking was impure according to Zoroastrian religious tradition. But she also remembered both men and women with long lighters holding cigarettes in the vestibule. Was Subhas telling the truth?

"Perveen?" Jamshedji said, as if sensing she'd drifted off into other thoughts.

Subhas shouldn't know this private thought, so she asked something else. "I heard about the strike yesterday evening. I wonder if there were any strange behaviors because of this?"

"The strike is over; they've all been paid. It's of no consequence."

Perveen heard the edge to the client's tone, so she tried again. "It would be helpful for us to know if anyone was left downstairs before you retired."

He closed his eyes, and Perveen imagined he might be recreating the scene. "Your friend, Alice Hobson-Jones, and her pet dog were sitting with Rochana. Also, my investor, G.K. Thadani, was chatting at the bar with Ajen. I wanted Ajen there to take care of drinks until all were gone."

"So it was a small group. What about Master Nishant and Marisa?" Perveen noted Jamshedji's blank look and explained, "Master Nishant is the male lead actor, and his daughter, Marisa Young, played a supporting role in the film."

"They must have gone back to their cottage earlier during a break in the rains. I don't recall seeing them except briefly after we finished screening the picture."

"Perhaps half an hour after the screening, I saw Mr. Becker and Morgan talking upstairs. Did Mr. Becker tell you about it?"

"No, but that is very likely because we had gone straight to work this morning trying to film a scene."

"I understand the desired scene had to be postponed because Rochana didn't arrive," Perveen said. "Have you talked with her this morning?"

"Not yet." When he realized the two of them were staying silent, he offered, "When I went in this morning, I kept the light off and went straight into the dressing room. I didn't want to disturb her."

Perveen wondered why Subhas wouldn't want his wife to be awake if there was a 7 A.M. call to set. His accounting sounded evasive. "Was anyone else missing from the company this morning who was supposed to be on set?"

Subhas shook his head. "No. Why so much emphasis on Rochana? The immediate problem is a police investigation of a death on this property."

"We need to know if she had any connection with Mr. Morgan, that's the issue," Jamshedji said.

"When he came through the receiving line, she introduced herself. He said something like, 'Very nice to see you again,' but I didn't think much of it at the time. Everyone tries to make stars believe they are old friends. Obviously, she didn't know him, just as she can't know the thousands of men who are infatuated with the screen version of her."

Perveen thought carefully about how to rephrase what she'd heard from Morgan. "The gentleman told me that he learned about the party from Rochana. That could indicate prior acquaintance—"

"Or perhaps a prior, brief meeting," Jamshedji said. "Perveen, did Rochana say anything about Mr. Morgan to you?"

Perveen shook her head, thinking, *Not to me, but maybe to Alice.*

Subhas's forehead furrowed. "Rochana and Hans and I met with the Bombay Board of Film Censors in May for the release of our previous picture. It's common process for the team at the top of the film to learn the censor's opinion, in case changes need to be made. At the time, just two men were there, and neither of them was named Morgan. That's why I was so startled when Miss Mistry said that about his job. He might be a recent hire, or . . ." Subhas shook his head. "That seems improbable."

"Or what?" Jamshedji asked.

"I wonder if Morgan might be lying about being a censor and actually be scheming along with ABC at Royal Indian Pictures. Shall we tell the police about the letter?"

"Possibly later on." Perveen thought that blaming the rival studio seemed unlikely, but she could see why he wouldn't trust ABC. "I suppose that Morgan could be a plant."

Jamshedji held up his forefinger. "And because Rochana worked at Royal Indian Pictures, we really must speak with her!

Mr. Ghoshal, would you be kind enough to go upstairs and see if she's ready to join us?"

"I could, but"—Subhas sighed—"if you are suspicious that Rochana had a secret meeting with Morgan outdoors, you may as well ask her directly. Don't put me in the middle."

Was he suggesting she make the interview because he wanted to be efficient, so that he could get back to filming, just as he'd wanted in the morning?

She considered the matter again. Subhas had said he had gone outdoors to smoke. Had he witnessed something he didn't want to talk about with Rochana? Perveen glanced at her father, who was maintaining a studiedly neutral expression. Slowly, she said, "We don't even know where Rochana is. I think locating her is the only matter of urgency."

There was a clattering sound at the front door, and someone shouted: "Police! Open up!"

"I think it's too late for that!" Subhas said.

"Don't worry. I am with you, and I'll make sure you don't answer anything unnecessary." Jamshedji spoke warmly to him and then glanced at Perveen. "It's best if you make yourself less visible."

Understanding that he wished to establish his role as Subhas's protector, she rose. "I could go upstairs and see if I can find Rochana. Mr. Ghoshal, would you mind?"

Subhas sighed heavily. "Not at all."

The police pounded again and Perveen hastily headed up the central staircase. The moment she was out of view, she heard the door open and Subhas affably greeting the police.

Asmaa was running a mechanical carpet sweeper in the long hall, carving deep lines in the plush Aubusson. Perveen came up behind her, and Asmaa's shoulders jumped before she turned and gave Perveen an appraising stare. For the second time, Perveen saw the magnificence of Asmaa's features, and thought to herself that twenty years earlier in her life, Asmaa could have played a heroine.

"What are you doing here?" Asmaa demanded: an atypical response from a servant. But Perveen realized she was no longer considered a houseguest by Asmaa. Perhaps the lady saw her as an enemy.

Gently, she said, "Sorry to startle you. Mr. Ghoshal said it was all right for me to look for Rochana."

"I see. But she's not in her room." Asmaa had softened her tone.

"No?" Perveen felt a sense of misgiving. "By the way, did you clean the bedrooms already?"

"Not yet. Why?" Asmaa's beautiful eyes seemed to grow wary.

"My father and I are helping Mr. Ghoshal manage the current situation."

"The dead Britisher. I've heard." Now Asmaa looked grim.

"Given the circumstances, Mr. Ghoshal gave me clearance to look through the bedrooms."

"All of the rooms?"

"Yes. Are they unlocked?"

"If people are out of their rooms, it should be so." Asmaa moved her hand to the waist of her sari. "I keep the keys."

*And a good deal more*, Perveen thought to herself. Perveen went to the bedroom door, and to her surprise, the enamelwork rose on the door's center swung when she touched it. A small circle of glass lay behind it. Perveen put her eye to the glass but saw nothing. She realized it was a peephole, allowing the room's inhabitants to check who had come to the door. She had seen this on some buildings in England, but never on an interior door. Whose idea, she wondered: Mr. Nanporia, or the Ghoshals?

Perveen turned the knob and found herself in a long room twice the size of the one she'd slept in and quite magnificent. An army of tall east-facing windows had a central pair of French doors opening to a long balcony that spanned that room's length. Perveen went straight to the French doors, which were locked, although all the other windows were partly open, perfect for allowing in air but not rain. It was only the edge of the floor's black marble border that shone with moisture.

The bed was covered in a grape-and-rose-checked silk coverlet. On top of that were masses of plump pillows, all made of embroidered silk and placed just so on one-half of the bed. The other side was rumpled. It was a double bed—in which just one person had slept.

She turned away from the bed, catching sight of her tired face in the tall, gilt-framed mirror at the center of the rosewood dressing table. Its polished surface was cluttered with cosmetics and a silver bell, the type used for alerting servants to come. She also spotted several velvet jewelry boxes emblazoned with the names of famous shops in Bombay and Calcutta. Holding her breath, she opened the first velvet box, and then the next. No jewelry was within any of them. In the small wooden rubbish basket, she saw papers and a bit of purple silk.

Had a robbery occurred? She imagined a burglar, perhaps who'd attended the party in fine dress, knocking out Rochana and taking the valuables. But if it had been a robbery, who would leave such a large sapphire ring? Perveen picked it up in her hand, lightly running her finger across the stone's surface. Scratched, like glass—and the golden metal setting around it wasn't genuine, either. Was all Rochana's jewelry an illusion, or had just the cheap stuff been left behind?

The en suite bathroom was strewn with a single towel. A speckle of hair clippings and shaving cream still marred the sink. These were surely the remnants Subhas had left from his morning toilette, along with a dark purple dressing gown on the floor. And where was a second towel, or a nightgown?

Not present. She noted a hand mirror made of fashionable pale green enamel had a long crack running through it. A broken mirror brought seven years of bad luck, didn't it? Seemingly the problems had already started.

Next to the bathroom was a half-open door that opened to a closet, which was a rare feature in Indian homes. Glancing inside the dark space, she saw a cord hanging from the ceiling and pulled it. An electric light came on, revealing two Vuitton valises lying tumbled on the floor. The clothing rack was tightly packed with suits, but no feminine attire.

Did Rochana usually dress elsewhere? This could be possible, she thought, as she left the bedroom and journeyed back to the guest room where she and Alice had been billeted. Here, she opened the almirah for the first time and saw women's clothing. Dozens of saris, all in highly lustrous silks. But the gold-leaf borders looked like machine stitching, not hand.

A second almirah held dresses, coats, trousers, and blouses—all finely made, some with labels from England and France. Rochana's Western clothing was extraordinary quality; the Indian apparel was good enough, although Perveen would never have worn paste jewelry. She imagined the dissonance meant that Rochana's customary clothing was that of a European woman—this was where she was most at home. The saris and jewelry were for performance; the film star, who was always seen at a distance.

The knob turned and the door opened; Perveen hastily sprang back from the almirah.

Subhas Ghoshal and Jamshedji walked in the room, followed by two tall, broadly built Britishers, one of whom she immediately recognized. How quickly everyone had arrived, and how unfortunate that they'd found her in Rochana's bedroom.

"And here you are," Jamshedji said with an effusive smile. "Detective Watkins from central headquarters has arrived. My daughter, Perveen Mistry. Superintendent McDermott, I heard you were already acquainted."

Perveen inclined her head in a slight gesture of respect. To date, her encounters with Bombay's police had been tense. Perhaps it was because most of the police didn't have degrees, and for them to deal with Indians who'd had the advantage of university and inherited wealth was an inversion of what colonialism meant.

"And why would this young lady be in your bedroom?" Detective Watkins, who had a hooked nose and beady eyes that reminded Perveen of an owl, peered sharply at Subhas.

"We asked her to go in," Jamshedji said quickly. "We were all looking for Mrs. Ghoshal. It's quite a matter of concern."

"Well, go downstairs now," McDermott instructed Perveen. "We are here to examine the rooms."

Room searching seemed premature. It could only help the police build a spurious case that Morgan's killer was a resident of the villa. Pleasantly, Perveen asked the policemen, "You've had a warrant drawn up, then?"

"No warrant at this time," said Watkins. "We thought it would be helpful to look throughout the house, and Mr. Ghoshal agreed."

"Yes," Jamshedji said. "The two of us will be right beside them, to answer any questions."

As Perveen struggled with the shock that Jamshedji was allowing a client's room to be searched without a warrant, his eyes bored into her, warning her not to keep talking.

"Well, then, let's get on with it." Detective Watkins's voice had become crisp, and his eyes lingered on her. "Was this the first time you met Sergeant Morgan?"

The detective must have made a slip of the lip. "Did you say the man was a sergeant?"

"Yes indeed." Watkins folded his arms across his broad chest. "Sergeant Joseph Morgan, Bombay CID. The deceased."

Perveen glanced at her father. Not because she needed guidance answering the question—but to take in his own surprise, carefully masked, but not impossible for a daughter to see.

The last time a white policeman had been murdered in Bombay was during her teen years. He'd been found with a bashed-in head behind a popular restaurant where he was known to be a regular. The fervor of the police response as they hunted through the city for his killer had been terrifying, and in the end an Indian he'd argued with in the restaurant was arrested, convicted, and executed. And now it felt almost impossible for Morgan's death to be ruled an accident; the question was whether they could keep Subhas Ghoshal and his studio alive.

"Miss Mistry?" Watkins prompted.

She decided to address her own inner question about Morgan's identity. "Mr. Morgan chatted with a number of people at the party. He didn't mention that he was a sergeant. Instead he claimed to be a censor."

"Censorship is a job within the police force," said Detective Watkins dryly. "And I knew him. I can vouch for his truthfulness."

She burned with embarrassment at her mistake—and also the possibility that Watkins would be less than detached about investigating the case.

Subhas cut in, "She's new to the film world. She didn't know."

Perhaps his description was meant to protect her from the police, but it only made her feel cast aside. Her father wanted her to take a backseat role, and probably now Subhas shared the sentiment.

## 11

## UNSCRIPTED LINES

Even after she'd left the villa and was walking down the drive to find Alice, Perveen felt herself shaking. Morgan's nationality was already a reason for the police to be agitated. Now there was the fact he was one of their brothers-in-arms. Killing a police officer meant not only a charge of murder, but possibly sedition. Both crimes could be punished by death. Alice's family could not avoid hearing about the situation of a dead police sergeant.

Inside the barn-cum-studio, her eyes needed to adjust from rainy gloom to the sharp brightness of a half dozen standing lamps. No sight of Alice. Hans stood with head and shoulders bent behind a large film camera on a stand. Two boys holding lights on poles were close to the stage. Ajen commanded the front of the stage, holding a card reading TAKE 1.

The artificial scene onstage looked cozy. Marisa was seated on a small Agra carpet, with her butter-yellow sari's pleats spread prettily around her. The slender young woman had her hands poised over a small wooden box brimming with sparkling ornaments—an image that reminded Perveen of Rochana's disordered jewelry in her own bedroom. Jewelry was the most portable asset, and about the only thing a woman could easily grab up if she intended to flee. Perveen herself hadn't left Calcutta without the jewelry she owned.

Would Rochana do the same?

Shaking herself, she returned attention to the stage. Behind Marisa stood a tall wooden screen painted to look like wallpaper. Clearly, the scene was supposed to be a wealthy drawing room. Nishant stepped up onstage and went to the far edge of the screen.

"One, two, three, take one, and . . . roll!" called out Ajen, clapping the wooden sign card.

The whir of the camera began. Master Nishant strode quickly to Marisa, his hands waving as he spoke. "Why are you misbehaving so grievously? You know nothing at all. One is enough, two will kill you!"

"Please don't speak of such things now. Anyway, you're wrong!" Marisa turned her head away from her father's bluster.

"I tell you that you're playing with fire."

Perhaps they were speaking so vehemently to look convincing. After all, when a film was released, one had to see the mouths and hands moving. Marisa's irate expression, and Nishant's bluster seemed so genuine, though, that Perveen felt her stomach tightening.

"Enough," called out Hans. "Cut."

Marisa grimaced and shot back, "Do tell him to stop, or I won't be able to act this scene!"

What audacity Marisa showed in giving a command to her superior! But Perveen's first shocked observation gave way to understanding that she'd witnessed a genuine argument.

"Yes, enough theatrics!" Ajen cut in. "We have wasted film already on your family problems."

"It is Marisa's debut as lead." Hans spoke decisively, his eyes on Nishant. "Let's not make her nervous about anything."

Perveen remembered Marisa proudly saying she was set to be the lead actress in the studio's next film. So what was Rochana's role?

"You, there!" Marisa called out, gesturing toward Perveen.

"It's disappointing, isn't it? Nishant brought me into this place to make my name—and now he doesn't want me succeeding."

Marisa didn't call him Abba, or Pappa, which was quite strange. Might they not really be related? Could Nishant be an older brother or uncle—or perhaps even a beau?

Perveen swallowed hard, considering the implications of a very attractive man in his thirties and a beautiful eighteen-year-old girl cohabiting. But she couldn't rush to conclusions. In her own mind, she sometimes thought of her father as "Mr. Jamshedji Mistry." It was a way to separate the familial from the professional—although it would be both rude and nonsensical to ever address him as such. Perhaps it was a matter of film culture that everyone used first names. "Sorry, I didn't mean to intrude. I came because I'm still looking for Rochana, and I've lost track of my friend Alice and her dog."

"Diana the Terrible!" Nishant said with a grimace. "Good riddance to that ankle biter."

"The dog responded to Alice's commands, but not anyone else," Hans Becker said from behind the camera. "Very sweet-looking, but the test did not go well. Very likely the tragedy is impacting everyone."

"So . . ."

"They left the studio about twenty minutes ago," Ajen said. "I told Alice that out of every hundred actresses who test for a role, we can only choose one. Same for dogs, unfortunately."

Perveen looked at Hans Becker. "Do you know how Alice was planning to leave?"

Shrugging, Hans said, "No idea. And the same for Rochana—the police already asked."

"The police seemed quite grim when they left," Ajen commented, putting down the take sign to come closer to Perveen. "Police went by. Are they making a thorough search for the killer? It's been very hard to keep our mind on work with the terror outside!"

"I understand." She could practically touch Ajen's fear and realized that all of them were working only because of orders from up above. "I know the police are motivated to find someone."

"That's the way it is when the dead man is European, isn't it?" Hans said. His tone was studiedly neutral, and she wondered if this was because he was being cynical—or perhaps was privately worried that he too could be a target.

She apologized one last time for her interruption and then stepped out of the barn.

After scanning the drive and area around the house, she didn't see Alice—though she did see Subhas, at a distance, going into a building marked FILM LABORATORY. She also saw the shadow of someone in the backseat of their Daimler. The figure turned out to be her father, copiously writing in his elegant cursive on a legal pad.

"Any sighting of Alice?" she asked through the open window.

"No. But I only came here five minutes ago."

"I want to give her a ride back home, but nobody knows where she is."

"Perhaps we'll see her strolling in the sunshine as we drive out," Jamshedji said.

"You're not still needed alongside Subhas, then?" She recalled seeing the forward set of the filmmaker's narrow shoulders and the tension on his face.

"His police interview is over. Hans will watch over him as they resume the filming. Sometimes work is the best way to stop from too much worrying."

Perveen hoped he was right. She seated herself next to her father, and as the car proceeded down the driveway, she took a long last look at the place where Joseph Morgan had been. The police vans were gone. Arman paused at the gate, and she asked the guard—one of the pair of elderly fellows she'd seen the first time they'd come through—if he'd seen a British woman with a dog.

The guard nodded. "About an hour ago. A sad-looking lady who did not answer when I asked if she knew her way to town."

"How will she find her way from West Dadar to Malabar Hill?" Jamshedji wondered aloud. "I suppose she might be going in her family car."

"I think that's unlikely. Her father always has business with the car early in the morning." Privately, she thought that Alice might have rung up Kitty Daboo from the post office and just not said anything about it.

"Well, the watchman saw her leave the property." As if sensing Perveen's downcast mood, Jamshedji patted her hand. "Alice is more or less accounted for. The watchman saw her alive. If only we could say the same for Rochana Ghoshal."

Her father's point was well taken. "What was the encounter like with Detective Watkins and Superintendent McDermott?"

"They were quite circumspect." Turning to her, he said, "We were together before they arrived, yet you withheld crucial information. You didn't inform me that the victim was a police sergeant! That made us look quite foolish—foolish and insensitive."

She felt heat rise to her cheeks. "I'm very sorry. It's exactly like I said to the police. Joseph Morgan was dressed in an ordinary suit and was drunk and behaving oddly. He only said he was a censor. There was nothing in his appearance to indicate he was in the police."

"And you think police can't be drunkards?" He snorted. "I'd hoped Detective Watkins would have confirmed whether he was on official business here—but they weren't giving anything away."

"You mean—because the studio was under suspicion for something."

"Yes. You'd better buck up and find out what, but it must be done very carefully. After all, we don't know whether the police have questions for you."

"Yes." Perveen knew it would be in the right order of things, since she'd discovered the body. But would they do it privately or call her as a witness in court? "They know I stayed overnight there—and that I was the one who reported finding the body. Must I hire a lawyer to represent me? I know that you can't represent multiple people in this case."

Jamshedji frowned. "Let's wait and see their next action. It's better for us not to look worried for ourselves."

That made sense. "I was surprised you allowed the room search with no warrant."

"As far as you were asking about the house—Subhas had no objections to room search, he told me ahead of time, and it made a good deal of sense because of Rochana's absence."

"So, you are also wondering about the disappearance of Rochana in conjunction with a suspicious death?"

"Quite. I made a point of having Subhas report it to the police, even though it's been less than twenty-four hours. There could be many reasons for her own disappearance—including kidnapping or murder. A husband would very likely be concerned about a missing wife."

"And Alice would be, too. She and Rochana became friends at lightning speed." Perveen stared out the window, looking at the lush green trees of Dadar. Just beyond them, the sea sparkled blue. Everything was beautiful; yet her own worldview had become cloudy. "And how did the police respond to the early report of Rochana's absence?"

"Without much excitement. I suspect the reaction would have been greater—after all, she is a famous film star—if they weren't involved in investigating a murder of their own man. They took down the facts and said they will be investigating quietly."

Perveen mulled over the words. "And what is a quiet investigation?"

"The office won't issue a press release about it to the public. At least, that was what Subhas requested." He gave her a knowing look. "The police did question him about whether Morgan and Rochana had spent time together during the evening. Subhas reported what he'd told us: that he and Rochana had welcomed him in the manner of any other newcomer during the receiving line. That was all he saw."

"Yes, many people saw that encounter," Perveen said. "But I saw and heard something on set today that made me curious."

"Oh?"

"When I walked into the barn, Master Nishant and his daughter, the actress named Marisa, were having a fierce argument that broke up the filming. I heard Nishant say, *One is enough, two will kill you.*"

"Probably talking about drinks," Jamshedji joked. "Why are you worried?"

"It sounded like Marisa was rebelling against his wishes, and she called him as 'Nishant' rather than by some version of 'father.'"

"These film people are so informal, aren't they?" Jamshedji scratched his smooth-shaven chin and then spoke. "If Rochana doesn't come back, Marisa's likely to become the leading actress."

"Actually, Marisa is already scheduled to be the lead in the new film. That makes me think, who will be her romantic costar? She could hardly play out love stories on-screen with a man known to be her father." Perveen remembered her shock at hearing Marisa speak so flippantly to Nishant and even use his first name. "I wonder if they are truly related."

"What are you insinuating—that a man and woman not connected by blood or marriage are living together?" Jamshedji demanded.

"No. I remember that Rochana said she was Nishant's daughter. It's just that—well, I'm not sure I trust everything Rochana says."

"I don't like to hear an educated solicitor mongering in rumor," Jamshedji said sternly. "Take a good rest when we reach home. Your mind must be cleansed of prejudice if you wish to assist with this case."

She didn't like his dismissal of her observations, but if Jamshedji meant that she wasn't out entirely, this was good news indeed.

BY THE TIME they reached Dadar Parsi Colony, the rains had returned as a light sprinkle. Perveen stepped out on the walk, pausing to breathe. It felt reassuring to be back on Manacher Joshi Street, where the air was filled with a faint grapey smell from yellow poinciana trees in full bloom. Looking up into the panicles of yellow flowers, she had a sudden memory of Rochana in her golden frock. She hadn't come across the dress discarded in the bedroom. Why?

The curtain in the parlor window twitched, and in the next instant, her mother had arrived outside, walking sedately toward her with Khushy in her arms.

"Just in time," Camellia said with a smile, and Khushy gave a soft gurgle at the sight of her aunt.

"Darling!" Perveen trilled, hurrying close so she could take Khushy into her own arms.

"Wait," Jamshedji called sharply from behind. "Don't take the baby."

"Why?" She stopped, and when he came up beside her, she saw the tension in his face. "What's wrong with me holding my dearest niece?"

"Your only niece," he reminded her. "Have you forgotten that we were both close to a dead man?"

Bathing after being in the unhealthy presence of death was a standard Parsi custom. Her joy at seeing Khushy had overcome her. Quickly, she stepped back from her mother.

"Just take the baby inside," Jamshedji said to Camellia, who was looking alarmed, now that she had heard mention of death. "I'll finish speaking with Perveen here."

As the grandmother and baby swiftly returned into the

bungalow, Jamshedji spoke gently. "You must not get ahead of yourself. After your bath, remember to check that Miss Hobson-Jones arrived safely home."

"Yes, I'll certainly call." She hadn't realized he was as concerned about Alice as she was.

"And there is more work. Before leaving today, I asked Subhas for a list of invited guests, which he has provided here." Jamshedji set his briefcase down on the hall table and extracted two sheets of handwritten paper. "Please go through it tonight and take notes on anyone listed you met."

Perveen looked at the elegant cursive writing that had the typical slant taught at convent schools. "He wrote this out for you so quickly?"

Jamshedji shook his head. "No. He said Rochana wrote out the list—the party was her responsibility, he said, as the studio's executive producer. He brought it for me from their bedroom after the police had gone through it."

Her father's mention of the marital bedroom reminded her of the uneasy feeling she'd had. "I have reason to think that only one person slept in that bedroom yesterday. The bed in the master bedroom appeared undisturbed on one side. I spoke to the housemaid, and she said she hadn't gone into that room to do anything before I looked at it."

Jamshedji's gaze narrowed as he looked at her. "So you really think Subhas is not giving a full accounting of where he slept last night?"

"It's more likely that Rochana was missing," Perveen said. "Subhas Ghoshal comes forward with some information to us—but not all. He kept quiet about his employees' labor strike, remember?"

"We must do a better job at making him feel comfortable speaking with us," Jamshedji said gravely. "Do look over the list I've given and try to recall more of the events of the evening. And tomorrow you've got the coroner's court."

Her stomach fluttered. "Did the police say the Morgan case will rise to the top of the coroner's list?"

"No. But with a head wound, it won't take long for the coroner to determine cause of death. I have my own business tomorrow morning. I don't want you to be absent from coroner's court and risk missing pertinent information I may need later."

"But what if they call me as a witness?" Perveen blurted. "I'd feel quite vulnerable, going into the coroner's court and not knowing what might happen to me."

Jamshedji put his hands in his coat pockets and rocked back slightly, as if putting distance between them. "We absolutely must give the appearance of cooperation. And if it happens that you are called, I can't keep you on as Ghoshal's primary lawyer."

Perveen felt stunned because it had seemed that he'd given his tacit assurance about her role just a few minutes earlier in the car. "Remember, you said I am the best suited for understanding the needs of a film studio. Could we leave my status on the case for Mr. Ghoshal to choose after we explain the situation?"

Jamshedji looked soberly at her. "Of course I decide. I am the firm's owner."

Outrage flared, but she steadied herself not to sound emotional. "Both of us are partners now, I thought—"

Jamshedji took his hands out of his pocket and held up three fingers. "You have just three years' experience. I have twenty-five, and I founded the practice where I hired you to work. Subhas Ghoshal originally telephoned for me, not you. And frankly, I am thinking overall about the appearance of a solicitor who has to account for her own movements near a scene of death."

Grudgingly, she knew all he'd said was true. "If there is a case, we need to hire a barrister. That's the lawyer who will come before a judge."

"But you understand the importance of hierarchy: how things appear."

His words triggered a memory; how the dead body by the driveway appeared to be Alice, how her life had turned upside down in an instant as she feared she'd brought her sweet, open-minded friend to the end of her life. Thanks to God, Alice was alive. How fortunate they all were to be in a position where the immediate problem was making peace with a father taking every caution to manage a police situation.

She should not feel this resistant to Jamshedji's power play. But was her resentment there because she feared that Jamshedji himself would investigate and find reason to point a finger toward Alice?

DURING HER BATH, Perveen scrubbed hard with the sponge, imagining all that was being rubbed off. She had perspired heavily during the previous evening, and even more so after discovering Joseph Morgan. And then, she'd had to answer to the police. If only there was a soap with ingredients to wash away her feelings of looming dread.

Perveen dressed in a comfortable house sari made of an airy cotton and went into the downstairs study, where the telephone sat in state on Jamshedji's desk. She picked up the receiver and gave the female operator, who answered in an Anglo-Indian accent, the Hobson-Jones telephone number.

As the phone rang, she hoped desperately that Alice had found a taxi that would accept her and the dog. Malabar Hill was a distance from Dadar; she couldn't have walked.

"Yes, she's here," Govind said after she had identified herself to him. His voice sounded shaky. "I'll tell her that you called."

Perveen breathed deeply, glad that Alice had reached home safely. "When do you think she might be available?"

Govind left a significant silence. "She is with Sir David."

Sir David was an even-tempered man, but he surely would be concerned about his daughter overnighting at a property where a man had been killed. How much of this would Alice tell him?

Morgan would have been a mid-level administrator within the Bombay Presidency government; perhaps Sir David had met him. And she imagined that if Morgan's death was ruled as murder, it could be conceived of as an attack on a representative of the administration.

Alice was surely hearing this from Sir David. But if she'd done something—would she confess it to him?

Govind's voice was steadier. "Miss Mistry? Is there any message?"

"Yes. Just tell her—please call me back tonight, no matter the time."

# 12
# AT CORONER'S COURT

Alice didn't call back that evening; nor did the Bombay Police. And in the night, after Perveen drifted off, she dreamed of a passionflower vine encircling her, tying her close to Colin. But just as his mouth was descending, a crocodile appeared, open-jawed. As the teeth closed around her face, she awoke, gasping for breath.

Her heart was pounding fast; the menacing reptile had seemed so real. Why had it come for her? Was it a representation of the Bombay Police, or fear itself?

Perveen arose, made her ablutions, and dressed in a sari of green chiffon dotted in yellow. As she opened the door, she saw the family's ayah Gita coming up the stairs with her bed tea tray and the morning newspaper.

"Awake already and dressed by yourself! I thought you would be tired, after being away from us so long."

"Do you have a minute to spare? Sit with me on the balcony."

Gita assented, following Perveen through the French doors that led to a wide balcony overlooking the lush garden behind the house. As Perveen settled on the swing with her tea, Gita went to the cage where the parrot Lillian had just awakened. Lillian squawked and Gita opened the cage, setting in the saucer of cut-up green beans and oranges.

"And how was your little holiday with the film people?" Gita spoke in a joking tone, as if to mitigate the household's anger.

"Not a holiday at all. How was Khushy? I missed her very much at bedtime."

"She seemed to be looking for you. Rustom-sahib played the game where he holds her flat over his head and spins about."

Perveen winced. "I'd never do that for her—not only out of fear but because she's got so heavy. Fourteen pounds on the scale last week."

Gita chuckled. "You sound like a proud mother."

"I'm trying not to be that at all!" Perveen retorted.

"Don't worry! The father's sister is a very important person in any child's life." Gita sighed. "Now the baby is starting to eat porridge, Hiba's not so much needed—but I don't know if Gulnaz-memsahib will ever come back to raise Khushy."

"Rustom seems hopeful about it," Perveen said.

Gita shook her head. "It's not right for a married man to live without comfort of a wife."

Perveen shook her head, thinking the situation was a good deal more complicated. Gulnaz and Rustom had been married five years and only developed trouble after their baby's birth. But maybe Khushy was better off without an emotionally explosive mother. Probably, Rustom thought about it even more than she did.

After Perveen finished her tea, she went downstairs for a proper breakfast; the scrambled egg and onion and green chili dish called burji, golden toast, and a plate of sliced mango dusted perfectly with red chili. It was a much smaller and faster breakfast than the usual; just as she was dining at seven, far earlier than the rest of the family. Folded next to her place setting was a fresh copy of the *Times*. Two front-page articles caught her attention. The first item, BRITISH POLICE SERGEANT DEAD AT FILM STUDIO, gave a succinct report of police being called early Thursday morning to the Champa Films property in Dadar to find the body of Joseph Felix Morgan, age twenty-six and employee of the Bombay Board of Film Censors. The report concluded with a mention that cause of death was yet to be determined by the coroner.

The second, much larger article, had a studio portrait of Rochana and a headline: FILM STAR ROCHANA DISAPPEARS.

The police had said they were keeping the matter quiet—which probably meant that someone had leaked the news. And that speaker had known exactly whom to approach, because this article was written by the same journalist who had reviewed Rochana's earlier films.

*Rochana Ghoshal, a starlet from Calcutta who moved to Bombay six months ago, has been reported missing by her recent bridegroom, Subhas Ghoshal, founder and owner of Champa Films. Rochana was last seen at a studio party on Champa Films premises in Dadar West. A source at the party reported the event's highlight was a preview for guests of the forthcoming film* Queen of Hearts, *at which Rochana appeared in sound health and happy spirits. The source did not comment on whether her disappearance might be linked with the sudden death of Sergeant Joseph Felix Morgan, a guest at the party.*

*Mr. Ghoshal was unavailable for comment on the disappearance of his wife. Any information on the star's whereabouts should be directed to the Dadar Police Station or Mr. Ghoshal's solicitor, Mr. Jamshedji Mistry of 10 Bruce Street, Fort.*

She sighed. Who was the chatty source from the party? She also wondered why Jamshedji hadn't alerted her to his speaking with the press. Chewing her toast, she mulled it over. Perhaps he'd deliberately wanted his address planted, in case anyone fearful of the police wanted to come forward with information.

AFTER PERVEEN DRESSED, she went outside with her briefcase full of papers and pencils, and her rain wrap and an umbrella. Arman was waiting in the Daimler, and the ride to court was quick.

The coroner's court was located in the vast property of Sir J. J. Hospital. Arman knew the small road that was closest to the hospital entrance. Upon reaching, she thanked Arman and took a short walk through the soggy green lawns to the Bombay Gothic, a gray stone building that served two duties: morgue on one side, coroner's court on the other.

According to a roster on the small veranda outside the court, Joseph Felix Morgan's autopsy was second in line. This was somewhat relieving to think that within an hour or so, she would not have to imagine Morgan's cause of death any longer. Another advantage was the early timing meant that there was less chance of the press arriving and asking her for comment. Although her name hadn't been listed in the paper, her identity as the city's first woman lawyer was widely known.

Yet the coroner's courtroom benches were almost full when she made her way down the aisle, looking for a seat. Either there were quite a few unexplained deaths in the city, or the story about Morgan had excited people. She believed the latter, because there was an outsize number of Europeans in the small courtroom. Some were wearing police uniforms, and she imagined they felt as if a brother had been lost. If the coroner put forward an argument for homicide, the two rows of Indian and British journalists present would quickly rush out stories for the afternoon papers.

Perveen withdrew her legal notebook, along with a well-sharpened pencil, from her case. No matter where she was, having these simple tools gave her both comfort and a sense of purpose. She tried to look casual as she glanced around the room. Subhas Ghoshal was not yet present, and she didn't see anyone else from the film company, although she did see the investors: G.K. Thadani and Ardeshir Nanporia, the man who'd been so upset about her using his umbrella. Now she wondered if the morning's lack of rain led Subhas to throw himself into filming. Or maybe his absence had something to do with Rochana: She'd turned up unharmed, or she had been found dead.

Swallowing hard, she turned her attention to the nine men sitting in the jury box.

To her eye, one of the men looked Anglo-Indian, with his uncovered head and European clothing. The other jurors wore turbans and caps and hats and traditional dress representing the city's various Hindu and Muslim communities.

Mr. King, the coroner, appeared to be in a cool mood. His role, as a quasi-legal officer, was to evaluate the evidence presented by the medical examiner, and sometimes others, and present his verdict of cause of death. The jury either agreed or disagreed with his cause.

He called for presentation of facts about the first case on the docket: an Indian dockworker of Koli background who'd been found wounded in a back alley. A constable was called up to testify about coming upon the body during nightly rounds. Then a medical examiner called Dr. Parker came forward to declare that the wounds were knife stabbing, and cause of death blood loss from a severed artery. The coroner and he then discussed the likelihood of a homicide; and then, after the coroner closed his argument for that case, the jury sequestered. Not ten minutes later, they were back, and the foreman gave the bailiff a paper with the jury's decision.

"Homicide," Mr. King said, "which puts the matter in the hands of the Bombay Police. Shall we move, then, to the second case of the day, that of Joseph Felix Morgan?"

His rhetorical question should have been met with silence, but there was a rumbling among the press in the first two rows. The coroner continued:

"The late Sergeant Morgan was found dead at eight-fifteen in the morning of Thursday, September 14, at Pearl Villa near Cadell Road, which is a property leased by Subhas Ghoshal for business and residential purposes from Mr. Ardeshir Dadhush Nanporia. Based on examination from the medical examiner, I shall present to the jury all evidence asserting a case of homicide."

Homicide was what she had unhappily anticipated—though it wasn't yet proven. Perveen didn't turn her head to look at Mr. Nanporia, who had been so scandalously named, but a rustling sound told her that many people in the audience were doing just that. As the coroner continued, she jotted in her notebook that the studio was mentioned as leased. She'd thought Subhas had said it was given to them by Nanporia; perhaps for legal reasons there was a nominal rent. The coroner outlined the details and then called up Dr. Parker, the medical examiner who had appeared earlier. Now she looked at the small, dark-haired man with deeper scrutiny. Parker looked in his middle-twenties but had the pallor of someone who mostly spent time indoors. He spoke in a monotone about the results of his autopsy of Morgan, aged twenty-six, an Englishman who had been in India for the previous two years: first with the the Bengal Board of Film Censors, and working for the Bombay Police's own censor board for the prior four-and-a-half months. Parker's voice was level as he estimated the time of death as between 10 P.M. Wednesday and 5 A.M. on Thursday as indicated by the state of rigor mortis. A toxicology report showed the presence of alcohol, cocaine, and various other substances in the bloodstream. His body showed bruises on his knuckles and back of the head; further investigation showed evidence of multiple blows to the head, including a skull fracture consistent with a fall of extreme force. Due to water present in the throat and lungs, Parker said, he'd identified drowning as the cause of death.

*So many factors*, Perveen thought, her pencil dragging slower than her mind. Intoxication, physical violence, and water! Any one of these could be a cause of death, but the doctor had posited that he'd drowned.

But there was no time to ponder this because Mr. King was summoning a police constable from West Dadar Station whom Perveen hadn't met, as well as Inspector McDermott, who had grudgingly taken her report at the police station. Today, McDermott's uniform looked freshly washed, and his manner was forthcoming and confident; he shot smiles constantly at the coroner and the audience. He answered in the affirmative when asked if he had responded to the call. "Sir, I found him lifeless."

King continued, "And how did you learn of the death?"

"The death was reported to me by Mr. Subhas Ghoshal's lawyer." McDermott looked over the audience, his eyes finally setting on her with a look that seemed accusatory.

Perveen's attention picked up. She'd been brought into the case.

"And who is this lawyer?" King's gaze sharpened as he looked at McDermott.

"A lady solicitor by the name of Miss Perveen Mistry," McDermott's tone made it sound like a joke.

"Indeed," the coroner said, following McDermott's gaze to look coldly at her.

Perveen's heart was thudding now. McDermott reported what she'd told him, but it was different from what the *Times* had reported: that Jamshedji Mistry was the lawyer on record. And what did King's one-word rejoinder mean? King probably recalled that she'd spoken up in an earlier coroner's court hearing with a point that had affected the jurors. And now a few people in the room were craning their necks to look at her.

It was inevitable for King to call on her. She felt herself sweating, waiting. But his words were: "Let us hear now from Detective Watkins."

Her pounding heart slowed as McDermott shuffled out of the witness box to be replaced by Detective Watkins, who'd left a bad taste in her mouth after her encounter with him the previous morning.

With damp fingers, she took up her pencil and recorded as best she could what the detective read out to the coroner and audience. Detective Watkins recited from a paper that, after finishing duties at central police headquarters, Sergeant Morgan had left his office at four o'clock and gone home, and after that, hired a taxi to arrive by six at Pearl Villa, the address of Champa Films.

Perveen paused in her note-taking. If Sergeant Morgan had left work so early, did that mean it was part of his duty to go to the party? It could have been undercover work of some kind. But she had sensed a deep attraction—mixed with cynicism—when he'd spoken about Rochana. He'd seemed personally involved.

"Sergeant Morgan was witnessed leaving the party at ten P.M. by Miss Marisa Young, an actress in the company who reports that she said goodnight to him in the villa's hall," Watkins said in a level tone. "Nobody in the film company reported seeing him after he left. His body was discovered at the edge of the studio's zoo by Miss Mistry, who claimed to be strolling the grounds with a dog on the property at six-thirty A.M. Miss Mistry said she informed Subhas Ghoshal and some of his colleagues before arriving at police headquarters an hour later, with the report of the body."

Detective Watkins then discussed the condition of the body, which appeared to have streaks of mud on the back of the suit. His pocket contained one hundred rupees in paper notes.

At this, there was a stir; it was a copious amount of cash for anyone to be carrying, especially a member of the police. At the end of the police report, the policeman said, "The presence of the large sum of money in the man's pocket makes robbery an unlikely motive."

So much for the theory about a common criminal wandering in through unlocked gates and taking advantage of an affluent man. She felt a lifeline slip away.

"And what was your impression of the body's state?" the coroner asked the police officer.

"Because of the knot on the back of his head, I thought he'd fallen hard."

"Fallen" could indicate an accident.

The coroner asked, "Can you please tell us more about any other physical details?"

"A red mark with the consistency of lip rouge was on his jaw."

At this, there was a great murmuring, and Perveen felt herself prickle. The involvement of a woman could point toward Rochana and many other ladies at the party, including herself. Now she despised herself for wearing lip rouge that evening. Would anyone besides Alice remember that? And thank goodness Alice's name hadn't come up in anyone's account. How fortunate that Perveen had not given her name in advance to be added to the guest list—the very list that her father said Subhas had provided at the police's request.

The coroner thanked the detective, who returned to the seats, and asked if anyone present wished to ask a question. Typically, family members asked questions first. But no one who looked like a possible wife or relative spoke up.

However, the press was holding up hands. The first one, a writer for the *Times*, brought up the matter that had struck Perveen: that there was no body of water nearby, and that there were several bruises that might indicate a fight. What could have caused the man to drown?

"May I remind the jury that a doctor's finding cannot be challenged," Mr. King said, his eyes shooting fire. It looked as if the questions were to be shut down, but Dr. Parker, who was sitting in the front row, raised a hand.

"Dr. Parker?"

"No offense is taken, sir. Please, may I elaborate?"

King exhaled heavily. "Very well. Come forward, sir."

Back in the witness box, Dr. Parker spoke, his eyes on the brash young reporter. "Hearing the circumstances of how the body was found at the edge of the zoo—and with laboratory reports indicating intoxication, I first considered the possibility of an accidental fall. But as indicated, there were too many bruises, including on the hands. This led me to suspect either a violent altercation between two men, or an attack. So your point is well taken, sir."

The reporter's shoulders relaxed.

"Yes, how can a man drown on dry land?" a second, emboldened, reporter called out, and there was more murmuring in the room.

"Order!" Mr. King said, sharply rapping a gavel.

When the room stilled, Dr. Parker spoke, his tone more animated than before. "Anyone who was in Bombay on Tuesday night will recall how hard it was raining. When it rains, puddles form. A person can die in a half inch of water, if they are unfortunate enough to have water rise into the nostrils and mouth."

*So why not accidental death?* As the thought came to Perveen, the coroner, Mr. King, spoke up from the bench. Solemnly, he intoned, "If a perpetrator should leave a disabled man with his face in water, or perhaps bring him to that source of water, it is a deliberate act."

Perveen looked at the jurors. Most of them were expressionless, but she thought she saw skepticism and curiosity in a few of the other jurors' eyes.

Another reporter raised his hand.

"What about the zoo animals? Could they have attacked, leading to a fall and the inhaled water?" Perveen recognized the lean, gray-haired fellow as a veteran Parsi journalist who wrote for the Gujarati paper, *Samachar*.

"Once again, we are not disputing Dr. Parker's finding. Detective Watkins, were any animals missing from their pens?" The coroner turned toward the policeman he'd just dismissed.

Watkins came forward again. "We were assured by the zookeeper that all animals were in their cages."

"Would Dr. Parker please explain in detail about the cocaine found in the body?"

Dr. Parker came forward, a slight frown on his face. "The alcohol reading was high, but there was also a low amount of cocaine. We could not conclude cocaine was administered that night, but very likely he was exposed to it within the last few days."

The repeated mention of the drug caused another murmuring in the audience. Although legal with prescription, cocaine was seen as a scourge. Perveen noted the passivity he had used to describe how Morgan had absorbed cocaine. She wondered if he was using this language in order to prevent making a policeman look like a member of the underworld.

"Doctor, what type of impairment comes from the combination of the alcohol and cocaine?" A second voice called.

"Potentially a rapid heart rate and high blood pressure. Such a combination might exacerbate anxiety and aggression. Use of one substance might lead to accidental overindulgence in the other." Sounding confident, the doctor ticked off the causes on his fingers. "But as I've said before, water was found in the throat and lungs, making a drowning the deciding cause in Mr. Morgan's death."

"I think we have answered more than enough questions," said Mr. King. Turning to look at the jury, he instructed them that they would now be able to view the body—an act that was done by looking through a plate-glass window into the morgue—and then sequestering for their deliberations.

Perveen watched the men slowly proceed to the window, which was in the wall close to the judicial bench. Some people lingered and others turned away quickly. And then, given the coroner's permission, they went for their recess.

Perveen got up, finding that her body had grown stiff as she had sat unmoving for so long. She'd been afraid of being called up—because she sensed that if she'd been questioned it could have gone badly for her. Yet because they hadn't asked, she wondered why.

Was it a simple matter of the knowledge she was a lawyer connected to Champa Films, and they reasoned that protected her? After all, Detective Watkins could have mentioned to the coroner that she'd challenged his inspection of Pearl Villa, although her father had ultimately allowed it. This might make her a problematic witness for their projected cause of death.

The sun had risen to a point where the air was quite warm, and the fans on the ceiling could not whir air fast enough to break the humidity. She wondered if the jury would take as brief a time to decide as they had done with the two previous cases.

Wandering into the hallway, she angled herself near the cluster of British police officers whom she'd noticed before.

"Not surprised at all," one of them was saying to the other in a grim tone.

"Quite right. Let's hope we won't lose more than a day over this."

Perveen could not come close to guessing what the men meant; but she did have the sense that they weren't mourning Morgan. The bailiff emerged into the hall, ringing a bell. The jury had reached a verdict. En masse, people came back in and settled themselves. The coroner called the court to order and asked the foreman of the jury to come forward.

The foreman was a small, nervous man wearing a British suit with a stiff black fetah, the Parsi men's hat that was usually worn for formal occasions. Swiftly, he handed the coroner an envelope.

After reading it, the coroner's eyebrows went up. So, he was surprised.

Clearing his throat, he spoke. "The jury was asked to affirm or to decline the verdict of homicide by drowning. They write that they have five in favor of the verdict and three against. This means the case will go forward to the Bombay city prosecutor's office, which will review the evidence and make its own determination of whether a police investigation is needed."

Cases would continue, so the coroner did not leave the bench. But in the recess, at least forty people, Perveen among them, stood up and proceeded into the aisles. The crowd parted, and as she walked along the veranda toward the stairs, she saw Messrs. Nanporia and Thadani huddled together on the lawn. She hesitated, not sure whether she should speak to them, but the decision was made for her when Mr. Thadani noticed her and bowed.

"Good morning," she said when she'd reached them.

"What a morning it's been, Miss Mistry!" Thadani's voice shook. "May I introduce you to Mr. Nanporia? He is the owner of Pearl Villa, and another investor in the studio."

"Yes, we've already met."

Nanporia grimaced at her. "Oh, yes. You are the one who took my umbrella."

"I am so sorry about that accident. I have my own umbrella today." She tapped it on the ground. Quickly, she added, "Does anyone know why Mr. Ghoshal wasn't here?"

Thadani made a helpless gesture with his hands. "I don't have a clue. Subhas should have come. That would have looked better in everyone's eyes. Now the police only have heard about him sending you, a lawyer, to report a death."

"It was my own idea to report. As you heard, I was the one who saw the—"

Thadani cut her off. "The police might have reason to think Subhas intentionally invited you to the party in order to assist him."

"You are insinuating something I don't believe," Perveen said, but she could see his point. "And I think it's likely my father didn't want Subhas to appear in the coroner's court because he could be hounded by the press."

"Not to mention, the crew needed to film today," Nanporia

said. "Subhas keeps to schedule in order to wisely use my investment."

"Yes," Perveen agreed, grateful for the support from an unexpected direction. "Subhas does like to work in the mornings. And films run on tight budgets."

"That is what I tell Subhas—keep to a budget, because my money's also in the pot," Thadani grumbled. "But with this prosecutorial investigation, who knows what will happen to the studio?"

"Champa Films is in jeopardy, that's for certain." Nanporia sounded mournful. "And this doctor seems to have had a shopping bag full of causes of death! That stupid copper was drunk and on drugs. How many men lie on Falkland Road, fallen down from intoxication? I did not give over my estate to Subhas Ghoshal to make it a deathbed for dirty farangs."

Perveen was shocked by Nanporia's casual usage of the vulgar term for foreigners, but Thadani chuckled.

"I also remember seeing that man misbehave at the party. I thought it was drink that loosened his tongue, but now I know it was a worse substance."

Perveen was on the verge of asking exactly what Thadani had seen and heard when a crisp British voice interrupted.

"Well done, Miss Mistry."

The voice belonged to Detective Watkins. Turning around to look at his scowling face, Perveen wondered whether he'd caught any of the critical comments about the deceased sergeant. Judging from Mr. Thadani's red cheeks and Mr. Nanporia's narrowed eyes, she guessed that they were thinking the same. But the comment had been made to her; she needed to answer.

"Hello, Detective Watkins. I don't know what you mean." She widened her eyes into an expression of incredulity. "I wasn't involved in the testimony."

He snorted. "What I mean is: You had the very good strategy

to be in the right place at the right time. You were on hand at the very crime scene when your client got in trouble."

She didn't like how he'd worded it. "Many of us were invited to the party. You have the guest list," she said, thinking of adding that Morgan was not on it. But she held her tongue, because that kind of comment could be used against her, later.

"Just as we—the film's investors—were also invited," Mr. Thadani said quickly, as if to bolster her. "By the way, Miss Mistry, did you also notice there was no guard at the gate that night? Anyone and his brother could have marched in."

She imagined that Thadani was trying to point blame away from party guests, but the way he'd phrased it made Subhas Ghoshal look negligent. What could she say: The guards that night had actually been actors? Reluctantly, she admitted, "When I arrived around six, I saw two fellows manning the gate."

Detective Watkins was looking intently at her, as if he'd sensed her inner struggle over the answer.

"Two fellows? Weren't they my regular durwans?" Nanporia shot back.

Perveen remained silent, not desiring to go into the details of the strike for anyone; especially since it had ended.

"Sir, it was gracious of you to introduce yourself to us, and best wishes for your department and the prosecutor in the investigation of the gentleman's death," Thadani said, even though there had been no introductions made. "Now, I must beg pardon, but my friend and I are traveling to a meeting. Good day, Miss Mistry."

"I'm back to the office, too," Perveen said, catching wind of a good exit strategy. "And let me say that I'm very sorry about Mr. Morgan's death. He must have been quite a valued colleague, and maybe even a friend. You worked in the same building, didn't you?"

Watkins looked appraisingly at her. "Yes. The censors are based at the Bombay Police Headquarters. I can't say I knew him personally, but in the force, we are all brothers. Do you catch my meaning?"

Was it a threat? Quietly, she answered, "I think it means that you will investigate this case with extra concern."

Raising a finger, he spoke in a hard voice. "Every case must be treated fairly. And in the case of a policeman's death, we have the responsibility to protect the force from insurrection."

His words rang in her head. Always, the government sought reasons to justify citizen suppression. "Do you think it was a politically motivated death, then?"

He gave her a long look. "It's more than an ordinary death."

*More than an Indian's death*, she thought, but did not say.

# 13

# A FRIEND'S DISTRUST

The threatening words of the detective still ringing in her ears, Perveen proceeded back across the damp grass, one hand holding the edge of her sari for protection, the other managing the legal case, just as the skies opened again to pour. She spotted the Daimler just past the stone wall bordering the campus.

"You always are in the right place at the right time," she said as she ducked into the car.

"I try," Arman said. "Where to, Perveen-bai?"

Having a choice after so much tension was a respite. Her first idea was to retreat to Mistry House. Yet she longed to see Alice—and it was important for her friend to know the coroner's verdict. "Let's call on the Hobson-Joneses," she told Arman. "If Alice is away, we'll continue on to Mistry House."

Alice's home was up on Malabar Hill, making it necessary to travel along Kennedy Sea-Face, the beautiful curving roadway that hugged the Back Bay. Normally this was a splendid journey, but today, several inches of water coated the surface near Chowpatty Beach. Traffic was light, due to the heavy rain, and as it thudded on the Daimler's roof, Perveen felt the start of a headache.

By now, the fragment of Alice's passionflower boutonniere

had probably been washed away from behind Pearl Villa. But there seemed no doubt that Alice had been behind the villa that evening. Perveen had found Mr. Morgan lying a quarter mile's distance down the driveway. There really couldn't be a connection, could there? Alice must have taken out Diana; that might have been why the flower was left in such an odd place.

The Hobson-Jones mansion had been built in the new century, possibly even within the last ten years. The house was notable for both its height and its lemon-yellow color. Because of the high rent the government paid for the bungalow, the Parsi landlord delivered outstanding maintenance. And the proof was that even in the gray day, Sir David Hobson-Jones's residence house looked immaculate.

Several durwans approached the car with the tight expressions that went with guarding one of the government's most important officials. Upon recognizing Arman and Perveen, the guards waved them through, hurrying back to the shelter of the guard box.

Arman dropped Perveen at the front and drove the car a slight distance to the parking area. Perveen didn't see the family's car. Perhaps Alice was out. It would be much better if Alice were in and her parents out. But with rainy season, people were home far more often.

Perveen summoned a smile when the butler answered the door. "Good afternoon, Govind!"

"Mistry-memsahib."

He looked at her gravely. She wondered if Alice was still looking as poorly as she had the other day. Or perhaps Alice was out. "Is Miss Hobson-Jones home?"

He hesitated a second and then spoke in a rush. "Will you come to the dining room? Wait there."

Perveen followed him down the glossy marble hall, so minimally furnished compared to her own home. They passed through an arch into the dining room and there, sitting with a half-finished plate of rice, dal, and chicken cutlet, was Colin Sandringham.

"Oh!" Putting a hand over his mouth, he coughed as if he'd been faced with a massive shock.

Perveen was just as startled. Why was Colin, who lived in Fort, dining alone at the home of her best friend? She turned around for an explanation from Govind, but his heels were already clicking down the hall toward the staircase. Trying to make sense of things, she asked, "Are you taking lunch here today? Where are the others?"

"I meant to tell you that I've moved in temporarily, but . . ."

"But why?" Perveen blurted before remembering Colin had said something about the Hobson-Joneses offering him shelter.

"Please sit down," he said, and she took a chair on the other side of the table, holding herself tightly. "I'm bunking in the original stables behind the house because of that ceiling leak in my flat that still isn't repaired."

"But this place is inconvenient for you. So far from the Asiatic Society." She stared him down until he looked away. "Why didn't you tell me? It's awkward to stumble upon you here when I only came to see Alice."

"It happened quite fast," he said defensively. "Yesterday evening Sir David came by the Yacht Club residency with the invitation. I said I'd only stay until the leaks in the flat were fixed. He was absolutely insistent!"

The timing of the invitation prickled her nerves. Alice had come home and must have been forced to reveal some details about her night out. Her guess was that the Hobson-Joneses had rushed in Colin in a desperate attempt to force the longed-for marriage that could put Alice back into a proper place. She struggled with a desire to keep silent, or to tell him the truth about her suspicions. She decided to turn it into a question. "I'm not sure if you realize that the lord and lady have their eye on you as an ideal mate for Alice?"

Colin frowned, making her regret the way she'd phrased things. "That's quite an assumption. In fact, if there is such a—misunderstanding—it's because you are the one who's always called me in to escort her to dances and parties."

It was true—but it was all a strategy for Perveen to have a way to chat with Colin without causing gossip. Grimly, she said, "It seems I've mucked up more than a few things. But you can't blame me if Sir David gets very close with you and tries to bring you back into the civil service!"

Colin laid down his fork and looked into her eyes. "He has been kind to me and is always asking about my future plans. Of course, he doesn't know that I resigned from the ICS because I'd wanted to move into Bombay to be able to see you."

"Remember, I never asked you to leave Satapur!" she protested, feeling he was turning things too hard against her. "You gave up a steady salary with a generous pension following. What you're doing here and there in Bombay isn't remotely comparable."

"To you, maybe. But I shall be fine. I have enough." He stared at her a moment longer and then took a forkful of rice. After he'd finished it, he said, "I think I mentioned that my grandfather died six months ago."

"Yes." She was glad for the subject change. "You were so close with him; he was a retired professor of botany and took you all around the gardens of England."

Colin closed his eyes for a moment. "Grandfather left my brother and me each an annuity. I've started to receive the money, and it's been very helpful."

Perveen held her tongue. She knew very little about Colin's family. Their name spoke of their ancestral origins in the Norfolk village where the British royal family had a castle, although Colin had grown up close to Oxford. Now she wondered if Colin had money as well as education in his background. This would be another reason for the Hobson-Jones family would approve of him for their daughter.

Colin leaned forward as if to confide something more, but there was an interruption.

"Good morning, both of you!"

They both startled at the sound of Alice's voice; Perveen's shoulders rose up fast, and Colin bounced back into his chair so quickly the chair skidded.

"I'm afraid it's already the afternoon! How long have you been there?" Colin sounded as disgruntled as Perveen felt.

"Long enough to hear you two talking about inheriting money." Alice was dressed in a lumpy dressing gown belted over pajamas. Her eyes were reddened, and she blinked several times as she regarded Perveen. Lowering her voice, she asked, "How did you get in?"

"Govind said I could sit here," she said, feeling unsettled by Alice's question. "I didn't expect to find Colin taking his lunch like the new lord of the manor. I needed to speak with you, actually. Did you know I called yesterday?"

"I didn't," Alice said.

Colin stood up, folded his napkin neatly and said, "Well, it seems like a time for you two to chat. Excuse me. Please tell your cook that I enjoyed the lunch very much."

"Well, you've cleaned your plate, so he'll know it," Alice said with a half smile, moving to take the chair Colin had vacated.

"Goodbye, then," Perveen said as Colin walked swiftly from the room. It had been distressing to find him here—but it was even worse to realize now there would be absolutely no chance for meetings outside of anyone's gaze. And she was troubled by Alice's anxious reaction to her presence. Softly, she said, "I hadn't known how you could make your way home without our car. I was worried."

Looking up at her, Alice gave a wistful smile. "I felt I had to flee. The filming was a disaster."

"Master Nishant complained about being bitten." Imagining

this, Perveen winced. "I guess it just wasn't meant to be. Diana is happy enough to stay at home with you."

"But I'm not happy at home. I—" Alice stopped when Govind returned to the room with a teapot. After he'd poured for them and departed, she whispered, "I don't want to stay here anymore! I really can't bear it!"

Perveen realized Alice might have her own suspicions about her parents' invitation to Colin. "It's got to be surprising to suddenly have another person in the house."

Alice pulled her mouth into a grimace. "Mummy and Pa are hoping he'll distract me from you and all the wild things we might do together."

Slowly, Perveen added milk to her tea. "So, they're wanting you to stay in with Colin and play chess, et cetera?"

"To do everything together! Actually, I'm not permitted to go out with you anymore."

"Oh dear." Perveen tasted her tea, which had gone unpleasantly cool. "And now my impromptu visit is going against that. Alice, honestly, I didn't know. As I said, I rang you yesterday."

"Mummy probably instructed Govind not to say if you called. But he also knows you're my best friend and doesn't have the gall to rudely send you off," Alice said. "He was kind enough to alert me that you were here."

"I could certainly leave now, but I've got news about the coroner's court."

"The hearing on Morgan's death?" Her voice dropped to a whisper. "Let's go to my little room. If Mummy arrives home, you can escape down the back staircase."

Quietly, Perveen followed Alice to the so-called little room, a small bedchamber originally meant for a governess on the second floor. But there was no bed, just a desk and a pair of chairs. Alice pulled the door closed and sat down in a chair across from Perveen.

"Do you have terrible news?"

Perveen tried to arrange her thoughts. "I've learned that

Morgan was a person of surprising consequence. Did you know that film censors are part of the Bombay Police?"

"Not until yesterday, when I was talking with Pa. Yes, there are many people concerned about him. But what was the verdict?" Alice's fists were tight balls on her lap.

"It was a split verdict," Perveen said, feeling surprised by Alice's urgency. "The coroner wanted the jury to find Morgan was a victim of homicide by intentional drowning. Five jurors agreed and three didn't, most likely because the medical examiner gave evidence of alcohol and cocaine use. The examiner also said Morgan had bruises and evidence of a fight."

"Quite a lot of other issues, then," Alice said. "If all these things were present, why would the coroner push for homicide by drowning?"

Perveen could see where Alice's confusion lay. "I'd thought to myself if he were drunk or disoriented, he could have fallen face down and drowned in a puddle. Logically, though, one might think that being beaten up around the head could have contributed to his falling and ability to save himself from drowning—especially if an assailant held him down."

"In a pond, or where?" Alice watched her closely.

"They are thinking the source of water could have been a puddle near the driveway. Remember how hard and long it rained?"

"Oh, yes." Alice sighed. "So, what happens, since the jury didn't agree?"

"A police investigation follows. And if what the police find supports the idea of homicide, they will send their evidence to the prosecutor, and then a charge is brought forward." As she spoke, she imagined how swiftly this could proceed.

"I admitted where I spent the night," Alice said. "Pa said how disappointed he was that I'd even been at the party. He said that if the police investigate my presence, it could have repercussions for his career. He's not on the best terms with the Bombay Police because of a recommendation he made to reduce their budget."

"Unless someone mentions you specifically, the police won't be looking into you. And you had the good fortune not to be on the guest list."

"You must be furious." Alice twisted the quilt in her hands. "If you'd gone home that night, it would have been fine for you—"

"I stayed because I thought you shouldn't be alone," Perveen said softly, because she'd noticed tears in Alice's eyes. "I didn't want anything to happen to you."

"I was mistaken about the film world being a light and happy escape." Alice wiped away a tear with a rough gesture. "And isn't it a shame that I really can't tell my cinema club students anything about the upcoming film, and what it was like to meet Subhas and Rochana Ghoshal?"

Perveen thought a change of subject was needed. "When are you starting up teaching again?"

"This coming week. It starts with faculty meetings only, which I used to dread but now welcome. I hope this won't be my last term."

"But there's no reason for that!" Perveen took Alice's hand in her own to comfort her.

In a wobbly voice, Alice said, "Pa was unhappy I'd been there overnight, but he didn't shout. He said he was choosing only to be relieved that I also hadn't been killed. Mummy was much worse. She says I'll be safer staying in England with her family in their home. Because of that, I felt I'd better say to them that it was your idea to stay out overnight."

"What?" Perveen was horrified.

"I said it was because you wanted Diana to have the screen test! I'm really so sorry—"

Perveen's face flamed as she realized that Alice had lied to save herself. Haltingly, Alice added, "We made a compromise. I can stay, but I must make a genuine effort to grow up and take my place in society."

"And this is why we can't see each other anymore." It was all about image. In a way, the Hobson-Jones family was performing a drama as complicated as anything Subhas might write for Champa Films. Sighing, she said, "I don't like you lying about me. But if telling that story is the only way to keep you in India, it's all right. I hope you'll not drink that way again. You weren't in your right mind, and that's why you pushed to stay."

"It's all true—but I remember thinking that if I'd left, the night would have just—ended." Clasping her hands together, Alice added, "I wasn't ready to end it."

Perveen recalled how Rochana's eagerness for them to stay had felt overpowering. Subhas and Hans both said that Diana needed to be available the next morning, and even Asmaa had strangely arrived to press cake on them and entreat them to stay. It couldn't have been because they knew Morgan would come to harm, could it? And that Perveen's assistance might be needed?

Feeling uneasy, Perveen recalled how she'd seen the Ghoshal bed, which had appeared to have had only one person using it. Was that typical? She asked Alice, "How late that night were you and Rochana together?"

"Probably midnight or so. I woke up on the sofa in the library with a splitting headache."

Earlier, Alice had said she'd slept in a spare room. What was the truth? "Did anyone else see you sleeping there—Asmaa, perhaps?"

"If I were asleep, how would I know?" Alice put her head in her hands. "All I can tell you is, I awoke feeling like death warmed over. And then I remembered I needed to get Diana to the filming stage by seven—and I had no idea where she was."

All of this was logical; but with Alice being downstairs, could she have seen or overheard something? "Did you happen to pass by the villa's back door?"

There was a long silence, and then Alice said, "This morning, I walked all around the villa because I was looking for Diana. Why are you asking, anyway?"

"Close to the back door, I saw the flower you'd worn in your jacket like a boutonniere."

Alice looked at her blankly.

"The passionflower from the garden at my house. You took it from Diana and put it in your buttonhole. Maybe you dropped it."

"I don't remember." Alice's voice trembled. "Did you pick it up?"

"No," Perveen said, noting the cloud that went over Alice's eyes. "Probably nothing will come of it. I've got another question, if you don't mind."

"Go on."

"Did Rochana ever mention Royal Indian Pictures harassing her?"

"No—she didn't say anything about them or even her time in Calcutta. She loves Bombay and being able to start over fresh."

Perveen noted the curious statement. "Did she say what the problem was in Calcutta?"

"No. For God's sake, you also were unhappy in Calcutta!"

Alice's retort reminded Perveen of her short, failed marriage. But she also sensed that Alice was keeping something from her. She'd already changed her story about where she'd slept, from a spare room to the library. Things had never been like this between them. Shakily, she said, "We have four solid years of friendship, you and I."

"We do," Alice said softly. "Why are you saying this now, of all times?"

"I feel like I'm stumbling in the dark. I think you're not telling me something that could be very important."

Alice bit her lip. "I shouldn't reveal the confidences of a friend."

"A friend whom you've met only once—"

"Twice. The first time was in Poona, at the Western Indian Riding Club. She remembered me very well."

Perveen decided to say what had been running under the surface. "Did you ever consider that Rochana might be after your friendship because she thinks you are useful to the studio?"

Alice's complexion reddened. "Useful! That sounds rather insulting. And I couldn't help them with Diana. She'd heard Hans speaking rudely to me—and from that moment, she was growling and refusing to cooperate."

"What did Hans say?"

"Look, I can understand him being upset that I wasn't there because of the dog. But he launched into a tirade about whether I was spying on the studio on behalf of the terrible colonial government. Someone must have gossiped about my father—you know I never introduce myself as his daughter or even talk about who he is."

"It's possible that Subhas told him—because when he asked me directly about your name, I acknowledged it. Sorry about that, Alice. But to explain more about Hans's way of thinking, it might be he's well aware that Bombay's government tries to discourage our theaters from screening non-British films."

"That must be an exaggeration. Look at all the American films we've seen!"

As Alice's pale brows drew together, she explained, "Americans must pay the British a heavy tax for permission to bring films into the country. The government's belief is, American films steal profits they'd wish to have themselves. Indian films both steal profits and have more power because they create visual stories in which Indian people see themselves."

"What does the last point mean, exactly?"

"Rochana fights a man—or men—in every film she makes. Could that not be seen as a metaphor for the downtrodden rising up against British power?"

"It's true that Subhas and Rochana are for independence and also for having the most success with their studio. But I don't see how that connects to me being used."

"You are the daughter of a governor's councilor." As Perveen said it, she wished she hadn't; Alice's expression had tightened even more. "Your father could be seen as possibly an influence over how Bombay Presidency treats filmmakers. There are matters around financing regulation that the Governor's Council does have sway." As Alice shook her head in protest, Perveen added, "They already met you in Poona, with your father. And the night of the party, Subhas double-checked with me that you were related to the Lord Hobson-Jones."

Alice's face crumpled. "Well, if Subhas said that, it still has nothing to do with Rochana."

Alice was defending Rochana, once again. She seemed more set on this topic than worrying where her new friend had gone. "I wonder about something. Do you know where Rochana might be?"

Alice's bleary eyes blinked again. "You're the one with better ideas."

"All right, then. That night, you were fast asleep. Maybe Rochana stumbled upon Morgan, and he laid into her. She could have successfully defended herself against him—or someone else did. In any case, he was dead, and there was a problem—and she ran away."

"It sounds like a film plot!" Alice protested. "Rochana and I were at the villa. He was found dead after he left the villa!"

"I'm not suggesting this is the only possibility." She paused to gather her ideas. "Because of the unguarded gate, anyone could have come onto the grounds. Morgan was a police sergeant and an ex-military man. He was trained in combat. If Morgan was outside and saw someone he didn't like, he might have rushed into a fight. Yet he was under the influence and could have fallen, and even without someone staying to kill him, he could have drowned." She recalled the water that had been in Morgan's lungs. "I wonder if the attacker might have had something to do with Rochana's disappearance."

"Do you mean—the attacker kidnapped her?" Alice looked off into the distance, as if picturing it. "I suppose anything could happen. And I hope against hope that Rochana turns up soon!"

Perveen swallowed hard. "My feeling is the same. I don't know when we'll see each other again. I feel like I'd better leave now, before someone like your mother sees me."

Alice looked soberly at her. "I wish you could stay. But I'm living under these terrible rules now. I brought the trouble on myself."

Feeling mournful, Perveen said, "It's also true that I invited you to the party. If only I hadn't rushed to tell you about it!"

"For a few hours, I was living in a dream come true," Alice said, leaving silent the conclusion: *and then, a nightmare.*

# 14

# A CARRIAGE HOUSE RENDEZVOUS

Outside, the rain was soft as it coursed through the tall gulmohar trees that dotted the Hobson-Joneses' walled three-acre compound. To bide her time, Perveen walked just around the corner, to the property's east side, where the carriage house lay.

When the British first developed Malabar Hill during the 1870s and 1880s, bungalows had been built from local wood, like this relic. Yet this aged building, on distant inspection, did not look as if it were falling apart. Its wood had been stained a yellow color, like the main house, but the hues didn't quite match. While the main house was a pale lemon color, this building was more like mustard. Sharp, just like her feelings.

As she gazed at the structure, the door opened, and Colin stepped into the doorframe. He looked at her without surprise and raised a hand in greeting.

After the brutality of the conversation with Alice, she didn't know whether she could bear another conversation; but at the very least, Colin needed a warning not to mention seeing her.

Taking a breath of damp, fresh air, Perveen walked steadily toward Colin's new home. Colin stepped back inside the house, allowing her to pass through the wide entrance.

Colin closed the door behind her, shutting out the view from the garden.

Perveen glanced about the room, furnished in the old-fashioned cane chairs and tables so popular with British colonials as they moved between camps. These homely pieces had likely been displaced by Gwendolyn Hobson-Jones's modern light-colored chairs, cabinets, and sofas. No art hung on the freshly painted walls; yet if she had seen Colin's pictures and maps hanging, it would have made her feel worse, as if he were settling in for the duration.

"Not bad, eh?" Colin asked, as if noting her long inspection.

"It could be cozy, except the roof is so high." She gazed upward at the pitched roof, imagining the long-vanished hayloft.

"My bedroom and bath are just beyond that wall," Colin said, pointing to the room's midpoint. "Fortunately windows were added, otherwise it would be quite hot."

"It feels a bit close." Perveen moved nearer to the whirring overhead fan, wanting something to cool her sticky skin. "Where's Rama staying?"

"Rama's on paid leave for the next three weeks. He's happy to return to his village."

"Yes, he lives so far." Perveen left it unsaid that Colin's clever, gentle houseman would not fit well into the complicated hierarchy of the Hobson-Joneses' many servants. And that reminded her of the household ban against her. "You were brave to open your door to me. It probably will be the last time."

Colin looked at her with concern. "Did you and Alice argue?"

"No, but now I'm persona non grata with Alice's parents. I can't see her anymore."

"I hadn't heard that. Come, let's sit down." Colin decamped to a long settee and looked expectantly toward her.

Perveen joined him, sitting a half foot away, close enough to feel the comfort of his presence. She made a brief account of how churlish Lady Hobson-Jones had been during her last visit, and how the lady now believed that Perveen had led her daughter to stay out overnight.

"That's unfortunate. Whilst you owned up to your family, Alice told a mistruth about you to protect herself." Colin pressed his lips together. "Anyone would feel quite injured by that."

"I'm embarrassed to have people think I'd be so silly as to put a dog's screen test over common sense," Perveen admitted. "But I know her parents have acted very severely in the past when she did something that they believed was improper. They had her committed in Switzerland for the year before she joined me in Oxford."

"Goodness!" Colin rocked back slightly. "What kind of a place?"

Soberly, Perveen said, "Alice said it was a sanatorium for wealthy women with supposed personality problems."

"But she's such a jolly, intelligent person. Everyone likes her personality. What sort of impropriety?"

Perveen weighed how much she should share. "Alice only spoke of it once, when we were together at St. Hilda's. She was expelled for breaking a silly rule at Cheltenham Ladies' College, and that's why she was sent to the sanatorium—a kind of punishment mixed with desire to keep her safe. After all, it was during the war, and they were here in India. Sea travel for civilians was impossible at times."

Colin raised an eyebrow. "And what was the silly rule?"

"Something about . . . being in a troublesome situation with another girl—" She paused, remembering Lady Hobson-Jones's reaction when she'd come upon the two of them in the dining room, just a few days earlier. What if it had been more than the clutter on the table, and more than the fact Perveen was Indian? Could the rage have something to do with Alice's history with women?

"Did the other girl accuse Alice of something?"

"Why does it matter?"

Colin looked closely at her. "Might it have been intimacy? These situations sometimes arise in boarding schools."

"She did say the two of them were found in bed. I—" Perveen felt her heart thudding. "But it couldn't be . . ."

"Why not? Maybe the reason Gwendolyn discouraged Alice from seeing you is because she thinks you are a lover."

Perveen wanted to protest, but Colin had raised a real possibility. "As you know, Alice is my dearest friend. I do love her. But I don't feel a *passion*."

"I didn't suspect that," Colin put his hand over hers. "However, I'm coming to see the wisdom of your own thoughts about my presence here. Lady Hobson-Jones has already suggested that Alice take me into the garden for drinks, or to have tea together by ourselves. Lord David told Alice to go with me when I wanted to go round to the Hanging Gardens for a walk, but she claimed fatigue. Yet as I was returning from my expedition, I saw Alice slipping out of one of the side doors and leaving the property."

Perveen felt her rage against Lady Hobson-Jones subside, because this was a new matter of concern. "With Diana?"

"No dog, but Alice was dressed in a Mac, as if to prepare for rain."

"What time of day was it?"

"Yesterday, around four o'clock." He slid his hand over hers. "What a somber face you're making. Where do you think she went?"

"I wish I knew. Alice's parents are worried about improper behavior ruining the family reputation, but I'm worried about her welfare."

"How so?"

Colin was so near that she could smell the faint aroma of his skin, and the starch on his shirt. She wanted to touch him—but she had to detach and put herself back into a legal frame of mind. "It's challenging for me to know what I can safely say to you—and what might cause legal problems. Have you heard of a film star called Rochana?"

"Just a bit from the morning newspaper. There's a report she's missing?"

Now Perveen retold him about Alice's longtime admiration of Rochana, and of the star's almost immediate mutual fascination. Colin's eyes rose when he heard how Alice had argued to stay overnight and how she hadn't returned to sleep in the guest bedroom. And finally, she told him about walking Diana in the morning and coming across the body she'd first feared was Alice, but then quickly realized was Joseph Morgan, an uninvited and unpleasant party guest who'd turned out to be a police sergeant working on the film censor board. And she said aloud what she'd hesitated to even say to herself before.

"I wonder if the reason Rochana's gone missing is because of Morgan's death. If she were involved, she might have run off to escape the police."

"Anything could have happened," Colin said. "But the first point would be to look at the verdict on Morgan's death, wouldn't it?"

"Oh, sorry. I haven't yet told you about the coroner's court." Quickly, she explained the outcome of the morning's proceedings—all of it would be in the papers the next day, so she didn't have to worry about confidentiality. Summing it up, she said, "Despite the official cause of death being drowning, the bruises and drugs and alcohol use could eventually point to manslaughter or homicide."

"How intoxicated did Mr. Morgan seem to you when he was at the party?" Colin asked.

"He could certainly follow a conversation and move about without any oddness of gait. At least, during the time period that I saw him." She summed up the details of his unpleasant face. "His pupils were overly large. He had a nervous mood and seemed to have a bad word to say about everyone. He was interested in speaking with Rochana but also implied that she was unfaithful to her husband. He was blatantly rude while talking with the company's cinematographer, Hans Becker, although I didn't catch what came before the insults."

Colin leaned back on the sofa and shook his head slowly. "What you say about the eyes and the energy sounds like cocaine. I saw men like that during the war."

"Morgan mentioned to me that he'd served in France. I don't suppose you ever heard of him?"

"Sorry. There were a lot of us fighting in France, not only from Great Britain but also from India and the other colonies."

"I only asked because he's close in age to you, and both of you recently arrived in Bombay. I thought you might have run into him whilst lodging at the Yacht Club."

"I hadn't. One's more likely to meet a superintendent than a sergeant at that club." Sighing, he took up her hand in his. "The late Mr. Morgan probably had what I'd call a hard war."

"The war was hard for everyone who fought or lost someone—or whose land was plundered."

Colin smiled wistfully. "Quite compassionately said. All the troops had a terrible time. Many of us endured physical pain, cold, and distressing work. And then there were those who became prisoners of war. War changed some men permanently. Those are the ones we say had a very hard war."

Perveen slipped her hand from his to touch his smooth-shaven cheek. "And how did you change?"

"The war gave me a love of geography and a hatred of guns." Colin straightened his shoulders and said, "Anyway, that's enough talk of the past. What about this film star, Rochana? If Morgan was stalking her throughout the party, might something have occurred later on in the night between them?"

"Yes, I think so," Perveen said. "And maybe that's why Alice is so bothered about things. In any case, Rochana's absence is a worry for Subhas and a setback for the film company. They are not only shooting a new film, but they are scheduled to start showing *Queen of Hearts* in theaters around Bombay and the rest of India in ten days' time."

"And that's if the censor's office approves," Colin said dryly.

"A police-run censor board might put resentment and suspicion of Champa Films ahead of professional duty."

"What a crisis!" Perveen laid her head on his shoulder. "I wish I could just wave a sword like Rochana and get everything put to rights. But that would be impossible."

Colin stroked her hair. "I was thinking . . . since nobody seems to know where Rochana is, do you think that she might not have run away but been taken against her will?"

"Yes, I think it's a possibility. I could ask others in the studio if they saw someone, but the police probably already have done so. I don't know that it's my role to continue asking those questions, either." Seeing his frown, she explained about Jamshedji's concern that the police were regarding her as a person of interest in an active crime investigation.

"You truly are up against it." His voice was sympathetic.

Perveen twisted the edge of a sofa pillow in her hands as she debated whether to ask the favor. At last, she said, "Alice should be getting ready to start teaching the new term next week. She's starting back this week organizing with the other faculty. Probably she won't be going off on mysterious walks in the rain."

"Maybe not. But if she does, should I tell you?"

He had guessed what she wanted to ask him, and that felt reassuring. "Yes, thank you."

"Will it be all right if I ring you about any of this? Sending a letter takes too long."

"Yes." She thought it through. "If Mustafa or my father picks up when you call the office, please just say you're calling from the Asiatic Society about some of my legal research. Don't give your name unless you can help it."

"But if I must—"

"Then do be truthful. And that it's about research. Mr. Dass, after all, has instructions to call because he's helping me with newspaper archive research." She broke away slightly so she could look again into his eyes. "The two of us. Always scheming to find a way to connect when forces are against us."

"Devious conspirators," he said, sliding a finger under her chin to tilt her face upward.

As Perveen's mouth met his, she could not help thinking, how many days?

More than a month had passed since the time they'd kissed in a secret spot in a private club. But someone had been nearby; they'd been observed, even in the dark. Here, nobody could peer through the high windows, and the door was closed—but not locked. And as Colin's mouth moved to her neck, she broke away.

"Is it all right?" he said, his breath coming roughly.

"Very much so. But just a moment." She slipped off the sofa, not bothering to straighten her half-slipped sari, and went to the door to bolt it.

Turning back, she saw a question in Colin's eyes. She smiled reassuringly at him and said, "A precaution. And help me remember that I must return to my car within twenty minutes."

As she joined him on the sofa, this time she moved her body over his. Time was short—they could lie together, holding each other, exploring the angles and lines, the places that gave pleasure.

Her blouse was still on, and so was her petticoat. But his shirt was off already, and she longed to explore more. But there would be time, she thought, as she rose slowly and began to rewrap her sari. Strangely, this reverse strip tease was arousing; she could see it in his eyes and feel it in her body.

How reckless to engage in intimacy so close to the literal doorstep of the Hobson-Joneses. She started to tell herself that she couldn't help it, but she knew that wasn't true. A film frame appeared in her memory: Rochana in *Queen of Hearts* facing Nishant playing the boat captain, a caring, watchful fellow who loved her. Why couldn't she have the same?

# 15
# AN OWL REPORTS

Twenty minutes turned into a half hour, and when she left, her cheeks were pink. She came around the side of the house quickly, glad that the steady downpour was keeping the durwans from their typical strolls around the property.

"You left me no time to bring the umbrella!" Arman protested as she dropped into the backseat of the car by herself. "Can't you see it's raining, Perveen-bai?"

"Yes, I noticed. That's why I came so fast." She shook the dampness from the loose end of her sari.

"And how is Miss Hobson-Jones?"

"Quite well."

"She just went off in the car like that," he said, snapping his fingers.

"Yes, she had to rush out." And was it just a coincidence that Alice's movement had directly followed their conversation?

"And she took the car herself!" Arman announced.

"What exactly do you mean?"

"She was driving herself! Why not have the usual chauffeur, what's his name?"

"Sirjit," Perveen answered.

"Yes, Sirjit-ji had only just gone inside with the lord and lady.

He is still there—and when he comes out, he will be shocked!" Arman turned the key, and the car loudly sputtered to a start.

"Well, the guards will surely tell them." And how much more trouble was Alice willing to throw herself into?

Arman rolled out of the driveway, slowing slightly to give a wave toward the guard box. "Does Miss Hobson-Jones know anything about the art of driving?"

"More or less. Her father taught her." She answered sharply because this was one of the very few things for which she envied Alice. "Did you notice which way she went?"

"In Malabar Hill, the only direction is down, na?"

She was glad that Arman's tempest in a teapot about Alice driving had diverted him from probing into why she'd stayed on the property after her friend's departure. But driving along, she thought his report of Alice leaving the house seemed ominous. It reminded her that Alice had told two different stories about how she'd spent the night.

Arman slowly navigated through three flash-flooded sections of roadway as he hit the bottom of Malabar Hill and then proceeded along the Kennedy Sea-Face to Fort, the low-lying neighborhood where Mistry House was located.

"Well done," Perveen said as he parked the car. Before he could get to her door, she sprang out, holding her own umbrella. Swiftly, she climbed the steps up to the building, trying not to think about whether Alice was still driving, and whether she might have got stuck in a puddle—or some kind of other trouble.

Mustafa always seemed to anticipate when she was on the doorstep, and today was no exception. As she stood under the portico, closing her umbrella, he opened the heavy door and held out a hand for her legal case. "No need to hurry. Your father is already here. He's in the parlor with someone connected to the studio matter."

She felt a rush of relief not to be faced with him immediately. "Let me quietly go upstairs, not to disturb."

"There's a fresh pot already in the parlor. I'll just bring the cup."

"But you said he's with a visitor. I'm not—"

Mustafa was accustomed to her and Jamshedji working together. It was unlikely her father would have spoken about the idea that he was thinking of taking Perveen off the case.

"But the visitor came to speak with you. Your father thought it impolite for him to have to wait alone."

Now Perveen was horrified. "Did I miss an appointment?"

"No, no. It's just a matter of respect for the aged. The gentleman walked a long way in the rain. His name is Dutt, I think—"

"Is it Mr. Dass?"

"Yes, that's the name he gave."

Perveen knocked on the closed door, and when Jamshedji arose to open it, she gave him a quick smile and came into the room. Her elderly friend was ensconced in a wing chair next to Jamshedji's usual spot. An open notebook lay between them on the coffee table.

"I'm so happy to see you. But you traveled in the rain!" Perveen said, feeling bad at the sight of his damp shoes. "Why didn't you telephone!"

"My friend at the Asiatic was away, so I couldn't get clearance to use the library telephone."

"What a bother," Perveen said, relieved that Dass hadn't mentioned Colin's name. "It was very kind of you to come."

"Never mind the rain showers. I am drying off and enjoying a cup of tea that tastes like home," Mr. Dass said with a beatific smile.

"Mr. Dass says our Darjeeling is almost as good as from his favorite shop in Calcutta," Jamshedji said. "Please sit down, Perveen. How about a cup for you?"

Perveen perched at the edge of the settee and poured a thin stream of golden tea into the third, empty cup. It was medium-hot, which meant that Mr. Dass had likely come a quarter hour ago, or even longer. Beside lay an open composition book full of spidery handwriting.

"I was just telling Mr. Mistry that, of course, translation is never completely exact," Mr. Dass said, as if realizing she'd been trying to guess what the two men had been discussing.

"Mr. Dass, is the notebook on the table a transcription you have made?" Perveen asked.

"Yes, indeed. I transcribed from Bengali to English. I found some articles about the film industry, just as you asked for."

"So many articles he has copied for us," Jamshedji said. "How useful it is to have the large sampling of articles he's brought. Mr. Dass is quite the polymath. Will you just read out to Perveen what you showed me?"

Her father could be very charming and kind. Seeing this, and thinking about the brusqueness he'd shown her, was hard.

"This column is a regular one in the Bengali newspaper *Ananda Bazaar Patrika*. It's titled: 'View from the Owl's Nest.'" Picking up the notebook, Mr. Dass brought it close to his spectacles and began reading solemnly.

"The Owl's eyes are sharp and open at night, so clear he can see North to South and back again. The latest sighting reveals that the Great Indian Bustard has alighted in Bombay. Who is this flamboyant bird? The one and only Mr. Abhijit Bipin Chatterjee, scion of Royal Indian Pictures. ABC, as he's known in the business, has taken rooms in well-known Green's Hotel in South Bombay for himself and his colleagues. ABC told the Owl in an exclusive that he has come to grace our shores in celebration of *The Warrior Queen,* an epic retelling of the story of Goddess Durga. In celebration, he is organizing an elaborate display in the Green's Hotel courtyard, where the public could pay respects to Ma Durga and buy tickets for the upcoming film. This raffle is to benefit the establishment of a Bengal Club in the Mahim neighborhood." Giving a small smile, he said, "This will be close to my home."

Perveen couldn't contain herself. "So, *The Warrior Queen* is going head-to-head against *Queen of Hearts*! That's bound to deflate Champa Films' sales—"

"But I am not finished," Mr. Dass protested. "The article's final line is: Will the audience approve of Patience Cooper taking over a role that Rochana would have easily slayed? Box office receipts will provide the last word."

"Who is this 'Owl'?" Jamshedji asked. "It's a shame he's so far away."

"Maybe not," Perveen said. "I reckon he's based in Bombay rather than Calcutta because of the line 'grace our shores' and the mentions of Mahim Green's Hotel."

"The paper is quite new, only established this year, and the columnist has been writing from close to the start," Mr. Dass said. "He has reported on other film gossip in the past. Perhaps he works in the industry."

"By calling himself the Owl, he maintains mystery!" Jamshedji looked thoroughly entertained.

Perveen remembered something Colin had once said, when they had been looking at gigantic vultures circling overhead in Malabar Hill. "The Great Indian Bustard is the largest bird on the subcontinent. It seems he's praising Mr. Chatterjee as being quite important."

"I wonder if Mr. Chatterjee always comes to Bombay for premieres—or if this is an unusual visit." Jamshedji picked up his teacup and sipped before continuing. "He may have come to directly negotiate some sort of settlement."

Perveen again recalled Subhas's comments about the trouble at Pearl Villa being connected to Royal Indian Pictures. "So, we now know ABC was in Bombay, even before the party." Jamshedji shot her a reproving glance, so she added, "I paid him. He's become a confidential helper to the firm."

"Yes indeed!" Mr. Dass said with alacrity.

Clearing his throat, Jamshedji asked, "Sir, is there anything else you wish to inform us about?"

Mr. Dass's other news was about the investors. He had located short mentions of the two men closely connected to the studio. The financial investor, Mr. G.K. Thadani, had recently bought several farms in the countryside that would be converted as a base for a factory. Also, Mr. Nanporia's business group, Nanporia Enterprises Limited, had lost ten percentage points on the stock market.

"That could be due to rainy season," Mr. Dass said.

Perveen thought about how Thadani and Nanporia expected *Queen of Hearts* to be successful and bring them wealth. This meant that the film's blocking or delay by the censor board would cost them; in fact, they might feel more strongly about the matter than Subhas himself.

"You are worth your weight in gold, Mr. Dass," Jamshedji said, leaning forward to shake his hand. "My daughter has been speaking about you for months, and now I am grateful to have the pleasure."

"I am most willing to help." Mr. Dass smiled widely. "Yet the truth is that at my age, I sometimes feel tired. I should be heading home."

Perveen glanced at her watch, and realized it was almost five. "You once mentioned where you live to me, and it isn't far off the route home for us."

"Yes, certainly we'll bring you home," Jamshedji echoed. "We can leave now. It's always better to try to get home in the rains before dark."

Poor visibility in the night increased the odds of driving into flash floods: destroying a car and potentially drowning. This was likely the reason Champa Films' screening party had started at five; although most guests still stayed till nine—and some, much later.

Once again, she thought that if she and Alice had left with Arman that evening, things would be so different. Perveen would still be chief counsel for Mr. Ghoshal rather than being a backup player, and Alice would not be skulking around with a difficult secret.

# 16

# THE BENGALI PERSPECTIVE

Mr. Dass's flat was in Mahim, an area very close to Dadar Parsi Colony, but one that Perveen hadn't previously explored. Many of the stone and stucco shops and apartment houses were similar to those built since the 1880s in much of Bombay. Yet the small street in which the retired postmaster lived seemed like an anomaly. Many shops had signs in Bengali lettering, and among the Bengali businesses with open fronts, she saw festooned goddess statues, ranging from a foot tall to life-size.

Traffic was slow because of partial flooding, and as the group waited for a constable at the roundabout to signal them forward, Perveen made a quick count of one statue's arms and came up with ten. "Let me guess—is that Goddess Durga?"

"You are paying attention," Mr. Dass said with a chuckle. "Our goddess of power has such a peaceful face, doesn't she? But did you know that Durga can also transform herself into Goddess Kali?"

"I didn't." Perveen tried to imagine it. "So Durga, who is pretty, is perhaps more like a girl, and Kali, who looks rather fierce, represents womanhood?"

"Not quite." Mr. Dass chuckled again. "Durga is a manifestation of shakti, or strength, as is Kali. Both are forms of Devi, the mother goddess worshipped in many different forms all over India. In Bengal, these two goddesses are worshipped as part of the Shiva tradition. Durga is very nurturing, and she can also be a strong defender."

"I must tell Gita about this." Seeing Mr. Dass's quizzical look, she added, "Gita is our ayah working in the house who came from Bengal."

"If she's Bengali, she must come to the neighborhood. Does she have Bengali friends here?"

"Only her mother," Perveen said. The two ladies chatted constantly in their native language but Perveen realized she wasn't aware that Gita had female friends who shared the Bengali perspective.

Now Jamshedji peered at the street. "Didn't the Owl's article mention something about Durga Puja?"

"Yes. The timing of the film's release about Goddess Durga is meant to coincide with the religious festival. Of course, a Durga story will attract the most filmgoers in Bengal, where she is so very beloved."

"Perhaps that is why Mr. Chatterjee came here—more publicity is needed to make ticket sales strong in less guaranteed areas," Jamshedji opined. "We can't blame him for being practical."

At the moment, Perveen didn't want to think about ABC. "Mr. Dass, were you born in Bombay?"

"I was fifteen when my family came." Mr. Dass smiled wistfully. "It was the mid-1860s, and the government wanted standardization and improved postal service throughout the country. My father transferred to Bombay from the post office in a very small town in West Bengal. The pay was the same, but the government had a flat for our family here, making it possible."

"Is this a government-owned building?" Perveen asked, looking at the plain but sturdy stucco building where Arman had stopped.

Nodding, he said, "Many postal families live inside. I am lucky to still have my one room to stay in after retirement."

"Do you have children?" Jamshedji asked.

He shook his head. "My wife and I were never blessed. But I have too many books and papers in the place. That is all I need."

Perveen felt melancholy as Mr. Dass got out of the car with Arman's assistance and made his way through the rain, up the steps, and into the building's vestibule. Perhaps she would also be alone at age sixty-eight. The potential to transform herself into another incarnation seemed impossible. She would surely be retired from practicing the law; what would be there for her?

Then she reframed it. By the faraway date of 1966, surely the Indian independence movement would have triumphed. But that would mean both Alice and Colin would be gone—not together, of course, but departed due to their country's irrelevance to modern India.

"So, what's next?" her father asked as Arman put the car into gear.

The bitter feeling was still inside her. Crossly, she answered, "How can I say what's next? You are in charge of the case."

"I see two areas of concern right now, and I wonder if you see the same."

Perhaps this was a small test of her abilities. "The chief worry is whether the police investigation of Morgan's death could be pointed toward our client. Morgan would have played a critical role in approving the release of *Queen of Hearts*. Therefore Subhas Ghoshal—and the financial backers of the film—have a motive."

"For things to go through—not to be derailed by death!" Jamshedji spoke emphatically. "Champa Films urgently needs the film signed off before offices in Bombay close for the festive season."

The festival he was referring to was Navratri, nine nights and ten days of exuberant Hindu worship celebrating the goddess

Durga and her associated nine female avatars. Although the British had no religious reason to avoid work, the season seemed to slow everything down, except of course the restaurants, florists, and musicians. "It's an understandable desire for the studio, but given the circumstances of a censor officer's death, there are bound to be delays!"

"Right you are. I cautioned that it would be unwise for either of them to meet censor board employees who might harbor grievance and suspicion about Morgan's death. Therefore, you'll carry in the film to the board."

Perveen felt uneasy but understood. Her name had been briefly mentioned in the coroner's court hearing, but she hadn't been called up to speak. It was quite possible that the people working at the censor office would think of her as a mere assistant. And in going to the office, she might pick up on some extra information about Morgan.

Jamshedji continued, "Mr. Ghoshal said the finalized film will be finished tonight. You shall pick it up at Champa Films tomorrow, and then go straight into town to the censor board."

She'd started to unlatch her legal case to get her notebook. "Did he tell you the censor office address?"

"Yes. Inside the CID building at central police headquarters."

"Arman and I could reach the Criminal Investigation Department blindfolded!"

He gave her a wry smile. "And whilst you do that, I'll make my own effort to meet Mr. Abhijit Chatterjee of Royal Indian Pictures."

"Have you written or called ABC?"

"Not yet. I shall leave a message for him at Green's Hotel this evening. I hope to transmit the idea that a civil suit against Subhas or Rochana would be a waste of money."

"Exactly right," Perveen said approvingly. "How will you convince him, though?"

"I'll ask that he share the original contract he had Rochana sign. My guess is, he didn't draw up a contract, just like Subhas didn't bother."

"I wonder if you can find out exactly when he came into town," Perveen mused aloud, watching through the window as they departed the Bengali neighborhood for their own. "His presence has coincided with a string of misfortunes at the rival studio."

"Oh? Setting Morgan's death aside, what other beads hang on your string?"

"The strike. The zoo gate was left open the night of the party. And what about the untimely death of Rochana's dog, Bubbles, who was also contested property? And finally, the missing star actress."

"Your string will break before you can tie him up in it," Jamshedji said. "All are misfortunes that could be blamed on Subhas and his crew."

She was tired of playing with metaphors. "What if ABC—or an associate—was on the Champa Films grounds the night of the party? Say that Morgan, who's passionately interested in Rochana, was outside and spotted ABC arguing with or even trying to kidnap Rochana. Morgan was a policeman by training and could have tried to fight the assailant—and, in the end, lost his life. And then—the villain carried on, taking Rochana away or worse!"

She stopped speaking, because the car was passing by a gap in houses where she saw the ocean sparkling beyond. There was a beach close to West Dadar. If the assailant had killed Rochana, he could have dropped her in the water, assuming she'd wash up much later, and far away.

"Or worse?" Jamshedji finished. "It sounds like a film story to me, Perveen. But I agree it would be most valuable to learn exactly what ABC has been doing during his time in Bombay."

Feeling encouraged, Perveen continued. "Joseph Morgan and Chatterjee might have had business dealings in Calcutta. After all, Morgan was once with the Bengal Board of Film Censors."

"I'll certainly ask," Jamshedji said. "And perhaps you might find out the status of *The Warrior Queen* while you are at the censor office. If the rival film's already been approved or is still waiting, it would be good for Champa Films to know."

THAT NIGHT, THE rain poured endlessly. The sound of water mixed itself into Perveen's dreams, and she saw herself in the center of a lake, moving her legs and arms in the powerful strokes that she'd seen boys make in the pool at the Willingdon Club. She'd watched them enviously. However, her family had deemed tennis more appropriate for her to learn than swimming.

In the dream, she'd almost got the swimming right. But ahead of her, a sea monster rose up; it had a cobra's head, but the arms were those of a businessman. Many arms, just like the figure of Durga. She heard herself screaming, but woke up, realizing that she was whimpering.

Someone else was screaming. Khushy, on the other side of the wall that divided the duplex house. After a minute she heard Rustom's voice, not cross, but consoling, and the wailing ceased. Turning over in her bed, she thought about how her brother wouldn't have known what to do two months ago. He would have shouted for a woman to help. But now, Khushy could rely on her father, and she probably had forgotten her mother.

Perveen checked her bedside clock and saw it was just after six. Saturday was a day off only for some people, but surely not for the people at Champa Films. She rose, took her bath, and after donning her petticoat and a white cotton eyelet blouse, she selected a rose silk chiffon sari that would dry quickly if she was caught in the rain.

Gita came in the room, carrying Khushy in the crook of one arm. "Why awake so early?"

"Pappa's orders," she said, while Gita came over to expertly adjust her sari's pallu. "I have two places to go. First, to the film studio, and then onward to police headquarters."

"And when is Arman coming with the car for you?"

"Eight."

"You could still visit with Khushy during her breakfast," Gita said, stepping back to look at the finished sari draping from all angles. "She has missed you. That's why she awoke so early today."

Perveen doubted it, but it was true that being with Khushy would cheer her up. She went downstairs carrying her niece and found Hiba, the baby nurse, waiting while John ladled out porridge into a small bowl. The baby's smooth wheat cereal, finished off with cream and dusted with brown sugar and cardamom, suddenly smelled very tempting.

Rustom was already dressed for the day, drinking a cup of tea and writing with his favorite fountain pen on plain stationery. He mumbled a morning greeting to her, and she sat down, while John came in with a plate holding poached eggs on vegetables for Rustom.

"And for you, Perveen-bai?"

"Is there enough porridge that I could take a bit?"

John looked startled. "Yes—but won't you also eat eggs?"

The Parsis loved eggs more than any population in India; it stemmed from the spiritual significance of eggs in Zoroastrian culture. "Yes, I will take one, with the vegetables."

"An interesting breakfast," Rustom said, looking at her. "Comfort and strength."

"Yes, I am in need of both."

"So you are going out to work, isn't it?"

"Yes." Nodding toward his paper and pen, she said, "And you are also at work."

He laid down the pen. "Just a personal letter. When it rains, my work dries up."

"The blessing is time with Khushy," Perveen said, gratefully accepting her breakfast from John.

"She wants both of you!" said Hiba, who had taken Khushy

into her wide lap for the feeding. "But first she must finish three more spoons."

"Let me." After the spoons were done, Perveen wiped up Khushy's porridge-smeared face with a wet towel. Perveen opened her arms wide, turning Khushy toward her and enjoying the feeling of her nestled close.

Chuckling, Hiba carried the empty bowl off to the kitchen.

"Mark my words. Put her close to your clothing, and my girl will spit," Rustom predicted while proffering a clean napkin.

"That's kind of you," Perveen said, smiling as she took the napkin. Her brother's occasional displays of parental expertise were amusing and also made her feel more reassured about being away.

Gita had returned to the dining room with a plate of eggs over vegetables, with an additional piece of toast. As Perveen readied her fork, she suddenly recalled Mr. Dass's mention of the upcoming religious puja.

"Gita, I hear there's a Durga Puja pandal coming up in Green's Hotel. Do you know about this?"

"I hadn't heard," she said, her eyes aglow. "Durga Puja is the festival I miss most. It's very beloved in Bengal."

"Well, a Bengali gentleman came here and is mounting a very fancy display."

"Oh! I would like to see it, but I don't know that place."

Perveen could understand Gita's insecurity about exploring such a large city on her own. "We could go together."

"Next Sunday Durga Puja starts," Gita said. "My day off. But it's Arman's day off, also. He won't be driving."

Perveen was hit by inspiration. "Rustom, you are also welcome to come."

Her brother wrinkled his nose. "Sunday is my own free time!"

She almost mentioned that he'd just been complaining about the lack of things to do for work, but she didn't think it would serve her. "What a kindness it would be if you drove us. And I wonder if you might teach me something about driving! And then I could be driving all the time and not bothering anyone about it."

Putting down his cup hard on the saucer, Rustom said, "You are no driver. You seem to believe that life should be like action films. Who is that daredevil driving female—Rochana, isn't it?"

"I didn't know you watched Rochana's films. Otherwise, I would have invited you to come with me to that party." *And Alice would still be safe.*

"I'm very glad I didn't go," Rustom said smugly. "Seeing how angry Pappa was when he had to fetch you the next day."

Perveen didn't take the bait. "So, what's your impression of the star?"

Rustom cocked his head. "On-screen, she is the perfect lady, isn't she? Until she pulls out the knife or sword or another weapon."

"I'm in charge of getting the censor to approve Rochana's newest picture," Perveen confided, watching his expression alter. He almost looked impressed.

"Really? Will you have a chance to meet Rochana?"

"I suppose there's a chance." Looking at her brother's interested expression, she realized he must not have read the last few days' papers. "Actually, she's been reported missing to the police."

"Publicity stunt, probably," Rustom said casually. "Well, maybe you'll find her when you're out at Green's Hotel on Sunday."

She shook her head, not understanding the connection. "Sorry?"

"I've seen her at Green's. Lots of film actors go, too. In the old days, Gulnaz liked me to take her there, and she would point out the various celebrities."

Perveen was surprised to hear that Rochana had circulated

so widely in certain public venues. "Was her husband there with her—Mr. Ghoshal, who owns Champa Films?"

"I can't remember hearing about any man of that name," Rustom said. "She's the one who matters. So many people fawning all over! Men, women . . . both Indians and Europeans. What a tamasha they made, laughing and drinking."

"I see." Had Mr. Chatterjee chosen Green's Hotel because he thought he might cross paths with Rochana?

"I only regret not going up for an autograph in those days—Gulnaz wanted one, but I didn't want to look like . . . well, one of those silly fanatics. Fans, aren't they called?"

"Yes, that's right."

Rustom took a second cup of coffee from John and stirred sugar into it, all the while looking at Perveen. "Will you get me a picture of Rochana signed 'With Love to Gulnaz'?"

"How can I do that when Rochana is missing to the world?" she grumbled.

Rustom looked slyly at her over the top of the cup. "I'm guessing—since you seem to be doing work for Rochana's studio—you need to find her?"

"I hope someone does," she said, being intentionally vague. "No promises, but if I ever do see her again and everything is—fine—I'll ask. Especially if you take Gita and me to Green's sometime to see the puja display."

"I suppose I might do that." Rustom grinned at her, and as if in appreciation, Khushy gurgled.

# 17
# THREE TINS

Half an hour later, Perveen gathered up her briefcase, laced up her ankle boots, covered her sari with a hooded rain cape, and set off in the Daimler.

Sitting back in the car, she pondered the surprising request that Rustom had given her for a picture of Rochana for Gulnaz. She had seen pen and paper in his hand; perhaps he had been writing a letter to Gulnaz. Did this mean Gulnaz had written a letter to him?

All the while through the drizzly drive toward Dadar West, she thought about the subtle way Rustom had indicated his feelings about Gulnaz. This was a new stage that followed the anger of the first months after she'd left him.

She imagined the scene he'd mentioned witnessing at Green's and thought about Subhas Ghoshal. Was his stated worry about Rochana being kidnapped a genuine belief? Subhas had seemed doting toward Rochana during the initial meeting they'd all had in the library. Yet most marriages in India were arranged for practical reasons—and even though this marriage hadn't been engineered by their parents, adding Rochana to his life was a boon for Champa Films.

Maybe, when Subhas had asked her to find out who Joseph Morgan was—it was because he sensed the man might be a threat to his relationship with Rochana. And if he found something out, to what ends would he go to prevent the disruption of his marriage?

As they pulled up to the gate of Champa Films, Perveen came out of her difficult thoughts and rolled down the window. She recognized the elderly guard from the last time she'd passed through, yet he stiffly requested her name.

"I'm Perveen Mistry from Mistry Law."

"Yes, I remember. But we are taking records now of everyone coming inside."

"A sound idea," she said.

The guard handed a clipboard with a paper attached for her to sign her name, the date, and time of arrival. Ahead of her on the paper were a few printed and scribbled names that she did not recognize, as well as those of Detective Watkins and Detective Vaughan. But they had come the previous day. She was the first visitor listed for the morning.

Slowly, they proceeded up the wooded driveway of the estate. As they approached the area where the zoo was, she felt her body tighten in memory. A worker was shoveling stones into a long pitted area, where she guessed the heavy police cart's tires had pushed down the mud. Just past him lay a second long depression that was still unfilled by stone and brimmed over with dirty water. This must have been where she'd tripped into a puddle. She hadn't noticed her feet were wet until much later—that was the power of shock.

Her father hadn't specified where she should go to obtain the film. Because lights were on in the barn, she asked Arman to stop the car. When he did so, she got out carefully, trying not to add fresh mud to her boots.

Inside, she saw Hans standing behind a camera on a stand. It faced the stage, which was framed with a black-and-white backdrop that showed a harbor fringed with palm trees. Standing in precise points in front of it, she saw Master Nishant dressed in a

Western suit, cut tight to emphasize his muscles, and two actors dressed as Marathi merchants.

Ajen stepped forward and held a cue card: SCENE ONE, TAKE SEVEN.

"One, two, three. Action!" Hans called from behind the camera.

Master Nishant strolled toward the men and pulled a paper out of his suit jacket pocket. The men looked at the paper, and one pointed a finger to stage right. As Nishant strolled in that direction, a heavily veiled, plump female actress came onstage now, holding a basket of fruit. Nishant stopped and spoke aloud the words in Hindi: "How much for the grapes?" The woman frowned and threw the contents of the basket at his face, then rushed off.

"And cut!" Hans said from behind the camera.

Subhas Ghoshal stepped forward, out of the darkness, to address the actress. "How many times must I tell you that you should be screaming? After all, you are afraid of Mr. Mehta. You believe he stole your boss's child."

"But nobody wants to hear my voice!" the lady said in Hindi, and Perveen suddenly realized it was a man.

"Sridhar, listen! The screaming is to get in the mood for the part. Your voice won't really be heard," Ghoshal said back in the same language, just as Perveen stepped into view.

"Excuse me, everyone," she said. "I've come to take the film to the censor office. And also, any accompanying papers and fees?"

Subhas rubbed his hand over his forehead. "Yes. And didn't I sign the papers?"

"Yes, you certainly did. Last night, after Ajen and I finished copying the film." Hans spoke in a gentle tone, as if Subhas needed extra care.

"Good. So much on my mind—"

"I'll give her the film," Becker said. Stepping away from

the camera, he smiled at Perveen. "We have it inside the house. Come with me."

PERVEEN FOLLOWED BECKER'S quick steps, stopping at the car to tell Arman to follow them up to the house. Hans hadn't broken his stride, and she had to pick up the edge of her sari so she could walk faster. Slightly out of breath, she said, "You are making quick work of it."

"Yes. Time is of the essence, as the British say."

As they stepped inside the house, Perveen saw that Asmaa had put everything to rights since the party's messy aftermath. The carpeted hallway and softly lit library looked the same as when she'd visited it before, but there was one difference. Before, there had been a smell of musk and jasmine and alcohol. But now the party was gone—and so was Rochana—and the great crystal vases that had held arrangements were unfilled.

She watched Hans take a key from the library's desk and use it to unlock a cabinet. He pulled out three short round aluminum tins; they reminded her of the tiffin containers used for transporting food, but these were much wider and had the company name "Eastman" stamped in the metal. The company name told her it was celluloid made in America, not Britain. A label on each container said, QUEEN OF HEARTS I, PROPERTY OF CHAMPA FILMS.

"Frankly, I'm nervous about being in control of these. Has the police's censor office ever lost film?" Perveen asked, making a note to herself that she must request the return of a total of three reels.

Hans handed her an envelope and shook his head. "Not for us, thankfully. And we always keep a copy behind, just in case."

Perveen checked inside the envelope and found a signed application for censorship, and some money. Sliding it into the first tin for safekeeping, she said, "How stringent has the censor board been?"

When Becker looked uncomprehending, she realized she might have used an English word he didn't know. "Are they tough about everything?"

"I think the whole business of censorship is—not well done," he said after a pause. "The reason the censor board was formed was because of accidents in some theaters. By inspecting the films, the board could know if the reels were unsafe and might catch fire. But then the censors wanted to make sure the film themes were moral."

Perveen was intrigued. "And what kinds of things do the censor boards consider immoral?"

"Nothing of real meaning. For instance, kissing is allowed—but to show feminine underclothing is not. Rochana said that Royal Indian Pictures was cited for showing her underwear once, and they had to trim out that scene."

The mention of underwear reminded her of Rochana traipsing about the island unclothed, and she blushed. "Is there anything else that censors routinely prohibit?"

"Oh, no film may include a gruesome murder or the appearance of soldiers or policemen."

Both events had just occurred in real life. All of Bombay knew about Morgan's killing from the papers, so it seemed ridiculous that similar stories couldn't be shown on film. She said as much to him, and he chuckled.

"Good for us that in *Queen of Hearts*, the villain is not a policeman. He is a gambling boss, and the death is just a crocodile's supper." Hans gave her a mischievous smile, which she returned.

"Will the police watch the film at their headquarters?"

"No, because they don't have the equipment. They watch the films at private screenings at the Imperial Theatre. Actually, it was your father's advice to Subhas that you bring the tins of film to them. Can you really manage it?"

She nodded vigorously. "I'm bringing it to protect you from

contact with Morgan's colleagues. They might convey things about you or what you said to the prosecutor."

"I wouldn't like that to happen." Hans's mouth drooped as he spoke. "I tell you that I entered this country legally and have worked hard and honestly. Perhaps it would have been better to stay in Europe. But it was so gray and sad after wartime. India was so beautiful and warm—it made me feel like living a new life. Even when it rains for months, I would rather be here."

Perveen's sympathy rose. "I was in England and France just after the war. I know what you are describing."

"You saw Europe?" He looked at her closely. "Which other countries did you visit?"

"Most of my time was in England. I passed through Belgium, which was quite destroyed. My friend Alice was in Austria when war broke out."

"You must see Switzerland sometime. It was neutral in the war and thus remained a haven."

"You were just saying you enjoy living in India. Are relations between you and the Indian members of the staff easy?" He looked at her with seeming confusion, so she added, "I mean, are people pleasant? It can be difficult to be the only foreigner in a community."

"Everyone is very kind, Subhas and Rochana especially." After a pause, he added, "The youngster, Ajen, chafes a bit; he's always got a silly joke, but behind it is a fierce desire to film each scene in his manner and rewrite some of Subhas's screenplays. He is talented, but he still must learn from us."

"Yes, of course." She was glad he'd mentioned Ajen, because this could lead to her next point. "Ajen struggled when Mr. Morgan made some rude comments to him. When I saw you and Mr. Morgan in conversation, it looked as if Mr. Morgan was being unkind."

"Not so bad. Our meeting at the party was just a few words spoken," Hans said. "Now, shall we—"

"I thought you were asking his opinion of the film—and he answered rather strangely."

"He was smiling during the film. Clearly, he enjoyed it! But when I asked him his thoughts, he wouldn't say."

"Maybe he was prohibited from saying something before the official censor process. What do you think?"

"If that was so, why would he come to this party?" Hans grumbled. "We still don't know how he learned about it. I remember him speaking of leagues. I could not understand his words or accent."

The sentence fragment came back to Perveen. "He might have said 'in league'—meaning collaborating on something."

Hans threw up his hands. "With whom? He was drinking heavily. That must be why his talk was so strange."

"You said you first worked in Calcutta. Did you encounter Mr. Morgan then?"

"Morgan was there?" Hans interjected. "What was he doing?"

"Serving on the Bombay Board of Censors."

"The first censor board in India. I made no appearances before them, because I was only a cameraman, in my earlier work." Hans checked his watch and gave her a quick smile. "Time for me to return to set. I'm sorry that I cannot continue chatting."

"Of course," Perveen said, remembering her own busy day. "Although, from what you told me, I'm sure Ajen would welcome the chance to help you."

Hans swayed restlessly, looking toward the door. "Ajen wants to replace me. Well, maybe his dream comes true."

Perveen hesitated, not wanting to inflame the situation. "I never heard him say that. He said he has appreciated learning techniques from you. But I got the feeling that he would rather be filming than acting, and certainly not making drinks."

Already at the library door, Hans turned to look at her. "Without enough staff that evening, we all had to help. I was involved in closing up the house."

This was a bit of significant information. Perveen arose and gathered her possessions, including the heavy tins of film. As she walked toward the door, she asked, "Who were the last people to leave, and when was this?"

"I brought you here just to give you the film. Really, Miss Mistry—"

"I'm sorry to be such a bother. But as the person who closed up the house, you surely know who left last . . ."

He paused for a few seconds, then spoke in a low voice. "I saw Ajen stroll outside with Mr. Morgan. But I don't think he would do anything to hurt another person."

"Did you see him come back?"

"No, Ajen wouldn't. He stays in one of the cottages. And after they left, so did I. No. I was tired and went to my cottage. Subhas hadn't yet gone upstairs, and I expected that he would lock the door."

"Or Rochana," Perveen pointed out.

"But she'd already retired upstairs—as had you and your friend Alice. Weren't you ladies together? Now, I absolutely must return to set."

Quickly, Perveen put aside her thought of how what he said went directly against Alice's account of waking up downstairs. "Of course, and I apologize for the delay."

Giving her a stern look, he said, "I hope you can submit the film easily. We need enough time to make copies to give to the distributors from the various regions. And of course, to open on time in this city."

"I hope so, too," Perveen said as she slowly walked, carrying the heavy tins of film out the door and into the car.

As Arman drove Perveen down the driveway, she saw Hans walking quickly toward the studio. It reminded her of the first time she'd seen him, a ghostly figure standing by the cottages. Now, as they rode along, she tried to remember which one it had been.

"Stop for a moment," she said to Arman, thinking that being five minutes late to the CID surely wouldn't matter.

"Did you forget something?"

"No, I just want to do a bit of exploring."

Exploring sounded a lot better than snooping, Perveen thought as she made her way along a small walkway of crushed stone to the cluster of cottages where the crew lived. Just one story high, and with tiny verandas, the places reminded her of modest holiday cottages.

She knocked on the doorway of the house where she'd remembered seeing Hans. There was no answer, and she hesitated for a moment before trying the knob. It was locked.

She had no right to search the place. Yet she could not resist a quick look through the window. The sofa inside was covered by a red coverlet with tiny mirrors and embroidery, and all the other furniture was low, wooden, and Indian. Castoffs from the Nanporia house, she wondered, or brought in from somewhere else?

She squinted, looking through the neatly arranged room. Then she looked harder, feeling puzzled by a silver and blue beaded scarf lying on the sofa.

Perhaps it was a prop that he had brought into the house; but she doubted it. It looked like part of Marisa's festive ensemble worn the night of the party. Had she been here and left in haste? No, it was not that, she thought, looking farther into the room and seeing a poster on the wall of Nishant. This was the home of the studio's star male actor and his ingenue daughter.

So if Hans had been standing on the veranda during the afternoon she'd driven in, this indicated he was visiting Nishant or Marisa.

Ajen had gossiped about Marisa playing up to Hans and trying to get favorable photographic angles. But during the party, Perveen had spotted Marisa in a private conversation in the hall with Subhas. She had sensed an intimacy between the two of them that put her on edge. Of course, she had to remember that Subhas was tasking actors with all sorts of jobs that evening.

She stepped away, almost stumbling as her heel slipped over a stone on the veranda. Walking back to the Daimler, she recalled the onstage argument between Master Nishant and Marisa. What was "playing with fire"? Perhaps Master Nishant was cautioning his daughter about men at the studio. But that was specious thinking—there was no reason to think it had bearing on Morgan's death. Her father didn't want her digging into private affairs, but what if Marisa had personal relationships with both Subhas and Hans?

Once inside the car, she told Arman, "Thank you. I'm ready to go to the police."

"Which station?" Arman knew the location of almost every station in the city.

"Central headquarters."

"Oh, very good. May I step into Crawford Market when you are there? I'd like to do a little shopping."

"Certainly. And that will be better parking, anyway." Although the police property was large, Perveen knew that their guards forbade most outsiders from having cars wait inside.

The car moved on smoothly, and Perveen nudged aside the film tins and reached for her legal case. Taking out her notebook, she began writing notes about the conversation with Hans Becker. He had spoken of Ajen stepping out of the villa with Morgan. She would have to check with others if the two men had been seen. It was disturbing to think that the bright and irreverent Ajen had been involved in Joseph Morgan's death; but if he was the last to have been with him, he was certainly a person of interest.

# 18
# UNCENSORED TRUTHS

Soon they were in central Bombay, passing stands overflowing with fruit and vegetables, and seeing the usual sights of the barbers on stools, waiting for clients, albeit under small shelters made of tarpaulins. Arman turned the car toward Crawford Market, where the shopkeepers were opening up and people were streaming in to buy. In the center of it all, Bombay Police Headquarters was a towering Gothic stone presence, heavily guarded. Arman drew up to the complex's entrance and stopped, coming to the back of the car to lift the three film containers.

"Shouldn't I carry them in?" he asked.

"Move along!" a guard said, striding over and waving his hands. "No stopping of vehicles."

"I'll manage," Perveen said, gasping as she clumsily loaded the tins into her arms.

"Go carefully, madam. I'll be parked on the side of the market by the jasmine wreath ladies," Arman called, though his voice was barely audible above the din. Even though it was a Saturday morning, the courtyard was bustling. Out front, a grand portico sheltered the khaki-clad officers as they came into the CID, some yawning from too little sleep, while others looked brisk. Indian police wearing blue uniforms filled the ranks of the constabulary, and they moved quickly to and fro, saluting any officers they passed by.

Perveen felt the dubious distinction of being the only woman as she waited in a long line at the reception desk. Everyone who passed by seemed to be looking her over and wondering about her purpose. At last, it was her turn.

The male clerk looked her over skeptically. His medium coloring and mix of British and Indian features made it likely he was Anglo-Indian, a population that was rising within the British-controlled police force. "You are making a criminal complaint?"

Perveen looked down at the load of tins in her arms, and then back at him. "No, sir. I'm looking for the film censor office."

"Are you, then." His eyes moved from her face and down toward her chest, which was fortunately blocked by the stack of wide tins. "And you are which actress, madam?"

"I'm actually a solicitor."

He chuckled. "If you say so. Second floor, third door on the left."

Perveen started for upstairs, thinking that the highest floor was not a very desirable location due to the amount of exertion required to reach it. She also felt heated by the recent exchange. She might be close in age to Rochana and Marisa, but she certainly did not have the willowy frame, fair skin, and oversized eyes that were typical for actresses. Probably he'd just said it to tease her.

Slowly advancing up the wide staircase, she was glad at least it was open air, giving her views along the passages out to the stormy sky. Crows swooped in, alighting on the balustrades, and she imagined herself flying out, too. She imagined escaping to a time before Mistry Law had signed on their famous client with so many complicated secrets.

The Bombay Board of Film Censors office looked very similar to other police administrative offices save for two British film posters on the wall: one for *Boy Woodburn*, the other for *Dick Turpin's Ride to York*. The waiting area held four chairs, only one of which was occupied. Sitting there, restlessly bouncing one crossed leg over the other, was a European man with two ladies' hatboxes stacked on the floor.

Perveen felt bemused, wondering about what a man in his thirties was doing with hatboxes, because they certainly weren't strong enough to hold tins of film.

An Indian police sergeant regarded her sleepily from behind a high counter. "Have you business here, madam?"

"Yes. I'm only dropping off a film for censor approval." As she spoke, she was aware that the European was staring.

"That still requires signing the ledger." The sergeant tapped a book on the counter before him.

She signed in as P. Mistry, representing Champa Films, before sitting down on the far side of the room.

To her shock, the European man stood and walked a few steps to the empty chair beside her. As she began working on a don't-bother-me frown, he spoke in an undertone. "You were at the coroner's court yesterday. Quite a shock, wasn't it?"

"Well, the situation is sad," she said cautiously. It wouldn't do to show any strong emotion about the finding that a man was possibly murdered on the grounds of her client.

"That's right," he said heavily. "A fellow's just three months in town and gets cut down, but not by the usual suspects."

Perveen pondered his words. "The usual suspects?"

"Malaria, cholera, fever of unknown origin."

Perveen wondered again at his presence. "Are you also in the film business?"

"No. I shared rooms with Mr. Morgan. I'm only picking up his things."

The chance meeting with a grieving yet talkative roommate seemed like a boon. Yet she didn't dare interrogate him with the sergeant just twenty feet away. Gesturing at the hatboxes, she said, "I noticed that your boxes are from Fawcett Millinery. Lovely shop."

"Thank you very much, madam! My father started it, and I'm the general manager. Murray Fawcett."

"My name is Perveen Mistry. All the women in my family shop at your store." It was a slight exaggeration, but Gulnaz, who wore Western dresses and hats for certain occasions, had brought Perveen to buy a few hats in the past.

Before Mr. Fawcett could answer, a door opened from the opposite side of the waiting room. Two European police officers emerged and, after both glanced cursorily at them, left the office without comment.

"Why are you here?" Fawcett asked in a low voice.

"Film business." She tapped the big steel tins containing the precious *Queen of Hearts*.

"A forthcoming film." His somber expression brightened somewhat. "Tell me the title?"

"*Queen of Hearts*. It stars—"

The receptionist interrupted. "Mr. Fawcett, Superintendent Stanley can take you in now."

As he arose and went on, hatboxes banging against his legs, she wondered what the police might ask him about Joseph Morgan. It was quite an advantage for her to have met Murray Fawcett, and she imagined the superintendent might think the same.

Once Fawcett was gone, she opened the envelope that Hans Becker had given her. The paper was filled out with neat printing: the film's name, a summary of the storyline, the names of the writer, producers, and director, and anticipated release date two Fridays hence. The film's running time was given as twenty-nine minutes.

About ten minutes later, Fawcett came out of the office, and from the way the hatboxes hung from his hands, it was obvious they were filled. She wondered what Morgan had kept inside the censor office that his roommate was permitted to carry out. Surely it was material judged insignificant for the death investigation.

"Goodbye, then," the man said brightly to Perveen, and headed through the door.

"Follow me," the receptionist said, and she rose and followed him to a different door on the other side of the office suite. He opened the door from her and announced, "Superintendent Stanley, this lady is representing Champa Films."

A rotund man with small eyes behind gold-rimmed glasses filled a wide chair behind a messy desk. Recognizing the fellow's soft profile, she knew he'd been among the government contingent at the coroner's court hearing. He grunted, "Name?"

Perveen introduced herself, adding, "I've carried a copy of *Queen of Hearts* for your board's review along with the signed paperwork and fees. It's my first time in this office, so please forgive me for not knowing much about the process. Would you be kind enough to tell me what happens next?"

"You are looking at the supervisor of censorship and film safety for Bombay Presidency," he said, seeming to puff up as he spoke. "Typically, review of films is done by me, as well as the Bombay Police commissioner and another police officer, typically a sergeant attached to this office. Unfortunately, our last sergeant has suddenly died, so the review for this particular film will be Commissioner Kelly and myself."

Two censors versus three made the situation potentially harder for the film, but that was nothing to state. "I'm sorry for your loss. And now it must be quite a lot to keep the censorship process going without your aide."

"Actually, it's relatively straightforward work." Stanley leaned back in his chair as he spoke. "Either the filmmakers follow the rules, or they try to test them. And in doing that, they only make life harder for themselves. Understand?"

She recalled how the waiting room had displayed posters of

favored British films. "Yes, of course. There's a film called *Warrior Queen* coming out from Royal Indian Pictures. Did that pass?"

Instead of answering her directly, he asked, "Have you *any* experience with film companies?"

"I really can't speak about past clients," she said, which seemed like an answer that alluded to client confidentiality without making her seem like an amateur.

"That is just how we treat information about other company's films," he retorted. "Just tell me about the topic of your film."

"A family drama mixed with an innocent love story," she said, thinking quickly. "*Queen of Hearts* also makes a condemnation of gambling and gangster culture."

"On the outset, that sounds fine. But no courtroom scenes or visuals of police!" he added, to which she nodded. "What is the timing you hope for?"

"Forty-eight hours would be fine." When she saw the incredulity in his eyes, she added, "If not that soon, we would be grateful to have the certificate as soon as possible, sir."

"My employee died inside your studio," he said evenly. "And you want me to cater to a breakneck schedule?"

He was the one who'd insinuated the censor board was willing to meet a timetable. Now she realized he was probably looking for a way to put her and the studio in the proper place. Softly, she said, "As I said, we are all sorry for the tragedy of your lost colleague. And as I'm sure you've heard, Mr. Morgan actually died outdoors, along a driveway—"

"Within the grounds of an estate that was occupied by the film company!" He shook his head. "DCI Watkins already knows what I think about the matter."

"And what is that, sir?"

"Sergeant Morgan was lured to the party, where someone then followed and killed him."

"Lured? Does anyone know whether Sergeant Morgan even had an invitation to this gathering?" She thought the fact that Morgan wasn't on the guest list was a protection for Subhas.

"He was often babbling about Rochana, and she even came here to bring their last film. Most irregular. Surely, she was the one who sent an invitation to him to go to the party." Stanley nodded, as if the matter was settled.

This was astounding news, but she didn't let her face change. "Do other film companies sometimes send actors and actresses to carry films?"

"As I said before, I don't give information about other studios. You people are always angling for it. I am only sitting at this desk today because of Morgan's death."

"Of course, sir," Perveen said softly. "But weren't the Bombay Police already investigating Champa Films?"

"What gives you that idea?"

She watched him, hoping her gamble would result in a change of his expression. "Mr. Morgan was wearing civilian clothing, and he didn't introduce himself as being a sergeant. Therefore I was wondering if your office had prior concerns about us?"

Stanley's face reddened and he huffed, "We are a censor office, not an undercover bureau. Now, please give me the papers, and the fee."

She guessed that he was being honest. "Yes, thank you so much. The studio owner included ten rupees. Is that correct?"

"No, it's three rupees, six annas." He took a paper from a pad on his desk and started to write. "But this is not a shop. I'm afraid we can't make change."

So perhaps that was how things worked. She watched him write out the paper and tear off the top, leaving the carbon copy underneath. "Tell them to to check with us in early October for a possible appointment. And I am talking about the director and producer themselves, not you."

# 19

# A HATMAKER'S TALE

Fawcett Millinery Company had a brass plate near the front door with date of opening: 1898. It was the year of Perveen's birth, which she took as a sign of good luck. Indeed, the last time she'd been here, it had been to prepare for the great voyage to England, which had been terrifying until she'd had the good fortune to meet Alice on board. Once in Europe, Perveen hadn't worn the wide-brimmed hat that she'd bought here more than a handful of times, just three years ago. Still, having the hats was a reassurance that if she felt it necessary to ever dress like the female students around her, she was prepared.

When they had pulled up in front of the proud white stucco building with a plate glass window full of hats, she sat for a moment. Mr. Fawcett's employees might gossip about a lady coming to see him for private conversation. After a moment, she asked Arman to check the glove box for an extra pen. When he held up the extra Waterman, she took it.

Inside, the shop was dominated by shelves holding the latest brilliant hat designs. Cloche hats hugged the head, had small feathers and bows, and a brim that almost obscured the eyes. Changes in fashion kept women constantly pressured to update their hats. This made dressing with a sari pallu pulled over the head, or dropped down, all the better.

At the counter, a middle-aged Anglo-Indian woman wearing a blue cloche that matched her dress perfectly looked her over appraisingly. "Yes?"

Perveen noted the absence of an offer to help her buy anything; perhaps the clerk had guessed rightly that she was not interested in the wares. This could get her bounced out quickly, if she didn't play her cards right. "My name is Miss Mistry. I've come to see Mr. Fawcett."

"Junior or senior?"

She looked at Perveen with approbation. Maybe she thought Perveen hoped for a job.

"Mr. Murray Fawcett, the manager."

"Will he know who you are?" The lady's voice had turned to superciliousness.

"I hope so. I'm returning something that he may have lost whilst leaving an appointment this morning." Perveen had tried carefully not to sound like someone who had a personal relationship with him, but the clerk was still giving her a sideways, disapproving look.

The clerk walked the length of the store, then disappeared through a door. A moment later the amiable Mr. Fawcett came out, looking blank until he recognized her face. Smiling, he said, "Very kind of you to come, Miss Mistry. What did I forget?"

She held the pen aloft. "I found this near your chair."

"I don't think—let me see—" He walked up to her, taking the pen in his hand. "A Waterman! Quite nice, but not mine."

*An honest man*, she thought.

"It's an expensive pen—you should take it to the police right now." The woman's words told Perveen she knew her boss's exact whereabouts.

As if she hadn't noticed the attempt at dismissal, Perveen gestured toward the lady. "You are brother and sister, I imagine?"

The woman drew in a sharp breath. "No indeed. I'm the shop's senior clerk."

"And a very excellent one," Fawcett said quickly. "Clara, will you please set up tea for Miss Mistry and me? After her good-hearted gesture, we mustn't send her out in the rain."

"It does look like a bad time for walking," Perveen said, peering toward the window. For once, the rains were cooperating for her purposes.

Mr. Fawcett led her to the area in the back that seemed almost a workroom. The hats on the shelves here were in various stages of progress, and there was a tall, straight basket holding peacock and ostrich feathers, and another spilling over with ribbons, and one holding silk flowers. Yet a lace cloth covered a small round café table with two small chairs set up on either side. Mr. Fawcett gestured for Perveen to sit with him at the table.

"Did you really think that was my pen?" he asked with a small smile.

"I wasn't sure. I'd hoped you would think I had a legitimate reason for coming." Perveen glanced at the half-open door between the workroom and salesfloor. "Do you mind if I close the door?"

"I'll hear about it from Clara, but . . . I suppose so."

Returning to the table, Perveen sat down again. "I came because I wanted to ask a few questions about Mr. Morgan."

Frowning, he asked, "Are you with the press?"

"Not at all. I am a solicitor in practice on Bruce Street. I met Mr. Morgan very briefly."

He gave her a long look. "Excuse me for saying so, Miss Mistry, but you don't seem his type—"

"What was his type?"

"Well, there was one woman. No chance for him, though."

She could guess who it was—but it wouldn't do to jump ahead. He needed reassurance. "Mr. Morgan had some communication with one of my clients. That's why I was at the coroner's court."

"Your client won't be getting anything past due from Joe. I

suspect he died without a penny—" He cut himself off. "I take that back. There was money found in his pocket, the policeman said in court."

"I'm not after money," Perveen assured him. "I'm trying to understand a bit more about who he was."

Giving a soft sigh, he said, "People say, 'Don't speak ill of the dead,' but I don't think Joe's feelings can be hurt at this stage. He had his good points, and his weaknesses."

"You are very compassionate."

He offered her a faint smile of thanks. "Not a lot of people understood him. It's no surprise that his own boss didn't think much of him."

"What did Superintendent Stanley tell you?"

"Not much. He said he was sorry for my loss of a friend. He said that even though they'd worked together a few months, he didn't know Joe well. He did mention that Joe had come into the police through a scheme to help war veterans, but I already knew that."

"I don't know anything about that program."

"Apparently a substantial number of police enlisted in the army at the start of the war. Many of them suffered severe injuries or died. The force needed new constables, so former soldiers were recruited. Joe rose quickly to became a sergeant, and when he was assigned duty working as a censor officer in Calcutta, he told me it was the best break of his life. I'd trade watching films for patrolling the streets of India, wouldn't you?"

Perveen gave a small chuckle. "Indeed. But why didn't he stay doing that work in Calcutta?"

"He had a problem with one of his bosses and transferred to Bombay about four months ago. Our government had recently assembled its own censor board modeled on the one in Bengal."

Perveen had glanced around for the hatboxes she'd seen at the office; however, the only boxes she saw were fresh ones that were empty, waiting in a corner of one shelf. "What will you do with his possessions?"

"His boss said I could pack them with whatever else Joe owned at our flat. Then I am to call him, and the government would pay to ship all of it back to Manchester."

"Manchester! So I was right that he had a Mancunian accent."

"Oh? I would not know how to describe his accent. I haven't ever been home."

From the injured tone in his voice, she regretted the comment. Some things she knew about England irked whites born and raised in India: the people who, like Fawcett, thought of Britain as "home" although they had not yet had the chance to visit. "Did Joe have a sweetheart here, or any close friends in India?"

"Not exactly." Raising his eyebrows, he said, "Joe had an unrequited pash for an actress who occasionally bought hats here."

"A famous actress?" Perveen felt slightly breathless.

"Oh, yes. Her name is Rochana. I waited on her the first time she came in, which was about five months ago. Clara waited on her the week after that."

"Did they meet in the shop?"

"No, it was a prior acquaintance. Interesting that you represent Champa Films, which is her company. Or should I say, her husband's?"

"You know a lot about the film world, for a man who makes hats."

"Only because Joe would spout off about things when he was drinking."

This raised another question for her. "How did you two gentlemen come to live together?"

"Joe responded to a newspaper advert for a share in my flat—I live on one of the floors above this shop. Pa was all for it because he thought anyone who regularly met film people could introduce me to actresses. Good for the business, you know?"

"I also work with my father," Perveen said, glad to find a

way to build their alliance. "He started a law firm, and it was his intention for my brother to join him. But my brother didn't particularly enjoy the field, so I went off to Britain to study law and returned three years later to help in the practice."

He glanced nervously toward the closed door. "Are you visiting me because there's some legal trouble?"

Perveen thought about the best way to answer. "A reputable lawyer is often dealing with some sort of trouble. But it's Joe Morgan's past life that needs to be untangled in order for the right thing to happen."

Fawcett shook his head slowly, as if still trying to make sense of the situation. "I didn't know women could be lawyers."

"And I didn't know men could design ladies' hats." She winked at him, and his mouth spasmed into a smile. Choosing her words carefully, she asked, "How would you characterize Mr. Morgan's relationship with Rochana?"

"He knew her from Calcutta, where he had developed this thing, but it seems to me she was rather a cold fish," Fawcett confided. "Twice he was out at a hotel eating and he saw her, but she didn't have time for more than a few words."

Perveen remembered what Superintendent Stanley had told her. "Did he ever see her at the censor's office?"

"Yes. I think that might have been the first time that he ran into her again."

Perveen itched to ask if she could go upstairs and look at Morgan's room. It was a difficult thing to ask, especially with the suspicious Clara on the premises. "Was it enjoyable to live with Mr. Morgan? When I met him, he seemed a bon vivant."

"He did like to raise a glass." Fawcett smiled, but his eyes were sad. "I'd thought that a fellow who got to see the latest films first would be jolly good fun when he moved in four months ago. But his moods were difficult."

"How so?"

"He was madly happy sometimes, not even sleeping in the

night, while other days he was more sickly and morose." After a pause, he added in a whisper, "Once I saw him sniffing a powder. He told me, 'It's not opium, so don't worry.' But I reckon it might have been cocaine."

"That sounds rather frightening."

"He's a veteran who fought in France; and although he didn't lose any limbs, he probably lost his happiness, then."

"So, he may really have been disappointed that Rochana didn't take him up as a—a friend," she added, for want of a better word.

"Yes. And like I said, he didn't have a girl here. He was lonely."

"So, what about his family in Britain?" Perveen asked. "Do you know if they've received a telegram—and perhaps news about any survivor's benefits?"

"Mr. Stanley had the name and address of his parents; I didn't. So it must be up to them, don't you think?"

"What had Mr. Morgan kept at the office that you brought back, if you don't mind my asking?"

"A nice crystal paperweight, an extra suit, and a shirt—I imagine they were there because of the rains. There was also an umbrella, but I decided there was no point in taking it back because one of the spokes was broken. There was also a police-issue uniform and raincoat, but that wasn't personal property."

"What about his things here?" Perveen asked. "Did he keep a personal diary or have letters?"

"Dunno. The police did come through earlier searching his room and left it in quite a tip. As I said, I'll have to pack it up and send it back to his parents."

What a shame she hadn't been to Fawcett Millinery a day earlier, before the police had come. "I'm able to help with that, if you'd like."

His look at her sharpened. "Why would you do such a thing?"

Smiling easily, she said, "Just an offer to help. We women are quite experienced in packing up trunks."

"But you don't work here," he said pointedly. "You have a very good position as a solicitor. And Clara is a very skilled packer. In fact—she might not take kindly to another lady stepping in."

"Of course!" She realized that her instinctive feeling that Clara cared for Fawcett had been right. "I suggested it only because seeing what he owned might lead to a better understanding of who might have wished him dead."

"Well, I could tell you that," Fawcett said. "He owed money to some rough men."

*Why hadn't he said that earlier?* she thought but merely leaned forward with an interested expression. "For what had they lent him money?"

"He never said. But it was more than his salary could handle. He was late on his rent to me last month, also."

An idea came to her that seemed entirely plausible. "Do you think he demanded money from Rochana?"

"Never said anything like that." Fawcett's voice was firm. "Anyhow, grubbing at her for cash wouldn't have brought her closer to him."

She returned to the idea of his debtors. "Did he mention any of the gangsters by name?"

"No, he didn't. They would ring the bell on the door in the evenings. He'd go downstairs, not bringing them up. But I did see two of them outside on the street once."

Now there was another way to point police toward both a motive for murder, and a pair of suspects. "Can you describe them?"

"It was night, so I couldn't see much except for what the streetlight showed, but I think that one of them was very fair . . . Parsi perhaps? Anglo-Indian?"

"And the other?"

"I couldn't tell. They spoke English, but they were from here."

To Perveen, this was very vague. "What kinds of accents?"

"Sorry, I couldn't tell you. And the only words I could make out were 'next time' and 'last chance.'" He crossed his left leg over his right, as if trying to get comfortable. "Soon enough, they should hear that he's dead. I only hope they don't pursue me to get money they might think Joe was hiding. I tell you—it's just not there."

"We heard one hundred rupees was found in his pocket, but that's for the police to dispose of. You don't owe the badmashes anything. Ring up the police if anyone bothers you—and I think they'd appreciate knowing about the gangsters, if they hadn't heard from somewhere already."

"The hell if I'll go back and see that pompous Superintendent Stanley," Fawcett said. "Do you have what you need, Miss Mistry?"

"Yes." He'd given her a possible pair of suspects, although their names were unknown.

Standing up, he said, "You should come back for another hat."

"Yes, I should, really." Putting a hand on the pallu of her sari, she said, "The thing is, I'm wearing a sari most days now, and hats obviously don't suit them."

"Ah, you're not like Rochana, then."

"Not at all!" she protested with a laugh.

"Rochana tried on everything we had, only to buy a simple white felt cloche, and then she had all kinds of instructions how it should be altered." Throwing his hands in the air, he said, "Feathers, diamante clips . . . She made us rework it into something entirely different. After buying from us twice, she didn't return to shop again. I wonder which other hatmaker she liked better?"

Or maybe Rochana hadn't returned because she'd learned that Joe Morgan was staying upstairs.

## 20

## A CALL FOR ALARM

When she stepped out, the rain had lessened. Arman was lounging under the awning of a building across the street, a cup of tea in hand. Seeing her, he tossed the clay cup aside and crossed the street.

"Back to Mistry House," she told him at the car door. "I'll update my father on these appointments and hear what else needs to be done."

As she settled in the backseat, Arman said, "It sounds strange for you to be assigned duties."

"Yes. You and I have more in common now than ever before."

"I applied to be a driver. My job is to serve."

Was he saying that she shouldn't mind, either? He had not wanted her to stay overnight at Champa Films; yet he had gone off, as she'd requested. And now she and Alice were embedded in trouble she couldn't fully explain to anyone. Pushing away the anxiety, she began to write down what Fawcett had told her. Considering the flatmate's account, she considered it even more unlikely that Rochana had invited Morgan to her party. Had he come to force a private meeting with her? She thought it likely. However, if he'd been killed, he would not be a threat to Rochana. So where was she? She remembered Subhas's worry about his missing wife, an issue that on top of all the other problems must be making his life unbearable.

The car pulled up to Mistry House in Bruce Street. In the damp air, the familiar scent of yeast and sugar coming from Yazdani Bakery was more intense. She wanted a sweet bun, but she could not tarry. Turning a last regretful look at the bakery's glass window, she went up the marble steps into Mistry House, where Mustafa greeted her and took her rain cape and umbrella.

"Is Mistry-sahib upstairs?" she asked Mustafa.

"Sorry, he isn't. He went in a rush to the bail court in Dadar."

"The bail court! What happened?"

"He was too rushed to mention anyone's name. And because you were in the car, he took the Central Line."

Should she be worried that Subhas might have been arrested? Certainly. Perveen started up the stairs, anxiety rising with each step. She almost fell when she heard the startling ring of the telephone in the hall below. Turning quickly, she grabbed the handrail just in time. She made it down the stairs, picking up the phone on the sixth ring.

"Good afternoon," she gasped. "You have reached Mistry House!"

"Miss Mistry, is that you?"

The tentative voice on the other end belonged to Colin.

"Yes indeed. And how are you, sir?" She spoke formally, trying to communicate that she was not alone in the family firm.

"A bit worried," he said rapidly. "Something's up with Alice. I need you to come straightaway to the docks near the Taj."

She was astonished by the audacity of his request. "Can we reschedule? I'm rather busy at the moment."

"She had an argument with someone and is now headed out in a tomtit!"

His slang sounded obscene. "Tommy who?"

Colin gave a short laugh. "A tomtit's a tiny sailboat."

"She sails with the Yacht Club's women's team all the time.

It's not reason to worry—" But as Perveen said it, she felt a trickle of unease. "How did you manage to see her doing all of this?"

"Sirjit, the family's driver, brought both of us into town. I came to this area to meet a colleague for lunch. Leaving the Taj, I recognized her huddled with another woman—smaller, dark, possibly Indian."

Perveen felt a surge of excitement. "Could it be Rochana?"

"I've never seen one of her pictures—and it was a distance. But the women seemed quite familiar with each other. The other one was gesticulating and shouting when Alice got in the boat alone. I think I could still catch up with her to see where she sails. There are all kinds of vessels for hire, and I could ask someone."

"Don't go without me." She hung up before he could respond. The words came out before she had time to reflect on the recklessness of the act.

Poking her head out the front door, she called, "Arman! We're off to the Taj."

IN THE SPACE of fifteen minutes, Arman had brought her to the Taj Mahal Palace Hotel's street-side entrance. "You are looking more suited for a storm than afternoon tea," Arman said, giving her rain cape and umbrella an appraisal as she clambered out of the car.

"It's bound to rain! Now, don't worry about waiting for me. You should go on to the bail office to be ready for my father."

Perveen walked straight through the hotel's halls and out its seaside exit doors. This would prevent the driver from catching sight of her as he drove away.

In the Front Bay, she saw small white specks of sail boats mingled with the low, open boats used by fishermen. She scanned past the almost-finished Gateway of India monument toward the area where dozens of yachts and boats belonging to Yacht Club members were moored.

She finally located Colin in the area where several larger

dinghies were docked. He was talking to a powerfully built Indian in sailing clothes.

Colin looked at her with relief when she approached. "I found someone to take us. We are set!"

"Greetings, madam!" The well-built gentleman wearing a skipper's hat and a natty uniform spoke jovially in mannered English. "My name is Sule, and my boat is the *Flying Fish*."

"Very good." She imagined Sule specialized in wealthy tourists, and the trip would be no bargain. Turning to Colin, she asked, "Is there even a chance to locate her?"

"Alice sailed west. The tomtit is about eighteen feet, so I'm hoping that Mr. Sule will be able to catch sight."

"I've my own binoculars," Sule said. "Standard equipment."

"And I have opera glasses with me," Perveen said, pleased she'd brought her legal case that carried them.

"Please come aboard, my good sir and madam," Mr. Sule urged, waving a hand toward the thirty-foot-long wooden vessel. "Let me show you Bombay's beautiful seas!"

In the next moment, the sound of fast-falling feet came up behind them. Feeling a surge of apprehension, Perveen stepped closer to Colin.

"Perveen Mistry!" A woman dressed in a wrinkled white skirt and blouse had run up to them and stopped short. It only took a moment for Perveen to recognize her as one of Alice's fellow faculty at Woodburn College.

"Miss Daboo, isn't it?" Perveen tried to hide her irritation. She'd practically got on the boat with Colin, and now that Kitty Daboo had arrived, there would be a delay. "Fancy seeing you here, of all places. How are you?"

"Actually, I'm feeling so distraught! In fact, I . . ." Kitty Daboo stopped speaking and wiped her eyes with her fist. Perveen realized the woman's skirt and blouse were in fact, a sweat-drenched tennis costume. She also wore a wide-brimmed sunhat askew on her wavy hair.

"Just a moment," Perveen said to Sule, ushering both Kitty and Colin to follow her a slight distance toward privacy. "I'm sorry, my dear. How can we help?"

"Yes. Didn't I see you speaking to Alice on the dock just a few minutes ago?" Colin asked.

Kitty nodded. "Alice rang me to meet her down here, where my brother keeps his boat. It was very inconvenient, but she said she would just like to take it for a quick ride. I finished my match and rushed here, and then I find she planned to sail it by herself! Why, my brother will have my skin—do you have any idea what the boat costs?"

"Tomtits are very expensive, I know that," Colin said. "Occasionally I see one in the environs of the Royal Bombay Yacht Club. Did you know the boats are moored in an area quite close—"

"Where did she say she was sailing?" Perveen interrupted.

"She didn't! But she had a compass with her, and all those boxes . . ." Kitty shook her head. "She truly looked like she was running away. She wouldn't say why. She won't tell me anything!"

"I'm very sorry, Miss Daboo," Perveen said. "I've had a bit of the same treatment, too. A lot's on her mind."

Colin spoke gently. "We shall do our best to catch up with Alice and after that, I'm sure she will speak with you again."

"Are you hiring a boat to follow her?" Kitty's eyes widened. "Do take me along. I can't bear it if anything happens to her."

Perveen cleared her throat and said, "I wish I could take you, but it's a matter with potential legal implications. Rest assured, though, we'll do the utmost to encourage her to sail back in your brother's precious boat."

"Oh!" Kitty moved aside her spectacles to wipe a tear from her eye. "That's right, you're a solicitor. Solicitors," she said, nodding her head toward Colin.

Perveen stepped on the edge of his foot, willing him not to correct the misunderstanding. "Alice hasn't done anything wrong, but whatever I say to her can't be heard by others. If you were considered a witness, it could be quite difficult for both of you, later on."

"My uncle's a barrister, so I understand what you're saying. But if she doesn't come to college tomorrow, it will be very bad for her!" Kitty's voice trembled. "It's a big faculty meeting."

"I shall ring you at the college tomorrow if we don't have a—a successful resolution," Perveen said. It was too hard to say: *if we can't find her.*

Colin bowed his head slightly to Kitty. "Perhaps we'll meet again, in a better circumstance?"

Perveen waved goodbye to Kitty, who stayed rooted, watching them as they boarded the *Flying Fish*. It had a roofed central section with bench seating underneath: rather more than what they needed. Still, it operated by motor and would be more comfortable than the rowboats and dinghies crowding the dock.

As he cast off, Mr. Sule started a tourist guide's talk about Bombay, compressing a half century of war between Maratha kings and the Portuguese, followed by the British acquisition thanks to the wedding dowry of Charles II's bride, the Portuguese princess Catherine of Braganza. That royal marriage had been strategic, as she suspected was the case for Subhas and Rochana Ghoshal. Yet Catherine was regarded as a pawn, while Rochana seemed to hold much more power.

Perveen looked back, just to see that Kitty Daboo wasn't following them in another vessel; but to her relief, she saw the woman in tennis whites walking back toward the street. She had not expected the woman's strong affection for Alice. Now she wondered with a jolt if it might be a truly romantic feeling; and did Alice feel the same?

"SORRY FOR MY botch-up," Colin said to her after they'd taken a seat midway in the bench: close enough to see the horizon, but distant from Mr. Sule. "I said too much, didn't I?"

"Yes, you did," Perveen said wryly, taking opera glasses out of her legal case—the best thing for distance viewing. "We could have chatted and sailed off without Kitty knowing the reason. But I suppose she's also gained a bit of security that Alice won't be lost at sea with her lawyers in pursuit."

Colin grinned. "She mistook me for a solicitor. I had to hold my mirth in check."

Perveen took the opera glasses from her face, because she didn't see anything looking like a miniature sailboat. "Tell me anything you noticed about Alice—I want to be prepared for when we find her."

"Alice was rushing along the dock carrying a basket and a box," Colin said. "And she looked different. When we got in the car to leave from her home, she was wearing a dress. But when I spotted her later, she was in trousers and jersey: proper sailing kit."

"She keeps her sailing clothes in a locker at the Yacht Club, and that's so close," Perveen said. "Did she have the basket and box when you came down in the car?"

"No. Because she was formally dressed and had her book satchel with her, I had no reason to think she was doing anything other than going to Woodburn College. But after Sirjit dropped me here, he might have taken her to another place."

"I don't think he'd knowingly abet her in an escape." Perveen tried the opera glasses again and shook her head. "There's nothing for me to focus on, but that might be because the lens power is too low."

"Maybe Mr. Sule can briefly spare his binoculars." Colin went forward to ask and came back holding the professional-looking instrument.

Holding the heavy instrument to her eyes, she focused and was delighted to see the bored faces of fishermen in a distant boat to their left. The islands in the distance were still just green-tinged blobs. "These are very good. Although I certainly can't see anything that resembles the what-do-you-call-it. Tomtit!"

"It's a rather charming name," Colin said. "Tomtits are birds native to the New Zealand islands that can fly long distances quite fast. The nimble nature of these boats makes them desirable racing vessels."

"Have you ever been in one?"

He shook his head. "I'm only an occasional sailor. My family spent time in Cornwall during some summers, and I loved being on the water, but I haven't sailed since I've come here. Probably I should. Sailing was a feeling of utter separation from the ordinary world."

"A lot of Parsis are fond of sailing," Perveen reflected. "Our people started out as boat builders in Gujarat, and then the most successful became involved in the sea trade between India and Hong Kong. But I don't swim, so I don't rush for chances to be in deep waters."

"Does this bother you—being here?" He put a hand over hers, and she felt its warm strength.

"As long as I don't think about it too much, it won't. And logically, I know this boat is quite seaworthy."

"There are probably life preservers nearby," Colin said, inclining his head toward a wooden box.

"It's not me who I'm worried about right now, it's Alice! Why would she go off on a sail by herself? Did she look depressed when she boarded?"

The wind whipped through Colin's hair, and he pushed it back with one hand while he continued staring out at sea with the binoculars. "I couldn't see her face. But she fumbled a bit with the motor when she headed out. It made me think she wasn't entirely familiar with that boat. And I keep wondering what was in the boxes and bags she carried: food or supplies so she can stay away?"

"She was so sad when I saw her at the house. She said she wanted to leave home," Perveen said. "But running off would be daft for someone who convinced her parents about the seriousness of her teaching responsibilities at the college."

"Good God, what will I say to her parents if she doesn't come back tonight?"

"I don't know." If Alice vanished, and the Hobson-Joneses learned that Colin and Perveen had set about to follow her without success, the question would arise: Why didn't you tell the police? Police boats and probably the Royal Navy would have been dispatched on her behalf. Feeling Colin's restlessness, she murmured, "Just a moment. I'm going to ask Mr. Sule something."

Perveen rose and walked forward to address Mr. Sule.

The captain looked anxiously at her. "Madam, feeling seasick already?"

"No. If one were to keep sailing straight, how far is the next country?"

"Days away," interrupted Colin, who must have had his ears pricked. "The tomtit couldn't make such a long trip to the coast of Arabia."

"But before that place are many small islands," Sule said, giving them both a worried look. "I think your friend surely is sightseeing there. I did not agree to sail to Arabia and back for a rupee six annas!"

"Of course not," Perveen soothed. "What can you tell me about the islands in Back Bay?"

"They are mostly unoccupied. Elephanta Island, which everyone knows, is close, and it has a strong dock and many interesting temples. Maybe your friend wants to see the Shiva sculptures."

Now she stood at the port side, and Colin starboard with the opera glasses. Several fishing boats were coming in toward the city. Here and there were merchant ships and fishing trawlers. In the distance, the small islands stood out like green jewels against the blue-black water. The dock at Elephanta had one tourist boat moored; Sule pulled his bell, as if greeting the other boat's captain, who tooted back. They continued west.

Through the binoculars, Perveen focused on an odd-shaped speck in the water. "Can you increase your speed slightly, Mr. Sule? I want us to close the distance."

As the captain did, the speck transformed itself into something wider. "I think I see a small sailboat with one sail!"

"Single-hulled!" Colin corrected. "I see it too."

"Mr. Sule, let's follow it."

Taking the binoculars back to identify the boat, he confirmed that he saw it. Then he looked at the two of them. "Two ideas about what to do. Tell me which of you to listen to."

Perveen looked at the islands, feeling like she'd seen them before. Three of them, right together. "I saw these islands in the film *Queen of Hearts*! They were in the backdrop of the scene as Rochana and Nishant sail toward sanctuary."

"Maybe—"

"She's meeting someone who knows that place well!" Perveen gave the binoculars to Colin and walked forward in the unsteady boat to speak to Sule. "Is it possible to pull into these islands for visiting?"

"You could," he asserted. "People were filming at one of them just before the rains began this year. The one with the lighthouse. There are also the ruins of a temple."

"That must be the one." Perveen felt excitement ripple through her. "Can you take us there, please?"

"I agree," Colin said.

Sule squinted toward the horizon. "The weather is still holding. But we're bound to get some heavy rain on the way back."

"Will passage back be safe?" Perveen asked.

"Of course." Sule spoke confidently. "And I cannot say you've had a boat journey if there is no stop."

Sule motored around a first island, which had a black speck near the shore; but Colin called out that it was a rock with a piece of wood caught in it. Sule dutifully brought them around the back of the island, and there was no evidence of a boat. They sailed on to the second and caught sight of the vessel. Colin held Mr. Sule's binoculars to his eyes. He identified it as a small, single-hulled craft, but said he was too far to identify anything about its captain.

Ten more minutes of watching; their conversation dropped. Perveen sent a silent prayer upward for Alice's safety. Any trouble could be worked out, as long as Alice lived.

And then, the island was closer, and the little boat headed straight on as if it planned to dock.

"It is a tomtit!" Colin declared. "And while I still can't see the pilot, the name on the hull is *Fast Madame*."

"Quite a name! Seems tailor-made for Alice."

"Yes," Colin said. "And the sailor has light hair, blowing all about!"

The boat's speed slowed as its navigator headed straight for the island. Because Sule was keeping the tourist boat half a mile back, per Colin's instructions, it took them a while longer to make out the shape of a short jetty on the island.

Colin strode to the bow to address Sule. "Can you just hold things here for a moment? Let's see if she manages to moor the boat."

"What a tiny island," Perveen said, marveling at the small, rocky surface covered with small trees. Yet there was a narrow, weathered lighthouse that looked at least a hundred years old.

"Why come here?" Colin's voice broke into her thoughts. "Maybe she's picking something up."

"Or someone!" Perveen suggested, her thoughts racing.

"Sir and madam, are you wishing to pull in and dock?" interrupted Sule.

"Yes, but let's hold tight a while longer. We don't want to alarm her."

They waited five minutes in position, and then Sule started up the motor again and proceeded further.

*Fast Madame* was close to the jetty now, and Perveen could see a blonde woman—Alice—standing up in the boat with a line in hand. And in the next moment, a dark figure appeared on the jetty. Alice deftly threw the mooring line toward the person, who caught it and tied the boat up.

"A dockhand working in such a tiny place!" Sule's voice was incredulous.

"Stop the motor, please," Colin said quietly. "We don't need to get close."

Sule stopped and they watched from a distance as the tomtit was safely attached. Alice bent to pick up a basket and came off carrying it. The supposed dockhand leaned into the boat, lifting out a box. After it was set down on the jetty, the dockhand rushed up to Alice to embrace her swiftly, then stepped back.

"So this is it," Colin said, his voice full of wonderment. "She's meeting a secret friend."

"It might be—" Perveen held back because of Mr. Sule's presence. "A very friendly deckhand."

"Looks like a dear friend or even a lover—"

"Hush!" Perveen said. They couldn't chat about this sort of matter with a fluent English speaker nearby.

"So, we have found the right vessel. What to do?" Sule asked.

Colin looked at Perveen. "Alice is safe and visiting someone she knows, so there's nothing to worry about. Do we really need to go ashore?"

The two figures were disappearing into the forest of green trees. "We can't just skip off without speaking to her!"

"Perveen, we should just let them be. How would you like to be caught out with . . ."

He left the last part unsaid, as if in deference to what Perveen had said a moment earlier. But what she wasn't able to say was that Rochana might be hiding because she had something to do with Morgan's death—and that Alice's secretive journey was connected to this issue, too.

"They won't see us pull in. Mr. Sule, please bring the boat all the way to the jetty."

As Mr. Sule started up the motor again, Colin spoke in an undertone. "I wish you wouldn't have suggested that! What if the fellow she was with is Indian? They are in the same terrible social position as we—"

"Neither of us could identify the . . . person . . . so let's not make stories." Perveen was being purposely vague. "I'll go ashore by myself."

"But Perveen—if Alice is meeting someone this far away from the city, it's because she wants privacy. It could be because they can't meet anywhere else."

"You are making quite a few suppositions at once," Perveen protested, calling louder to the front. "Mr. Sule, could you please quietly pull in?"

Sule looked uneasily from one to the other. "You or he will need to step off to secure the boat—"

"I'll try. It's like double-knotting bootlaces, isn't it?" Perveen looked casually at Mr. Sule, who looked horrified.

"No!" Colin said, wincing. "Ship's knots are a bit more complicated than that. Against my better judgment, I'll do the necessary."

When the boat was a few feet from the jetty, Colin stepped off and then straightened up, facing the boat as Sule threw a coiled line. Colin caught it and deftly whirled it in an elaborate figure eight around an iron post. Holding out a hand to Perveen, he said, "Come off, then. But I won't be stalking them through the island."

Perveen held the edge of her sari with one hand and used the other for balance as she stepped over the gap between the tourist boat and the wooden jetty, and walked a few feet to look into the body of *Fast Madame*. It held a jug of water, a tarpaulin, and a tin biscuit box.

Colin regarded her with a serious expression. "Will you be needing your legal case during your visit?"

She knew he was rubbing in her earlier comments about the criminal investigation. She thought about carrying it for a moment, then thought about how she could hardly take notes without alarming them. "Don't be silly. This is just a matter between women."

After a moment, Colin added, "Then it might be her actress friend? I can see why Alice didn't want Kitty to meet her!"

Perveen was just as curious, but it was no time to speculate. "Let's not jump to any conclusions. If it was Rochana we just saw, the question is, why is she here? It's a very tricky situation because of my role representing the studio. And there's also the matter of protecting Alice—"

"From what? She sailed all the way from the city because she wanted to be here."

"She needs to hear a few words of common sense." Perveen looked seriously at him. "At the very least, I can recommend how she might gird herself for any police scrutiny, not to mention her parents' wrath."

"I see," Colin answered, sounding a bit less aggrieved.

Perveen continued down the jetty, her thoughts in a whirl over the possible excuses for interrupting the two on a deserted island. She paused at the jetty's end, where she saw a pair of abandoned brown leather boat shoes. This man-sized, wrinkled pair of shoes was the one Alice used during her Yacht Club activities. She must have wanted to protect the shoes from getting sandy. The carefully placed shoes, and the items still left on the boat, gave her hope that Alice intended to leave the island, perhaps quite soon. But was that her own wishful thinking?

Glancing over her shoulder one last time, Perveen waved to reassure Colin. Even at the distance, she could see his expression: steady but concerned.

As she turned back toward the land, she realized that her view toward the lighthouse was at just the same vantage point shown in the climactic scenes toward the end of *Queen of Hearts*.

She was standing in a film frame and felt transported. She was Rochana: the runaway almost bride, and then a fleeing film studio wife. But was she escaping one kind of danger only to find a new, unknown one?

# 21

# THE ISLAND HIDEAWAY

After two minutes of walking through the sandy brush, Perveen glimpsed a bamboo shanty with a tarpaulin roof. Nearby, she saw a pile of rubbish: some of it construction materials, and other parts colorful. She guessed that the studio had just left its waste behind; and on a deserted island, there weren't the city folk to descend on such matter to use for themselves or sell.

A trio of small, gray-faced monkeys casually came toward her. From the look in their eyes, they seemed to anticipate contact: evidence that they'd been exposed to humans who'd perhaps left food scraps. Langurs, they were called. But only Colin could have told her the exact names of the small, orange birds flitting through the trees.

As she continued forward, she suddenly caught Alice's voice.

"—Can't hurt you now! Why won't you come back?"

Perveen halted, her right foot crunching on a tuft of rough grass.

"Because now it looks—you know how it looks!" Rochana's voice was a wail.

"But staying here looks worse—much worse!" Alice scolded. "It's too difficult for me to keep coming out."

"But you like sailing! To be on the open seas is better than being in jail, isn't it?"

Perveen felt faint and reached out to feel the sharpness of a tree trunk under her hands. She needed something to steady her, now that her worst suspicions were materializing.

"If you don't come back with me tonight or tomorrow, you'll run out of food and water," Alice continued. "I'd rather have Pa call up the police boat than let you stay here and die, Rochie."

"Dearest Al," Rochana murmured. "Your Pa wouldn't ever think me important enough to order a rescue."

Perveen tensed, feeling her fears had been justified. Not only did the two women already have pet names for each other, Rochana appeared to be pushing her power, just as Perveen had witnessed at the party.

"But I can't manage this back and forth alone." Alice's voice was plaintive.

"We'll do everything together," Rochana said. "We promised, remember?"

"Yes, Rochie, we did." Alice grunted, as if exasperated.

"Let's just go for a swim. The sun beat down on me coming over on the water. I'm burning up," Alice said. "And I brought you a swimming costume, too."

As their voices faded, Perveen guessed they were walking away. Her thoughts were in a jumble. What was the promise—and would Alice really withhold something from Perveen for the sake of a friend she'd made only so recently? She needed to think over what she'd heard and prepare herself for the inevitable conversation.

The small, ruined stone temple lay ahead; Perveen recognized it as part of the scenery from the film. She decided to go inside, just for a moment, to get out of the sun and calm herself. Alice's help given to someone who asked for it should not be something to resent. The difference was that it had taken months for them to become close enough friends to get to the point of sharing secrets.

The temple was dim, but the entryway provided enough light for her to see remnants of old pottery and what had once been a large stone statue. All that was left of the statue was a sinuous body shape and four arms. Perveen guessed the poor goddess—either Lakshmi or Saraswati—had lost her head to some European collector.

The disfigured statue heightened her sense of discomfort. She sucked in a long breath, and then another. Her memory now shifted to what else had been spoken. Alice seemed to have digested what she'd said to her about how Rochana's presence in Bombay was crucial for Subhas. She'd also seemed to talk about "coming and going," rather than departing for good. This was all good news—although she couldn't disregard Rochana's comment about returning home to be thrown in jail.

If Rochana and Alice were connected to Morgan's death, it felt unwise to confront them about it while the three of them were alone on the island. She resolved to go back quietly to the jetty and leave a note inside the little boat for Alice telling her the importance of speaking together as soon as possible.

As she crept out of the temple and began walking toward the water, she again heard voices.

"I bet the swimming here's fantastic. Race you!" Alice called out playfully, and Rochana laughed like a schoolgirl. And these sounds made her angry; how could they be so carefree after a man's death, and with the studio in turmoil?

A crashing sound came through the brush, and Perveen pulled behind a tree so she wouldn't be seen. It was just in time, because both women strolled by briskly toward the water. Alice was dressed in her sporty blue swimming costume, and Rochana was wearing a black suit that must have been Alice's because it was a few sizes too large, ending loosely over her slim knees.

She should have turned away; but she kept looking. She couldn't help noting the broadness of Alice's shoulders, and her straight strong body with a strongly muscled back and athletic thighs. Rochana, about three inches shorter, also had a similar strong set to her shoulders, but her hips were more rounded, giving her a classic, statuesque femininity. The final shocking revelation was that when the strap slipped from Rochana's shoulder, it showed that she was evenly tanned, as if she might regularly sunbathe without clothes. Perhaps even at Pearl Villa!

It appeared that the two were off for a swim. And what a shock it would be for Colin and Mr. Sule if they walked out! Her anxiety over the humiliation that would be suffered by all rose up so high that she forgot fear for herself and called out: "You'd better stop! There are men near the island."

The footsteps crashed to a halt.

Alice turned first. "Perveen!"

"Don't move a step closer!" Rochana threatened. "You've no right to be here."

"I'm not looking," Perveen said, which was true of her action at the moment. "I'm here to protect you."

"Does this mean you've come in a police boat?" Alice responded. "Oh, God!"

"No, no!" Perveen called out, hearing the rising panic. "I wanted to warn you that I came by a boat, and a captain is waiting on board. Alice, I followed you because someone saw you cast off and was worried."

The two women conferred in low voices, and then Alice spoke loudly. "Give us time to go back and dress ourselves. And then we will meet with you."

"Where?" Perveen asked.

"There's a lighthouse on one side of the island," Rochana said.

"Very good," Perveen said, then wanted to take back the words that sounded so silly. As the two women rustled farther toward the shanty, she considered the difficulty of the situation. She was being led to meet them at an area distant from where the boat was docked. Was this a strategy of Rochana's? Rochana's need for secrecy might be so great that she believed Perveen was a risk that needed to eliminated.

No, she told herself sternly. She must not panic. They might be checking with each other to affirm what they could tell her. She walked back through the green, accompanied by monkeys loping through the trees, witnesses to whatever lay ahead.

Rochana and Alice were already at the lighthouse, seated on folding chairs similar to those she'd seen in the studio. These were director's chairs: Had they been left behind, after the filming? The scene was almost amusing. Rochana had put on the same spangled dress she'd had on at the party, while Alice was dressed again in her sailing clothes, including a cap pulled low on her brow. Perveen couldn't see Alice's expression, but Rochana had affected a friendly smile upon her arrival.

"Dearest Perveen. You wished to track me, and you succeeded," Rochana said. "Congratulations! Especially for catching me out in a swimming costume. If you've brought a camera, you could sell the negatives to somebody."

"There may be someone leaking information, but it's not me," Perveen said, wishing to deflate Rochana's self-importance. "I was actually just following Alice. She departed from the Back Bay all by herself. Her good friend Kitty was utterly distraught—anything could have happened during Alice's solo sail!"

"Who's Kitty?" Rochana sounded peeved.

"I never saw you following me. How did you do it?"

Perveen caught the slight hint of respect in Alice's tone. "Two people saw you and the vessel. It took a while to catch up, and you were in such a tiny vessel that it was hard for me to see it. Eventually, I recognized the island from the film and made a guess to sail a bit closer."

"Well done," Rochana said, but her tone was flat.

"If I found you, anyone else could," Perveen said, looking meaningfully at the actress.

Wrinkling her nose, Rochana looked away from Perveen toward Alice. "You haven't told me who Kitty is and what she knows about—things."

"She's my—very good friend from Woodburn College," Alice said, keeping her gaze averted from Rochana. "The tomtit is her brother's boat. I promised Kitty up and down and sideways that I'd take good care of it, but she still really wished to come along. I felt wretched saying no."

"But your decision was right." Rochana's fingers tightened on the arms of the flimsy chair. "How much does she know?"

"I only said to Kitty I had an errand to run to a nearby island." Alice's voice was plaintive. "I know it didn't make sense."

"Borrowing a friend's boat for a private reason doesn't seem as large a matter as some other things," Perveen said, sensing an opening. "And I'm so very glad that you are alive, Rochana. I'm legally bound to help you and Subhas. Because Alice has some ties to our firm, she's protected from testifying to anything that might be discussed today."

"I hope that's true." Rochana's tight mouth visibly relaxed. Now her gaze shifted to Alice, as if to urge her to be the one to speak for them.

"Let's start at the beginning, then. You probably want to know how Rochana arrived here." Alice spoke forthrightly, the way in which Perveen was accustomed. "We came here on Wednesday at four in the morning."

She'd named a time that was three hours before Perveen's discovery of Morgan. "But how did you manage passage in the dark?"

"We had both sobered up. And I know this island from filming." Rochana's voice was cool. "We drove to the beach at Dadar just as fishermen were getting ready to set sail. One of them transported us. Didn't think anything of it; the fisherfolk are used to us film people asking for favors."

Perveen added to herself that the population was largely illiterate and thus unlikely to see the headlined stories about Rochana's disappearance.

"The fisherman dropped Rochana off with the few things she'd carried over," Alice said.

"Clothing and jewelry from your room, Rochana?" Perveen interrupted.

"Well—yes," Rochana said. "I didn't know how long I'd be away."

"Let me finish, please." Alice looked at Perveen reprovingly. "The fisherman brought me back to Dadar, and I drove the Hispano-Suiza back to the villa."

"Oh!" Perveen strained for a distant memory. "During the time I had stepped away from the body and just into the zoo entrance, I heard a car engine."

"That was I," Alice admitted. "But I didn't notice you. I was intent on looking straight ahead—hoping nobody near the house was out and would see me."

Alice had scraped in before the guards had returned to their posts: lucky for her. But how long would her luck hold out? Perveen looked back at Rochana, who met her gaze evenly. "I'm still wondering why you came here and didn't let anyone know your whereabouts."

"It was my choice to get away. We'd been quite shaken the previous evening."

Reluctantly, Perveen pushed aside her earlier inclination to avoid speaking about the dead censor. "Shaken because . . . you have some knowledge about how Joe Morgan died?"

At this, Alice flinched and Rochana's eyes hardened. The actress's voice was chilly. "But Perveen, Alice said you're a champion of women. Now you don't sound like that at all!"

Perveen felt gratified by Alice's praise, but that was not enough of a reason not to suspect her. Softening her voice, Perveen said, "Whatever happened can be handled. I'll help you find legal representation. But Rochana, it's a fact that you and Morgan were previously acquainted. Others know it."

After Perveen spoke, Rochana seemed to shrink in the chair. Alice put her hand over Rochana's, as if to comfort her.

"Who told you?" Rochana said in a small voice.

"Joe Morgan claimed you'd invited him to the party. And the man he shared quarters with backed up the story that the two of you once were close in Calcutta."

"'Close' is not the word for it," Rochana said stonily, and Alice glared at Perveen, showing her disapproval of the line of questioning. "After Joe Morgan met me, he made things so— bad—that I had to find a way out, to get away. With Subhas, I got my new start—but Joe had the audacity to come forward and push himself on me again."

"So, it's a case of former—harassment?" Perveen chose a mild word, giving Rochana a chance to say more if she wanted. Then Perveen glanced at Rochana's tanned left hand, where a slim band of diamonds still circled her left ring finger. "Does Subhas know anything about this?"

"No." Her voice was vehement. "Subhas thought he was just an uninvited British fan coming through the receiving line. It was hardly the time and place to tell him that I'd seen Joe by chance when I was out having drinks with our friends. He tried to chat me up in the hallway, but I managed to get away. I pretended I didn't know him in front of the others, and I'm sure he resented it."

"How long ago was this?"

Rochana ran her tongue over her lips, which were still pink without the rouge. "Two months ago. It was like a nightmare come back."

As Rochana's perfect lips quivered, Perveen felt a rush of sympathy. She had her own experience trying to put a difficult man in her past. Although Cyrus lived more than a thousand miles away, as long as he lived, she could not consider herself free.

"Do you know how Joe heard about the party?"

"I don't—know!" Rochana's voice cracked. "We invited scads of people in the business. Because he worked in the censor office, he could have heard chatter about it from someone else—perhaps another studio owner or director."

Perveen remembered Superintendent Stanley saying Rochana had been to the office. She thought about asking Rochana if she'd seen Joe Morgan when she'd gone, but decided to focus on the night of the death. "At the party, did you give Joe Morgan any money?"

She shook her head. "Why would I give money to a man I hated?"

"I don't know, but one hundred rupees was found in his jacket pocket."

"That is quite a random accusation!" Alice interjected.

"Never mind, I'll tell her. That money was from me. He probably brought it to the party for a reason."

"Like what?" Perveen asked.

"Buying drugs from one of the guests, maybe. And you know, I wasn't the only lady who caught his eye. Earlier in the night, I noticed him come close to Marisa: just like this." Rochana put a hand on the side of her buttock. "Then he leaned in to say something into her ear. Shortly after that, she caught up with me and asked if she could please leave the party early. I thought she might have succumbed to some kind of offer from him. On the other hand, she could be trying to get her distance."

"Rochana told Marisa she could leave if she wanted," Alice said. "I heard it myself. We thought Morgan might have done something horrible, like ask for her to spend the night in exchange for money. And if Marisa had refused him, maybe that's why he made the attack."

The word "attack" made Perveen want to jump in with her own questions, but Rochana was already speaking.

"Women must help each other," Rochana said, looking at

Alice warmly. Turning back to Perveen, she said, "When I saw you and Alice in the reception line, I knew you'd be a good excuse for walking out of the line. But Joe was never far from me that night. Always in the same room, watching."

"I saw him, Perveen," Alice spoke indignantly. "He was like a hungry cat watching a bird."

Perveen recalled how, during the receiving line introductions, Rochana had appeared very startled by the sight of Alice. Now the party felt like a game of people watching each other for reasons she couldn't understand. Taking a gamble, Perveen looked at Rochana. "Why did Alice say that Joe Morgan attacked you?"

She reared back so the chair almost tipped over. "It wasn't my fault—"

"Of course it wasn't. He attacked you." Even though Perveen's words were meant to calm, she could see from the way Rochana's eyes flickered that she was highly nervous.

"Very well." Rochana spoke haltingly. "You'd gone off to bed, and Alice and I were still downstairs drinking and chatting, trying to ignore him, although he was always coming in and out of the library getting drinks. There was a moment when I ran up to my bedroom suite to do the necessary. Morgan must have seen me go in because he caught me coming out of my bedroom suite. He pushed me back in and he started in. I screamed and Alice heard it."

"That's right. I had been minding the dog downstairs but decided to go upstairs for Rochana's bathroom, too. I heard Rochana's cry, and that's how I knew which door to open. I saw him push her onto the bed, but his back was to me. I picked up the first sturdy object I saw to hit him with." Swallowing, she added, "It was a hand mirror."

"Hence the bruise on his head!" Perveen said, now understanding the significance of the cracked mirror she'd noticed in the room.

"I only meant to stun him for a moment—but he didn't

come to," Alice said in a rush. "We talked over what to do and decided to slide him along the hall and down the back stairs. He let out a snore in the process, so I tell you he was alive."

Perveen thought Alice sounded truthful—but the fact that she'd participated in moving an unconscious man from one location to another would not play well with the police. "Why ever did you move him?"

Rochana looked at her incredulously. "He couldn't be found in my room."

"But he had behaved monstrously toward you in an attempted sexual assault. Everyone downstairs would have been outraged and concerned for your well-being!"

"He was injured by us," Rochana said evenly. "And I'm sure a lot of people would think I led him upstairs. After all, he was in the library with us and saw me go. That's the way people think."

Perveen had to admit that society would think the value of a white police officer was worth more than that of a film star only recently arrived from Calcutta. Film stars were admired, but they weren't seen as nice women. Rochana's ease with weapons was another reason she might not seem a victim. "Did you think Subhas would also doubt you?"

"I really don't know. But I know he would be quite upset about how all of this would affect the film."

That night, if Subhas had learned about Morgan's assault on Rochana—or had put two and two together, perhaps with Morgan's help, about Rochana's past in Calcutta—he'd have an obvious motivation for vengeance. Now she wondered whether Subhas had been so unpleasant when they'd met that morning because he had hoped the body would be discovered much later.

Yet Rochana's mention of Subhas's concern for film showed that she doubted his emotional connection to her. Was this because when they were alone, he didn't really care for her? Perveen remembered the evidence of their keeping separate bedrooms. Perhaps Rochana had herself bought into the value of a marriage for the sake of appearance. Such a union brought extra profit to Subhas—and it could also allow either of them to have affairs on the side.

Perveen shook herself back to the matter at hand. "Will either of you please give some more details of how you brought Joe Morgan outside?"

Rochana shook her head. "I can't. It's hard to remember more than I've said. The night was just so awful!"

Alice picked up the conversation. "He was obviously intoxicated, so the best idea was to leave him somewhere close to the bungalow but not able to get back inside. Rochana took his feet, and I took his shoulders, and we brought him down the servants' staircase to the first floor. The stairs go into a little hallway by the kitchen, but no servants were there."

"Because of the strike," Rochana added. "I suggested that we leave him on the back step. There's a small roof over the door that would protect him from rain. When he woke up, he would be fine. In case any staff saw him sleeping there, they'd take over and help. They would think he'd gone out for fresh air, and then just . . . fallen down. Just in case he was too severely injured, or . . ."

*Dead*, Perveen thought. "And when did you move him to the zoo?"

"That's just it! We didn't move him *there*," Alice interjected. "The fact that he was found by the zoo gate absolutely proves he came to his senses and was able to walk off. Because the party was over, he was trying to find his car, and kept going down the drive—"

"He didn't come with a car and driver," Perveen said.

"Well, then, he might have been going out to find a taxi or something," Rochana interjected. "They can be hailed just outside the gate."

"I heard a thumping noise near my room shortly after eleven."

Alice winced and muttered, "We'd thought you were asleep. You must have heard us moving him."

"All right, then. And where was Subhas?"

Rochana blinked, as if considering the question for the first time. "I don't know where he was after the screening finished. It's not our style to hang onto each other at parties."

Perveen still felt something was missing. "If you thought that Mr. Morgan was alive and would simply wake up, you weren't in danger anymore. So why did you leave for the island that night?"

"I didn't know what he might say about me—about what we did to protect ourselves." Rochana's voice trembled. "I thought it better to be away, just until we were sure he wasn't going to charge me with anything."

But Alice was the one at real risk, Perveen thought. She had struck the man. Yet Rochana might believe that because Alice was British and the daughter of a senior administrator, she had nothing to worry about. Still—the story would be a public relations nightmare. Joseph Morgan could have wreaked all kinds of revenge on Rochana, Alice, and Subhas. Perveen jerked her mind back to the chronology of events. "What was your reaction when you were going down the driveway and passed Morgan's body?"

"We did not see him there," Alice said firmly. "Nor did we see much of anything. It was pitch-black and Rochana was driving with the headlights off. We didn't want to attract notice going by the staff cottages."

And the two of them had been drinking and were highly upset. Perveen asked, "So, now that we have talked, what do you think you'll do?"

"I'm still thinking about things." Rochana regarded Alice with a serious expression. "We have a lot more to talk about. I can't return till that's done."

"You can also tell me," Perveen began, but Rochana shook her head decisively.

"Not this."

"But everything's on hold with you gone. Subhas and Hans

are trying to start filming the next picture! As executive producer, surely you are worried."

"Marisa is taking the female lead, and she'll do fine." With a small smile, Rochana added, "Although I can't say she'll manage the scenes with Tora as well as I would have."

"Who?" Alice asked.

"Our studio tiger. Perveen, you must tell Asmaa to make sure Tora's getting enough food!"

Perveen wondered why Rochana was talking about such a mundane issue, but perhaps it was because she knew about cost-cutting measures Subhas had made for the staff. She said, "The strike's over. It's likely the zoo worker is taking care of everyone."

"Still—tell Asmaa what I asked you," Rochana said.

Perveen lifted her hands in a conciliatory gesture. "I shall the next time I'm there."

"Yes, go back. But you really mustn't tell Subhas where Rochana is," Alice cut in.

Perveen was legally responsible not to keep secrets from her client, but she wasn't going to bring this up now. Trying a new tactic, she asked, "Are you afraid of Subhas?"

"No, of course not!" Rochana blinked and looked uncomprehendingly at her. "He adores me. I could never find a more handsome, clever, and understanding husband! Do you really have to tell him where I am? What if the police ask and he has to tell them?"

Alice's eyes narrowed, and Perveen wondered if her friend had heard something else. Changing the subject, she said, "ABC has come to the city. Did you know, Rochana?"

"I didn't. ABC is a true bastard." Rochana's voice hardened. "He would do anything to get ahead of someone else in the film business!"

"Things can be worked out, and you can play a role in it." Perveen scrambled for a solution. "I've heard those little sailboats can carry up to two passengers. You could both go back together, but there's room aboard the tourist boat I hired."

"No, thank you." Rochana was dragging her fingers through the sand, as if she was utterly engrossed in the pleasures of a beach. "Alice has supplied me nicely. I'm staying here for a while."

"Even if Rochana wanted to come back this afternoon, I couldn't risk it. There's a storm coming. I'm staying till it's passed."

Alice's words made Perveen realize the island was also a respite from her parents' unhappy home.

Perveen looked upward. The sky had been cloudy before, and now it looked a bit darker. Did this mean they'd all be trapped on the island? She put aside that worry to concentrate on Rochana's declaration. "If you feel uncomfortable staying at Pearl Villa for any reason, we can look for another place."

Rochana lifted a handful of sand and watched it run through her fingers before answering. "Nowhere is safe. I've known that since I was a girl."

"That is very sad," Perveen said, unable to suppress a shiver. "I'm so sorry, Rochana. And I think you've only told half the story—"

Alice's arm crept around Rochana's shoulders. "Perveen, there's no more point in investigating. We both know you're not representing her interests."

Perveen felt the pain at Alice's words, as well as the sight of her friend's physical closeness with the actress. "Technically I'm representing Subhas and the studio, but because Rochana is an executive producer in the same company, of course I am here to help."

"I took a great risk in speaking to you, and now you are telling me I'm hiding things. Tell me, are you truly an open book? I doubt it!" Rochana shot back, her eyes filled with the fire she showed at the start of every film fight scene. "Believe me when I say, I'm not speaking another word."

## 22

## PLEASURE AND PERIL

Feeling rattled, Perveen walked back down the sandy path. The experience of listening to Rochana and Alice's story, in an uninhabited island so far from the city, felt surreal. Yet she had a sense it was true. Unfortunately, her last comments to Rochana had been a mistake; they had blown up all the work she'd done trying to forge an alliance. She'd been thrown out; and there was no escaping the challenge of a journey home across rolling waves, with windy skies that were darkening.

She raised a hand to signal to Colin, but he'd already spotted her from the jetty.

"You were gone for ages," Colin said by way of greeting. "With the impending storm, I almost went ashore to look for you."

"Yes, the sky looks bad. Mr. Sule really wants to go, instead of waiting it out?" Perveen asked, remembering Alice's words of caution.

Perveen boarded the craft before Colin and then held out a hand to him as he climbed aboard, landing with a slight roll.

After he'd quickly righted himself, he spoke. "So glad you are back. I'll confess that from the moment you left, I'd been worried. What was going on for so long?"

"Sorry," Perveen said. "It was a difficult conversation between the three of us. As you and I both thought, that was Rochana on the jetty."

Colin blinked behind his glasses. "So! What brought her all the way here? Has it got anything to do with Morgan's death?"

Taking a page from Rochana's book, she withheld a full answer. Anyway, her mind was still struggling to remember all that had been said. "I've got to write down what was said in my notebook. After that I'll figure out if I can say anything to you without comprising the case. Just know that it was—tumultuous."

"Just like the water," Colin said, as a surprise wave caused them both to grip the side of the boat for balance.

Mr. Sule finished untying the ropes and called to them, "We must go—no more sightseeing. The storm is coming."

"I understand. And I'm very sorry about the delay on the island," Perveen said.

She and Colin went to sit in the stern, as they'd done before. Settling down next to her, Colin asked, "Now that we're properly alone, can you at least tell me something about Alice?"

Perveen relented, because Colin was Alice's friend, too. "Alice needed to bring Rochana supplies. And I shouldn't say much more, for legal reasons."

"Very well." Colin seemed to be studying the advancing gray clouds on the horizon. "Can you tell me at least whether she's coming back? It's such a tiny boat she's in—it could be tossed about like a toy."

"Alice said she'll wait for the storm to pass."

As Perveen spoke, she imagined that Alice would stay as long as she could. The image of her and Rochana embracing on the dock returned. She felt her body tighten again as she realized she was questioning the nature of the embrace. Now she didn't know if she was unduly suspicious or sensing a truth that Alice couldn't tell her. Had Perveen not done enough to earn her trust?

"Sturm und Drang," Colin said, interrupting her thoughts.

"You're speaking German. I can guess the meaning of the first word, but I can't the second."

"I believe that 'Drang' means turmoil. The emotional kind. The phrase was the title of a play by—oh, I can't remember anymore. I had to know it for a test in school."

"And years later, you quite like using German words in everyday life," Perveen teased.

He winced. "Do you think it's pretentious?"

"No," she said, quickly putting a hand over his and feeling glad to be at a distance from the boat's captain. "I was just thinking that you don't have trouble speaking German, even though you were in the war. At the screening party, Joe Morgan took such a dislike to Hans Becker due to a misperception of his nationality. Anyway, it's not the time to be thinking of it. I must return to my business at hand. I'll just make a few notes about my conversation."

"Right. I kept an eye on your legal case while you were gone." Colin stood up and limped along the shifting deck to a heavy box affixed to the boat's floor. Unlatching the lid marked LIFE PRESERVERS, he brought out the case. Upon returning, he half-fell against her as a wave roiled the boat. "Sorry. Are you all right?"

"Yes indeed." Perveen steadied him and herself, before moving a slight distance to open the case and find her notebook within to write down what she remembered hearing. Alice had struck Morgan with the hand mirror to stop him from hurting Rochana. The women had claimed they'd dragged him downstairs and out to the steps by a back door of the villa. If that was true, it would have seemed likely for one of them to check through the window if he was still there. Although it was dark— and perhaps fear drove them to stay away.

Another possibility was that the women had gone back to

check and discovered he was no longer alive. And that they'd decided not to mention that they'd moved his body, which could have easily been done in the Hispano-Suiza.

Perveen recalled the deep tire tracks she'd seen in the muddy drive—a tiny ditch that she'd tripped in. Now she wondered if the depression had been made because, after bringing Morgan down to the zoo, the Hispano-Suiza had reversed and gone straight back to the house. All of this before Rochana and Alice used it again to get off the property for Rochana's escape.

Perveen thought their story contained a hole as largeas a swimming tank, and despite everything that had passed between them recently, she didn't want Alice being thrown into its center.

If only Rochana hadn't pulled Alice away from Perveen that evening! If the two friends had stayed together, Alice would certainly have gone home at the right time and not be suffering any of the terrible repercussions. But then she remembered Rochana saying that Alice had saved her life. Because of Alice's presence and strength, Morgan was stopped from completing his assault on Rochana. The fact that she had brought Alice to the party might very well have saved the actress from physical trauma, at the very least.

After the hard conversation, she felt compassion for Rochana, but she wasn't ready to give her full trust. Rochana was the one sharing the story that they had made a run for the island because of Morgan accusing Rochana of something. How believable was this argument? The more obvious reason to run off was flight from the police.

Feeling sick, Perveen closed her notebook, and with clumsy fingers, she slipped it back in the legal case. The water was slightly choppy, and she didn't feel steady enough to walk the distance to the box Colin had opened that she knew also contained the life preservers. Additionally, the business of writing while the boat was rolling slightly had made her queasy. She pulled in air through her nose and then saw Colin had moved to the tail of the boat. Between clenched teeth, she asked, "Do you see anything interesting?"

"It looks as if a storm was already going through your mind."

As Colin spoke, a few drops of rain began to fall.

"Please take the ladder to the cabin!" Mr. Sule called from the bow.

"But don't you need a hand here?" Colin said, moving toward him.

"This is just another monsoon afternoon for me." He gave them a half smile. "Yet I will feel better with the two of you safely below."

Perveen latched her legal case and cautiously followed Colin, who was moving toward the hatch. Then it was only two steps down to a small space with a long, cushioned berth. It had a security rail that could be lowered, which Colin did, to afford them both sitting space. What a funny little place this was—the cabin, Mr. Sule had called it. Perveen remembered the word from childhood reading. Had it been *Treasure Island*? It felt awkward to go into such a small space, where Colin lit a lantern, revealing varnished wooden walls marked by a calendar showing a picture of Durga, Lakshmi, and Saraswati, the goddesses celebrated in Navratri. A shelf with a guardrail contained some bottles and maps. There was a scent of tobacco and mold; not the most pleasant, but Colin's nearness made it better.

"Is your stomach bad?" Colin asked. When she shook her head, he said, "Now I remember. You've said you don't like tight spaces."

She gave a soft sigh, releasing some of the pressure. "It's frightening only when I'm alone."

Colin pressed her hand briefly. "Now, it took twenty minutes to reach the island, so I can't imagine the trip back will be more than forty-five minutes, even at the worst."

"We will exceed the time we contracted with Mr. Sule," Perveen said. "It doesn't matter. I have a bit more money."

"That's a relief, because I've turned out my pockets already! Is anyone waiting for you at the dock?" Colin's breath was in her ear.

"No. I sent Arman off to the bail court. He thinks I'm having a meeting with someone inside the Taj."

"So, tell me this," Colin said, stroking a strand of hair away from her hot face. "What does Alice know about my involvement?"

"I told her nothing about you," Perveen assured him. "She didn't ask anything, either."

He glanced at the legal case. "Did you take notes?"

"Just about the conversation held with the women on the island." She smiled at him. "You are far too much to compress into writing, anyway."

"During the war, I kept a diary." Colin eased himself back against the cushions on the bench seat. "I thought I should because it was such a huge experience. But all I really could record was what was within ten feet. I couldn't name the events the fellows and I were in. Hard to tell if it was an exchange of fire, a skirmish, or a battle. All that was defined after the fact."

"Did you ever have times when it felt like you had victories?" Perveen asked. "I mean, times when you were in a fight with someone and everything came through all right."

"I won't venture to tell stories about it. Many of my memories have faded. It's easier to erase the faces of men who came close to killing you—and those you might have killed. I'm sure it's self-preservation."

"I could never forget you," Perveen said. "I've tried, because it would be easier, but I can't."

"And these are good memories?"

"Memories of great joy—but always mixed with Drang."

The waves rolled, throwing her against Colin. Now they were no longer sitting side by side—she was half atop him, with one leg dangling off the bench. The waves pitched them again, and she fumbled for the berth's guardrail, raising it to ensure that they both were tucked securely into the space.

Perveen looked down at Colin's face. His eyes were on her, yet he lay with his arms not touching her, as if he worried that she'd think he was taking advantage. He didn't know that she no longer felt claustrophobic, and the feeling in her belly was not nausea, but desire. She wanted to forget this adverse time, what she was caught up in without escape.

Perveen lowered her mouth to touch Colin's—butterfly light. As she kissed him again, the boat rolled, and Colin's arms wrapped tightly around her, steadying her. Now they were sideways, and their hands were underneath clothes, touching hot skin. Why here, when she had been to his flat before, and she had pulled away so many times at the final moment?

"The captain can't possibly come down here," Colin whispered into her ear. "But are you sure about this . . ."

"Yes!"

They were not on soil—they were in a strange in-between world, a time of possibility. And perhaps Colin wanted to shake off the melancholy of war, just as she wanted to escape the troubles of her work. They fit together so well; they understood each other's rhythms, sensitive points. It had been more than a year that they'd known each other; what had seemed impossible before now felt natural.

His hand moved between her petticoat and her thighs, and joy rippled through her, and she moved her own hands under Colin's shirt. The roaring of the wind and pounding of rain overhead was deafening. If she had tried to say "I love you," her words would have gone unheard. So she drowned herself in love, gave up to the pleasure of touch, and let the sensations inside build until it felt like the world exploded; and then, using her lips and hands, she helped Colin journey to the same place.

"I feel like we are both whole," she whispered right into his ear afterward. "United in a way we weren't before."

"It's the same feeling for me," he said, his voice rough. "I can't live without you. Why would you ever worry about me staying with the Hobson-Joneses?"

"Well, I shan't think of it again," she said, kissing his neck.

The world was no longer rocking, and they could hear each other more easily.

"It's safe to go upstairs," Colin said, but his voice was heavy with regret. "Though it sounds like it's still raining."

"Yes, let's show our faces," she said. It was far better to present themselves with clothes tucked back in correctly to Mr. Sule, than for him to come upon them and suspect the obvious. So they dressed, and first Colin went up, and a few moments later, Perveen. She made her way shakily to the outdoor bench, which was thoroughly soaked.

Bombay was just ahead, the boat moving steadily into the harbor. Perveen knew that once they docked, their romantic escape would be finished.

AT THE HARBOR, Mr. Sule was paid several rupees past the agreed price, at Perveen's insistence. "You did not expect to be delayed on an island to the point that you had to navigate through a difficult storm."

"I agree with her. Please take it, sir."

"Thank you kindly, madam," he said with a chuckle, pocketing the money. "Any time, I will take you traveling. Remember, my pleasure boat is always moored where you saw me."

"Pleasure boat indeed," Colin said, as they walked off the boat and along the dock, which was bustling with activity; more boats readying to leave, some carrying goods and other passengers. The busy throng masked them somewhat from public view.

"I was more expecting us to be seasick than what happened," Perveen answered. She was still feeling lightheaded.

"Sick with love. I can't imagine when we'll ever be so lucky again."

"It will happen. It must. If only it weren't so difficult a time—"

"Difficult, yes, but it's our time. We must accept that. And darling—it will get better. All of it."

PERVEEN'S EYES TEARED up as she watched Colin walk away toward the stand where horse-drawn taxis waited. They were in public now—hence the separation. She went into the Taj, where there was a cubicle where one could pay to make a telephone call.

How many hours had passed since she'd left Mistry House? Five. Not good at all, but as she'd said to Colin, she could present her father with the good news that Subhas Ghoshal's wife was alive. How would she phrase it, without giving away the damning details of Alice being pulled into Rochana's flight from Joe Morgan? As the operator put her call through to Mistry House, she pondered it.

As she expected, Mustafa picked up. "And where have you been? I hope you weren't caught in the heavy rains."

"I'm near the Taj, and the rain is tapering off," Perveen said. "I was getting some interviews for the case and have something to tell Mr. Mistry."

"You just missed your father and Arman. He gave up on waiting and went off on some business."

"Did he return from bail court?"

"Yes. He argued on behalf of Mr. Subhas Ghoshal. But it was not a good outcome."

"So that's why he went off so quickly." Now she realized that the tension she'd felt earlier in the day had been because she'd feared this ever since she'd heard the words "bail court." The police must have gathered some misleading evidence to have an arrest warrant.

"Very well. I'll walk to Mistry House. I'm sure that Arman will come back for me, once he knows I've reached the office."

"But the rain—"

"Remember, I've got my gumboots and an umbrella."

# 23
# A TYCOON'S TORMENT

As she walked, water soaked her, and she felt almost too overwhelmed to think straight. Perhaps the cracked mirror Alice had mentioned was the evidence seized—especially if it had blood or hair. But it was circumstantial evidence—not enough to link to him. It had to be something else.

Entering Mistry House, she stripped off her wet gear and told Mustafa she was going upstairs.

"A good idea," he said. "Fresh towels in the bathroom upstairs, and I'll bring you tea."

The hot cup of Darjeeling mixed with creamy milk was comforting. After finishing the cup, she took the papers out of her legal case and spread them across the aged mahogany partners desk that she shared with Jamshedji. His side was usually tidy; but today a raft of papers were left out, along with a pencil and notebook. The notebook lay open, and her eyes strayed to its content. Written in his flowing, clear hand was a line of names:

*A Hobson-Jones*
*L Young*
*Ajen*
*Becker*
*M Nishant*
*ABC*

The existence of such a list caught her off guard. Were these people the witnesses he thought could give Subhas an alibi? Or were they persons he wished to gather enough information about to raise doubt about their innocence in the matter? It was especially troubling to see Alice identified, and no mention of Rochana.

Perveen had watched Ajen and Joe Morgan the evening of the party. She'd thought the men had no prior acquaintance. But that didn't mean a first acquaintance wouldn't lead to something violent later. In fact, Hans had mentioned Ajen leaving the party during a time when Morgan was outdoors.

Hans Becker himself had been subject to verbal abuse from Morgan. At the same time, Hans was practical; he wanted his film to go through. The murder of a censor would cause a significant disruption in the film's clearance. She couldn't imagine the beleaguered man hurting the production this way.

Nishant was a likelier possibility. He might have heard that Morgan had touched Marisa and felt the need to avenge family honor. Or, if Morgan had accosted Marisa outside, Nishant might have come upon the scene and done the needful. But if that had been the case, Nishant and Marisa's argument the next day did not make sense.

"Your father rang," Mustafa said, interrupting her thoughts.

"Oh, good!" She was eager to talk to him about the list.

"He said he's heard reports the road by the mill is too flooded. He's not sending Arman back to us and suggested you take the Central Line from Victoria Terminus out to Dadar Station."

Perveen had noted a pause between the sentences, as if Mustafa had been reluctant to say it all. "Are you concerned that he suggested I ride the train?"

"Quite so! For a lady to ride without a family member—" He shook his head. "It does not seem right. I should come along."

Her father hadn't ordered that, though—and she didn't

want minding. "Plenty of ladies will be riding because of the flooded roads. Best that I go immediately. Shall I ring you when I reach?"

"Certainly. If I haven't heard from you in an hour, I will be very worried."

AT VICTORIA TERMINUS, trains headed north were delayed. Crowds of impatient travelers grew, even in the ladies' waiting room, which was quite full, as she had expected. She settled on a corner of a bench next to a toothless old lady who was snoring loudly. No danger to her privacy, she thought, taking out her notebook to go through her writing from morning up to the point of talking to Rochana and Alice.

The process gave her time to think about the account of events. Alice had confirmed striking Morgan, while Rochana hadn't specifically done so—except by alluding that they had done him injury.

And what was Alice's reaction to this? She thought about Alice's silence, her downcast expression. And she also thought about the sunburn on Alice's neck and shoulders from the long journey she'd made. She could only hope that Alice made it back safely and that she'd set things right with Kitty Daboo.

A clacking sound of the titles changing in the overhead arrival board alerted her that some trains were running. The crowd surged toward the board, and the good news arrived a few minutes later about a departing train to Dadar.

Perveen stood up and was swept along in the crowd toward the platform for the Dadar-bound train. Aboard, she found a seat next to an older woman, and soon, a ring of women and girls took hold in that section of the compartment. They had staked a claim, she thought, as the conductor rang the bell furiously, and the door finally closed.

With the crowding, her instinctive anxiety began burning inside, a small flame that she prayed would not grow to a blaze.

She was afraid of herself—how she might panic and rush out at an early stop, just to have some space.

The train set off, like it or not, and her internal fire continued to burn. And when the older lady got out a few stops along, the space beside Perveen was quickly filled. She was a little girl of about nine years, with smooth braids hanging to her waist, dressed in a bedraggled school uniform. Perveen caught the girl peering up at her, and she smiled by instinct.

"Why do you have that?" The girl was now looking at the legal case in Perveen's lap.

Where to begin? As she spoke, the fire seemed to weaken. "I practice law. Do you know anything about law?"

In the minutes that ensued, Perveen found herself calming and waving off a new friend two stops before Dadar. Like that, the anxiety had collapsed into embers, and she'd remembered who she was.

"TAXI?"

"A ride?"

"It's raining, better ride!"

When she disembarked at Dadar Station, people left and right were being solicited by men representing various taxi drivers waiting outside with their horse-drawn carts. One wizened fellow tapped her shoulder, saying that his owner's car was waiting in the side street for her, and that this would be a more comfortable ride.

Perveen simply glared at him. What nerve he had—did he think she was the kind of female who would ride with strange men? She wished she'd had enough time on the train with the little girl to mention that corrupt people would propose things that must be declined.

Her home was just fifteen minutes' walk. She trod on, realizing as rain fell that she'd forgotten her umbrella inside the waiting room at Victoria Terminus or even aboard the train.

The legal case, now soaked, felt heavy and uncomfortable clutched to her. At least it wasn't a baby she was carrying. An infant would be wailing. She imagined Khushy taking her pre-supper nap or waking with her arms and legs waving, and a small cry announcing herself.

The rain was a steady downpour, a thick rushing sound that masked almost everything else. She breathed heavily as she walked fast, eager to get out of the deluge. But there was another sound in her ears, one that sounded out of place. Fast steps. Someone else trying to get out of the rain? She debated whether to turn her head. No, she decided. She'd always felt that showing fear was an invitation to making danger a reality.

In the next moment, she was turning into the Parsi Colony, the wide streets full of tall, new homes with lighted windows. The steps continued, and her resolution not to look turned into a consideration of foolhardiness. She would take shelter and let the man pass on by. The family's favorite chemist shop was just ahead. As she opened the heavy glass door, she felt a surge of relief from the presence of Mr. Lalit Veerkar behind the high counter, making his medicines.

"Eh? You have a prescription, or what?"

"It's me—Perveen Mistry. I don't need—"

The door that she'd let fall behind her opened, and from the clutter of soles on the tile floor she realized her follower had arrived. She could only widen her eyes to show Mr. Veerkar that danger had arrived, but he was merely greeting the stranger. "And how may I help you, sir? This lady is not ahead of you. She only needs to buy an umbrella!"

Reluctantly she turned and saw a familiar pinched face: also wet like hers, although his fetah and coat weren't soaked.

"Mr. Nanporia?" she croaked, trying to catch her breath.

"Yes, indeed, Miss Mistry. Why were you rushing so fast?" he grumbled.

"It sounded like I was being chased," she said, not entirely willing to believe he meant well.

"Chasing?" Mr. Veerkar interjected, looking askance at Nanporia.

Nanporia shook water off his umbrella. "I'm surprised that a solicitor as successful as Jamshedji Mistry would have his daughter traveling without a private car or funds to take a taxi!"

Perveen bristled both at the insult to her father and Nanporia's paternalism. "Leave him out of it, please. And wouldn't you agree that sitting through a coroner's court hearing seems more trying than a ten-minute walk home from the train station?"

"Sir, we are not filling any more prescriptions today," Mr. Veerkar cut in, as if wishing to add to her defense. "I am closing early, in fact."

"I am not looking for medicine!" Nanporia said impatiently. Turning back to Perveen, he said, "A person of great importance, a dear friend of mine, has been arrested. It's imperative that you hear about it. I have been waiting an hour for that train to come in, and then you refused to go with my driver."

He had to be talking about Subhas. Carefully, she said, "I just heard also. It's very kind of you to make sure I knew."

From behind the counter, Mr. Veerkar clucked his tongue, and his expression remained skeptical.

"I was at my Bandra flat when I called your office," Nanporia continued. "The houseman said your father was out on business and that you were already on your way home. He told me the main road was reported flooded and not to attempt driving into the city."

Perveen knew they needed to get out of hearing range of the chemist, who was known to dispense gossip along with his tablets and salves. "Please do come for tea at my home. My family would be glad to offer hospitality." For Mr. Veerkar's benefit, she added, "Thank you for your patience. I'll send our servant here tomorrow to pick up some sundries."

"Sunday, we are closed!" Mr. Veerkar called reprovingly, as she stepped out the door that Mr. Nanporia was holding open.

Ardeshir Nanporia had offended her the first time they'd met, when he'd accused her of taking his umbrella. It had been true, of course. How ironic that now she was getting shelter from him, holding the selfsame umbrella over her as they walked out to the waiting car.

Nanporia's car was vast and quiet—a black Rolls-Royce. The rough-looking fellow from the train station gave her a reproachful look as he held the door open. He seemed to be silently saying: *You didn't trust me, all because of how I looked!*

Yet caution was the way of the world—especially for women, who had to rely on instinct for safety. In the car, Nanporia stayed quiet. Perveen appreciated it and used the five-minute drive to prepare herself. The financier had a vested interest in protecting Subhas Ghoshal's ability to keep working and for Champa Films to succeed. But would he only speak about this, or did he have more pertinent information that could point toward another person who had reason to kill Joe Morgan?

They drew up to the house, where lights were glowing in the windows. The door was opened quickly by Gita, who gave a yelp of surprise at the sight of an unknown gentleman behind her.

"One of our clients," Perveen announced, to give her the message they needed discretion. "How do you take your tea?"

"Milk and sugar, of course." He looked perturbed at the idea there could be any other way.

"Gita, after you take this gentleman's coat, will you please bring him into the parlor? I'll just go upstairs for a moment." She would change out of her rain cape, gumboots and drenched sari into a fresh, dry one and give a quick kiss to Khushy.

After dressing herself in a blue silk sari embroidered with hummingbirds, Perveen tiptoed into her parents' bedroom for a peek. Khushy was soundly asleep in her cradle.

"Don't kiss her, lest she wake. She's been fussy today," Camellia said in a whisper from the hallway.

"I've got someone downstairs I need to chat with privately," Perveen whispered when she'd joined Camellia in the hallway. "Could you please ring Mustafa at the office to tell him I arrived safely?"

"Certainly." Camellia looked dismayed by her daughter's deshabille. "You're so wet, Perveen-jaan—were you walking outside?"

"Yes. Pappa told me to take the train because he was off with the car."

"That is quite unfortunate." Camellia went to the long French windows in the hallway and peered through the downpour. "Ah, yes, the Nanporia family's Rolls. Quite comfortable, isn't it?"

Perveen was stunned that her mother had quickly guessed what she'd been trying to keep private. "There are quite a few Rolls-Royces in the city now."

"Not in the green color. Mrs. Anita Nanporia often comes to our committee meetings at the Parsi General Hospital in that car. Are you meeting her for some reason?"

"No, Mamma, not her. I really can't say more." Perveen had to acknowledge that the Parsi community was sometimes much too small a world. Yet this was another strength to remember during the upcoming conversation.

When she returned to the parlor a few moments later, Nanporia was ensconced in the velvet settee with a steaming cup of tea in his hand.

"Thank you for waiting," she said, going to sit across from him in an easy chair.

Smiling, he said, "This colony is such a nice place. Beautiful views from that window, even in the rain. I am buying a house in the next street."

"And you have a flat in Bandra and the estate in West Dadar," she said admiringly. "How can you decide where to go home at night?"

He smiled self-consciously. "Well, that was why it didn't seem so difficult to share the estate with Subhas. We have plenty of places to stay, and we always need a new place for my wife, who has a penchant for modern decoration."

Perveen imagined that her house—full of inherited brass, silver, and mahogany, much of it from the 1890s through the prewar years—would strike him as out of date. But she loved its familiarity, and there was no doubt that every stick of furniture was well-made. The Mistry family's set was a far cry from the flimsy wood and paper constructions she'd seen onstage at Champa Films. And here, she saw an opening. "And you are also investing in film—a business more ephemeral than real estate, isn't it?"

"We had no problems until this film, but you are right; it can be worrisome." Shaking his head gently, he added, "My wife thought so. We must listen to our wives, at least occasionally. I was saying as much to Subhas."

She nodded, encouraging him to go on.

"Rochana has vanished. Why is that?" he asked, then rushed to answer his own question. "Because Subhas must not have behaved correctly. I see your mother—she was smiling. She is a pillar of the community, just like my own wife. Why? Because Jamshedji Mistry and I provide affection and attention, as well as the necessary."

He was right that Rochana was gone—but she couldn't say that she'd seen the woman, just that afternoon, and that Rochana had expressed love for her husband. Trying to sound easy, she said, "Yes, of course. But could you tell me anything more about the arrest? It was Subhas you meant, wasn't it?"

"The police came with a warrant to Pearl Villa. I was already there because I'd wanted to speak with Subhas. He was still filming, so I was biding my time walking through my place when the police came."

She wondered if "walking through" was a euphemism for snooping. "Would you say that your house appeared in order?"

"Not as spick-and-span as when my wife and I lived there," he said, with a note of irritation. "But Subhas and Rochana have only the one housemaid, Asmaa—I imagine to economize. Actually, I'd wished to talk with my old servants, the ones still caring for the rest of the property. I'd heard they had been unhappy."

"Had you known about the labor strike?"

He shook his head, looking sorrowful. "Subhas had promised from the start that he would naturally pay for their work. It turned out he expected them to wait for pay when he's waiting for box office receipts. Yet something changed—they were paid after all, I believe starting the day after that disastrous party."

"I heard the same thing. Will you please tell me more about Subhas's arrest?" she prompted, trying to get him back on course.

"They declared they were arresting Subhas on suspicion of involvement in Morgan's murder," he said. "I watched as those dreadful coppers stormed into the barn. Everyone was afraid!" he said, raising up his hands in mock surrender. "Nishant and the rest of the men fell silent, I'm sure not wishing to attract accusations of interference. Marisa, the young actress, ran to weep in Ajen's arms. Hans said that he would let the lawyer—meaning your father—know right away."

"What grounds did they have?"

"Morgan's necktie was found in a wastebasket in Subhas's bedroom. Apparently, they also found a button in a corner of the stairwell."

"Such weak circumstantial evidence!" Perveen said, realizing that Rochana and Alice had neglected telling her about this dangerous detail. "However, the police have the power to hold people in jail without any evidence of having committed a crime. This is a very difficult situation."

"Isn't it, just?" Nanporia tapped one leg restlessly against the other. "*Queen of Hearts* should be releasing next weekend but has no censor approval yet. I'm also funding another picture that's halted because the studio head is in jail, and the star is missing—"

"I thought Rochana wasn't acting in the picture. It's Marisa's turn."

"That's right," he said gloomily. "Let's hope she's up to the task. Anyway, you and your father need to know that Subhas couldn't have killed Joe Morgan. He must have had other enemies."

"Why do you think that?"

I know that he is a blackmailer. And usually those types have people to pay." As Perveen stayed silent, Nanporia exhaled and then said, "Morgan demanded money from me."

Perveen tried to keep her face still. "When and where did this happen?"

"Two weeks ago, he arrived by himself at the Orient Club—do you know it?"

"Quite well! A lovely place." *With lots of witnesses.*

"Well, he arrived wearing his police uniform as if on duty, even though it was seven at night. He asked the manager to find me. When he came over, he said not to worry, it was a social visit. All I could do was offer him a drink and pretend to the others around me that I'd invited him."

"How dreadfully unnerving!" Perveen's sympathy was rising.

"Morgan asked me to join him at a table in the back," Nanporia said. "Then, he didn't waste time with small talk. He said he knew that I was an investor in the film. He told me that he'd been appointed to the censor board, and there was a tremendous onslaught of new films coming in. If I wanted the film's swift approval with minimum cuts, I needed to pay him an advance fee of two hundred rupees. And of course, I couldn't send it through the mail or appear at his office, because it's in the police building. He wanted it that night."

"So, he was an extortionist," Perveen said, the picture becoming clear in her mind. "Why would he ask you rather than Subhas?"

"So there would be no direct tie between him and the company."

"Do you think any club members or employees would remember seeing him and even hearing his words?"

"When a British police officer comes in, many of us cast a wide berth," he said with an ironic smile. "I have been asked plenty of times for baksheesh, but never by someone who looked like him. I bluffed, saying that the request was something I would have to take to the film company. My thinking was that I would tell Subhas and perhaps he could go to someone else involved in the censor office to report the man—but as I found out, that would carry risks."

"I don't understand why Morgan settled on you, in particular."

"I'm the money behind Champa Films—it's been in the newspapers." Nanporia looked down at the lace tablecloth, his expression morose. "And I realized the cost of having the film disapproved—or in a best case, just delayed—would allow ABC's *Warrior Queen* to open before us and perhaps get the better theater locations."

"So you agreed to pay him?" Perveen asked the question, realizing that Nanporia, in his honesty, was making a very good case that he himself had reason to want Morgan dead.

"Worse than that." He rubbed a finger against the lace, as if testing its strength. "I said for him not to come to my club again, but just to meet me at the screening party. So many people there, all drinking, meant that I could pass him the money without it being noticed. He stepped out to the back, and I followed and gave him an envelope with the money. I had decided not to tell Subhas about it; you know what an idealist he is."

"So you're the reason he found out about the party!" Perveen said. "But something I wonder about is that Mr. Morgan was found to be carrying one hundred rupees, only. Had you bargained him down?"

"No!" Nanporia exclaimed. "I wouldn't have dared. Feeling quite sickened, I paid him the full two hundred. I wonder what happened to the rest. Maybe—taken by his killer?"

Rochana and Alice hadn't mentioned going through Morgan's possessions. She recalled that the women had already told her their theory that Morgan had emerged from his stupor to walk away down the drive. She could imagine a thief killing him and going for his pockets, but why would he leave so much behind?

"It seems possible," she said, continuing to think. Morgan might have used some of the money to pay off the gangsters that night, but only if they had followed him onto the property. Another possibility was that Marisa and Master Nishant's argument onstage the day after the murder had something to do with taking money for sex. But why would a man pay one woman so generously when he'd used sheer force on another woman a few hours earlier?

She laid the theory aside and returned to the present crisis: Subhas Ghoshal. "What else can you tell me?"

"Nothing. But don't you think, because only part of the money was in Morgan's pocket, it means he was robbed? And that whoever did it was the one who killed him?"

"Are you willing to speak about the blackmail?"

He shook his head. "I don't think I can come forward lest it appear I was behaving illegally. My reputation will be ruined."

"I won't put you at risk," Perveen said. "What happened between the two of you might not have bearing on his cause of death. The trouble is, we can't easily find a thief by ourselves."

"All those actors live amongst the trees," Nanporia said,

rubbing his chin. "They had to go home that night. Perhaps they saw something."

Perveen sat quietly, thinking about it. So much could be done, including calling on Rochana to show herself alive and well, and explain that she was not a willing lover to Morgan. But would she cooperate?

"And what are you pondering, Miss Mistry?" Nanporia prompted.

She shifted into the present. "There's the matter of bail for Subhas. We don't yet know if it's been granted or if so, what the amount is."

"His funds have been tight, so he can count on me. I'm not aware of Rochana's holdings, though."

The mention of Rochana gave Perveen a slight jolt. "Does she have substantial funds?"

"She worked in Calcutta for the early years, and she was amongst the highest-paid actresses in India. There lies a chance she has funds kept in a bank or somewhere else."

"But a woman can't have her own bank account without her husband or father's permission," Perveen said, thinking about her own situation. Now she wondered if the scattered jewelry meant that Rochana had left with her most valuable pieces.

"True," he said glumly. "And how could we tap Rochana for aid to her husband if she's nowhere to be found? Thadani, the other big investor, also has cash problems."

Perveen thought the bony-faced man's face looked sunken—perhaps from worrying or missed meals. "I'm sure that my father has done his very best to bring down the bail. And of course, you'd get your money back. If only . . ."

She shook her head, deciding not to finish her thought: that Subhas might not be granted bail, and all filming at Champa Films would be over and done with.

# 24

# AUDIENCE WITH A TIGER

After finishing his tea, Mr. Nanporia left, resisting Perveen's entreaties to wait to see her father. She watched after him as he took his fetah and umbrella and left through the front door, wondering at the turnabout. He had trusted her enough to give masses of information; but the story was so incredible, about the bribery and whatnot, it was perhaps not true. Had he come to her because he thought she'd more easily digest the story that painted Mr. Morgan as a villain?

Jamshedji Mistry arrived home an hour later and went straight to the dining room. Perveen had held off eating so she could join him. After he'd tasted a bit of everything—a spiced pork chop, okra-mutton curry, crispy zucchini bhajias, and a creamy onion dal—he spoke.

"The judge ordered three hundred rupees to be paid for bail. Outrageously steep; but I was unsuccessful in convincing him that Subhas had the right to be at liberty to earn his livelihood. The prosecutor argued that Subhas was a wealthy studio owner and certainly not lacking. So, until the money is raised, he is sitting in the lockup."

"Mr. Nanporia has committed to assisting with bail." She explained what the businessman had pledged, as well as his confession about paying the bribe Morgan had demanded.

"I'm surprised that he was so forthcoming." Jamshedji's gaze showed grudging approval.

"Yes. But isn't he protected by being your former client?" Perveen asked.

Jamshedji seemed to think a moment. "He asked me for help with a property matter years ago—you were in school then. I had practically forgotten."

"And Subhas said Nanporia is the one who recommended Mistry Law to him."

"Yes, but I am not sure why. Nanporia must have employed other lawyers since." Jamshedji frowned. "It's not ideal to have a past client so deeply involved in our current client's case. But will you ring up Mr. Nanporia tonight and see whether he can deliver three hundred rupees to the bail office tomorrow morning at nine? I'll meet him there."

"I will do just that." Perveen didn't want to end the conversation without delivering her own big news. "And may I ask your opinion on something? How much do you think Subhas's situation might change for the better if someone reported seeing his wife alive?"

Jamshedji pursed his lips. "Remember, he's not been charged with doing harm to Rochana. Is this a tip from one of the film fans?"

"No. I found her! Ever since she disappeared, she's been staying on a small island where *Queen of Hearts* was filmed."

Jamshedji paused in cutting his pork chop. "You didn't tell me this straightaway? And what led you there?"

"Well, you were the one who wanted to discuss Subhas's arrest—the priority issue," Perveen protested. "To answer your second question, I hired a tourist boat to follow Alice, who was sailing solo from the Front Bay docks out toward the islands in a very small racing sailboat. She led us straight to Rochana."

Jamshedji lifted the piece of pork to his mouth and thoroughly chewed and swallowed before answering. "And why didn't you know earlier? Why would your good friend withhold such crucial information from you?"

Perveen caught the judgment in his tone. "Alice was overwhelmed. Apparently, Rochana asked for assistance to go there after the party was finished. Rochana was also frightened—"

"Of what?" he interrupted. "A charge of manslaughter, or homicide?"

She frowned, not liking his terminology. "The ladies said emphatically that they last saw Joe Morgan alive. They did bash him up slightly, but they believed he was alive."

Jamshedji's eyes narrowed. "Bashed him up? Do explain."

"I'll try."

Perveen told him about Rochana's description of Morgan's power over her during her time in Calcutta, and how the night of the party he'd attempted to rape her—and Alice had to strike him to get him off the actress's prone body. Jamshedji's expression darkened as she repeated the women's account of moving the unconscious man to the backdoor steps, and Alice's relief later when she saw that he was gone. "I know this account will sound suspicious to the law."

"We should assume they will regard a dead police sergeant as a hero."

"But there was another side." She went on to describe what she'd learned from Murray Fawcett about Morgan's drug use and debt to gangsters.

"What a sorry specimen of a man," Jamshedji said after her account of the conversation in the millinery shop. "Do you think Mr. Fawcett would be willing to be a witness for us?"

"I think so," Perveen said. "But it would be a stronger argument for Subhas if we could find somebody who mentioned seeing unidentified persons on the property that evening. I want to pursue this, if you agree."

"Yes." Jamshedji closed his eyes for a moment, as if trying to work through the chaotic accounts she'd just delivered. "All in all, the biggest trouble is that the women fought Morgan to the point that he was unresponsive. Then they chose to remove his body from the scene of the attempted rape. We must find a reason why two women would do that, instead of just rushing downstairs to announce to one and all their success against a villainous attack."

"For a woman to claim attack—especially a married woman—would raise the question of her virtue—you know it would!" Perveen protested. "They told me they thought removing him out of Rochana's bedroom was the only way to avoid scandal."

Jamshedji rubbed his chin. "That is also true. Now, I've thought of another point. We could argue that another reason for the ladies moving the body was to protect the reputation of a government officer. After all, Alice Hobson-Jones is daughter of a councilor. Do her parents know about this?"

When she shook her head, he said, "I will assure Subhas that we've located his wife, alive and well. That will be reassuring for him. It would be good if someone could convince Rochana to come back—but without your traveling to the island again. You must speak again with Alice."

"Of course, in good time—"

"Tell your friend that if Rochana doesn't show herself, we will tip the police to her whereabouts. But I expressly forbid you to travel to that island again. The area is remote, and there's no reason to think Rochana isn't dangerous. She could make it so you disappear."

"I thought that first, Pappa. But I've told her repeatedly that we have her interests in mind and will protect her from the law as best we can."

Shaking his head, he said, "She's trained to fight. Even I've seen it on the screen."

"When did you go to the cinema?"

"Subhas and Hans played the most recent film at the party.

There's a boat scene where she throws a man overboard to his death."

"I'm nervous the film might not immediately pass the censor approval," she said, thinking about the high stakes involved. "Most people have very little extra money for film tickets, and if ABC's *Warrior Queen* makes it into theaters first—"

"Yes," Jamshedji said glumly. "There won't be anything left in their pockets to buy a ticket to see our *Queen*. And if filmgoers believe Subhas is a murderer, it's a potential reason for them to boycott the film."

"A situation ABC could profit from," Perveen mused.

"Correct." Jamshedji pushed the cleaned pork bone to the side of his plate. "And ABC's not yet responded to my letter delivered to Green's Hotel. Either he's ignoring us to play the upper hand, or he's gone off without us knowing."

Perveen thought about her father's busy day working on behalf of Subhas. "Would you like me to find out about this, too?"

Jamshedji laid down his fork and gave her a long look. "You could check at the hotel, but don't try for an appointment with him. Whatever you do, don't call too much attention to yourself."

*EASIER SAID THAN done*, she thought to herself when she awoke early on Sunday morning, noting with relief the quiet outside: no falling rain. Surely Alice had reached home safely, sometime over the last few hours.

She couldn't call the Hobson-Jones household to ask to speak to Alice, let alone Colin. On Monday, though, she could look for Alice at Woodburn College and try to learn what Rochana had revealed after she'd left. That question still burned, but she needed something else to do today. She could go to Champa Films to speak to Asmaa, as Rochana had asked her to do—and also to a few others who were gaining prominence in her mind.

When Arman arrived at eight-thirty to take her father and her out for the Sunday morning activities, a plan came together. First, her father would be dropped at Dadar Station, where he would meet Ardeshir Nanporia, who was coming to personally deliver bail money. She'd told him her thoughts about doing more interviews of actors and staff at the studio, if she could.

After Jamshedji disembarked at the Dadar Police Station, Arman drove on to Pearl Villa. The customary guards were at the gate and let her through. This time, instead of going up to the main house directly, she asked Arman to stop at the entrance to the zoo.

"Who will you be seeing here?" His voice sounded dubious.

How silly she'd look to give the tiger's name. "Just looking around at the zoo. Not more than five minutes."

Stepping out of the car, she tucked the folds of her lime-green chiffon sari tighter against her waist. If a cage gate was ajar and a tiger loose, she was ready to run.

To reach the cages, she walked along a trail strewn with straw and passed through a variety of pens, with short wooden fencing to enclose a family of chital, the dog-sized deer that were native to forests in the northwest. These deer were clearly tame, coming close to the fence as she passed. Farther along were enclosures holding a pig and a water buffalo, and then a riding ring with three horses. A small cage held a family of monkeys whose expressions seemed resentful. The largest one took up a mocking call and lunged toward the bars as she passed.

She kept her pace steady, even though she'd been startled. She reminded herself of the hundreds of times she'd been within a few feet of monkeys, even shooing them from Colin's veranda when they came too close to a plate of snacks. She was annoyed by the persistent entourage, but perhaps it was because they didn't recognize her and felt like telling her so.

Or—were they warning the others? There had been a lot of commotion around the zoo since Morgan had been killed. For all she knew, they'd seen Alice and Rochana, and then whoever else might have come.

The tiger had been sleeping in the back corner of its cage, but the monkey's calls awakened it. Tora had a splendid cream-and-orange coat, with flared cream markings around her huge golden eyes. She collected herself, rising and padding a few steps forward. But then, as if changing her mind, she turned and went back to her corner.

So, the tiger wasn't bothered by her. Perveen felt a rush of relief, even though she'd never been in danger. Then she heard the crunching of straw and turned to see a thin young man in a vest and lungi carrying a pail.

Smiling, she asked in Marathi, "Are you Sridhar? The assistant who also played a role in the film?"

He nodded a bit shamefacedly. "Yes—it is embarrassing to put on pillows and a sari and play ladies. But then I get a bit of pay that's better than for this work feeding animals. Are you the lawyer's daughter?"

"Yes." No need to mention her own credentials; it would just seem officious. "I was wondering. With all the hustle and so on in the last few weeks, how has it been for the animals?"

"The animals don't like strange people coming around and say so." He swung his bucket, looking ready to go.

She imagined he was giving her a hint, but she wasn't ready to leave. "I heard there might have been a cage open during the night of the party."

"Yes. It was our tiger's cage," Sridhar said in a low voice. "Very strange because I'm sure I latched it that night."

"Where do you keep the keys?"

"Hanging by the hut." He waved toward the crude structure a few yards away. "Always there in case of emergencies. But there is no danger from Tora. She didn't leave her cage, and she is not the type to be looking for extra food with the treats she gets."

"What kind of treats?"

"Rochana or Asmaa brings leftovers from the kitchen at least once daily. Chicken, lamb, whatever is cooked. The other animals see and smell and are jealous."

Perveen thought again about the monkey's reaction. "So Asmaa and Rochana really like tigers?"

"The tiger is Rochana's partner in some of the films. Therefore, Rochana wants the tiger to love her."

"Ah, I see." And now she understood why the tiger had come close enough to look at her and then walked off. She wasn't the right person.

Not Rochana.

She bade Sridhar goodbye and, as she exited the zoo, scanned the drive. Arman was parked in the same place. A tall, powerfully built man was strolling rapidly toward the staff cottages. Master Nishant was dressed in a tunic and trousers, looking far more Punjabi than he had on the party night.

"Master Nishant! Hello!"

He halted and then turned to deliver his trademark brilliant smile. "Miss Mistry."

"Do you have a moment?" Seeing his smile fade, she added, "I have some important news."

His expression relaxed somewhat, and he gestured toward the cottages. "Very well. I'll give you a cup of tea."

She hesitated. To go into a building alone with a man was questionable both in terms of reputation and safety. "I'll tell my driver where I'll be, and to wait ten minutes."

Perveen walked back to the Daimler and explained the situation. Arman still looked dubious. "Master Nishant is a professional fighter—I've seen him in the films. So why don't I drive closer to the cottages and keep my window open?"

"A good idea," she said, relieved by his foresight.

"You don't suppose—he could give me a signed picture, also?"

His request made it clear that he didn't anticipate trouble. Winking, she said, "As long as he doesn't kill me, I'll do that."

Moments later, she and Nishant were at the cottage threshold. But as he put his hand on the knob, the door swung open, causing them both to step back. Asmaa had emerged with a towel over her arm and looked just as surprised.

"What business have you here?" Nishant asked Asmaa in Urdu.

"I was checking on the dhobi's delivery of linens," Asmaa answered crisply in the same language. "You have extra towels. This must go to Becker-sahib instead."

Asmaa might have directions to adhere to a tight budget—or was she snooping, just as Perveen had, albeit through the window? She decided to mount a distraction. She chose to speak in Hindi, which she knew they'd both understand. "Asmaa, I just went to meet the tiger named Tora. That tiger is Rochana's favorite, isn't she?"

"Yes." Asmaa's tight mouth relaxed. "After Bubbles passed on, Tora became Rochana's beloved."

"I was wondering about the amount of food she receives."

Asmaa looked at her with surprise. "Why are you asking this?"

Keeping Rochana's existence secret was becoming a burden. "I know that staff weren't paid for a while, so I thought perhaps food was scarce."

"Never for Tora. She's the most important to the company, after Rochana."

Nishant harrumphed as if offended. "Tora wasn't in the last film."

"Coming in the next," Asmaa retorted.

"Yes. I'll be teaching Marisa how to act with her," Nishant said in an officious way.

"Tora has been getting enough. She won't eat your little girl!" Asmaa said sharply as she squeezed past the two of them and walked swiftly away from the cottage.

"Asmaa doesn't like Marisa. Not at all," Nishant said as he ushered Perveen inside.

Perveen thought back to the argument she'd seen between Nishant and Marisa. "The older generation thinks the younger ones are too bold, isn't it? Where would you like me to sit?"

"Why not that chair?" He pointed to an upholstered chair with fine carving. It was the best chair in the room and looked like it had been made in another city, perhaps Lahore, where he and Marisa came from. As she sat down, he stationed himself on a worn settee that was placed across from her. "Marisa does have a bad trait of speaking out of turn. But how rude for a servant to punish us by taking away the towels!"

Folding her hands in her lap, Perveen asked, "What was the trouble last Thursday morning?"

He regarded her with a neutral expression. "I don't know what trouble you mean—beyond the death. You know all about that."

She could tell he wasn't in the mood to be candid. "Sorry, but it may be important. You and Marisa were having a very loud argument onstage. You said something like, she was playing with fire." When he didn't elaborate, she pushed on. "Did anything happen during the party that caused conflict between you two?"

Narrowing his eyes, he asked, "What did you hear happened?"

"I don't know anything. I'm just guessing, was it something to do with a man?"

"If only just one man!" He shook his head wearily.

"What do you mean by that?" When he didn't answer, she said, "Does she have several beaux?"

He looked searchingly at her and then spoke. "I doubt you know this, but in our world of acting, dance, and music, there has always been a tradition of patronage."

"A source of income by appreciative fans," she said. "I've heard that there are performers who live quite well in cities like Lahore because of their patrons."

"Yes. In our home city, rules are established, and things proceed easily between men and women, with each getting what they desire," he said. "I admit to instructing Marisa she would rise at Champa if Hans truly liked her and appreciated her beauty and talent. I saw Hans as a good choice, because he is alone."

She wanted to clarify it. "Without a wife?"

"Yes, as far as we know. He's never spoken of one."

Perveen searched to find words that wouldn't offend. "Do you think relations went too far between Hans and Marisa?"

"As I've said, I had no argument with Hans Becker." After a pause, he added, "She was involved with a second man. I can't say his name aloud. It would be disrespectful."

Perveen remembered Marisa seeming to spy on her own conversation with Subhas Ghoshal. "The big boss?"

"You guessed it. How she can be so reckless!" He raised his hands up, shaking them as if reenacting an argument. "His wife is the star of the company—and my costar!"

"So, was there anything else about the party?" Perveen prompted, sensing his reserve had dropped in the presence of a sympathetic listener.

"Honestly, I had a good time at the party. I was very happy about how well the film turned out. People in the business were praising me. We had plenty of drinks. When I came back to my place, I was quite tired but I saw . . ." He closed his eyes tightly for a moment. "I didn't see, but I *knew* Marisa was with someone under my own roof."

Feeling apprehensive, she asked, "How so?"

"She'd left her dupatta on the knob of the door. That is supposed to mean stay away—someone has company inside. I use the signal quite a bit myself. But that night, I was annoyed because it was so late. I wanted to go inside, but I couldn't possibly interrupt."

Perveen decided to voice the question she'd had about their relationship. "It's . . . unusual to have such an arrangement with a child, isn't it?"

"Who are you to judge me?" he snapped.

"Let me rephrase it." Perveen sensed her instincts had been right about doubting the relationship. "I am not accusing you of anything. One woman is already missing—Marisa's safety could also be at stake. I must know who she is to you—whether she is actually your daughter."

Nishant stood up then and walked toward the windows. Looking out at them, but not at Perveen, he began. "You likely know that Subhas had hired me two years ago, right when the studio started. He was using male actors playing women, and some minor actresses. No big female star was yet attached to the company. Then he landed Rochana! She is an indisputable star, but I also thought: My sister's daughter is almost as pretty."

"Of course," Perveen agreed, though her feeling was that no other actress she'd seen exhibited the sensuality and intelligence that Rochana had, on-screen and in real life. It was a kind of magic.

"Marisa was eager to try films, but she has four younger brothers and sisters, and neither of her parents could leave them to travel to Bombay to chaperone their eldest. I was the obvious choice, because I have a home here and could convince Hans and Subhas to let her screen-test. From the moment I introduced her to the studio, I spoke of myself as her father, so that there would be no trouble about getting her housing with me in this estate. Many of our junior actors must live outside the studio grounds. Her mother wouldn't have agreed to her living with strangers."

"So many of us have parents who worry about our movements," Perveen agreed. She found it ironic that a community of women were expected to reside with family for protection and social approval—yet still had freedom to pursue financially beneficial romances with men.

"Will you tell this to Subhas? He might not trust me anymore."

Perveen looked at Nishant's troubled face and thought it through. "I don't believe the fact that you two are uncle and niece pertains to any of his troubles. Now, I was asking what happened after you noticed the dupatta hanging on your doorway. You thought someone was inside with Marisa. What did you do?"

"I thought it must be Hans, and I resolved that I would talk to him. I walked the length of the cottages to his place, intending to wait for him and tell him he had gone too far—if he wanted my daughter that way, he should marry her. But he was already inside his place, sitting at his table, weeping. He would not talk about anything, but I guessed that he felt broken thinking that Marisa had gone off with someone else."

"Is that what he said to you?"

"No, of course not. After all, he thinks I am her father—it would be quite awkward. I patted him on the back and said that I was sorry. I sat with him for an hour or so, until his crying ceased. Then I walked back to the place and saw Subhas walking off through the trees, and the dupatta was gone from the doorknob. So I knew he was the one! When I got inside, Marisa was in her room already. I was angry and still partly drunk, so I didn't go to her. I thought it better to wait and speak to her when we were having morning tea."

He was admitting himself to be a man of emotion who had chosen restraint. But was he wise enough to really know how Hans felt about his niece? The cinematographer's breakdown could have occurred because Morgan had told him the film was going to be rejected—or some similar threat. Slowly, she asked, "Are you very sure that Marisa was romantic with Subhas, and that Hans felt romantically betrayed?"

"Marisa said to me the next morning that she and Subhas are in love!" He raised his hands helplessly, then let them drop. "She shouldn't cause such upheaval among people who work together. It's through Rochana's good grace that Marisa is starring in the next picture. Why would she give some perks to a husband stealer?"

Perveen's eyes were soft as she regarded Nishant: a glamorous man, heroic and strong on-screen, who seemed broken with disappointment and worry. He had brought in his niece to Champa Films with the same kind of hope that Jamshedji Mistry had when he'd opened the office door for her at a time nobody else in the city would hire a woman solicitor. All she could do was suggest that things didn't always match up with the way they appeared.

"Mr. Morgan had behaved in a most unsettling way at the party. They could have been discussing this and what to do next?" she suggested.

"My niece is hardly one for Subhas to turn to for advice. I imagine you are actually thinking that one or the other was involved in his death." Nishant looked soberly at her.

"Of course not," she answered, although her heart rate had quickened. "Never mind about them. Didn't you say that it was one o'clock when you came back from Hans's cottage?"

"I did. I'm sure of the time because Hans has one of those special wooden clocks from Europe that make noise on the hour." He paused, as if making more calculations. "Today's newspaper said that the medical examiner said Morgan died sometime between eleven and four in the morning. So Subhas could have been involved—but don't you think of blaming Marisa!"

# 25

# THE ALPHABET, ACCORDING TO CHATTERJEE

It was hard to continue the conversation after that; she could not put the case at risk, especially since she was defending Subhas. Perveen said a subdued goodbye and went outside, back to the waiting car. The next stop was bail court in Dadar.

It was a ten-minute wait for Jamshedji to come out of the low white building guarded by an unsmiling constable. Walking right behind him was Subhas, in a crumpled suit, and Marisa, smiling and fresh in a pale pink sari.

Perveen blinked, not quite believing her eyes. "A good morning to you, Marisa."

"It's a horrid morning—I have been so worried!" Marisa cried. "But your father says everything will be all right."

Jamshedji was pointedly not looking at the young actress, who was clinging to the studio head's arm. Subhas seemed oblivious to Marisa's expression—he waved excitedly at Perveen.

"You couldn't have come at a better time!" he said warmly.

"I'm so glad you are out," Perveen said, because there was no point in saying "free" when it was only bail.

Jamshedji took the front seat next to Arman. That left Perveen on the far left of the backseat, with Marisa in the middle and Subhas on the other side. Marisa sidled close to Subhas, who, again, didn't show any reaction to her.

"When did you come to the jail, Marisa?" Perveen asked, trying to get a sense of things.

"Just about an hour ago. I cried all night!" she added. "But unlike others, I will stay by this man's side."

The comment seemed a dig at Rochana—but how could Marisa know she was alive and hiding out? Choosing not to take the bait, she spoke to Subhas. "How was your night in lockup, sir?"

"Not as pleasant as a suite at the Taj," he said wryly. "This morning, when I learned that Mr. Nanporia had so generously bailed me, I was high as a kite. And I have a tiger's appetite for breakfast."

"You need a big lunch, too!" Marisa declared. "I will ask Asmaa to prepare it. Such a happy day today: Look, everyone is already anticipating the festival season."

Perveen followed the line of Marisa's slender hand, which was waving toward a shop entrance festooned with marigold garlands. "Mr. Ghoshal, will the documentary film Hans will make about Navratri also have to be reviewed by the censor office?"

He nodded glumly. "It certainly does—even though our main purpose for the newsreels is creating films meant for distribution in Europe. There's a great deal of interest in India—that's how we met Hans in the first place, when he was working with Pathé Studios before the war."

She'd heard the name somewhere before. "A French company?"

"Yes, and they are interested enough in India that they have an office in South Bombay. Champa Films compete against them just as we do with Royal Indian Pictures. I will have to talk with Rochana about other documentary ideas."

Perveen caught Jamshedji's gaze, and he blinked one eye, as if to intimate to her that he'd informed Subhas about Rochana's safety.

"Such good news that Rochana was found," Marisa said silkily. "And of all places, on the little island!"

"Please keep the matter under your hat." Jamshedji gave both Subhas and Marisa stern looks. "We are already in conversation with Rochana about returning."

"And let's not forget the power of Rochana's new friend Alice, the daughter of Lord Hobson-Jones!" Subhas clasped his hands together. "So many advantages to having a government family in our corner."

As the car traveled swiftly onward, Perveen felt herself start to burn. As she'd thought, Subhas regarded Alice as a tool to gain favor with her well-connected, wealthy father.

They had reached Mistry House.

Perveen was the first to get out of the passenger door Arman had opened. Marisa trailed behind her, followed by Subhas. How was she going to separate the two, so Subhas could have a private legal conference with the two of them?

As she started up the steps, Mustafa opened the door. Looking past her, he winced.

In a low voice, he said to her, "Isn't that Mr. Ghoshal with you?"

"Yes. And his, ah, employee . . ." She trailed off, seeing the tension in his face. "Is something wrong?"

"There's a visitor without an appointment. I don't know if it's good for Mr. Ghoshal to come in—"

"Who is it?" Perveen asked, her stomach tightening.

"Yes, who?" Subhas echoed. "Someone from the censor office?"

"No, sir. It's Mr. Chatterjee of Royal Indian Pictures."

"Oh Khodai!" Perveen blurted.

Jamshedji, who had been coming up the steps behind her, bumped into her. Quickly, she delivered Mustafa's news.

Jamshedji's expression was tight as he gestured toward the parlor window that faced Bruce Street. Perveen saw what he had: the shape of a man standing inside, looking out at them.

"How could he know we were coming here with Subhas?" Perveen asked quietly.

"I saw a man who looked like ABC in the bail court," said Subhas, who was still standing a bit farther down on the road. "I wasn't entirely sure—I was trying not to be rattled, so I kept my eye on Jamshedji and the judge instead."

"Oh, he's ruining Subhas's welcome home!" Marisa bleated.

"Quiet, everyone." Jamshedji motioned for both Subhas and Marisa to proceed in the direction of the parked car. "Perveen, you stay."

"Why run? It makes us look weak!" Subhas muttered as he stomped back toward Arman, who jumped out of the car and started opening the doors again, as if in anticipation of their flight.

"We cannot allow you to lose your head," Jamshedji instructed. "We aim to sort out the matter with him about Rochana's contract and then will give you some choices of ways to respond."

Perveen shot a glance at the actress, who'd arranged herself in a flattering pose that was attracting stares from the lawyers walking toward court from their street.

Subhas persisted, "But he wrote the letter to me!"

"You can speak with him later, after all is settled. At this time, he thinks that you are a suspect awaiting trial, and that puts him in a position of power over you. I have a proposal.

"I'll bring you and Miss Young to my club for a hearty Sunday dinner. Perveen, go inside to ring Pearl Villa to find out if the press is still hanging around the studio gates. We want the area to be clear for the homecoming of Mr. and Mrs.—I mean, Mr. Ghoshal and Miss Young."

Jamshedji had tried to cover up, but Perveen guessed that he was embarrassed to have accidentally identified the studio owner and ingenue as the couple. She thought Subhas and Marisa both seemed unruffled. Clearing her throat, she said, "ABC's still on the premises."

"That's right. Deal with the man as politely as you would with any visitor. Find out his agenda and then send him off."

Perveen chose her words carefully. "You mean—work in my capacity as a solicitor?"

Her father grunted, "Yes, you may."

Perveen felt gratified by the trust he was placing in her. Smiling, she watched the men and Marisa get back into the car and drive away. Glancing back at Mistry House, she still saw the man standing at the parlor window. They had put on quite a show for ABC, who had very likely read their faces and hand movements. Feeling sick, she went back up the steps and let Mustafa open the door for her to go inside.

"I'll be glad to meet with Mr. Chatterjee," she said, taking a notebook and pen out of her bulky legal case, which Mustafa took into his hands. "I take it you have already brought him tea?"

"The kettle's on the hob." Mustafa pressed his lips together, and she guessed he was taking an intentionally long time with it.

Lowering her voice, she said, "Pappa has taken our client away for reasons of discretion."

Mustafa nodded sagely. "I thought as much. Please let me dry your legal case for you in the kitchen. It's quite wet."

She stepped into the parlor and addressed the portly man who was still peering out the window. "Good morning. Are you Mr. Chatterjee?"

He gave a slight bow, the hemline of his long kurta sinking lower over his neatly draped dhoti. "Yes. And who are you?"

"Perveen Mistry. I'm my father's partner in the practice."

"And the other girl who was vamping for her audience on the street? The very pretty one, is she your sister?"

"No," she snapped, then tried to reset herself. "Please sit down. Mustafa is making tea for you."

He smiled, revealing a broken tooth. With his portly figure and yellow-green skin, he didn't look quite healthy. Holding out a square box, he said, "I brought something for you and your father."

"How kind of you." The square red box wrapped in ribbon

was the right shape for sweets, but she was loath to take food from someone she didn't know. "I shall give it to Mustafa to set aside for my father's enjoyment this evening."

"But you yourself must enjoy it now!" he exclaimed, his voice rising with emotion. "Bim Chandra Nag is one of the most famous sweet shops in Calcutta."

Perveen recognized the name on the box from the historic confectionary. Now what to do? He surely wouldn't attempt anything as bold as food poisoning. And it was true that a rush of sugar could help with concentration. Untying the red string that held the box closed, she beheld a glistening line of golden-brown ovals. "These look like ledikeni."

"Hanh!" He looked at her with approval. "How did you know?"

"I stayed in Bengal for a little while." She hoped that would be enough; he didn't deserve the story of her short venture into married life.

"These sweets are named in honor of Lady Canning. Did you know that?"

He was referring to the wife of the first viceroy of India. "No, sir, I hadn't heard it. Although it seems a curious choice of name for a golden-brown delicacy."

"Creamy white would be a better color for a white lady, isn't it?" He chuckled. "People say that Mr. Nag named the sweet for political advantage."

"Just as one might think Royal Indian Pictures is a name that gives a good impression to the government," she said with a small smile.

"Not quite. My patron is a rajah; actually two rajahs, who are both my financiers," he said with pride. "It would be rude to favor one over the other, hence I used 'royal.'"

"Very diplomatic." She wished she hadn't asked; she was only fishing to see where he swam politically. A matter irrelevant to the case. "Excuse me for a moment, while I take these delicacies to be served on a proper plate. By the way, how do you like your tea, sir?"

"The Bengali way, of course."

Memories of milky sweet tea served in clay cups on the road still gave her a phantom toothache. "Three sugars and milk?"

"Khub bhalo!" Chatterjee proclaimed, a finger in the air.

"Very good," she translated back to him; and he chuckled in approval.

It was not the Mistry way to boil tea with milk and sugar; but glumly she told Mustafa what needed to be done. She would drink from the pot as well, in order that Chatterjee would continue to think her as someone in alignment.

After she'd returned to the sitting room and Mustafa served the tea from a pot and the sweets laid out in a circle on a matching plate, she took a ledikeni and nibbled the edge. It was so sweet that pain shot through her teeth. But it was also soft and delicious, so she murmured, "Very tasty."

Taking one of the same, he munched it. "You can't get anything as good in Bombay. We are offering these sweets as part of the prasad at my Durga Puja pandal."

She remembered what Mr. Dass had said. "Is it the one in Green's Hotel?"

"Yes—and I believe the only pandal in this city. We are introducing this style of celebration to Bombay."

"Really?" She didn't know if this was correct, because she wasn't part of the same religious community.

He smirked, stretching his round face wider. "Yes, that is what the local Bengali community tells me. And quite happily, I've landed approval from the Bombay Board of Censors allowing me to release *The Warrior Queen* in time for the Durga festival."

"Is yours a mythology film?" Maybe it wouldn't be as much competition as she'd feared.

"One could also call it a bio-epic," he said grandly. "It's the story of Durga's life, and her victory against the demon

Mahishasura, with tremendous special effects. Ticket sales are at the Grand, and also at Green's Hotel."

"I see," she said, remembering that Green's Hotel was where the Durga Puja pandal was being set up.

"Shall I reserve complimentary tickets for you, your father, and Mr. Ghoshal? All of you must need something to lighten your spirits, with the police charge."

So there, the first arrow. "That's very kind. I can't speak for anyone's availability at the moment—"

"And Ghoshal afraid to show himself," he added with a chuckle. "He was about to enter the building not ten minutes ago, and then he ran away. Tell me more about that girl who's not your sister: his new mistress?"

"That is a very minor actress in the film company," Perveen said sharply. "They were only dropping me off before going on to business elsewhere."

He gave her a disbelieving smile. "Your father sent me a letter begging for a meeting. But he chose to step out?"

"We are partners representing Champa Films," Perveen said with emphasis. "Please let me take notes on what you wish to say. Then my father will know just the same as me."

As he grimaced, showing his bad teeth, she thought about sharks. "I came to talk about Rochana's contract. My most important employee ran away from my studio—and what has become of her now in Bombay?"

Instead of responding to the second question, she asked, "If she hasn't taken salary for the last nine months, she's not your employee anymore, is she?"

"Rochana left before the filming of *The Warrior Queen*. Her runaway act caused me a financial loss. I had to hire Patience Cooper at a usurious price. And there is no replacement for Bubbles!"

If he'd caused the dog's death, he was playing games with her. But this wasn't the point to bring up now. "Have you brought a copy of any document showing the terms of employment for Rochana?"

"No; that is hardly necessary. I came on a matter of business, but now it is a matter of the heart."

"My goodness!" Perveen feigned shock. "You can't be saying that you love Rochana. She's a married lady . . ."

His eyes shone with indignation. "No! I care for her like a father. I am desperate for whoever has harmed her to be punished." Pointing a finger at her, he said, "I think you must know the truth. Tell me."

"The law requires us to keep all matters about Champa Films confidential."

"You don't understand," he fretted, his fingers furiously rolling sweet crumbs on his plate. "From the day I discovered her, I treated her like my own daughter!"

"But I thought she's the daughter of a military man," Perveen countered, recalling what Rochana had said about a British officer for a father. "She has her own family."

"Her father was said to be British, yes, but he never married her mother, a Bengali Muslim." His dark eyes seemed to glow with excitement. "And that lady I speak of—who I've seen with my own eyes—was of a good family who naturally cast her out, and after the man's death she turned to domestic employment. The only reason Rochana speaks English so prettily is having gone to La Martinière on scholarship for poor girls of mixed heritage. She learned to fence there, too; that was the important thing."

"Rochana mentioned the school, but none of the rest." Perveen tried to look less shocked than she felt. "You are a master storyteller, sir. How can I know that you aren't offering me such a tale?"

"Listen." He shook a finger at her. "I rescued from a chawl the only child of an unmarried mother working as a seamstress. I gave her work, paid for her clothes and athletic training. I made her into India's fierce sweetheart."

"How young was Rochana?"

"Thirteen at the time. I saw her riding quite nicely in an annual talent show at her school. Her mother agreed to her coming for an audition, and then she lived off my good graces for more than six years, you know."

Perveen still needed to put more pieces in place. "But if Rochana's mother is Bengali, why do the newspapers and magazines say Egypt?"

"The story about exotic parentage is for the public." Looking sagely at Perveen, he added, "It only built her glamour. How could she compete against the likes of Patience Cooper, Sulochana, and Seeta Devi?"

Perveen put down her cup abruptly. She had believed Rochana's story of being thrown out of her family for marrying Subhas. Perveen had thought how brave the two of them were to live in a way that she and Colin couldn't—and perhaps Alice and Kitty couldn't, either. And that was because Rochana and Subhas's world—film—was one where romances could take forms that were far from what civil society demanded.

Perveen tried to pull herself back to the present. This conversation was an important opportunity to gather information about Rochana's history at Royal Indian Pictures—she could not let herself become trapped in a wistful reverie. "Do you have an idea of how many times Rochana was injured during the making of your films?"

"There were no serious injuries!" He shook his hands vehemently as he spoke. "Everyone gets cuts and bruises now and again making action pictures. Rochana was thrilled to show off her fencing skills to slash with swords, and her swimming prowess in the river. And didn't our cameras do her justice, and thrill thousands of viewers throughout India!"

She wanted to pull him down from his pedestal of ego. "Yet this work wasn't enough to keep her happy. She left your studio. Why?"

"It had nothing to do with my leadership. It was because of Joseph Morgan." He said the name with obvious distaste.

*Just as Rochana had said.* "How well do you know him?"

"I wish I didn't have to!" ABC said, shaking his head. "He's a jumped-up sergeant who landed a plum spot as a film censor. Morgan came to one of our film parties in Calcutta uninvited, and I was forced to accept him. He spent some time eyeing Rochana up and then chatting to her. I thought it well and good because the next day, there was a censorship screening. After meeting her at the party, he invited her to accompany me to the evaluation. And after she came, it was the first time any of my films had a swift pass by the committee; no alterations needed for the film. He then asked me to be sure that she be the one to drop off the next film to the office."

"It sounds like you might not have attended that meeting?"

"That's correct—he didn't tell me to come along, did he?" ABC shrugged and went on. "Rochana told me afterward that all was well. But the next time we had a film ready to bring there, she concocted a story about a shoulder being in too much pain for her to lift the tins of film. I sent a lackey with her to do the carrying, but she'd started trying to avoid those censor screenings altogether."

"And you didn't wonder why?" Perveen could imagine a situation of intense pressure, if not abuse.

"She had become a *dilettante*!" He fairly spat out the word. "She would come to work, only doing certain scenes, and asking me to have one of the male actors do fight scenes, car chases, and water scenes. I said no—if we falsified the scene, her loyal fans would be disappointed. I worked hard to find Rochana. I invested more money in her than any other actor—she had the highest salary. And she had the physical abilities. That is what people paid to see."

"I understand," Perveen said, toying with the sweet on her plate. "You must know quite a bit about Mr. Morgan. He is such a mystery to us."

Looking self-satisfied, he said, "Morgan was an English bachelor who'd had a rough time in the war. He told Rochana his troop was captured, and he was sent to a prisoner's camp in Germany. The inmates had very poor food and were made to work very hard. He hated Germans very much because of it."

As he spoke, she remembered Morgan's tension in the hallway with Hans—and also the ghost of something else she'd heard. But it lay too far back for her to muster: and now Chatterjee was reaching for another sweet and indicating she should take one as well.

"No, thank you. My hands will be too sticky to take notes if I do." Turning the page, she continued. "How close in communication are the Calcutta censor board and Bombay boards?"

"They don't make unanimous decisions, because there are different political situations throughout the country. There are three places in India now where most films are being made, and they all have censor boards. It is utterly ridiculous for us to have to travel like this, but the truth is, what flies past the censors in Bombay might be stopped dead in Calcutta."

Perveen made a note of this. "Does anyone know why Mr. Morgan was shifted out of Calcutta to Bombay?"

ABC gave a small, mean smile. "Perhaps the bastard was caught."

"Caught doing what?" She wondered if his pressure on Rochana had been detected by others in the office.

"During the end of his time in Calcutta, he had demanded some studios pay fees to him ahead of time to guarantee he wouldn't object against their picture during the censorship process. Morgan represented one out of three police votes on the project. Therefore, he would be the deciding vote, if the other two disagreed."

Perveen recalled Nanporia telling her about the same extortion. "What amounts did you pay him typically per picture?"

Chatterjee raised a finger. "I never said that I bowed to his demand. That would be participating in an illegal activity."

"Of course not!"

"But if he extorted other filmmakers, the truth could have somehow been exposed." Chatterjee sounded smug. "I just kept on making films. I make my mythology so entertaining that there's nothing for the British to be frightened about. Whereas your client is different, isn't he?"

"I really can't comment on the films," she said stiffly. He had confided so much—she'd almost thought she had him in hand. But now she saw his sharp edge had reemerged.

"But you've seen *Queen of Hearts*, haven't you? What happens in it? Do tell!" he pressed her.

"I'd hate to spoil the story for you," she demurred. "But maybe I can procure you a free ticket . . . and it would be so easy on everyone to move on from any past arguments. The more Indian studios that are producing films, the better for the Indian population."

"I understand you speaking such nonsense to bolster the position of Champa Films, but that studio will fall apart now that Rochana is gone." ABC's wide smile again revealed the broken front tooth, making him look ghastly. "Subhas has just got too much trouble, doesn't he?"

*And you might be the one who came to Bombay to cause such trouble*, Perveen brooded. But she would not let her face show this. "Your cup is half empty, Mr. Chatterjee. Would you like some more?"

At this, he snorted. "Oh, there's no reason for me to stay any longer, is there? Do tell your father that I'm waiting for him to make the next move."

# 26

# THE FACES OF PRISONERS

During the time that Perveen talked with Chatterjee, every bit of her attention was on him: his amiable yet superior manner, his desire to gossip about Rochana's past, and even the way he'd slurped his *s*'s and his tea. He was a grand storyteller, all right.

She had been so caught up in the conversation that her note-taking had dwindled, and after he had departed, she scribbled down what was missing. He'd dropped lurid tidbits about Morgan's interest in Rochana and his interest in taking bribes. The latter part seemed likely to be true, given what Mr. Nanporia had said about the man's demands for money. Morgan might have decided there was a greater chance of success demanding money from a film's investors rather than the filmmaker himself; and less chance of being caught.

In a way, Morgan's actions reminded Perveen of the situation within *Queen of Hearts*, where Rochana's character was poised to sacrifice herself by marriage to a gangster.

And Morgan had just seen this film. Maybe he'd believed the storyline was concocted by Rochana as a reference to her past in Calcutta. *No!* she decided. That was too much introspection for such a miscreant. But was she unfairly judging Morgan? It was too easy to dwell on his nastiness and overlook his past emotional torment.

She closed up the notebook and went out in the hallway. Her phone call to Pearl Villa was picked up by Asmaa, who confirmed that the press were no longer waiting at the gates. This meant the coast was clear, at least temporarily, and she could inform Jamshedji, Subhas, and Marisa.

THE RIPON CLUB was located on Esplanade, just a few minutes' walk from Mistry House. The august Parsi establishment was situated on the upstairs floors of another law practice building almost as handsome as Mistry House. She rode up in the elevator, all the while hearing the chatter of diners growing louder. Here, her old friend Nariman had now shifted from being a head waiter to the maître d'. Beaming at her, Nariman said, "Good afternoon, Miss Mistry! You've just missed your father."

"They aren't here?"

"Sunday lunch is becoming our busiest shift, and they could not wait for a table." Nariman lowered his voice conspiratorially. "Also, I think Mr. Mistry was perturbed by the number of people badgering his famous guests for autographs."

That, she could believe. "Do you know where they decided to go?"

Nariman shook his head and chuckled. "Your esteemed father is too polite to mention the names of other dining establishments in front of our patrons. Now, Miss Mistry, I could gladly squeeze you into a private table somewhere. Today's menu includes your favorite dhansak!"

"You are tempting me, but I've eaten." It was a white lie, but she had made up her mind. In the last minute, the memory she'd tried to dredge up during ABC's visit had surfaced. This meant she had something to investigate before she found them, and the place to go was back to the Royal Asiatic Society.

The marble steps leading up to the Asiatic entrance in Bombay's original town hall had long slicks of water on them, which meant she took her time going up, pausing to allow faster people to move ahead. Sunday was also a big day for patronage at the Asiatic Society. As she passed the tall Doric columns and proceeded into the cool entry hall, she signed the membership book and then ventured further inside. The head librarian had disappointing news: The materials that had been displayed during the recent Thinkers Lecture were no longer available in the reading room. "One of our vice presidents was involved in the disposal."

She thanked him and, feeling a sense of foreboding at the word 'disposal,' headed downstairs. She certainly hoped Colin wouldn't have thrown anything away.

She trod carefully down the spiral staircase to the ground floor, where she saw Naim, the library peon she knew best, mopping water from the very end of the corridor. *It must have been from the previous day's storm*, she thought, and she felt glad that he didn't look up, that he wouldn't catalog she had visited Colin's office again so recently.

As she approached Colin's small office, she felt a surge of nerves. Not fear—but excitement. She couldn't expect Colin to be in—but if he was, it would be perfect.

He sat at his desk, which faced the open door, papers and a typewriter in front of him. At the sound of her creaking the door open farther, he raised his head.

"Oh! This is a nice surprise."

"To me as well. Why are you here on your day off?"

"Things have been tense up in Malabar Hill, and I suppose I had nothing better to do," he said with a half smile. "Perhaps we had a bit of telepathy about where we could see each other again?"

Smiling, she stepped into the room, closing the door behind her.

Colin looked from the closed door to her in wonder. "You always want the door open."

"Sometimes, not always." Perveen suddenly realized that she was flirting. Had she picked up this skill from Rochana? *What did it matter?* she thought, as Colin drew her close for a long, satisfying kiss.

After he'd released her, she said, "I've actually come on business."

"Truly?" he asked, looking at her warmly. "But before we address that, let me assure you that Alice reached home safely. I didn't have an easy way to tell you."

"I understand." Perveen nestled back against his chest.

"I rang up my landlord this morning to check about the leak in my flat—he's got someone looking at it tomorrow," Colin murmured into her hair.

"Good on you," Perveen said. "Now, I must be quick about my mission here."

"Yes, do tell me!" Colin pulled away slightly to look at her.

"You mentioned that the Asiatic is considering acquiring some folios with war pictures. What's the book called?"

"It's titled *Prisoners of the Great War*, and the acquisition was vetoed." Breaking apart from Perveen, he went to the bookcases and touched a thick volume placed flat on the high shelf. "It's soon on its way back to the dealer who hoped to sell it to us."

"What was the cause for veto?"

"The book includes several German-made photographs of our men in the prisoner-of-war camps." Soberly, he added, "At the Thinkers Lecture, there were police and other officials in the audience who insisted having such a book in our collection means having anti-British propaganda on the shelf."

The lecture he mentioned had occurred the same night as the party, so Joe Morgan hadn't been there. Perhaps some of his colleagues had gone.

"But I'm interested in seeing the book. May I?"

Would she recognize Morgan's face? She had only seen him a few times that evening. The newspaper hadn't shown a picture of him.

He lifted the heavy folio bound in red cloth from the shelf and carried it to his desk. Clearing some papers, he placed the volume squarely in the center. "I'd allow you almost anything."

"Silly," Perveen said, coming closer to the desk.

When she reached it, he held the book aloft and said, "Price."

"Very well." She gave him another kiss, and he put the folio back down on the desk.

Immediately, Perveen flipped to the title page, where the photographers' names were listed. "I see surnames that look French and possibly English, but not anything that looks German. How could that be?"

"And various anonymous photographers," Colin said. "Well, it will take you some time to go through. Why don't you take the chair?"

Slowly, she flipped the pages. Many of the first pictures were distance shots of buildings set in fields, and battlefields with badly wounded soldiers. And there were shots taken inside, where men were posed, as if for intake, many dressed in shabby uniforms. Quite a few had obvious wounds and bandages and looked somber.

"So this is what's objectionable," Colin said. "Seeing our men down and out. And look at this next picture—prisoners scrubbing floors, another cleaning latrines."

"Logically, they would have been photographed by the men in charge: probably their guards or German soldiers. I have seen plenty of prison cells here in Bombay, and this is about the same—except the people look cold. Look how those two are huddled for warmth." She was closely examining the faces for anyone who looked like Joseph Morgan.

"War is the definition of inhumanity, isn't it?" Colin mused. "One of the fellows at our library discussion thought that these could be posed pictures taken by the Central Powers to send to newspapers and show humiliation of Allied men. But does that mean it's not part of history?"

"I agree with you," Perveen said, turning the page. Colin was just behind her, so close she could feel his breath.

"How does this tie with your work?"

Since it didn't involve the Ghoshals, there wasn't much risk in telling him. "As you already know, Joe Morgan was in a prisoner's camp in Germany. It was an off chance, but I thought he might be recognizable in this book. I really don't see anyone who resembles him."

"What good would that do your investigation?"

Again, Perveen deliberated how much to say. She had begun to think with pity for Joe Morgan; but she felt at war with herself. "I don't like to think ill of the dead; especially someone who had his life forcefully taken. I want to feel sorry for him—but it's been hard."

"I understand that. And looking for a particular British soldier in this book would be searching out a needle in a haystack. At the peak in 1918, there were 3.8 million soldiers fighting in North Africa, the Middle East, and Europe."

"It seems all the more reason for this book to be here—although if there are Indian soldiers in these pictures, I've missed them."

"Indian forces were held in some German prisoner-of-war camps—I think for certain one called Wünsdorf."

Perveen turned the pages to the index, her fingers running along the alphabetically listed place names. German was an interesting language with so many long words that needed patience to be sounded out. But then she stopped. A name appeared that was part of a half-forgotten memory.

"Colin, can you pronounce this for me?"

"Oh, dear. It's got an umlaut, which makes it very difficult to pronounce. Shny-de-mool."

"Aha, then! I believe I heard Joe Morgan speak that same word." Colin's eyebrows rose. "When?"

"At the party, Morgan was having an argument with the cinematographer Hans Becker. I was at a distance and overheard that word, although I thought it was an epithet."

"Why would you think Schneidemühl is a bad word? It's the name of a town in Prussia."

"I translated it in my mind to 'snide mule,'" she said with a grin. "But Morgan must have been bringing up the town, or more likely, this particular prisoner of war camp. After all, he'd been a prisoner of war." As she spoke, Perveen had been turning pages carefully and reached the section showing Schneidemühl—a picture of men with heads bent working with hoes and wheelbarrows on a field, with a long, low building in the distance.

"I see!" Colin was nodding. "And you told me some time ago that Mr. Becker is Swiss German."

Looking up from the book, she said, "Exactly. Hans made out to me that he couldn't remember much about the conversation, but now I have this to ask him about."

Colin cleared his throat. "Becker might not like being pressed about his nationality. Should I come along just to be sure you're all right?"

She hesitated. "I'm so grateful to you for helping me yesterday, but I'd rather not bring you over to Champa Films. I can't risk losing any more ground with my father."

Colin's disappointment showed in the set of his mouth. Slowly, he said, "Surely you don't have to worry about your standing with your father. He knows you found Rochana—that's a major coup."

She had also gathered intelligence from Murray Fawcett and Nanporia, not to mention ABC an hour earlier. A picture of Joe Morgan was coming together in bits and pieces. And while she could not excuse his aggressive conduct toward women, she could at least see a possible base for his misery.

# 27
# INTERVIEW WITH ALICE

Colin's question about where her loyalty lay remained in her mind as she rose and dressed early on Monday morning. It was going to be a hard morning. She resolved that she must remain detached, not only for her peace of mind, but the justice of the situation.

Gita came to help her dress and frowned at the midnight-blue tussar silk sari that Perveen had taken out of the almirah.

"If it rains, that silk will show every spot."

"Bombay people cannot live in fear of the rain, and I haven't worn this in months."

"So stiff and big," Gita said, starting to unfold the sari, still frowning. "For an older lady."

"It's not bad to look mature," Perveen replied as she stood still while Gita began the draping. Tussar wasn't a refined, softly draping textile. It was a more rustic fabric from weavers in Bengal Presidency who used threads woven from the empty cocoons of silkworms that had been allowed to grow and escape.

She imagined that the moths who'd escaped had free spirits. The moths hadn't fled because of fear, the way Rochana had. It was time for them to go. Turning to view herself in the long mirror on the almirah door, she saw that the stately dimensions of the wrapped, coarse silk gave her a more filled-out profile. For a young woman, she looked authoritative, an illusion that she hoped would serve her well when she visited Woodburn College.

Perveen had visited the college many times, so she approached the guard's booth to sign the college's logbook. She was required to sign as a record of her visit, but it was also useful for her own quick check of who was on the premises, both visitor and faculty. Alice's name was in the book ahead of hers, exactly as she'd hoped. After signing, Perveen stated her destination as the office of dean of students. The guard waved her through. All of it appeared ordinary and respectable; the opposite of how things really were.

Perveen hurried past a few students milling on the veranda and climbed two flights to Alice's corridor. Her door was closed—an unusual sight for the faculty member who was popular with students. Feeling misgiving, she pressed her ear to the wood. No voices came, so she knocked. There was no response; but when she turned the knob, she found the door opened. Alice was seated in her desk chair, but slumped forward with her head and arms on the desk.

Perveen's interpretation was the same as when she'd seen the pale corpse lying near the Nanporia estate driveway. *Alice was dead.* Her heart began pounding, yet she felt unable to move her feet. She heard herself crying. "Damn it! Oh, Alice—"

In the next instant, Alice's shoulders jumped up, and she turned her head, looking in shock at Perveen. "Why are you here?"

"I—I—" Perveen was unable to further the sentence. She was overcome with gratitude that once again Alice was alive, albeit distressed.

"I must have fallen asleep," Alice said, looking with panic at her watch. "Oh, God. Almost time for the faculty meeting."

"You must have nine lives!"

Alice was running fingers through her mussed hair. "I don't follow."

"You're like the cat that slips past danger every time," Perveen said, her heartbeat finally slowing. So much for her attempt at detachment. "I saw you lying motionless. I worried that . . ."

"Last night I didn't sleep much, so when I came in and started looking at papers, I dozed off."

"I'm glad it's only that." Perveen stood rigid, feeling that Alice's normalcy was a kind of reproach. "And I know you must have a busy day ahead. I'm sorry for waking you up, but we must talk."

"Will you at least close the door?"

Perveen did so, returning to sit in the small chair meant for Alice's visitors. Trying to find enough room for her capacious sari, she shifted several times as she spoke. "Subhas Ghoshal was arrested on suspicion of killing Joe Morgan."

"Oh, I know!" Alice rubbed at one eye. "At breakfast, Mummy made a point of mentioning what's front and center in the *Times*. Just trying to make me feel worse."

"May I tell you something confidential?" After Alice nodded, she said, "It's not mentioned in the article, but apparently the police found Morgan's necktie in the bedroom's waste bin."

In a low voice, Alice said, "When we first tried to move Morgan, it was very hard. While we were dragging him, I heard him moan and worried that he might choke. That's when I said to Rochana to stop a moment so I could take off the tie and unbutton his collar. I don't recall what I did with the tie."

Perveen did not want to leave Alice as the only one culpable. "Did Rochana agree with you about moving him?"

"She was worried that I was taking too much time, but yes, she waited."

"I see. And his collar button is what Asmaa found on the stairs."

"I didn't see that he lost a button. I really bungled it, didn't I?" Alice stared past Perveen toward the closed office door, as if contemplating escape.

Perveen felt a pang as she heard Alice's words. "You were only in that predicament because you tried to save Rochana."

Alice pressed her lips together tightly. "We didn't know he

would die. Now I wish—I wish I could have taken her away without knocking him out cold. Then we could have raised a storm downstairs, even though she wouldn't have liked it."

Perveen sensed from Alice's words that she might be slightly less aligned with Rochana than before. "Is Rochana coming back from the island anytime soon?"

Alice looked up sharply. "Let's not talk about her, shall we?"

Perveen shook her head. "Why not?"

"Please. I don't want her in my life anymore."

Perveen wasn't ready to give up. "You seemed unified when I left. Did you fall out about something in particular?"

"That's not anything I'll ever tell you."

Alice's words landed hard, like stones.

"Oh," Perveen said, trying to think of a better rejoinder, but failing.

"What do you think she said?" Alice pushed.

So Alice, underneath the bluster, still wanted the communication. But the ball was in Perveen's court. She took a deep breath and said, "I can't begin to guess. But I'm not sure about the emotions flying between Rochana and you. I wonder if these feelings might not be . . . platonic."

"*Not. Platonic.*" Alice repeated the words in a deliberately slow fashion. "It sometimes astounds me how you trip over yourself speaking. And look how you put things in the negative! This is why I've never said anything."

Perveen bristled at the accusation; but she knew Alice was right. "What you're saying about me is true. I'm sorry."

"You are always so quick to say sorry." Alice sounded pensive. "It's what we are raised up to do, isn't it? When I told you about what happened to me at boarding school, you said that you were sorry that I'd been sent to a place so unreasonably strict. But you didn't understand that I loved a girl, and I lost her forever. I still dream about her."

Perveen's eyes moistened. She remembered what it felt like

after she'd left Colin in the mountains, a year earlier, believing they'd never meet again. "And did she . . . look like Rochana?"

"No. Verity was a redhead." Alice exhaled heavily. "Rochana wants us to be like sisters."

"And that's why she would tell you something she doesn't want anyone else to know." As Perveen paused, a memory surfaced. "I was watching a chameleon a few days ago, and it strikes me that Rochana is just the same type of creature. She can change her appearance and story so easily. You and I aren't like that."

"That's right. I'm more like a worm," Alice said grimly. "Lowly, plain, tunneling underground."

"What's wrong with being a bookworm?" Perveen waved her hand toward the crowded bookcase, the desk covered in papers. "None of this is glamorous or beautiful—but it is solid. Your true habitat."

There was a clicking, and suddenly Alice's door was wide open. Standing with the light streaming in behind her was Kitty Daboo, whose gaze shot past Perveen and toward Alice. Her expression was that of someone who'd been in anguish and just been relieved. "So you are here! Why didn't you tell me you were back safely?"

"Kitty!" Alice's voice cracked. "Don't worry, your brother's boat's back in place, and there's not a scratch on it. Sorry I didn't ring up. I've no excuse."

"And I thought, after you'd found her, you also could let me know," Kitty said, scowling at Perveen. "I've been waiting—worrying—"

"I do apologize!" Perveen felt awkward, as if the situation now was that she and Alice were secretly in league. "When I got back to shore, I had bad news—a professional matter. That's why I forgot."

Alice unfolded herself from her chair and went to take the lecturer's hands into her own. Alice whispered something to her, and then Kitty raised Alice's left hand and kissed it.

Perveen quickly looked away, knowing she'd correctly intuited Kitty's feelings for Alice. And it seemed that Alice felt the same, because she was now gripping both of Kitty's hands and continuing to murmur something.

"Time for me to go on," Perveen said hastily, rising from the uncomfortable visitor's chair. "Kitty, I'm sorry again for not ringing."

"I regret my sharpness," Kitty said, breaking the gaze with Alice for a moment to look kindly toward Perveen. "I've been so worried, and now I'm still worried that she's missed the first quarter hour of the new term's faculty meeting."

Alice winced. "Oh, God! I have that presentation. I meant to write up some notes on what to say—I'm utterly blank."

"It's supposed to be about upcoming student events. I suppose you could say that you're postponing because there is so much more information to come?" Kitty suggested.

"Thank you for the good idea. And also, for coming for me." Alice looked tearfully toward Kitty, who held her hands even more tightly.

It struck Perveen that despite the faculty meeting, the two of them didn't seem to be in a rush to leave Alice's office. She was also surprised by the genuine sweetness she felt seeing their reunion. And it struck her that what the two of them had—a secret relationship that could roil society—was exactly the same kind of dilemma that she and Colin faced.

Perveen paused at the door to say goodbye again, but there was no answer.

WAITING FOR A break in traffic, Perveen crossed the Seaface Road to Chowpatty Beach, a stretch of golden sand that shone against the Back Bay during good weather. Today, the sand was damp and closer to brown in color. Would Kitty and Alice walk on the beach sometime—perhaps watching the sunset after day's end?

The sea's surface was smooth, and she imagined the fish

underneath, some lazily resting themselves and others swimming in search of food. The desire to live was part of all beings: It was just that people twisted things in their minds to make survival more of a struggle. Bad things happened along the way, and people were more likely to save themselves. She thought about the Great War, and how it had been much more brutal for Joe Morgan than it had Colin. And as she considered Rochana and Marisa, she understood that the murky film world they swam in was one of the few places that they could rise against expectations. Still, lurking in the shadows were sharks, men who watched carefully and knew when to bite.

So many stories were flooding her that she consciously shifted to considering what had just happened across the road. Kitty Daboo's interruption had turned out to be such a blessing; it had given Alice hope, and herself clarity. But she kept in mind that Alice still hadn't told her what Rochana had privately confessed. Or was that word she thought of—confession—an unfair assumption?

Turning back to look at the college, she saw the Daimler had returned. She crossed the road, and Arman came out of the car to meet her. "Finished?"

"Yes. Thank you for returning for me." She smiled at him, thinking here was yet another helpful person in her life.

"Well, it's better not to go to the office. When we arrived, the police were already there."

Perveen felt herself tighten. "What about?"

"I recognized DCI Watkins, so it must be a matter concerning your father's case."

"Well, they can't take him back into jail because he's on bail. I only hope the interview goes well." As she settled in her seat, she reminded herself of her father's skills.

"Mr. Mistry acted as if quite pleased to see them. You know how good he is at that."

"Yes," she agreed. "And as you said, he doesn't need me there. Let me think . . . Can you please take me to Green's Hotel?"

"Green's?" He wrinkled his nose slightly.

"Well, there is a Durga Puja celebration that may have started." She might also see ABC while she was there.

"I heard your brother say something about taking you there for that exhibition with Gita and the baby."

"I hope we can go later in the week. I'll get an advance look today, to see if it's suitable for Khushy to come with us."

There was good reason for her words. Although built right across the street from the elegant Taj Mahal Palace, Green's Hotel was known for mixed clientele—sailors, and local people who liked a good party. Perveen had only been through the hotel once before, so she took her time entering and looking around the hotel's open courtyard with a number of occupied tables. Aromas of crisply fried bhajias and the sourness of beer rose up as she passed a group of sailors speaking Italian. In the corner, a band of Anglo-Indian performers was playing a song she didn't recognize. Several couples were dancing vigorously and touching in a manner that was a far cry from the sedate ballroom dancing she had seen at the Ripon Club.

*Monday morning, and these people don't give a fig about society!* she thought while passing a tiny table where a single Indian man and a European lady had their heads bent close over drinks.

Nobody around them seemed concerned by this disruption of social convention; their eyes were on the band, or the card games, or on the pouring of the pungent beer. Perveen recalled how her brother had spoken of Rochana sitting in state at a table here surrounded by friends.

At the far end of the courtyard, she glimpsed a stage with a small bamboo roof and proceeded toward it. The Durga Puja pandal was as large as some of the neighborhood Hindu temples she had seen in Hindu neighborhoods and was extravagantly decorated with wreaths of marigolds. At the center was a throne holding a painted clay statue of Goddess Durga, with her ten arms holding slender spears. Durga was seated astride a golden lion, and Perveen couldn't help thinking of Rochana and Tora. Would the two of them ever be together again?

When a group of men wearing fine brocade sherwani coats came close to the pandal, she stepped aside, not wanting to obstruct their possibility of worshipping. However, they looked at the pandal curiously, laughed, and moved on. Maybe they thought an exhibition of religion so close to people drinking alcohol could not be genuine.

Someone with a familiar voice called out a boisterous hello to another man, and she moved forward more slowly to see the two of them shaking hands like old friends.

Ajen was the one with the voice she recognized, and the smaller man, with a bent head, seemed familiar, too—but from a different world. As she moved closer, she saw that she did in fact know both, because the aged man with him was Mr. Dass.

How could it be that the two of them were here today? She stepped behind a potted palm, where she could continue to watch without notice. Neither man had mentioned knowing the other, but they were both Bengalis. Had Mr. Dass taken it upon himself to investigate Ajen? And it came to her then that she had trusted Ajen because she had liked him, but maybe she shouldn't have. And now, because she'd given Mr. Dass instructions to research company doings, she felt anxious not knowing what he was saying.

"Drink, madam?"

A waiter had spotted her and looked expectant.

"No, thank you." She could have retreated and worried about what it meant; but then she would have a hard time questioning both of them without looking like she'd secretly spied. The only thing to do was the obvious; make the best of a chance meeting.

Perveen rearranged the pleats of her sari, which had been slightly crushed in her hiding place, and strode forward.

When she was five feet away from the men, who were still intently talking, she called out, "Hullo."

"You found the way to see Durga!" Dass answered, beaming. "This is another Bengali, a new acquaintance I have admired for some months. May I introduce this young fellow?"

"Dass-sahib, she knows me already." Ajen's eyes flickered past her as if looking for someone else.

"Miss Mistry has enjoyed your recent writing," Dass said quickly. "Isn't it true?"

Perveen wasn't ready for pleasantries. "The only writing I know of Ajen's is the title cards for films!"

"Mr. Biswas here is the Owl, published in the local newspaper for Bengalis. I have pulled out the truth!" Dass announced with a mischievous grin.

"They wanted a Bombay correspondent," Ajen said hurriedly. "It hardly interferes with my duties."

"I am surprised to see you here this morning, though." Perveen looked hard at the young man, who was clearly annoyed by the revelation. "Isn't morning when the light is best?"

"Hans gave me leave when I asked. I hope you won't tell him the reason." Ajen glowered at her.

"In your recent column, you interviewed ABC," Perveen continued. "Was it done right here at Green's?"

"Of course."

Mr. Dass was following the exchange with a startled expression, as if belatedly realizing that Perveen had suspicion of a writer he admired.

Clearing her throat, Perveen said, "So, Ajen, it seems you have friends everywhere. I believe that ABC may have used you as a conduit to Champa Films."

"Not to speak with Subhas. That is all done through lawyers, he said to me."

Yet the way he'd chosen his words triggered an instinctive feeling that she was partly right. Taking a guess, she said, "But you were the one who helped ABC lure the workers away from the Nanporia estate to this hotel on the day of the film party."

"The workers needed pay to live, so they were willing to take any kind of work," he said in a hard voice. "They'd started ABC's job a few days before the party. That night, it was crucial that this installation be finished for press photographers scheduled the following day. It couldn't be helped!"

"What day did the work start?"

"The Thursday before the party. He came with his car and got the people."

"And Rochana's dog, Bubbles, took sick that evening, and was dead the next day." Perveen felt indignation rise within her. "I'm sure that if Bubbles were out on the property, he would have recognized Mr. Chatterjee."

"Yes, the dog greeted him," Ajen said slowly. "He had a treat in his pocket—but you can't think he would . . ."

"He certainly might have killed the dog if it slowed the production of his rival's next film." Perveen shook her head, unable to hide her contempt for the self-serving young man. "Why are you even pretending to be interested in the success of Champa Films? You have so many outside interests."

"I don't understand, Mr. Biswas," Mr. Dass interjected. "Do you work at a film studio? I thought you were a journalist."

"Yes, I am a cameraman, screenwriter, and occasional actor. I thought film would be my future," Ajen confided with a wistful air. "But I do not have as much freedom of artistic expression as I hoped, and the salary is unstable. Hence, I'm also a newspaper columnist."

Perveen asked, "I suppose you are on Chatterjee's payroll, too?"

Ajen shook his head vehemently. "I'm not. Although I suppose you will be telling Subhas everything about this, and then he'll make a complaint to the Bengali newspaper, and I'll lose my writing job, too!"

"You know that I'm duty bound to help him." She struggled

for the next sentence because she felt at risk of causing Ajen to storm off. "The conflict Subhas carries is with Chatterjee, not you. And I think you might know things about all sorts of people's activities that could help clear Subhas of the murder charge."

"Hardly. It seems that nothing I do matters!" he complained shrilly. "As long as Mr. Becker is at the camera, nobody else gets to rise. It will be European American cinema to the end. I may as well write my column about all sorts of people and events. I was given a chance with this paper because it's new and they needed a cinema critic for this city."

"Come now, young man. Everyone knows that Bengalis are India's best artists and writers," Dass reassured. "Your writing is greatly enjoyed!"

She couldn't hear Ajen's reply because of the sudden blaring of traditional music, empowered with a drum.

"This must be the celebration procession!" Mr. Dass exclaimed.

Coming through the door was a procession of about six Indian men. With their lower parts draped in white dhotis and their bare chests wreathed in blossoms, they looked like worshippers, except for the man in front of them, who was carrying a placard that said, "Best Tickets! Buy Early!"

"Profit in the guise of religion," Perveen said with contempt.

"You turn up your nose at it, but it works!" Ajen shot back.

"So, if you aren't being paid, what is ABC giving you in return for giving him access to the estate and its staff workers? I don't suppose it's an early ticket to their show?"

Perveen spoke jestingly, although the situation was serious. And from Ajen's silence, she guessed that he understood the seriousness of the situation.

More people were coming through the hotel's doors, forking in two directions, some for the ticket salesman, and others for the pandal itself. Looking at them, Perveen shook her head.

"So now *The Warrior Queen* is getting press that will overcome *Queen of Hearts*."

"I had nothing to do with how ABC chooses to advertise."

"But then why did you come here today?" Perveen prodded.

The parade was attracting attention, with some of the courtyard diners clapping and cheering. Other people rushed forward to get close. Perveen stood rooted because a new man had appeared in the midst of the parade: Chatterjee. Dressed in a white dhoti and a formal jacket, he was wreathed in marigolds and had a smudge of white ash on his forehead, as if he'd just been blessed at a temple.

Chatterjee did not see them, because he was speeding toward the ticket seller and speaking in his ear.

More crowds followed, and waiters rushed around to the tables serving drinks and food. Perveen felt torn. She'd come to the hotel in the first place in order to speak to Chatterjee, but this moment in front of so many people wasn't the fitting time. As she turned toward the door, she saw that there was a new, thick ring of people blocking the way. They moved in a slow formation toward the center of the hotel, their progress blocked by people jumping up from the tables to insert their way into them. Perveen caught her breath at the sight of a slim woman in a sky-blue dress spangled in silver who was lightly holding the arm of Master Nishant.

Her eyes were heavily ringed with kohl, and her rouged lips parted in an inviting smile as she walked smoothly along. What a difference from the last time Perveen had seen her on the island.

"Is that Miss Patience Cooper, the actress playing Durga? She looks like a true goddess!" Mr. Dass was staring, enraptured, just like everyone else.

"No, it's the missing actress, Rochana," Perveen told him. And what a dramatic entrance she had created. But so many questions remained. Was Nishant with her because he'd always known, and come to her rescue? Or had Alice brought her back and not said anything about it?

## 28

## FALLING STARS

"So, Bombay's beloved star is back in our skies," Ajen exclaimed from the other side of Perveen. "I'd call that throwing a bombshell on the festivities, wouldn't you?"

"You sound almost triumphant," Perveen said, looking into his gloating face. "Did you know that she was safe all along?"

Ajen put a hand to his lips. "Of course not. I feared we had lost her forever."

"I would normally have been in the library at this hour and missed everything. What a lucky moment!" Mr. Dass looked to Perveen for agreement, but she couldn't smile. From the elegant appearance of Rochana, she guessed she'd returned to Pearl Villa to bathe, dress, and make up. But the question remained: Why would Rochana appear with Master Nishant, rather than Subhas, who, after all, was living free until his trial?

Maybe Subhas thought her appearance with Nishant was a way to disrupt ABC's event. Another possibility was that Rochana had caught wind of the budding romance between her husband and Marisa, and therefore cut him out of her big moment.

Perveen craned her head, searching through the crowd, but she didn't see him or anyone else from the company. The crowd was going wild, cheering and coming to cluster around Rochana, who waved them off.

"Rochana always wants to be noted by the press," Ajen said into her ear. "This must be why she's come!"

Hans Becker's words about seeing Ajen walking around outdoors after the film party came back to her. She said to Ajen, "This really is a perfect story for the Owl."

"Oh, I know when the story is better told by someone else," he said, looking steadily at her.

"So you're a secret keeper—for a lot of people, including Rochana?" She couldn't help thinking that the young man who clearly prized being of value to the studio could have been involved in the death of Morgan.

"I rarely speak to Rochana," Ajen protested, but his words sounded hollow.

Perveen scanned the crowd again and saw that Chatterjee had left the ticket stand and was furiously regarding the photographer beckoning Rochana to pose with the pandal behind her.

As if to change the subject from Rochana, Ajen pointed at the sight. "ABC is gobsmacked. Maybe he thinks Rochana's done away with his precious star Patience Cooper!"

"It's not a time for joking," Perveen reprimanded, although it felt like sweet justice to see Chatterjee receive a comeuppance.

Perveen watched ABC's furious eyes travel from his film ticket stand, where nobody was buying, toward the mobbed star who'd left his studio. If she could take him aside, she imagined it would be an excellent moment to convince him to drop his insistence on getting Rochana back to his studio.

But before she could move, there was a new surge of excitement in the crowd; another important arrival to the hotel. She saw a second lovely woman coming through the door, smiling and nodding at her applauding audience.

"As you were just saying, Mr. Dass—here's the one who's supposed to be here: Miss Patience Cooper." Ajen clapped his hands together. "What will two wildcats do when confined to the same courtyard?"

Patience Cooper was a lissome woman with fair skin, dyed black hair, and a beauty that was strikingly similar to Rochana's. She had swanned in a jet-beaded black dress, surrounded by an entourage of men, both European and Indian, all dressed in black tie. She approached the pandal quickly, waving to people at the tables, who began clapping. A free show. Then, she stopped dead as she saw Rochana.

Rochana merely smiled, her teeth gleaming white against her plum lipstick. Taking her hand, she pressed it coyly against her mouth and blew Patience a kiss.

"The greatest stars of Indian cinema, pose together, please!" a photographer called out.

Chatterjee shook his head, no longer the center of his concocted drama, and proceeded toward the far edge of the courtyard, where a flight of marble steps led upward.

"I'm going up to talk to him," Perveen said aloud to Ajen and Dass. "It won't be a minute!"

"But why?" Dass said. "Everything exciting is happening right here. We are both observing and making the news for tomorrow's newspapers!"

But now was the time to approach Chatterjee about his onsite presence at Champa Films, a fact that could lead the police to him.

As Perveen climbed the stairs, one hand on the railing and the other holding the edge of her sari, she felt an urgency to confront him. She could see him move away from the stairs, heading down the hall. If he disappeared without her having seen his room door, she would lose the opportunity.

"Hello there, ABC!" she called out quickly in a happy tone.

He turned, a polished smile on his face, ready for the film fan or journalist who'd pursued him for a quote. But as Perveen drew closer to him, he recognized her, and his face hardened. "I told you to send your father to speak to me."

"If you wanted Rochana back working, and she's right downstairs, why are you running away?" Perveen challenged.

Folding his arms across his chest, he stared her down. "She's trying to ruin my show and make trouble for Patience. I won't be part of it."

Seizing the advantage, she said, "So, you don't want Rochana to work for you anymore, then? It seems a rather wise idea—"

He shook a finger at her. "I've no reason to talk to you about what I want. Go!"

"But you are quite a person of interest to me." Perveen advanced up the stairs slowly. "You were on the property when the dog was poisoned. And you came back the night of the party, didn't you?"

His expression was stern, but his hands were trembling. "You're speaking nonsense. Go home!"

She had reached almost the top step, and from where he was on the landing, he flung out his arm. "Go away!"

She stepped back to protect herself and suddenly felt herself slipping.

Her right foot hadn't found the surface it expected and instead was starting to slip off the stair. As she struggled to balance, the stiff silk of her sari fought against her feet.

She would fall.

She was falling.

It was all so fast—*faster than a film stunt*, she thought. Why couldn't she grab the handrail?

ABC's face receded as she tumbled backward. Somewhere, she heard a woman scream, just as she felt a sharp twist to her left shoulder and back.

She'd landed: not to the faraway floor, but somewhere along the staircase. At the same time, she felt a whoosh of air and saw a glimpse of blue-and-silver spangles pass by. Rochana was heading upstairs.

Perveen tried to call out for Rochana that it was pointless to speak with ABC, but her voice was no longer there. And she felt strange; like there was a ringing in her ears, a voice telling her something else. She reached out to one of the strangers who'd come up to surround her, but suddenly realized she couldn't move her arm.

She saw men's faces around her and saw herself rising in the air. *Surely I'm not dead,* she thought as they began carrying her. No, it was not a funeral shroud around her but a tablecloth; she could even see an oil stain on it. But then she wasn't sure: *Awake or dreaming?*

## 29

## A BAD BREAK

A day later, Perveen was startled to awaken in Sir J. J. Hospital. The tablecloth was no longer wrapped around her body. When she moved her head, she caught a glimpse of white sheets, and a strange blue cotton gown covering her shoulders.

"Hello? Is anyone there?" she spoke aloud. She heard the sound of a scraping chair and then saw Jamshedji rising up from the room's corner to come forward with a wide smile. But as her father kissed her forehead, she saw deep lines of worry etched on either side of his mouth.

"So. You are awake." And then he told her what happened—that she had a broken arm and a possible concussion from a dreadful fall at Green's Hotel. The police were inclined to think the fall an accident, something that frustrated him.

"But he didn't break my arm. I fell," Perveen said, because at least she had that memory.

"Chatterjee hit you—a clear assault. An action that contributed to an accident that could have been fatal." Jamshedji rattled off the offenses in a staccato fashion. "It's possible that you have suffered a concussion. At the very least, a broken arm affects your health and, temporarily, your livelihood!"

She considered what he was saying. "It's true that a solicitor needs a working hand to write. But I can still speak with people, and I will be walking about soon—" After he cut himself off, she felt anxious. "I hope you're not thinking of suing him for my injury. It will complicate the current state of affairs!"

Jamshedji patted her shoulder. "A civil suit is certainly a possibility any father would think about, when the police fail to see the damage done to his daughter. But I want you to rest and gain strength before you worry about another thing!"

If she wasn't working, it would build evidence for a civil case. But that small, possible gain would eclipse the serious matter at hand. "Please, Pappa. You know that if I lie around here not working, you'll fall behind schedule on the work trying to build Subhas's defense." His face was stony, so she added, "Let me at least tell you the thoughts I have."

"But you're not prepared," he said, the concern deepening on his face. "You had a severe break and were in deep shock. You've awakened after more than twenty-four hours here."

"But I'm fine!" Speaking rapidly, to avoid further interruption, she said, "I hadn't fully debriefed with you about my time with ABC, and then my conversation with Ajen Biswas. ABC lured Pearl Villa's essential staff away to build up the pandal in the hotel in the time leading up to and during Subhas's big party. And Chatterjee also entered onto the Pearl Villa premises at least twice, making him a suspect in the sudden death of Rochana's dog. He certainly might have encountered Morgan, who was also a thorn in his side."

"Worth pursuing," Jamshedji said. "But the trouble is, he could claim we are framing him because of the claim he's trying to make against Subhas for employing Rochana. It all could look very silly in court—especially if we throw in the homicide of a dog named Bubbles!"

"I can write a legal brief in a very serious manner," Perveen said. "That is, if I could dictate to a secretary. Tell me, what is going on now with Subhas and Rochana?"

Jamshedji clasped his hands and smiled. "They are once again living together as man and wife, so there is every hope for stabilization of the studio."

"But that sounds like an announcement for the press! What about the close attachment Subhas was recently showing with Marisa?"

Jamshedji leaned forward and spoke in a more confidential tone. "That was nothing serious. Apparently, Marisa had been hanging near Subhas because she was frightened by Joe Morgan's behavior at the party. That's what Subhas said to me, and he offered her some comfort when at her place that evening."

"The word 'comfort' could cover a multitude of activities," Perveen said sarcastically. "The more important thing is whether Marisa and Nishant and Subhas will all honestly confirm for the police their whereabouts that night."

"Subhas feels such an admission of going to an actress's cottage for several hours is too damaging for his reputation—and it could put the situation with Rochana's homecoming at risk," Jamshedji said.

"Have the police questioned Rochana about whether anything happened between her and Mr. Morgan that night?"

"Not yet. And she hired her own lawyer to represent her, as I recommended, to prevent conflict of interest. She is fortunate: Her popularity has risen since she was photographed restraining Mr. Chatterjee at the top of the stairs."

"Sounds like a scene in a film, doesn't it? The first stunt is me falling, and the second stunt is Rochana knocking him down."

Jamshedji rolled his eyes just enough to show her he didn't approve of her cynicism. "The other important matter is that Hans and Subhas were called earlier today to the censor office to receive word of the board's decision. The board asked for just one small cut, and the film will be released as planned with the first screening this Saturday at the Imperial Theatre."

"I hope I'm out by then."

"Never mind about that," he said briskly. "Now, let me tell you a bit more about various employees at Champa Films."

He said that Ajen had agreed to testify that Chatterjee was on the grounds twice before the death of Morgan. And with no guards working the gate, that information could present a possible scenario that Chatterjee could have been there the night of the party and become embroiled in a confrontation with Morgan, who could very well have tried to solicit payment from him, too.

"All that falls apart if Chatterjee has a strong alibi for his whereabouts," Perveen said. "There are still some people like Asmaa I never got to properly interview."

"The housekeeper?" Jamshedji's voice rose, and then he shook his head. "She has no motive."

"I think Asmaa knows more about Rochana than others do—and Rochana seems unusually connected to her. The two of them take special care of the tiger. And do you remember that Rochana even mixed the cocktails for us when Asmaa couldn't? That's an unusual behavior reversal between mistress and servant."

"But Rochana makes drinks because she is worldly wise, a completely different sort of woman!" Jamshedji said.

Perveen felt instinctively irritated by her father's interpretation. "I'm not aware that Rochana has ever left India. And isn't it ironic that Rochana isn't being charged by the police for hitting Chatterjee, while he is being charged with causing my accident?"

"The difference is that Rochana is Bombay's sweetheart—and ABC is not."

The new male voice snapped Perveen's attention toward the door. Subhas Ghoshal was standing there, holding a bouquet of marigolds. He had likely overheard at least the last few sentences. Hans Becker was standing slightly behind him.

"Hello, sir! Thank you for the flowers," Perveen said, adjusting the covers to hide her hospital gown.

"She will find water for those blooms," Jamshedji said, rising from his chair and looking at the nurse who'd accompanied them in. "Let's get another chair for you, my good man."

Jamshedji took a commanding position, standing near the head of her bed, urging Subhas to take his vacated chair. Hans waited, sitting down gingerly on the extra chair the nurse brought. The three men filled up the small space of the patient room; Perveen was no longer at ease.

"You did too much for us!" Subhas said, looking at Perveen.

Feeling apprehensive, she asked the filmmaker, "How so?"

"I mean that you should not have gone to such lengths to help," Subhas said, looking rueful. "Your terrible injury was in pursuit of ABC, and that makes me feel quite guilty for putting you in the kind of jeopardy Rochana used to suffer."

"Thank you for your concern, but I am recovering quite well," Perveen said, putting it in mind to remind him later not to use the word "guilty" so freely.

"We came because we learned your father was here. We have good news, and both of you can hear it."

"Oh?" Perveen's spirits raised.

"The censor board reviewed our film early, thanks to the grace of God." Subhas raised his hands heavenward. "They asked for one small cut, which we will make—and then the film is free to be shown throughout India and worldwide!"

"I'm so glad!" Perveen beamed at him. "But what scene was cut?"

"Part of the crocodile scene was judged too graphically violent. We will not be able to show the actor's head disappearing into the jaws," Subhas said.

"Oh. I thought it was an artificial crocodile in close-up?"

"Yes—a large puppet," Hans Becker added. "But that did not matter. Fortunately, our existing footage shot at a distance, of a crocodile rising and grabbing the villain, was allowed."

"We plan to open this weekend at the Imperial," Subhas said. "What a relief that is. And seven distributors will be sending

*Queen of Hearts* on a tour of almost one hundred tent theaters nationally. Our largest ever," Subhas said. "It should clear all our debts and perhaps give enough money to buy a bit of land to the north to make a studio."

"After the trial," Jamshedji said, giving him a cautionary look. "We still have that on the horizon. Best not to put the cart before the horse, isn't it?"

Subhas gave his typical, careless shrug, but Hans Becker nodded soberly, as if he was looking at the situation more realistically than the studio owner. And this made her want to ask him about the final piece. Glancing at both her father and Subhas, she asked, "Could I have a moment alone with Mr. Becker?"

Subhas raised his eyebrows, and Jamshedji glared as if she'd made an etiquette breach.

"I would rather not speak about the company without Subhas here," Hans said, and his eyes bored into her.

Perveen was startled. Did he see Subhas as his prime defender—or did he think she would be afraid to bring up something confidential? Maybe he thought she was covertly trying to get information about Subhas or Rochana.

"All right, then," Perveen said. "I only wondered if you'd thought any more about the conversation you had with Joe Morgan during the party. I remember you telling me that you'd try."

"I would tell you what I know," Hans said, "but it was such a wild night. I was very busy taking pictures of people and answering all kinds of questions."

"He said a word that I first thought was an insult."

"Yes, he was very rude!" Hans looked at Subhas for confirmation, and the filmmaker wrinkled his nose.

"He mentioned Schneidemühl. Does that mean anything to you?"

Hans looked quizzical. "In German, 'Schneide' means tailor. And 'Mühle' means mill."

"I've also heard that Schneidemühl is the name of a town in

Prussia which was controlled by Germany during the war," Perveen said. "A town where a prisoner camp was set up. There's a chance it's where Joe Morgan spent his war years."

"Ah!" Subhas said. "So Morgan might have been unfairly blaming Hans for his past misery! All on the basis of a Swiss man sounding like a German."

Hans's cheeks flushed, and he added, "The Swiss have a dialect. Germans say the Swiss don't speak properly."

"Just as there are so many dialects in India," Jamshedji chimed in.

"I think he's explained it well enough," Subhas said, looking meaningfully at Perveen.

"So tell me, what is the future of Indian films, then?" Jamshedji said in a jovial voice, looking toward Subhas. Clearly, he was trying to steer the conversation back to general topics.

"Indian theaters still mostly screen American pictures; but brilliant Indian films will surely dominate in a few years. As long as you can keep me out of prison, Champa Films will be part of this magic."

"I think the case against you is weak," Jamshedji said emphatically. "If we can catch a few more details about Morgan—perhaps relating to his drug debts—I'm sure we can put doubt in the judge's mind. That is the reason Perveen asks so many probing questions—she wants to understand Morgan's past in Germany—and perhaps his time in Calcutta will also be important."

Perveen knew from her father's words the mission was to put both men at ease. After all, they'd come as a kindness to her. Smiling, she said, "Now that Rochana's back home, has she resumed work in your company?"

"We've talked about her writing more stories and training up the younger starlets like Marisa to take primary roles," Subhas said. "I was surprised to find her interest in documentary films. It will be a small challenge in getting the investors not to mind seeing her name on the marquee for all our films, but I'm confident we can do it."

His cautious statement made Perveen wonder if Rochana truly was tired of acting. Or was it a matter of him pushing Marisa forward? Subhas privately could be quite angry about Rochana's secret exit to the island.

"Documentaries will be cheaper to make, because of their shorter length and lack of salaried actors," Hans added. "A top studio should be able to provide a mix of films."

"Quite true," Subhas said. "And even after you return to Europe, our studio will have benefited from the lighting techniques and camera work you've taught Ajen and me."

"What's this about Europe? Are you leaving Champa Films?" Perveen said, looking at Hans.

After a quick glance at Subhas, Hans said, "I'm not sure where I'll land, but I feel wanderlust to take my camera to yet another world. And Ajen is already well trained and happy to take over."

"Do you think he's a strong enough cinematographer?" Perveen was still thinking about Ajen's double-dealings with ABC.

"But of course. He is an excellent talent," Subhas said.

Perveen looked at Jamshedji, wondering if he hadn't explained to the studio owner exactly what Ajen had done.

"Later," Jamshedji said, and she understood the message meant for her.

"Yes, let's go now," Hans said, rising from his chair. "We have tired her too much."

"Thank you very much for coming." Perveen watched them say goodbye and then turned to her father when they were alone. "What do you think?"

"I will tell Subhas privately about Ajen. Maybe he could get Becker to stay a bit longer. I can certainly understand why he wants to leave now, having experienced trouble at this studio. He will have more artistic freedom elsewhere."

"That could be," Perveen assented. "But maybe there's something else—I really do believe that Hans knows something about Morgan's past he's afraid to tell us."

"He's spoken about British government oppression—likely he's afraid of becoming involved in any kind of court case," Jamshedji said. "Our best option is to direct attention toward the gangsters mentioned by Mr. Fawcett. But given the population of our city, finding the particular miscreants will be like finding needles in a haystack."

"Very true." And though she wouldn't voice it to him, Perveen felt disinclined to spend energy on something that a judge might think irrelevant and refuse to include as part of a defense. Usually, the answer in a killing was more obvious.

Closer to home.

# 30

# THE GIFTS OF VISITORS

The next day, Colin and Alice came.

The pair of them appearing together would never raise any questions. But it was frustrating, because their joint appearance meant Perveen couldn't ask Alice deep questions about Rochana, nor could she tell Colin how much she loved him, and how afraid she was about losing the mobility not only of her arm, but her way of life. It struck her then that these two, both foreigners, had become like her sort of relatives. Although not to each other.

"I can't imagine why they haven't let you go home yet," Alice asked, bustling around looking for a place to set down the crystal vase of roses that she'd brought. "It's just a broken arm."

"I think they are watching for other possible developments," Perveen said. "Concussion, et cetera."

"I've brought you a pillow!" Colin pulled a tan silk-covered bolster out of a shopping bag and put it in her arms.

"My goodness. It's about the weight of Khushy when she was born, and it rattles—" She shook it lightly with her left hand.

"That's rice inside. It's an Indian pillow that can mold to you, your back, your neck, whatever you need."

Perveen came forward slightly so he could tuck the rigid pillow behind her and the bed's iron headboard. "Alice, whoever holds this wins the pillow fight."

"It's the film premiere tonight," Colin said. "Alice got her hands on tickets for Kitty Daboo and me. If only you could be there, Perveen."

"Well, I've seen it already." She didn't really want to go; but her curiosity couldn't stop her from inquiring of Alice, "How did you get the tickets?"

Alice gave a light snort. "Are you trying to find out if I'm speaking with Rochana?"

Perveen realized how easily Alice saw through her casual question. "I suppose so. I heard from Subhas the other day that she's very busy at the studio."

"She asked if she could ride horses with me one morning at the Turf Club," Alice said shortly. "So we did that, and afterward we had another talk about how—how things could be going forward. She presented the tickets then. I think she intended for Mummy and Pa to be the ones attending, but I thought that would rather be rubbing their faces in a problem they'd rather forget."

Perveen guessed Alice was referring to the scandal of the overnight stay—or was it something more? In any case, Alice wouldn't reveal it in front of Colin.

"By the way," Alice said, "My father told me that Mr. Chatterjee tried to make a police complaint against Rochana for hitting him on your behalf. They laughed it off."

Perveen was grateful to Rochana for standing up for her—but that bit of aggression hadn't changed anything after the fateful tumble. "The trouble is, I'm not entirely sure what ABC did to me. He raised his arm, but after that, I don't remember anything other than tripping backward."

Alice looked incredulously at her. "Rochana said everyone saw it happen. Hearing what we've said—reading the newspapers—don't you feel furious and enraged?"

"Everyone has their own reaction," Colin said quietly.

Perveen wondered if Rochana's past—from her early days, up until the attack from Morgan—had given her the feeling that she had to save Perveen. She could have seen herself on those steps facing Chatterjee. But all she said was, "I don't feel angry. I wore a sari that didn't fit well and was difficult to move around in."

Alice interrupted, "Don't say these things in front of us! If there's a civil case, Colin might be called by ABC to testify as to what you said."

"You have really taken to heart all my lectures." Shifting against the hard pillow, Perveen smiled at her.

Alice rose from her seat in the chair closest to the bed. "I'm stepping out to the washroom for a long ten minutes."

"Thank you very much, Alice," Colin said with a grin.

"You're welcome. I can't count how many times you've been my beard!" She winked at him before swinging out the door.

"What was she saying? Is it a new slang?" Colin asked Perveen after Alice had gone off, quietly closing the door behind her.

"Beard means a cover-up or disguise," Perveen said. "When you go with her to parties as an escort, it appears to others—including her parents—that you have a fondness for each other. Alice and I saw the ways in which this misunderstanding benefited her, as well as you and me. But it also created misunderstanding."

"Yes, you're right." Colin slipped into one of the guest chairs and leaned down to kiss her for a long, delicious stretch. When they parted, he said, "To be able to still have you here seems like such a gift. I'm shocked about what happened to you. I keep thinking: if only I had been there at Green's Hotel!"

Perveen put up her good hand in protest. "Please don't tell me you would have been like a cinema hero engaging in fisticuffs!"

Colin shook his head. "You can control a lot, Perveen. Yet you cannot stop me from feeling the way I do."

"I won't try." Perveen stretched her left arm up to pull him down for a kiss, one that lasted all the time until they heard Alice's light knock on the door.

AFTER HER FRIENDS left, she took dinner and then dreamed about the marble staircase at Green's Hotel. Instead of leading to guest rooms, it was leading into clouds, and she felt anxious that she couldn't make it all the way. There was a figure at the top: not ABC, but a taller man, fair in color, though she could not see his face. He wore long white robes that reminded her of her religion's founder, Zarathustra. But he had no head covering; she knew it wasn't him.

She awakened gently to the sound of steps in her room. Someone was in the room, perhaps a nurse.

"Hello?" she said, and then the wall light was switched on.

"Excuse me. I didn't know you'd be asleep." Hans Becker spoke quickly.

Perveen blinked to adjust her eyes toward the light. Hans looked strange, because he was wearing a long white coat like a doctor's. He looked ghastly in the bright light, and the hollows under his eyes seemed to have deepened since she'd last saw him.

"What time is it?" She squinted at the distant clock. "Does it say a quarter past twelve?"

He didn't answer, and she suddenly noticed that he was holding the heavy pillow that Colin had brought her. Hadn't that been at the foot of her bed? She had a sudden misgiving about things; his strange costume, the late hour, the fact that he'd been inside her room with no light on.

The bell for the nurse was on the table on the left side of her bed, near her working arm, but if she reached for it, he could easily stop her. Even if she did try to ring the bell, its noise could be smothered quickly with the pillow—and then, he could use the pillow on her.

Nishant had spoken about finding Hans weeping in his cottage the night of Morgan's death. She'd questioned whether the actor was right about thinking it was about trouble between his daughter and the cinematographer. Now she felt even more strongly that Hans had something to hide.

As if watching a film, she saw the upcoming scenes. After Hans had suffocated her, he would walk through the hospital in his white coat like any other physician. Outside, he'd abandon the coat. He'd get his papers and leave the country like everyone was expecting him to do. Her death would be inexplicable: perhaps related to something happening internally that hadn't been diagnosed.

The crystal vase with marigolds was also on the same table. From under the sheets, she edged her body toward it, but as she did, he moved closer, too.

How could she manage it with just one working hand? Impossible.

Hans was leaning over her, so close that she could smell his breath, a mixture of tobacco and sharp, stinking alcohol. His eyes were somewhere on the wall. He was trying to detach.

"Please," she said. "Please don't—"

He breathed in and seemed poised to act. Then he exhaled and stepped back. "I'm sorry."

He seated himself in the guest chair, keeping the pillow on his lap. Was this because he knew she'd figured him out and was trying to convince her otherwise? She summoned up a scream, but it came out weakly, like a deep sigh.

"I wanted to speak with you alone, but you have visitors almost every hour. That is why I'm so late."

"Oh." She could barely manage the next part. "Is there something you wish to talk about?"

"I—I—" He fell silent for a moment. "Why are you so interested in Schneidemühl?"

He was waiting for an answer. Trying to sound calm, she said, "I heard the word spoken aloud, as I've already told you. And then I saw a book that had the place name spelled out."

"What book?" His voice was sharp. "Where is it?"

"It was recently published." Her mouth was dry. "Photographs of many places and people. It won't be going into the Asiatic Society Library, though."

"But you still saw it. Who took the photographs?" He spoke casually, but she saw that his body had gone tight and still.

"The section pictures were not . . . attributed." Getting the words out had been tricky, with her decreased breathing. Seeing his face tighten, she went on. "I think . . . you were the photographer? But how . . ."

"Why should I tell you? Ever since you started working for Subhas, there's been trouble!" His words tumbled out after each other, a torrent of panic.

The longer she kept Hans talking, the greater the likelihood a nurse or orderly might notice the light and open the door. She spoke lightly. "Were you traveling through Schneidemühl as a photographic journalist?"

"Not traveling through—staying there." He stayed silent for a while, but eventually said: "It was a military job. I'd been a filmmaker, and becoming an army photographer, taking pictures of prisoners and their activities, saved me from the front."

She had the sense that he'd held everything in for so long that it was a relief to unburden himself. And now she understood why Joe Morgan had recognized him.

"What else did you have to do?"

"I didn't ever hurt anyone." His tone was still aggressive, as if in reaction to the implication he'd killed Morgan. "I followed orders about photo assignments. Some photos were for record-keeping about inmates, and others were used for pamphlets that our planes dropped over the British troops."

"Everyone believes you are Swiss." She hoped this would reassure him; bring him back to the present.

"After the war, I arrived in Switzerland, and they gave me citizenship."

"That was fortunate," she said, filling the gap. It would have been hard for a German to be admitted to British India.

"A Swiss passport meant Pathé Studios in France hired me. Pathé brought me to India as an associate cinematographer for one of their films, and I happened to meet Subhas. He heard from me how I loved this country and offered me the spot as the lead cinematographer for his new film company." Hans seemed to be relaxing, now that he was speaking of the present. "Anyone would have joined him. India was a fantasy of colors and joyful people."

This was the timeworn foreigners' description of the country, but she chose not to fault him for it. When people stepped into a world that seemed happier than their previous place, it could feel like a magical transformation. She could point to Colin, for certain. And Alice's journey to India had brought her a prestigious academic role she might never have had in England. Not to mention Kitty. She ventured, "Have you felt peace here?"

"Not entirely. But I was grateful to do the work I love."

"And then, Joe Morgan showed up. Please tell me what he said to you . . . the truth."

Hans cleared his throat and then spoke.

"Morgan said he remembered I took his picture when he was raking filth from the latrines. He said that he had become a film censor and was part of the police. And that if I didn't pay him, he would expose me as a . . . war criminal." The last words were choked out, as if each one came with a knife stab.

Perveen felt the pain, too. She knew what it was like to be trapped, and to have people in power who would only make things worse if one spoke up. "He knew you were vulnerable. And he was desperate for money—extorting others beside you." Perveen thought about the two hundred rupees that should have been found in Joe Morgan's pocket, instead of one hundred. Why?

"Hans—I heard that you went forward and paid the villa workers with one hundred rupees for their back wages. It was a generous thing to do." Because he didn't acknowledge the compliment, she asked, "Was it the money that you found on Morgan?"

He was still for a long moment, and then said, "I only took half of what he had. Subhas thought it was necessary to delay paying the staff, but I saw them growing desperate. It made me sick to know that Morgan could do whatever he liked."

"Did you know that Germans are still being held in prisoner-of-war camps just outside the city?" he interrupted, his voice low and enraged. "Even after the peace treaty was signed."

"How can they?"

"Ask your English friend whose father is so high up," he said bitterly. "When I realized she might become close to things, I was rather worried. I didn't know coming to work in India would be a risk for me—and that is why I must go, leaving no record, of course."

"Does Subhas know about your past in Germany?"

He shook his head. "Subhas wouldn't have hired me because he operates in British India and could not put his company at risk. But I felt I couldn't live with the uncertainty as the prosecutors keep working. They are set on finding Morgan's killer."

Perveen felt chilled as she saw him circling back to the reason he'd come. He'd planned to eliminate her. "I really didn't put two and two together about Schneidemühl until you spoke to me. Really, what you need is your own legal representation . . ."

"To kill a British government employee means hanging. I've done the act that I tried so hard to avoid during the war. I disgust myself."

"It was such an odd way that he died," Perveen said. "Seemed like a series of accidents, really."

"I've thought about it a lot and written something down." He pulled a small envelope from his jacket pocket and held it toward her.

He'd come with the intention of killing her because he believed she was close to uncovering the truth of his shared past with Joseph Morgan. What was the note about—his reason for killing her? Why would he do such a thing, to raise attention, when he still needed to escape India?

"There is light. You can read it," he said when she didn't take it. Her pulse raced as he opened the letter and leaned forward to place it in her right hand.

"Can't you read it?" he said.

After she read it, he would kill her. Feeling nauseated, Perveen picked up the letter with her left hand and brought it close in order to decode his curling script. Hans had written an account of the night of the party. He described the conversation with Morgan in almost the same words he'd said aloud to her. Then she reached the part that mattered: his account of departing the villa at eleven o'clock and heading toward the cottages.

*Ahead of me I saw a man, stumbling like a drunk. Coming closer, I recognized the striped suit and knew it was Joseph Morgan. He must have heard me because he turned and spoke my name. I didn't want an encounter so I changed my path, avoiding the cottages to go into the zoo. My idea was to get away by running through the cages and out the back, and then on to my home. But he followed me, screaming my name. I stayed in place near the gate because I wanted the shouting to cease in order that others wouldn't hear him.*

*Morgan came up close and threatened me with angry words. He said the problem of my past would be exposed unless I paid him four hundred rupees. I said to him that I didn't have such money—that nobody was taking salary until the film was released. He said that he would make sure the film was approved quickly and that when the money came from the first box office weekend, I could get it from the company. To this, I didn't answer, because I knew I must speak with Subhas. Then Morgan swung his fist toward me. I blocked it and then hit him in the stomach. Then he fell into a small ditch, landing on his face.*

"Morgan drowned in water," Perveen said, shooting a look at Hans. "An accidental fall into this ditch?"

His eyes were on his own hands, twisting in his lap. "Just read it."

*When Morgan had been close to me earlier, I'd seen the edge of some papers in his breast pocket. I looked because I was worried that he might have written down my name. But the paper was around a clip of two hundred-rupee notes. I took one hundred rupees to pay the overdue wages of the house staff. The next morning, early, I gave the money to Vikas, one of the Pearl Villa workers. I told him it was for everyone's back pay. Vikas was grateful to accept and said he would have everyone working again.*

*I apologize to the family of Joseph Morgan for his death. I was told by so many in my country that the war was necessary to save Germany. Mr. Morgan also heard the war was necessary to defend Britain. However, war makes prisoners of us all.*

"Just one thing," Perveen said after coming to the end of the account. "In your words, there was a single blow from you, and he did not get up again."

He nodded, but did not answer.

Perveen remembered the scrapes on his hands when she'd seen him the day after the death. "And to get the money from his breast pocket, wouldn't you have had to lift him?"

"Not lifting," Hans corrected. "I turned him, I took a bit of money, and I put the rest back. As you know, the police found it."

Perveen did not think it was as simple. When she'd seen Morgan, his face was not turned to the side.

"Are you leaving India because you fear being charged with assault and robbery?" she asked.

"The coroner's court verdict was homicide." His voice shook as he said it. "The detectives are hunting a man they think is a—a cold-blooded killer."

On the contrary, she thought it was manslaughter. But the

prosecutor could argue that it was an act of sedition. Hans's original German nationality would make it a very easy argument for them. "The thing is—his face was in the mud. There was more water there that night, wasn't there?"

Silence stretched between them.

"Yes," he said heavily. "He was alive when I took the money—I saw his eyes move. But I let him stay with his face in the ground. I heard him choke, but I didn't move my hand. All too soon, it was over."

"It is very brave of you to tell me," Perveen said, looking up.

"Madness, really." His voice was bleak as he reached out to retrieve the letter.

Perhaps she really had gone too far. Heart thumping, she spoke. "When you were in the room earlier—holding the pillow—was your intent to kill me?"

"I came wearing the coat from our costume collection," he said, touching the white lapel. "I didn't want to have anyone question me. Yes, I was afraid of what you could do. But when you opened your eyes, I saw the fear in them. Your fear was as great as mine. And it made me feel very sick. I couldn't."

Perveen hoped that his last words were sincere. It seemed that way—but if he had premeditated enough to wear the doctor's coat, he might still go through with the plan.

"I am a Catholic, and I grew up with confession each week," Morgan continued. "Yet nothing I ever said to one of those stern priests was as hard as what I just said in this hospital room."

"You were honest," Perveen said, still feeling on edge. As if she had any more way to dissuade him, she added, "I thank you for your mercy. And like I said, I do want to help you speak with a lawyer, if you are willing. It's not a hopeless case!"

"Goodbye, Miss Mistry. Thank you for listening. I know that your account will be believed."

"I will certainly repeat what you've told me, if you wish. Anything, Hans—"

Hans Becker shook his head, giving her a brief half smile. Then he turned, quietly opening the closed door as he stepped through. The door stayed open, and she could hear the rhythm of his swift footsteps until they finally faded away.

HE'D LEFT THE room's central light on. With the brightness, it took a long while for her breathing to slow and for her to decide what to do. When a nurse eventually came to switch off the light, she knew she should have told her about Hans. But she was no longer in danger. And she wanted to make sure he had legal representation. Her senses settled as she thought about this, and she slept.

When she awoke, the sun was shining through the sheer curtains in the room, and Jamshedji was sitting in the visitor's chair next to the bed. She readied herself to tell her father about the dangerous midnight visit, but he spoke first.

"Good morning to you, my dear. I bring serious news from the studio. I wanted to tell you before you read it in the papers."

She felt herself tense. "Are Subhas and Rochana all right?"

"Yes. But I'm very sad to say"—he broke off, slightly choking—"that Mr. Hans Becker was discovered dead in the darkroom this morning."

A chill ran through her as she remembered how he'd declined her help the night before. He was so desperate that he'd moved from wanting to take someone else's life to ending his own. Or had he? Haltingly, she asked if he knew any more details.

"Becker had vomited, so poisoning is suspected. He had wrapped himself in one of the white backdrops used for filming, as if he anticipated the sickness and didn't want to make a mess." Jamshedji's voice was heavy with grief. "There were several open bottles of chemicals, and a half-filled glass. Subhas said that there was also a sealed envelope. He knew enough not to open it, just to give it to the police."

"I think it might be suicide," she said. "I can also guess the content of the letter Hans left."

"And why is that?"

"Hans came here a little after midnight and showed me a confessional letter about what happened between him and Mr. Morgan. Then he took it with him."

Slowly, she told her father about Hans's nocturnal visit, including his halting admission that he had caused Morgan's death. "My questions drew him out more than he expected, and it moved him away from the initial thought of hurting me—in order to cover up," she added, sensing Jamshedji's alarm. "Nothing happened but a long conversation. And by the end of it, no matter what I said about helping him legally, he thought he had no possibility of a future. I wish I'd convinced him."

"I shan't allow you to take blame for it!" Jamshedji interjected. "He was very likely facing a death sentence for his actions toward a policeman. He chose to end his days in an easier way than festering in the government's jails and then meeting a hangman."

"I want people to understand the strain he was under—and how he made some very hard choices—including letting me live on as a witness. Please, will you take notes on what I remember about his visit? I want it all to be very clear for the police."

Jamshedji sighed and bent to open the legal case he'd carried in. Taking out his own notebook, he said, "The police do know that we are defending Subhas. For us to bring forward a confession from a man who's no longer living may not be taken seriously."

"If the envelope near his body holds the confession letter that was read to me here—there won't be any question." Perveen recalled the last quiet moments with Hans. "At first, I was annoyed he took it—but now I understand the importance of it being found with him. He staged everything perfectly, like the brilliant cinematographer that he was."

# 31

# A CHANCE TO HEAL

Two days later, jurors of the coroner's court unanimously agreed with a suicide finding in Hans Becker's death. The note he'd written was a key piece of evidence. The document was just as Perveen had read it, and was authenticated by her and the office of the prosecutor. The suicide note also led to a dismissal of all charges against Subhas Ghoshal. Mistry Law's work was seemingly closed.

Perveen learned through the papers that Subhas, Rochana, and their crew had celebrated with a ripping party at Green's Hotel. Alice was invited, but she demurred due to a prior dinner commitment at Kitty Daboo's home. A family dinner, Alice had told Perveen with satisfaction.

Perveen hated the minutiae involved in writing up bills, and this one was a doozy. The original retainer covered the cost of Rochana's contract trouble. Happily, it had been put to rest. Jamshedji had gone to meet ABC in person, and the producer, anxious over Perveen's condition and the threat of a civil suit, agreed to sign a document acknowledging that Rochana Ghoshal had left his company on good terms and had not violated any informal or formal employment agreements.

The rest of the bill went to cover the costs of representing Subhas in the matter of Joe Morgan's death—from Perveen's attendance at the party onward through the Green's Hotel accident, and Jamshedji's work at bail and coroner's court and the prosecutor. Three hundred and twenty rupees seemed a massive amount—but when Perveen eventually brought the bill to Subhas at Pearl Villa, he didn't seem shocked.

"A drop from the bucket," he said, counting out rupee notes for what he owed her—as well as payment for the prior bad check. "Our box office returns are outstanding, and we have new investors wishing to sponsor three more films."

"So, it looks as if we are settled up!" Perveen said as Rochana entered the library.

"I'm sure there will be more work ahead. Happier kinds of contracts." Rochana smiled at her, and Perveen wondered if Rochana had guessed how much Alice had told her about their misunderstanding. Today, Rochana was dressed in off-duty clothing; a pair of flowing men's trousers and a collared shirt that were sized just right for her slender frame.

"I would be honored to continue serving the studio." Perveen still felt unnerved by the death of Hans, but it was also true that she and her father had worked hard in a difficult situation. Rochana's husband, once accused, was now free.

"Are you in a rush to return to the city? I'd like to speak about something else." Rochana leaned against the bar, affecting a casual look.

Perveen felt a surge of excitement. Perhaps Rochana was ready to share with her the same secret she'd told Alice earlier. "Of course we can talk. Off the clock," she added to make them both chuckle.

"Ladies' talk is not my talk," Subhas said, smiling his goodbye and leaving the library.

"It's such good weather—what do you think about a walk on the property?" Rochana suggested.

"Why not? It's a treat to enjoy this splendid property without rain drenching everything. Let me leave the case with my driver, though."

After Perveen had left the locked legal case with Arman—as well as the unneeded instructions to guard it with his life—she rejoined Rochana, who was standing a bit farther down the drive.

"The driveway is so much nicer to walk on without mud puddles and police markings." She shot a glance at Perveen. "Was it the zoo gate where you found Joe Morgan?"

Perveen was startled for a moment but then remembered Rochana had been away during most of the investigation. "Yes. Do you want me to show you?"

"Please. My feelings—I can't quite understand them," Rochana said as they walked along toward the place. "I didn't like him, but I still grieve his death."

"I think—I think he would have been grateful for that," Perveen said. They were now standing at the zoo gate.

Rochana stared fixedly toward the cages holding animals, and then she spoke. "You've heard that Joe had been captured by the Germans and gone to stay in a camp for three brutal years. Afterward, he left Europe to come here to make his memories seem further away. But he still needed help, and that was alcohol and drugs. I sometimes think getting me was part of that escape."

Perveen considered the actress's words, spoken in such a gentle tone, and imagined the fear she must have had at being taken against her will. "Having a relationship with you must have made him feel powerful. So many other men saw you on the screen and could only dream of such moments."

Rochana pressed her lips into a wry half smile. "You compliment me too much. Joe had loved films as a young man before the war. During his imprisonment, he diverted himself replaying the films he had enjoyed—from Chaplin's comedies to *The Perils of Pauline*. He went to India as an ordinary police sergeant, so being given the chance at the censor office was too much of a dream come true. He couldn't act in a picture—but he could have an actress."

"And he also pushed producers to pay him bribes," Perveen added.

"ABC is someone I really don't know. First he was good to me, then he was like a dreadful bully, and now he's let me off." Rochana wrapped her arms around herself, as if for comfort. "I really don't have a sense of what ABC might have done if he met Joe again. Now that we're here, do you recall where exactly you found the body?"

"He was lying here, to the right," Perveen said, noting the way Rochana had deliberately changed the subject. "When I came upon the body, I thought it was Alice. At that moment, I felt like I'd lost everything."

"Oh, yes," Rochana said, pushing open the gate. "I know how you felt, because I feel the same. Come, let me show you the zoo."

They walked toward the deer, who danced delicately up to the pen's edge, as if looking for food, but Rochana passed by, her attention ahead.

Perveen recalled the caged tiger was just up the path. "How has Tora been, now that you're home?"

"Quite happy to be visited every day. Frankly, it's easier to count on her affections than those of Subhas," she said archly. "But I am staying busy. Ajen and I are working on the outline for a short documentary film about tigers."

"That sounds exciting! Can you tell me about it, or is it top secret?"

"The working title is *Tigers Must Be Loved*. It will start with footage of tigers roaming freely in the wild and then have footage of tigers fleeing cruel sportsmen. We haven't figured out everything, because as Ajen says, it's got to feel like a newsreel for people to believe it. We are fairly set on the film ending happily with me cuddling close with Tora. Tigers are really just big cats—they are not marauding killers, as the ignorant think."

"I, for one, would be happy never to see a tiger-skin rug again!" Perveen said.

"Yes—we pulled Mr. Nanporia's rug from the library and put it in storage," Rochana said wryly. "Now, would you like to properly meet Tora?"

Perveen walked alongside Rochana as she came up to the cage, cooing a greeting. The tiger, who'd been quietly lying in the back, padded forward. Rochana opened the cage and Tora ambled out, looking appraisingly at Perveen before making her way to rub against Rochana's leg.

Meeting a tiger on the loose was not what she'd anticipated. Trying not to meet the tiger's eyes, she calculated the distance between them. Three feet? What would happen if Tora decided she was a threat?

"You're frightened?" Rochana asked, seemingly in surprise.

"It's just that—without a leash, how do you control her?"

"Oh, she's absolutely tame! Would you like to pet her?" Rochana asked. "Or, I could ask Sridhar to bring some meat for you to feed to her. Then she'll really love you!"

Stepping back, Perveen bumped against the open cage door, and it made a dull clanging noise. Tora's head whipped toward the noise, and her throat rumbled.

"Tora was just afraid for a moment. She isn't going to bite you. She can tell when people are threats or safe. Just like any intelligent pet," Rochana added, with a casual laugh that reminded Perveen of Alice.

"Dogs are easier for me to pet than tigers," Perveen said. She was flooded with the initial unease she'd felt about Rochana and tried so many times to suppress. Perhaps Rochana truly did think she was a threat—and this was a strange sort of endgame.

"Go on then—look at the ducks. I'll join you after I've given Tora her snack."

Perveen walked to the duck pond, trying to still the shaking of her body. It had felt like a close call.

From a distance, she watched the well-built tiger and Rochana proceeding slowly together toward the zookeeper's shack, where Sridhar emerged with a bucket. Tora sat docilely, and Rochana dropped a piece of something from the bucket into her open jaws.

Perveen turned away from the toothy chomping and only began to relax while watching a small family of ducks swimming leisurely in a small pond. These were the kind of animals she would have enjoyed feeding, but she wasn't going to go over to Rochana and Sridhar while the tiger was loose.

At last, Rochana led Tora back to the cage and closed it up before strolling toward Perveen.

"You fed her very skillfully," Perveen acknowledged. "She does behave like a pet with you."

"Well, that she is," Rochana said shortly, as if disappointed by Perveen's abandonment. "Now, shall we go back to the villa? I'm not quite finished with what I need to share."

The two women strolled back up the drive, passing the parked Daimler, where Arman was napping across the front seat. All was as it should be. But as Perveen entered the house, she saw Asmaa in the back of the hall, watching her, and that reminded her of her own question for Rochana—something the lady might find offensive and that might break apart the fragile peace. But somehow, she needed to know. Delaying, she asked to use the washroom.

"Why not use the lav in the guest room upstairs? There's a very pretty flower arrangement I made there that I'd like you to see."

Perveen went in the marble bathroom where, on a side table, an arrangement of pink roses was entwined with Krishna Kamal flowers. Coming out, she found Rochana sitting on the velvet-covered stool by the dressing table. Feeling startled that Rochana had followed her up, she spoke quickly. "A beautiful bouquet. Are all the flowers from the property?"

"No, they come from a flower seller who's just beyond the gate. We can afford fresh flowers all the time again. Alice introduced me to the Krishna Kamal—she was wearing it in her buttonhole the night of the party. Go ahead, you can sit down on the bed."

As Rochana spoke, she looked innocent; but Perveen wondered how much Alice had shared of her own confidences.

Perveen settled uneasily on the edge of the bed. "Yes?"

"I adore this bedroom, which is why I wanted you and Alice to have it during the party," she said. "And I also keep some of my things here—you may have guessed that I sleep here from time to time."

"There are all sorts of marriages," Perveen said, hoping to soothe Rochana's nervousness. "Who's to say one can't benefit from a quiet night alone?"

"It's the British style for husband and wife to have separate rooms," Rochana's voice was firm. "Quite proper and safe. And what's good for the goose is also good for the gander."

Perveen wondered if she was hinting that she felt free to have her own love affairs.

"What does Asmaa think?"

"Why would you ask that?" Rochana asked sharply.

"She wanted me to give a message to you about Tora. I think she did that because she knew you had gone away but weren't killed." Perveen watched Rochana's rosebud lips tighten. "Did you tell her because she's like a mother to you?"

Rochana recoiled very slightly, but then she regained composure. "So you have noticed our resemblance?"

Perveen nodded, waiting for more.

"She raised me by herself until I went off to La Martinière to board—but she lived nearby and was at my side after I left school and my acting career started. But ABC said it was better for her to play my maid, which is why I call her by her first name."

"Does Subhas know?"

"I saw no reason to tell him, because he adores the story about my English military father and my Egyptian mother. Will you tell him?" Anxious violet-blue eyes bored into Perveen.

"It's a personal matter, nothing to do with the company."

Rochana blinked with relief. "There are many reasons I have to be grateful to you, but the most important one is Alice."

How could Alice be so angry, and Rochana just the opposite? Perveen stared at her, trying to make sense of it.

"Did Alice tell you about us? What we truly are?"

*First the loose tiger, now this.* For the second time in a half hour, Perveen felt a prickling of sweat. Carefully, she said, "What do you mean by that?"

"Ah. I can tell she hasn't told you. Of course she wouldn't! But I will."

Perveen felt mystified as Rochana walked slowly to the cupboard and came back with a small album bound in red velvet. "There are some pictures I wanted to show her—but she wouldn't look. I'll show you."

Perveen hesitated, wondering if looking at the book Alice didn't want to see meant betraying her friend. But curiosity won out, and she let Rochana put the book into her lap. An aged brass pin showing a horn, topped by a crown, had been screwed into the center cover. Perveen tapped it lightly. Solid brass. "An interesting decoration."

"It's a military badge once belonging to my father. He was a junior officer in the army, then, and this was all my mother had from him before he transferred out."

"How old were you at that time?" Perveen asked, watching Rochana turn the cover to the first page.

"I wasn't even born. He'd left six months before my mother

gave birth. But he knew she was pregnant, and he left her with quite a bit of money. Kind of him—it helped for a few years."

A British officer father, just like Rochana's biography stated. "How did they come to know each other?"

"Since she was fourteen, Asmaa did all kinds of traditional Indian dancing—both Muslim and Hindu schools—in the theater. My father was captivated, and waited after the show to invite her for supper with him. She was seventeen then. Here, I've got a picture of her," Rochana said, reaching across Perveen's lap to open the album, passing the cover page to show a second page with a newspaper clipping glued in.

It was a browned, tattered piece from the Calcutta *Statesman* dated April 12, 1902. The newspaper fragment contained a boxed picture of Asmaa and another lovely dancer in traditional full-skirted costumes. "Glorious Gayatri's Festive Dance," read the headline.

"She looks like a real goddess!" Perveen said, recognizing Asmaa's fine bones and luminous eyes.

Rochana gave her an approving look. "Actually, Gayatri is a Sanskrit word for song and is also the name of their goddess of speech—ironic, isn't it, because my mother is always so quiet! She was born a Muslim and called Noor, which means brightness or beauty. She chose Gayatri as her artist's name, just as I go by Rochana."

"And what is your real name?"

"Rowan," she said with a grin. "It doesn't sound very girly, so it's not a good name for the cinema. Rowan is the name of my father's sister, and she chose that because of how much my father spoke of her."

Rochana turned the page and spoke quickly. "Here's another one. Me at the school with the others."

The teacher in the back row held a sign showing *La Martinière, First Form*. Two rows of little girls; Rochana, slender and bright-eyed, was recognizable in the front row.

"Did you like school?" Perveen knew her question sounded trite, but she didn't know what else to say.

"Not at first. I was a boarder, like many of the full scholarship girls. We had been brought there to become more English, to have more of a chance in life. We rode and fenced and played tennis and studied, learning to speak with the right accent. But there was no money for university for me—and my marks weren't quite high enough, compared to the others, for a full scholarship locally."

"What happens to such girls—so well educated, but nothing more ahead?"

"Those with socially acceptable families could marry. But most went into jobs like hotel clerk or telephone operator. Not enough money in those jobs to live independently, and we were told over and over not to go back to our slummy roots. I believed that message with all my being. ABC was a wealthy man who donated to the school and sometimes came to the sports days and had congratulated me on my skills. I was thrilled when he offered me the chance."

"I understand." Perveen watched Rochana turn the page to show a picture of her wearing a white graduation dress, with Asmaa looking sober on one side and ABC beaming on the other. One could almost imagine them as a family group, except for the simplicity of Asmaa's dress.

The next page contained a staid, organizational photograph of military men. "I grouped the pictures in the order that they were acquired," Rochana said. "In Calcutta, there's a library that holds old newspapers and military books from all over India. All kinds of treasures."

Perveen interrupted, "Do you mean the Royal Asiatic Society of Calcutta?"

"Yes. I found this there and had to create a distraction in order to cut the paper so I wouldn't get caught. I hope you won't tell?"

Perveen imagined Colin wincing. "Of course I won't. Please show me more."

Six British-looking men were seated in a row. The photograph caption said: "Junior officers, Bengal Light Infantry 1901."

"You don't see him?" Rochana sounded disappointed.

"I'm not sure who to look for?"

"My father's the second from left in the third row."

Perveen looked at the small image of a man whose face was mostly obscured by his cap. She couldn't tell anything from it at all. "How did you learn about your father?"

"Asmaa knew his name, and in fact she used it in order to get me enrolled as a free student at La Martinière School. I started there at age four—so, gosh, I've known it for ages. Now, I only have one more picture. It was added recently."

Another page turned, and here was a crisp new photograph with a high-gloss sheen. Pictured were Alice and Sir David Hobson-Jones standing together at the Poona Racetrack with Rochana and Subhas a few feet away, beaming.

"I heard about how you met Alice at the races." Perveen was puzzled by the picture's inclusion in an old book. "You aren't saying . . ."

"Yes. We are half sisters."

Perveen felt dizzy with shock and swiftly turned back to the page with the group of military men. This time, she endeavored to read the names in tiny print. She hadn't tried before because the script was small to the point of being illegible. This time, she set the book on a patch of sunlight on the bedspread, so reading was easier.

"Third row, I had said." Rochana's voice was quavering. "Left to right: 1st Lt. Walter Fisher, 1st Lt. David Hobson-Jones . . ."

Perveen felt the shock of what this meant. "Do you think that he's your father?"

"I know he is," Rochana shot back. "Ask Asmaa! You could even go back to the nuns at La Martinière and they'd have the record, although now it would be a mite scandalous to bring up. When I entered school, he wasn't very important. But then he joined the ICS. Did you know that men in the military and the ICS who have sexual relationships with Indian women can be thrown out? Lose everything!"

"Yes. I was just—I heard about it from Alice." As she spoke, she realized that Alice had been thinking about it.

"I told Alice all of this on the island. I would have told her, regardless, because we need to be together. But at that time, it was so important—if we were in danger, her father needed to help us. We would not make it public that I was his, but I know he'd be able to protect us both."

Perveen sat with that. "And was Alice . . . what did she say about this idea?"

"At first, she didn't believe it. But then her feeling changed. But she wouldn't tell her father about me—she said she wasn't ready. We sailed back to the city together—but without saying much. Clearly, I'd played the scene wrong."

Rochana's use of stage language reminded Perveen that, despite the photographic evidence in front of her, she should not simply accept what was said as truth. "You mentioned that Sir David left your mother's life before you were born. And at the time you were four, going off to live at school, I believe the Hobson-Jones family was living in Ceylon."

"Yes. He'd left the Army and had entered the ICS by then. And as you know, Alice is a year older than me—and she was born in Calcutta, too."

The thought that Sir David had been unfaithful with a wife and small child at home made her stomach turn. And now his seeming appreciation for Indian cultural aspects seemed sinister.

"I always wanted to meet my father. Coming to Bombay, I knew there would be a chance. I hadn't known that I had a half sister until the meeting at Poona, and when we met, Sir David clearly had no idea of our connection. That day, I was mainly jealous of Alice. That was all I could think of! Then you brought her to the party with Diana, and I started to see how she was so clever and fun and then, well, she saved me from Morgan. Those traits must come from our shared father, don't you think?"

Perveen would rather have done twelve hand feedings of Tora than push the next question. Haltingly, she asked, "So how does Alice feel about this?"

Rochana fiddled with the bedspread's fringe. "I don't have a clear idea. Alice agreed to take me riding with her at the club, after I wrote to her about it. Sir David was there briefly, but he didn't say anything of consequence. Just the usual pleasantries, which either means Alice hadn't told him, or he refuses to recognize me."

And how long would it stay that way? Softly, Perveen added, "Sometimes the hidden past can unravel lives. All three of you could lose your social standing, your work, and most importantly, your connection to each other."

"Do you think I don't know that already?" Rochana pulled the bedspread's edge tightly into her fist. "I haven't told Subhas. Believe me, if he knew that I had a father in government, he would push him for better terms for Indian filmmakers. I won't take advantage like that—another reason I won't be the one to tell Sir David I'm also his child."

Perveen felt a rush of relief that Rochana wouldn't cause a scandal for the family—and at the same time, she felt that Rochana must have felt all the more rejected. "Does it hurt—not to be accepted by her?"

"Quite a bit." As Perveen rose from the bed and went to the door, Rochana took her place on the bed, looking mournful. "What will you do now?"

"Nothing. You had asked me to keep things confidential, and I will do that."

"And maybe—maybe Alice will come back to me. It just might take time," Rochana said hopefully.

"I think you're right. One last thing. I know that you are downcast over this rejection. I beg you not to go to lengths."

"Such as?"

"Please don't run away again. Or do what Hans did."

Rochana delivered her a wan half smile. "Don't worry. Now that I know Alice, why would I do such a thing? That would be like cutting myself out of a family photograph."

## 32
## December 1922

FROM *THE BOMBAY CHRONICLE*, DECEMBER 20, 1922:

**New Double Feature at Empire: *The Young Rajah* and *Tigers Must Be Loved***

Last night, the Empire Theatre held the first screening of *The Young Rajah*, the latest American film to open in Bombay starring Rudolph Valentino. This headliner film with screenplay by June Mathis and direction by Phil Rosen brings an outsider's eye to the Subcontinent. Picture a handsome young Indian rajah who's been hidden away in America under the name "Amos" since childhood. He's been in America, the birthplace of his mother, due to the murder of his Indian father during a hostile takeover of the family's princely state. Amos grows up in America handsome but undeniably brown, thanks to cosmetic enhancement. The character also has a white spot on his forehead, a sign of mystical powers that he can ultimately use in a fight for the kingdom. What happens to the rajah's romance with a racist white woman from America is also to be expected. A poor film for Valentino's talent, although this film's saving grace is a splendid array of costumes designed by Natacha Rambova (wife of Valentino).

On the other hand, *Tigers Must Be Loved*, the newsreel short that played before *The Young Rajah*, is magnificent. The documentary, which uses daringly close film footage of India's varied and proud tiger species, possesses the suspense of an adventure film. Many audience members screamed in fright during this reporter's viewing of the film due to the whisker-tight cinematography by Ajen Biswas. Perhaps the most crucial message of the film is that the tiger in India has overwhelming love for its family. One of the film's most poignant scenes involves a maharaja's party relentlessly hunting a handsome Bengal tiger, interspersed with footage of its pack members sadly watching from a thicket. Yet the film ends optimistically with the charismatic actress Rochana walking casually through a garden with her own pet tiger, Tora, and then demonstrating the grooming, training, and feeding of this domesticated, well-cared-for tiger. It's this writer's hope that coproducers Subhas and Rochana Ghoshal will continue blending reality with suspense in more newsreels revealing myriad aspects of our country.

"So, will this review go into your scrapbook?" Perveen asked, carefully refolding the newspaper page and handing it back to Alice. The two friends had a table in the back of B. Merwan, a popular Irani café in Nana Chowk. With a plate of mutton puffs between them and a mixed rice pilaf on the side, it was just a quick lunch meeting before Alice's afternoon of teaching.

"It's up to the kids," Alice said calmly. "I'll give them the clipping, and I've donated the scrapbook to the student film society. I didn't want to keep it in the house."

*Just as Alice's mother would have liked.* "Have you told the student club members anything about meeting Rochana?"

"Of course not! Leave well enough alone, at this point."

Perveen studied her, thinking it was good that she could even say this much. Perhaps it meant the storm had finally settled.

It had been a rough few months. After absorbing Rochana's revelation, Alice had taken a hard look at her father. As she told Perveen, he'd served five years of military service before joining the ICS; and throughout his rise to the top, he'd traveled constantly. It made her uneasy to think that there was a whole secret life and a cast of children and mothers who'd been cast aside.

"I know my mother's difficult to live with—but honestly, I feel Pa cheated on me!" Alice had railed to Perveen. "He could have come home to see me a bit more often than he did. Instead, he was running through the theaters and bars of Calcutta seducing dancers and leaving them with the hard work of bringing up children alone."

It struck Perveen that Sir David's interest in theater aligned with his daughter's passion for film. And despite the innate biases of colonialism, they both had made meaningful relationships with Indians. In fact, Alice was now deeply entrenched with Kitty and had brought her as a guest to the opening of *Tigers Must Be Loved*. Thinking about this, Perveen said, "You could have sat with Rochana at the screening—why didn't you?"

"Kitty preferred to be a bit apart, and I'm not wishing to upset her again."

"Was she worried about Rochana?"

"Yes—she misunderstood what it was about. I explained I was thrilled to meet Rochana and helped her when she asked, but that was the sum total," Alice said firmly. "I hadn't realized how much Kitty cared for me."

"Do you think you might"—Perveen trailed off, fearful of being rebuffed—"ever love Kitty?"

"Of course." Alice grinned and said, "Kitty has said it to me most beautifully, and I am looking for the right moment to say it back."

"That's how it was with Colin and me," Perveen said, reaching out to clasp her hand. "I'm very pleased for you."

Alice clapped her hands together. "Thank you for that, Perveen. I wasn't expecting it from you. I thought maybe . . ."

"I'd be jealous?" She shook her head. "You've already called me your sister. That's enough for me."

"Dearest Perveen." Alice pressed her hand over Perveen's. "The glorious thing is, Kitty and I could get our own hideaway. You can come visit me there, since my parents are still in such a snit about you visiting."

Perveen had been wondering why Alice hadn't had her over; it was sad to hear the reason. "What kind of hideaway? Not the island, I hope."

"Don't be silly. The architects are almost finished with building Woodburn College's very own faculty quarters!"

"I've seen the construction going up! Rustom was annoyed not to get the contract," Perveen added, intrigue rising. "Will Kitty have a flat?"

"No, she's quite content in her family's place. But I'm eligible, especially since I'm a dean. Frankly, after the way Mummy's been during the last two years, I'm tempted to sign up."

Perveen noted Alice's omission. "Your father will miss you."

"That's all right." Alice's voice was sharp, and Perveen wondered if, underneath the surface, her friend wished for Sir David to experience a bit of the loneliness he'd caused for her, Asmaa, and Rochana.

"Where is this housing?"

"In Nana Chowk, just ten minutes' walk from the college. I'm in rapture over the possibility of keeping my own hours and having a place where Kitty and I can be undisturbed. And just think about not needing a driver to bring me to and fro! Really, the only time I might rue not having Sirjit's service is during rainy season."

But it would be quite a while until the next rainy season. The winter's pleasant temperatures would continue, meaning plenty of chances for Perveen to enjoy taking Khushy outside in the perambulator, maybe even all the way to one of Alice and Kitty's tennis matches. And winter might also bring legal work that was so routine she'd be able to slip off to Colin's flat early in the morning before the city properly awoke.

Yes, she would continue sidestepping the rules; and she couldn't think of a better partner to do such things with than Alice.

# ACKNOWLEDGMENTS

This book took longer than expected, but I am happy that it was made possible with the thoughtful insights of family, friends and kind experts in the field. My deepest thanks go to Amrit Gangar, the noted filmmaker, film historian and Consultant Curator of the National Museum of Indian Cinema. I'm indebted to Dr. Madhu Mitra, a retired literature professor and scholar of Calcutta history, who helped me understand the meaning behind Durga Puja. Caleb Franklin, my terrific film agent in India, thanks for the never-ending promotion of Perveen Mistry in Bollywood—not to mention the inside view of film life in India that helped shape this book. I also thank Saahiti Shrikant, a former agent at Matter, for arranging a research tour for me at Mehboob Studio. Deepak Rao, police historian, I so appreciated your informal tour around the remains of the Imperial Theatre in Mumbai.

Thank you to Bharat Parekh, my dear stepfather, who shared his film books and memories at the start of the project. I thank my local friends, Shireen Mathur and Farida Guzdar, for Parsi cultural expertise and many wonderful afternoon teas. Marcia and Barry Talley, the boat would not have left the dock without your maritime know-how. Lynn Bowman, Claire Banerjee and Catherine Stewart were all generous manuscript readers with important insights that helped me during the rewrite stage.

Vicky Bijur, my longtime agent and friend, thanks for your patience and wisdom throughout this long process—and your commitment to getting Perveen into the hands of readers worldwide. Finally, the team at Soho. Starting off with my brilliant new editor, Alexa Wejko, I am so grateful for the care and effort put into the pages of this book. I extend my gratitude to Bronwen Hruska, Juliet Grames, Paul Oliver, Rudy Martinez, Steven Tran, and Lily DeTaeye for outstanding support over the years for the Perveen Mistry series. Finally, I thank my husband, Tony, who is becoming a great travel-research partner, and my son, Neel, who is happily launching his own artistic career. I am grateful to my trustworthy pals in Crime Writers of Color, the Mystery Writers of America and Sisters in Crime for being there, every day, all the way. And to anyone I've forgotten to name, I offer you thanks and a giant hug!

India film history buffs will probably recognize within my fictional characters some similarities to real film luminaries like Himanshu Rai, Devika Rani, Ashok Kumar, Fearless Nadia, Merle Oberon, Niranjan Pal and Franz Osten. I learned about these legends from reading scholarship on many aspects of film history and journalism. Some of the books I consulted were: Age of Entanglement: *Germans and Indian Intellectuals Across Empire* by Kris Manjapra; *Bombay Hustle: Making Movies in a Colonial City* by Debashree Mukherjee; *Love, Queenie: Merle Oberon, Hollywood's First South Asian Star* by Mayukh Sen; *Mercantile Bombay: A Journey of Trade, Finance and Enterprise* by Sifra Lentin; *Niranjan Paul: A Forgotten Legend & Such Is Life: An Autobiography* by Niranjan Pal; *The Observant Owl: Hutum's Vignettes of Nineteenth-Century Calcutta* by Hutum Pyanchai Naksha and Kaliprasanna Sinha, translated by Swarup Roy and *Wanted Cultured Ladies Only! Female Stardom and Cinema in India, 1930s–1950s* by Neepa Majumdar.

Most Indian films from the 1920s were made from fragile film and did not survive, except in bits and pieces. You can find some of these films online in the India Film archives and on YouTube. The National Museum of Indian Cinema in Mumbai has brought many such fragments on long-lost Indian films back into dazzling life as part of their fabulous displays. If you're in Mumbai, you should go.